FINAL PAYMENTS

Mary Gordon

BALLANTINE BOOKS • NEW YORK

Library of Congress Catalog Card Number: 77-90259

ISBN 0-345-29554-4

This edition published by arrangement with
Random House, Inc.

Manufactured in the United States of America

First Ballantine Books Edition: January 1979
Seventh Printing: February 1981

First Canadian Printing: February 1979

For Kathleen Biddick

I

My father's funeral was full of priests. Our house had always been full of priests, talking to my father, asking his advice, spending the night or the week, leaving their black shaving kits on the top of the toilet tank, expecting linen towels for their hands. A priest's care for his hands is his one allowable vanity.

They prided themselves on being out of the ordinary, the priests who came to visit my father. One of their jokes was that non-Catholics thought that they argued about how many angels could dance on the head of a pin, not knowing that that was a ridiculous question: angels were pure spirits; they did not dance. No, it was the important questions that absorbed them. They argued about baptism of desire, knocking dishes of pickles onto the carpet in their ardor. They determined the precise nature of the Transubstantiation, fumbling for my name as I freshened their drinks.

All these priests wept at the cemetery, and I did not weep, for my father, whom I loved. I stood behind Father Mulcahy and concentrated on the way his pink skull showed through his white hair. I liked his shoes; they were edible-looking, winking out from under his perfect cuffs. Even as I observed these details, I knew I was wrong to do it; I knew the clarity of my mind was unseemly. They lowered the body of my father. I would never see him again.

Do not think that because I did not weep, because

I

I am capable of ironic statements about his behavior,
I attach to my father's existence less than a murderous
importance. I gave up my life for him; only if you
understand my father will you understand that I make
that statement not with self-pity but with extreme
pride. He had a stroke when I was nineteen; I nursed
him until he died eleven years later. This strikes everyone in our decade as unusual, barbarous, cruel. To
me, it was not only inevitable but natural. The Church
exists and has endured for this, not only to preserve
itself but to keep certain scenes intact: My father and
me living by ourselves in a one-family house in
Queens. My decision at nineteen to care for my father in his illness. We were rare in our situation but
not unique. It could happen again.

My father's life was as clear as that of a child who
dies before the age of reason. They should have had
for his funeral a Mass of the Angels, by which children are buried in the Church. His mind had the
brutality of a child's or an angel's: the finger of the
angel points in the direction of hell, sure of the justice
of the destination of the souls he transports.

For my father, the refusal of anyone in the twentieth century to become part of the Catholic Church
was not pitiable; it was malicious and willful. Culpa-
ble ignorance, he called it. He loved the sense of his
own orthodoxy, of holding out for the purest and the
finest and the most refined sense of truth against the
slick hucksters who promised happiness on earth and
the supremacy of human reason.

In history, his sympathies were with the Royalists in
the French Revolution, the South in the Civil War,
the Russian czar, the Spanish Fascists. He believed
that Voltaire and Rousseau could be held (and that
God was at this very moment holding them) personally
responsible for the mess of the twentieth century. He
believed in hierarchies; he believed that truth and
beauty could be achieved only by a process of chas-
tening and exclusion. One did not look for happiness
on earth; there was a glory in poverty. He would often

talk about the happiness of people in the slums, although he had never visited one, and he ignored the struggle of his own family against poverty, a struggle that ended in his mother's madness. But if I had pressed him about his family, which I never dared to do, he would have said that the misery was worth it, for they were working to uphold a standard that was more important than their individual lives. The pyramids were more important than the deaths of the individual slaves. To question the price that had to be paid was simply an admission of softmindedness that was only the excuse for a paltry vision.

And now they were burying my father, because something had to be done with the bodies of the dead. It was the end of my life as well. After they lowered his body, I would have to invent an existence for myself. Care of an invalid has this great virtue: one never has to wonder what there is to do. Life is simple and inevitable and straightforward. Even the tedium has its seduction; empty time has always been earned. One can, if one chooses, leave it simply empty. My life had the balletic attraction of routine. Eleven years of it: bringing him breakfast, shaving him, hating to look at his face, twisted from the stroke in a way that made me forget the possibility of beauty. And the bath. Moving his body around, the incredible weight of that body even though it appeared so thin, his left side paralyzed because something had gone wrong with the right side of his brain. Sliding bedpans under him, looking at the misery of his buttocks. And the smell of his urine and his feces that, loving him as I did, I ought never to have known. And then I would put him in the chair and wheel him into the kitchen because, after all that, the morning was gone and it was time to make lunch.

And with his mouth twisted and his eye half shut he would try to talk to me. If I did not understand him, he would throw or break something, so that I would pretend (my ironic father to whom irony was no longer possible) always to understand.

In the afternoons he would try to read or sleep, and I would go to the store and try to clean the house. But it always seemed impossible. Life had accumulated around me in the house before I was old enough to fight it; life had grown into the walls so that I began to confuse it with the dust that was everywhere and the magazines that collected, that my father did not want thrown away, and the old letters and the grime that I could never get out of the furniture.

At supper I would cut my father's food up for him and wheel him into the living room where I would read to him for an hour. And then it would be time to get him ready for bed. The slow, long business of dying tired him daily. It is impossible to explain to anyone how long it takes to do the most ordinary things for an invalid. The whole day goes into the needs of a dying animal. And as with each new stroke he was able to do less for himself, the days were filled, and I grew dull. I slept whenever he slept. Sometimes he slept most of the day.

Neighbors would come in, and there would be a semblance of talk. And Father Mulcahy would come on Thursday nights. But with him I would have to make up a life: I would have to be the Isabel he had always loved. It would have been unbearable for him to know how dull I had grown, how distant, how tired, so I kept up the semblance of a perfectly false cheer that he needed, which to anyone but someone of his kindness would have seemed impossible.

You may wonder, as many have wondered, why I did it, why I stayed with my father all those years. Does it suggest both the monstrosity and the confusion of the issue if I say that the day Dr. MacCauley told me about my father's stroke was of my whole life the day I felt most purely alive? Certainty was mine, and purity; I was encased in meaning like crystal. It was less than three weeks after my father found me with David Lowe. Perhaps after the dull, drowning misery of those weeks, the news that brought me the possibility of a visible martyrdom was sheer relief: a grapefruit ice that cleanses the palate between courses of a heavy meal. During those weeks we barely spoke; neither of us could invent the mechanism of forgiveness. Then my father had his stroke. In its way, it suited us to perfection.

He had three more strokes between his first stroke and the day of his death. Can you guess how many times in those eleven years people suggested that I get someone in to help, that I get on with my life? I developed a technique for responding to those suggestions: I would close my lips rapidly and say how well we got on this way, and how my father would hate a stranger. And it was true; it was terrible enough that he should strike out at me for the failure of his body, for its simple and complete betrayal, but if he were with a stranger he would have been deprived even of the consolation of his rage. And we were connected by the flesh, so if anyone should minister to the decay of my father's, it should be I.

If, at night in my bed, it suddenly came upon me that he could go on like this for twenty more years (his heart is strong, the doctors had said), and if it came to me that I too was dying, and if in the bathtub I looked at my breasts and my thighs and saw the first signs of aging, and if I realized that for days I would go on not knowing what day it was, having no reason to know, and if I smelt his sick breath and wished for him only to be dead—still, I knew this was mine. This was my life, inevitable to me as my own body. I could not share that life any more than I could give my own body over. It is too simple to say, but I must say it: I loved him very much; I loved him more than anyone else.

And then there was the nightmare of my father at the door, seeing me with David. That would come back to me if I thought of getting someone in. Or the time in 1965 when I wanted to go to the Bahamas with my friend Eleanor for a week and spoke to my father about having one of the nursing sisters in. He wept and took my hand and looked at me with the pure terror of a child who has found himself lost in a department store. And his lop-sided mouth opened and closed like a child's before he cried. My tall father, my father who had been so sure and so stern, and how his sternness, at the mercy of his body, had turned to a child's weeping, "Don't leave me." It was the only time Eleanor has ever been angry with me. It was a shock to have my friend say perfectly gently, with no hint of excess, "You are letting him eat you alive."

But Eleanor continued to visit me regularly, coming out to Queens from Manhattan, bringing fruit. And we would sit in the kitchen, talking, Eleanor gesturing with her clever fingers. We never talked about our lives, we talked about ourselves, about our natures, checking on one another against our childhoods to see what we had become, as though external events had no consequence.

At the cemetery, Eleanor stood at my right side, Liz at my left. The path of the life of someone one has loved from childhood always seems inevitable, enviably straightforward, far simpler and therefore far more highly valued than one's own. One's own seems, in contrast, a crafted and yet random mix of calculation and chance. That day, at my father's funeral, I believed myself more formed by chance than by calculation. Or, rather, my adulthood seemed to be so. It was precisely the failure of my calculations that marked the exit of the child.

At a funeral there is always at least one person one does not wish to see. I looked over at Margaret Casey, who had kept house for us, whom I had not seen in seventeen years. Her coat fit her like a cheese box: an aggressively bad fit. Even *she* wept, and she had no right to be there. If I were Margaret, I would have had the good manners to stay away. But the poverty of a life like Margaret's relieves one of the responsibility of good manners; there is nothing to lose, therefore nothing to safeguard. I looked at Margaret, remembering her as she was seventeen years before, when the touch of her damp fingers could sicken me for the afternoon. We will never forgive each other. And we are right. What we have done to each other has been unforgivable. People at the cemetery comforted Margaret; people spoke to her before they spoke to me. She was weeping, and I was not. She seemed to be taking everything more seriously than I was.

And David Lowe was there, whom I had forgiven, whom my father would not forgive. They would all be coming back to the house; all those priests kissing me, all the neighbors who had, for years, given me cakes and casseroles in return for the romance of devotion that my father and I had triggered in their lives.

I stood near my father's grave, my black heels cutting holes in the grass. I kissed and was kissed; I answered people's expressions of grief with coos and cluckings, animal noises, which seemed at that moment the only appropriate response. They had buried my father; I would never see him again. That I continued to breathe air surprised me. I had borne the impress of his body all my life. Walking past statues of St. Michael and St. Gabriel, archangels, I felt light, as from the removal of a burden, light as a spaceman in a gravityless universe.

"Shall I drive you home?" asked Father Mulcahy.

"I'll go with Liz and Eleanor," I said.

I could see he was disappointed, but I needed to be with them. They were the only people in the cemetery who did not seem to me anachronisms. I sat between them in the front seat of Eleanor's car. There was Eleanor beside me, driving the car sensibly, taking on an adult's acts, and yet the same girl I had walked next to at First Communion. Eleanor and I took the Sacraments very seriously: Penance, Holy Eucharist; we were concerned for the perfection of the outward form. Standing on line for Confession, for Communion, we were careful to keep our spines straight, to fold our hands so that they were Gothic steeples, not a mess of immigrant knuckles. Liz, I remember, was slapped by the principal for passing notes during the

Consecration. Eleanor and I were frightened by the stories that the nuns told only to frighten us: Sacrilege, doing profane things with sacred objects, like the woman who secretly spat the Host into her purse and took it home to jab it with a pencil. The image was made extraordinarily clear to us by Sister Immaculata —the small black holes in the white bread, and the fate of the woman. This depraved soul had been found mysteriously dead the next morning with a circle of black dots around her heart.

Eleanor and I looked at each other when we heard that story, as we had looked at each other when the pastor came in to tell the first grade the procedure in case of atomic attack. But Liz raised her hand. When Sister Immaculata called on her she asked, "Why would anyone want to jab the Host with a pencil?"

Sister Immaculata grew very red. She said she had never heard a child preparing for First Communion say anything so rude. She asked Liz if she were sure she was really ready for First Communion. The threat cowed even Liz. We had all imagined ourselves in our blue serge uniforms standing outside the line of white angels, white brides, on their way to what everyone told us was the happiest day of their lives, watching, being mysteriously, implacably punished.

But there was Eleanor beside me now; there was Liz. I had always thought Eleanor's face of all faces the most perfect. Such susceptibility to heats and colors! The shade of the eyes, the whole meaning of the complexion, could change in a second. One thought of phrases from old novels to take the measure of that face: "suffused with pretty blushes." She had the kind of face that would have driven a Victorian paterfamilias to strangled fantasies. And a mouth that was barely a line, thin Irish lips invented for mourning.

Liz sat on the other side of me, appealing as an Indian brave or a good saddle. She was not fond of Eleanor. "She always seems so goddamn breakable. There's no excuse for that," Liz would say, with a real sense of outrage. Liz was the mother of children, the only one of us who had reproduced. Which, I thought, made her far more vulnerable than either Eleanor or I. Her mouth was another kind of Irish trick, brimming with mockeries as her eyes flicked up and down, scanning for foolishness like radar. Then, when there was something she could settle on, her face became fully alive. She would tell stories and pause seriously in mid-sentence, after parts of the verb "to be," as if she knew that her natural eloquence would make her audience suspect the truth of her narrative. She ought to have led men across the Antarctic; she ought to have run a factory. Instead, she had married a politician. No, that's wrong. It is impossible to think of John Ryan as anything other than a Fordham boy.

Eleanor stopped for a red light next to the subway we always took to the city. I went to the city with my friends. A deceptively simple statement, yet it changed my life, all our lives, and marked us as different from anyone in the neighborhood. If it is hard for New Yorkers to believe that people live in places called Nebraska and Kansas, it must be impossible for all but a relative handful to understand the difference between Queens and "the city."

My neighborhood is one of those urban pockets that feigns a fine suburban detachment while abutting on the mouth of a slum. But it was not always so. Its changes became more visible as I drove through it with Liz and Eleanor, who had left it. For I had not left it.

I went to the city with my friends. I went out of the neighborhood. Like too much in my life, the neighborhood drew its existence for me from its relation to my father. My father stuck out in the neighborhood, the neighborhood intellectual. Every neighborhood does not have one, as every village does not have an idiot, but if he is there he serves the same outsize function. The village idiot would not be equally idiotic in another village. My father would not have been such a marvel of brilliance outside the parish. It is important to note that *he* never went into Manhattan. If I went,

I went with Eleanor or Liz (one or the other, not both). My father claimed to be devoted to upholding Western civilization, but in the thirty years of his life I knew, he never went to a museum, or an opera, or a concert, or a ballet. What he meant by Western civilization was the Church. So it was natural for him not to want to leave the neighborhood where the Church was so predominant it did not need to be upheld. It needed only the occasional refinement: gargoyles or the replacement of a pane of colored glass. At which he was an expert. He knew where he belonged. His complaints about the ignorance of his neighbors were a sham, like the complaints of the husband of a beauty who exhibits the bills for his wife's cosmetics at a party.

The neighbors always told me how they looked up to my father. I suppose I believed them. For many years I tried to suppress my envy of Liz and Eleanor, whose fathers worked for the phone company, played baseball, were young, watered the lawn in the summer. My father's distinction was at times an embarrassment, particularly because it was so marginal. The neighbors valued having my father among them, a professor of medieval literature at St. Aloysius, where they hoped to send their sons. But they were uncomfortable because they did not understand exactly what he did all day. They had to place him alongside the professional men: MacCauley, the doctor, with his wet blue eyes like a dog's or a stage Irishman's; Delaney, the lawyer, with his beef-steak of a face. But they had clear need of MacCauley and Delaney when they were selling houses and giving birth. They had to invent for my father an authority to which they could defer. So they were shy with him—particularly the men—and they looked to him—particularly during the McCarthy years—as the person who established "the role of the Catholic in the modern world," who kept intact that interface between the sacred and the secular. He addressed the Holy Name Society and the Rosary Society and the Catholic Daughters. He spoke at Communion breakfasts and potluck suppers; he advised the priests on the Liturgy and the State.

No one went to Liz's father, to Eleanor's father, with such complicated issues. And in return for being spared such vexations, Mr. O'Brien and Mr. Lavery showed up every year to put in our storm windows, were available to unclog the gutters, to shovel the snow.

The day of my father's funeral we rode up the street we had all been born on. Dover Road. Each of us had our split-number Queens addresses. Eleanor had the green house: 50–18; mine was the mock Tudor: 50–12. And, almost up to Meadowbrook Parkway, Liz had the red brick with the winding pathway we all envied: 50–04.

"It's like riding through a time capsule," said Liz. "And all those people, John Delaney, Margaret Casey, Father Mulcahy. I thought they were all dead."

"What's happened to Margaret?" asked Eleanor.

"She's living with her sister or something. Upstate somewhere. I think she works in a box factory."

"A box factory," Liz said. "I love it."

"I wish I didn't have to see all these people right now," I said.

I had looked forward to walking into the house for the first time without my father. I thought I could trap myself into some kind of understanding which I could then have preserved, like a photograph at a surprise party that reveals the face of terror and outrage at having been invaded, in the dark, by one's dearest friends.

"I think it's supposed to be good for you to see people," said Liz. "Except these are all the people you don't want to see."

"Maybe we can encourage people to leave soon," said Eleanor.

"Fat chance," said Liz.

We weren't even the first ones to arrive. The O'Hares, who had lived next door to us since 1952, were sitting at the kitchen table. One of the reasons

our block was spared the interracial tensions of the
sixties was that nobody ever moved out. Changes in
status, although they were rare, did not encourage
people to move. They simply added things to their
existing houses: patios, swimming pools, fountains,
statues of the Virgin bathed in iridescent light. If children moved away, their parents did not contemplate
small apartments. The rooms were kept and dusted
weekly, even, perhaps, redecorated for grandchildren.

Bobby O'Hare still lived with his parents, an embarrassment. I could like him now, sitting at my table
with his mother and father, as I could never have
liked him ten years before. I liked him because he
had been in some way devastated; the boy who had
spilled his souped-up cars and his skinny girls onto our
lawn, into our driveway, had become, with age, defeated. The sexy sullenness of the teenager had turned
into a morose inactivity. He had begun to get fat. He
had become kinder.

Boys like Bobby (I call him a boy although he is
only five years younger than I) are capable of a kindness that undoes me. It is connected to their muteness;
it is part of their stupidity—yet it springs from the
kind of perfectly good heart that is lost directly one
becomes articulate. Bobby would sit with my father
longer than anyone else. It seemed to soothe him. If
I wanted to go out with Eleanor to dinner, to a movie,
I knew I could ask Bobby to stay. For one thing, he
was always there: he never went out. He stayed in his
room, composing country-and-western music on his
guitar, writing it down on staved paper, mailing it to
stars. His belief in fate was as brutal as the way he
looked at his mother. It was the morose faith of a
primitive or a desert father: there was no need to *act*,
action would not change things and could conceivably
harm the direct flow of the preordained.

Bobby could have become nearly what he was by
the simple process of aging: that kind of teenager is
bound to be disappointed in adulthood. For Bobby's
girl friends, life's peak is hit at sixteen; boys like him,

even uninvaded by history, have a few more good years, but not many. They begin to decay at twenty-two. But Bobby's decline was not simply the natural deliquescence of his character. He had gone to Vietnam.

If Vietnam divided the country, it did not divide our neighborhood. People who were against it got out. Like Liz, whom I now see would not have had to marry John Ryan in 1966 had she agreed with her parents about Vietnam.

I remember Liz talking to Bobby O'Hare before he went away. Of the three of us, Liz was the only one Bobby had ever wanted to talk to. I suppose he always loved her; I suppose, given his nature, he still does. She stood by the door of his car and said, with perfect heartlessness, "What you're doing is immoral. You're going off to kill people who are fighting for something you ought to believe in."

He didn't argue. He was smart enough not to try to outargue Liz; he knew her too well to doubt her inflexibility.

Liz and I talked about the war in my father's house, under our breaths, as other women talked about their love affairs. Secretly, I addressed envelopes for the Women's Strike for Peace as I might secretly have sent away for contraceptives. I did not try to argue with my father. He was already sick. For him, President Diem was a Christian hero, Madame Nhu, a lady and a saint. The issue was simple for him; the North Vietnamese were Communists, and Communists hated the Church. How I envied my father the clarity of his enemies, even as I watched the peace marches on television, looking for Liz and her babies in the crowd.

I was the only one who understood Liz's jokes about the peace movement: nuns in Ship'n Shore blouses who made her want to join the Green Berets just to be on the opposite side; priests with no sense of irony losing their virginity in their forties; concerned laity, all overweight or underweight, with bad taste in shoes and bad complexions. And, of course,

Eugene McCarthy was the man every Catholic girl had
dreamed of marrying, as Dan Berrigan was the priest
we yearned to seduce. There was no one on the picket
line who could laugh with Liz at all of that. I became,
during those years, invaluable to her.

Looking at Bobby O'Hare in my kitchen, I remembered his going-away party. 1967. Everyone was
fiercely, dangerously proud of him. I was afraid of the
sounds coming out of the house next door; the aggressive jocularity of people defending a position has
always menaced me. And working-class Irish are always defending something, probably something inde-
fensible—the virginity of Mary, the C.I.A.—which is
why their parties always end in fights.

It was August; the windows were open; my father
couldn't sleep. He had been sick for four years then,
but he could still speak quite normally. I was by his
bed and let him read me Céline to drown out the
noise of breaking glass, tires, anger, sex that was going
nowhere. Finally my father became enraged. I had to
go next door and ask them to quiet things down, a
proposition that I knew, even as I walked through the
hedge that separated our houses, would end in violence.

I walked into the O'Hares' house like the angel of
death. I am sure that for all the years I took care of
my father I carried the smell of his sickness with me,
a sour, male smell unnatural to me as a woman.

The bottom floor of the house was covered with
signs: GOOD LUCK BOBBY, BOBBY O'HARE
U.S.M.C., GIVE IT TO 'EM, LEATHERNECK. Red,
white and blue crêpe paper stretched from ceiling to
ceiling. Bobby and his friends were dancing in the living room. He was pouring beer over the head of Carol
Gambino, to whom he had given his high school ring.
The O'Hares were in the kitchen, telling jokes to their
friends. And there I was, at the door, the same generation as the people dancing in the living room.

Mr. O'Hare got up and embraced me, the drunk's
embrace that made me feel I was drowning. I was

only twenty-three, but it was unthinkable to anyone that I should be encouraged to go inside with "the young people." Mr. O'Hare brought me a stool to sit on; Mrs. O'Hare brought me a piece of cake. I was becoming more and more uneasy. I was here, after all, to censure their exuberance, to press the claims of an invalid, to demand an invalid's rights: silence, order, predictability.

"How is your father?" someone sitting at the table asked.

I had to say it then. I put down my cake and looked at no one. I tried to make my face perfectly blank, a nun's face, a nurse's.

"He's having a bad time right now. Especially to-night. Which is why I was wondering, Mr. O'Hare, if you could ask Bobby to turn down the record player."

Everyone at the table was silent, which made the laughter and the music coming from the living room seem a deliberate offense. Everyone around that table was the parent of one of the children in the living room. Children my age. I could see the resentment in their eyes, resentment of the kill-joy who is perhaps finally the greatest bully. But so great was the author-ity of my father that they did not question the pro-priety of sacrificing their children's pleasure to his comfort.

"Tell those kids to knock it off, Ray," said Mrs. Flannery, the wife of a policeman.

Mr. O'Hare ran over to the record player. The needle made a noise going over the record that was as dangerous as an air raid siren.

"What the fuck do you think you're doing," said Bobby, towering over his father, whose height, in the tradition of postwar sons, he exceeded by six inches.

"Ya hafta stop making this goddamn racket. He can't sleep next door."

Bobby's face looked massive, the side of a building.

"What the fuck do I care. Some old fart who should've been dead years ago. I'm going into the fuck-ing Marines. I could be fucking killed. And all you care about is some old bastard next door who has to piss through a tube."

Of course, an Irish father would have to strike his son for such a monstrosity. I did not feel, standing at the door of the living room, that Mr. O'Hare was fighting his son to defend the honor of my family. I thought Bobby was right. But it was the shape and purpose of my life to be on my father's side, to defend him from whatever dangers he had imagined. I thought Bobby was right; I also knew I had done the right thing. I slipped out the kitchen door, back to my father. Soon after, we heard cars starting up. Everyone was leaving. We had stopped the party. My father slept only when the last light was off at the O'Hares'.

Was Bobby thinking about that night, sitting at the dining room table on the day of my father's funeral? Of course not; he was thinking of my father, being simpler than I, and more loving. I could see he had been weeping, as had his parents, as had everyone in the neighborhood but me. I do not understand why, that day, my mind was able to focus (but with impeccable clarity) only on the past.

I was grateful to the O'Hares for their concrete acts of kindness, but I was grateful even more because they had kept my two secrets. They knew I did not go to church; they knew I was not a virgin.

They could easily have told my father what I did all those Sundays, all those years, but they did not. I know it was not loyalty to me that had kept them silent, but the desire to spare my father more pain, and perhaps their sense of superiority that the daughter of the man who had thought, without being a priest, to speak to them on spiritual matters, had lost the faith.

Among the most complicated ways in which I had deceived my father were my Sunday walks. The only absence he would tolerate without petulance or accusation was the necessary hour for Sunday Mass. But I had ceased to believe. It is possible to pray for faith when one is grappling with a crisis of faith, but when loss of faith comes gradually, as it did to me, the issue seems plain and no longer compelling; no prayer is possible. And so it was not that it was torture for me to sit through Sunday Mass at Assumption Church, it was simply boring. It had occurred to me in high school that it did not make good sense for there to be only one possibility open to men. And when the Church ceased to be inevitable, it became for me irrelevant. And then there was the Council, with its sixties relevance and relativity that interested me not a whit.

So, with the one hour in the week that was not exacted from me, I deceived my father; I took a walk. Each time, for eleven years, I took the same path: up Glasgow Turnpike to the very top of the hill, into the small park, once around the pond and home again. Given the extreme and enforced circumspection of my life, I was sometimes tempted to try different walks. But since I had only the one hour, I could not risk it on a walk I might not enjoy. I would walk, each Sunday, from eleven to eleven-fifty, looking at the trees and the pond of Dwyer Park. Unless it was raining, in which case I would go to Milt's luncheonette and have a cup of coffee and a raisin bun.

Although they sometimes tried to talk to me in the kitchen, tried to trap me into discussions with priests, the O'Hares were silent to my father. And they were silent on the matter of David Lowe.

It was astonishing that David Lowe had come to my father's funeral. He had called and asked if he could come; he happened to be home from California. He would like to honor my father. Would I mind if he came? I said that he could come if he liked. After all those years it surprised me that he had a real existence. Having acknowledged his existence, it became too real for me to imagine I could have any effect on it.

David Lowe compensated my father for years of professional neglect. My father taught at St. Aloysius from 1934 to 1962, and in all that time David was his only disciple. It isn't difficult to understand, considering the make-up of the St. Aloysius student body. Parents saved to send their sons to St. Aloysius to be doctors or lawyers or accountants, insurance men, if all else failed. Their daughters went to be elementary schoolteachers and to meet Catholic boys. If boys had aspirations of a more purely intellectual nature, they would not have gone to St. Aloysius; they would have gone to Fordham so they could be with the Jesuits and still live at home. Girls occasionally slipped in with higher intellectual pretensions, but my father was too skittish around his female students to attract them to his feet. Although he protested that his students were the salt of the earth, no one was devoted to him until David Lowe.

David's devotion made up for years of unpopularity. He was born to be a disciple. He was tall and dark, his hair was too short, and he was almost spuriously thin. For three years David and I, unable to think of any manners that would allow us a possible relation, stayed away from each other, acknowledging one another with uneasy smiles of recognition when we met. I worked hard to avoid my father at the college, and David was always with my father.

How did we get together then? When did I first speak to him? Oh, yes, the movies. We met at the movies. It was 1962: *West Side Story*.

What was my father's reaction to my seeing David? He did not seem to think it extraordinary. And yet he was the first boy I went out with. The only boy. At that time it did not occur to my father that I was ready to be in any danger—old enough to have relations in which sex played any part. I'm sure he felt it was the same thing as bringing one of my classmates home for lunch from kindergarten.

Such a high-toned courtship we had! Dates at the Cloisters and the Museum of Modern Art. Did we ever eat together? No. It was a wilderness of talk, a paradise of talk. We saw each other every day, and we would talk—but not about ourselves and never about my father. How strangely absent from it all my father was, although he was at the center of it. And then kissing in the movies. Dear God, the pleasure of that. That was it, that was the truth of it: the proximity of his really rather foolish body was to me a pure joy.

"Make love to me," I said. Of course, I was the one who started it. I had no doubts then. It was right; I wanted it. It was the strongest thing I knew. Driving in his black Volkswagen he would hold my hand on the gear shift, he would hold me as he drove. When I said that "Make love to me," he held me against his small bird's chest. I could feel his heart. I said, "I want you very much," and he said—so like him, the kind of thing I loved him for—"Well, I feel the same way about you." In his scholar's voice.

How odd it is to think of myself at nineteen in David's black Volkswagen, predictably in love, not, for once, the daughter of my father but someone's girl friend. The simplicity of that identity allows me no small measure of self-love, allows me to believe for a moment that whatever happened was the result, not of my brutality, but of an innocence I have always doubted, even in childhood, as possible to my nature.

It was not the first time that David and I were in bed together when my father found us. But after it happened—David weeping, unable to move, my father shouting outside the door, "Get out of here and never come back!"—I did not see him again. I remember the bed shaking with David's weeping, causing my naked breasts to jiggle absurdly as I covered them with his T-shirt. I remember his saying, "I'll marry her, Professor. It will be all right; I'll marry her." And my father turned to him in hatred. I have never seen such a pure emotion. Even to speak of it now frightens me.

"You will never see her again," he said. "You have ruined her life. You have ruined mine. Never come near us again."

Weeping, out of control (or I would never have gone to a woman), I ran next door to Mrs. O'Hare. I told her what had happened. She ran a bath for me. She got me two clean towels. I don't remember her saying anything. We never spoke of it again. Three weeks later, I came home from school to see the ambulance at the door. My father had had a stroke.

She would think of all that now, when she saw David Lowe, as I had thought of Bobby's going-away party. It was inevitable; all these people in this room would bring back the past with a vividness that might be unfortunate.

David and his thin blonde wife were the first people I saw driving up. He was thinner than ever, with a thin gray beard that was too long for his chin. Why was there so much gray in it? He was only thirty-four. And why had he kept that beard when it was such an obvious disappointment? His head hung forward between his shoulders, the head of a man who is having trouble satisfying his wife. Now that he was actually there, I resented his being in my house. His actual physical presence made me remember that time with an intensity that his image spared me.

To remember that time is to remember a flood: the waters of my act surrounded me. I was drowning in that time, and drowning my father in impossible consequences. He dragged me to Confession, but I did not confess, and he never knew that I did not, and I never went again. He was silent those weeks but for his weeping, and to say, "If you should have a child, we will keep it. We will move away somewhere and raise it."

I had never thought of a child, and those days took on a new frenzy. I could have a child. But of course I did not.

Perhaps it was a disappointment to my father for several reasons. What would have pleased him more than going into his old age taking care of my child, discreetly hinting at rape or virgin birth as its origin? The violence of either possibility would have sustained him. And it must have disappointed him that for my act there was no clear punishment. So he had to invent one: the stoppage of his brain, the failure of his own body as a result of the pleasure of mine. Had I had a child (a son, of course, named after him) he would have been able to embrace an impossibly hale old age, walking his small grandson to the rectory every day where I would have worked, growing daily as pale as Magdalene, through the charity of the parish, who would never mention my crimes.

And perhaps I wanted that, too, or if not that precise fantasy of public penitence, some scene that skated near melodrama with all its florid components: discovery, punishment, above all the chance for a clear, new life. What was I doing with David, in my own bed, in my father's house, in the middle of the afternoon? In the middle of the afternoon in the middle of summer when my father would of course not be teaching and liable at any moment to walk through the door? I have never been able to understand why, given the precision with which up to that time I handled my life, I made such an amateur blunder. Perhaps it is that the intrusion of sexuality marks the end of precision. Or perhaps it was something more complicated, for I have never given myself the luxury or insisted upon the humility of thinking my motivations simple. Was I trying to punish my father for something; for his lack of attention to my obvious adulthood, for his lack of jealousy at the intrusion of so clear a rival? He didn't even tease me about David. Perhaps I was outraged at his lack of outrage at what could so obviously have separated us. Would it be so easy for him to let me go? Perhaps the prospect so deeply appalled me that I had to construct the scene that would forbid me marriage during my father's lifetime, that would make impossible the one match he might have approved.

It is clear to me now that what I most feared was the possibility of my father's and my relationship becoming ordinary, or even assuming a texture that might seem comprehensible to an onlooker who had not known us all our lives. Did I fear, even as I embraced my nineteen-year-old lover, the picture of myself in

an apron, cooking Sunday dinner for my father and
David and our children with the names of early Christian martyrs? My father's discovery of me that day en-
sured that no man would ever enter my life in any but
a professional capacity. I would see priests and doctors
and policemen and lawyers and eventually the under-
taker who would come for my father in his discreet
gray Buick. But I would remain intact.

Walking with surprising confidence through my living room, David shook my hand. Did his wife know
we had been lovers? I wondered what other women
he had had besides her and me.

"I owe everything to your father. My whole career,"
he said. His wife's chest was so flat that I had fantasies
of walking up it.

"Yes," I said, nonsensically, "he was very devoted."

Liz came up behind me, holding a plate of cake.

"Well, David," she said, "how's your research?"

"How did you know about my research?"

"Why would someone like you not be doing research?"

"As a matter of fact, I'm doing a book on the *Pearl*
Poet and the tradition of alliterative verse."

"A significant contribution?" said Liz, passing cake
to his wife.

"I like to think so," he said, taking a napkin from
the table.

"Isabel, there are some people who want to see
you," Liz said.

"That little squirt," she said. "What's he doing
here?"

It was painful to hear her talk like that about someone who had been my lover. Even though I agreed
with her. Now I could never tell her about David. Because I had kept the secret from her for so many
years, it was an oddly vivid loss.

"He owes my father everything. Everything," I said,
imitating David's earnestness.

"I thought your father had more sense than to loose David Lowe on the world."

"David sat at his feet."

"Look at the shoes on the wife. Do you believe it? Bows. Manhattanville 1962. I bet she has a miraculous medal pinned to her bra."

"I don't think she's ever worn a bra."

"Right. Her slip. Can't you see it? God, I haven't had a cheese bun in years. Since I left Queens. Now that's significant. I think we should tell David Lowe about that. It might be a big break-through for him, researchwise."

"Dear God, here's John Delaney."

"OK, I'll keep him from you for a while. As far as I can see, you have four major tasks before you. One, keep Margaret Casey away from Father Mulcahy. Two, keep Father Mulcahy away from the booze. Three, keep me from Eleanor before I say something mean. Four, keep my mother away from me before she drives me crazy."

"This day is much less clear than I had hoped."

"How do you feel?"

"Dazed."

"Sad?"

"No, not nearly mournful enough."

"Shit. Here comes my mother. Now you'll have to talk to John Delaney."

Delaney the lawyer. It was astounding how someone could so completely represent the body and yet give no suggestion of sex. Whenever he approached me, I felt as if I were drowning in flesh. He always managed to cover a great deal of territory in his embraces, and yet his hands never approached any dangerous areas. And how did he manage to conceal his age? The truth of it was buried in that smooth, expensive flesh, an immigrant investment.

"God love ya, honey, God love ya. You're a little saint."

He was patting my back as if I had the hiccoughs.

He took out his handkerchief. Did he think he was going to make me cry?

"You stop by the office tomorrow, sweetheart. You just lean on me. I'll have you all squared away in no time."

"Thank you, John," I said, backing away from him into the oxygen. That was John disposed of. What was next? What had Liz said I had to do? Keep Margaret away from Father Mulcahy and keep Father Mulcahy away from the booze.

He was holding a glass with a gold-colored liquid in it. For an hysterical second I thought it might be ginger ale. But I looked at his eyes. They were as unfocused as a fish's looking up from a bed of ice. When he saw me, his eyes turned entirely liquid.

"We've lost our best pal, both of us," he said, falling into me.

"Come and have something to eat," I said.

"No. I don't want to eat. I lost my best pal. I've got no one to talk to."

I wished he would stop. I wished all of them would stop. The excesses of their grief prohibited mine.

Liz's mother came over to him with coffee. They sat together on the couch.

"How's that fine daughter of yours? A fine girl, a fine Catholic mother."

Mrs. O'Brien snorted. "How should I know. She never talks to me."

"Now, Grace, I'm sure that's not true," said Father Mulcahy, looking around for his glass.

I could see Margaret walking toward us. I had to protect Father Mulcahy from her, so I approached her, the person I most wanted to avoid. My hatred of Margaret brought me back to myself, broke through the haze I had lived in since my father's death. Hate made memory solid, made it sharp, like glass fruits preserved in a bath of acid.

In my living room, on the day of my father's funeral, I looked back with perfect triumph at what I had taken away from that woman. I had kept her from my father. But in my triumph there was fear that such clever thefts are not, cannot be, permanently unpunishable.

I should feel some sort of gratitude to Margaret. She kept house for my father and me. Eleven years. After my mother was killed (a tragic accident, people said, run over in front of the house; I do not think of it; my father and I never spoke of it), Father Mulcahy sent her over. I was two then. She stayed until I was thirteen. Until I got rid of her. She did, I suppose, a great deal of helpful and necessary work for us. But she was paid, I want to say. Not enough, of course. That network of Irish daughters, orphaned in their forties by the death of an invalid parent, works always for less than minimum wages at jobs found by some priest, some lawyer, some doctor, among their own kind. But I knew what Margaret wanted: she wanted to marry my father, and I would not allow it. And that was why she was at the funeral, to reproach me with her tears, with the egg-colored pockets under her eyes, with the bad fit of her raincoat.

I once caught her telling Mrs. Keeney, the rectory housekeeper, about my father. She and Margaret wore identical slippers with holes cut out for bunions. I heard them talking in my father's kitchen.

"I am not one to complain, Mrs. Keeney," Margaret had said, "but I ask the child to put down her blessed book for one moment and pick up her room and she does not, does *not* give me the courtesy of looking up from her book even. And the father can't see the forest for the trees. If ever I should, mind you, after enduring this abuse a hundred times, point it out to the man, he apologizes to me, he's always a gentleman, and says, 'But Margaret, she can always get someone to pick up after her, but she can't have anyone else do her reading and thinking for her.' "

"It seems to me that's not the only way he can't see the forest for the trees," said Mrs. Keeney, winking at Margaret.

"I'm sure I don't know what you mean," Margaret said.

"It seems to me, Margaret Casey, that if Joe Moore wasn't so wrapped up in his old books what he'd see is that that child needs a mother, and how much he's come to depend on you."

Margaret giggled and rubbed her palms together in a way that was to me not only sickening, but dangerous. Then Mrs. Keeney caught sight of me, listening on the landing. Margaret's face turned pale and ugly with hatred, and it frightened me so that I wanted to run away. But I didn't; I used my good manners, which I believed kept back terror. I nodded to the women; I told Mrs. Keeney it was nice to see her. Even at thirteen, I had perfected the gestures of *noblesse oblige.* I had learned them naturally, growing up the daughter of a professor in a neighborhood where everyone else's father worked for the Transit Authority or the phone company. Margaret and Mrs. Keeney imagined that the tilt of my head was triumphant, but it was at that unnatural angle out of fear. The idea that anyone hated me so much made me ill. And the idea that I was hated by women made everything incalculably more menacing. The idea that these two women, Margaret with her damp yellow skin, Mrs. Keeney with her enormous bosom, her moles, thought about *my* father in *that* way was unbearable. But I knew myself, even at the moment of my greatest fear, to be powerful. I knew I could prevent what these women were planning. Margaret would not marry my father.

It was Father Mulcahy who finally gave me the courage to do it. Father Mulcahy, my friend, my father's friend, Margaret's friend, the confessor of all of us. All those connections, coming from that one man, like a spider's web from its own body. All those possibilities for betrayal.

The certainty of my childhood I owe to Margaret, for it was after she left that I ceased being a child. And it calls for gratitude, that clear transition. And Margaret's unattractiveness and stupidity made the shape of my life possible. I always knew who I was; I was not Margaret. It gave me a great freedom. I could do whatever I wanted. Her reading the *Sacred Heart Messenger* allowed me to read Mary McCarthy; her damp, immigrant pieties opened the way for what I believed was the ironic, elegant austerity of my adolescent prayer life. Her dull-witted absorption in my father granted me the range and timbre of my devotion. I invented myself in her image, as her opposite. It was immensely helpful. Without her, I would have had to invent myself entirely. An exhausting process with the charm, perhaps, of originality, but with very little prospect of real quality.

It was from her that I won my father. But my victory was twisted, like the twisted end of some punishing German tale. I won my father and my wish. But he was too much for me. The life he cut around me (it is painful, but the truth) would have been, particularly during his illness, the perfect life for Margaret.

You can imagine how unbearable the brown patches on her skin—they were not moles but large, irregular in shape, like the beginning of a cancer—were to a child, or even worse, to an adolescent. I wondered how she managed to keep the house so tidy and yet look so inevitably germ-ridden herself. All her clothes seemed damp, as if her body were giving off a tropical discharge. I believed it to be contagious, although I could neither isolate nor identify it. Her feet were flat as a fish, except where the bunions developed like small crops of winter onions. The sound of her slopping around the house in her slippers is the sound of my nightmares. She would come upon me, thinking she had surprised me, but she was not clever enough to be successfully furtive. Or I was too clever for her. But she made me *feel* as if she had surprised me, as if she had found me with my hand somewhere shameful: in the cookie jar, in the money box, in my own private parts.

Her attempts to turn my father against me were as clumsy as her attempts to catch me in some illegal act.

She would complain to my father that I read all the time instead of helping her with the housework. This showed her complete misunderstanding of what my father wanted in a daughter. He was breeding a Mary: he knew that Christ was right in telling Martha that her sister had chosen the better part. Margaret could never understand that my father didn't care if I cursed or chewed gum or asked for beer with my lunch. He always said he was raising a Theresa of Avila, not a Thérèse of Lisieux: someone who would found orders and insult recalcitrant bishops, not someone who would submit to having dirty water thrown on her by her sisters in Christ and die a perfect death at twenty-four. I would say something like, "That goddamn Sister Evangela. I know more French now than she'll die knowing." (The instruction in my high school was so deficient that it allowed my natural intellectual priggishness a beautiful prosperity.) Margaret would raise her eyes—to God? to one of His more forebearing saints?—and say, "When a Catholic girl uses bad language, the Blessed Mother in Heaven weeps."

I would storm out of the room, cursing more loudly, and my father would follow me saying, "Calm down, calm down. You're right. I know you're right. But what school would be better?"

"Anywhere. Jamaica High."

My father would draw himself up to what he imagined was the posture of Ignatius Loyola: "What doth it profit a man, if he gain the whole world and suffer the loss of his own soul?"

"Do I have to lose my soul to learn some goddamn French?"

"There is plenty of time for that. Right now you are sowing seeds at Anastasia Hall that will bear ripe fruit in your womanhood."

"Yeah, stupidity. That'll do me a lot of good."

But Margaret would have been long left behind, listening to our argument at the kitchen door. Why wasn't she cleverer? In some ways, it would have turned out much the better had she been more subtle, more careful, had she had a complexion or a bosom.

She had certainly aged as badly as could be expected, although I could see at the cemetery that she had begun going to a hairdresser. Why had she done that? For whom did she want to be more beautiful? For my father on the day of his burial? For the priests?

Poor Father Mulcahy. She had been able to *get* him as she had not been able to get me or my father. But he was not clever either, although, unlike Margaret, he was perfectly good . . .

Certainly, it did me no good to be so clever; nevertheless, even at this point I take a not inconsiderable pride in the way I got rid of Margaret. I stood in my father's living room, on the day of my father's funeral, flushed with pleasure at that remembered cleverness.

It was 1956; I know, because that was the year Grace Kelly made *The Swan*. She had just become engaged to the prince. This had seemed to my father, who was normally fiercely on his guard against vulgarity (he had never, for example, liked the Kennedys) the emblem of everything he wanted for the Church. That marriage symbolized power and being in the mainstream. One of the crowned (Catholic) heads of Europe was marrying a chastely beautiful American Irish-Catholic girl, a daily communicant my father would say every time the subject was raised. I, too, was delighted, but for entirely different reasons. Normally, I had to sneak out to the movies. My father was convinced that movies were responsible for the spiritual and intellectual degradation of a generation. He had written an article for *The Sign* called "Movies: Pap or Poison?" But I loved them, they hinted of a world where people were glamorous, cared about clothes, spent money, weren't Catholic. I was amused that my father had fallen for the press's snow job like any shanty Irishman, but to point this out to him would have been to lose a tremendous advantage.

I had prepared for weeks for the day when my father and I would go into Radio City. Is it possible that

my calculations were so exact? I knew that after a
Grace Kelly movie was the perfect time to bring up
the image of Margaret: how bad she would look in
the afterlight of a beautiful woman, especially the ice
goddess who had married the prince. I have lost that
quickness of mind, that sureness of primacy. Perhaps
the rest of my life will be a slow decline from having
been a clever girl.

The following Saturday I confessed to Father Mulcahy that I had committed sins against charity thirty
times in the past week. He knew whom I was talking
about and asked me to come to the rectory for tea
after Confession.

I wept in the rectory office; he took me on his lap.
He would do anything to stop my weeping. He promised he would talk to Margaret about finding another
job.

When the scene finally came, it was quite as grue-
some as I had imagined but less climactic. Both the
men I had trusted failed me. Neither my father nor
Father Mulcahy had the courage to speak to Margaret. In the end, I was the only one able to act.

It happened on a Sunday. On Sundays, Margaret's
presence annoyed me more than it did normally, because there was nothing for her to do. My father and
I, of course, would be going to Communion. We could
let, as the directives from Rome would have it, only
water pass our lips from midnight the night before
Communion. At least on weekday mornings, Margaret
had an ostensible function: she made breakfast. Like
everything else she did, her breakfasts were a poor
showing. How I hated her method of waking me. My
adolescent sleeps were long, dark and sullen. Never
once in those years did I wake of my own accord. It
was Margaret, always, knocking on my door like some
rodent trapped behind a wall. This would bring me to
a rage of wakefulness and I would stomp into the
bathroom, bad-tempered and clearly in the wrong,
while Margaret, who had been up and had gone to six
o'clock Mass, would watch me with a silent and

superior reproach. That would increase my fury; it is impossible to feel the equal of someone who's been awake longer than you.

She sat at the kitchen table, going over prayers in the little prayer books she always brought to Mass with her. I despised those prayer books: Perpetual Novenas, Devotions to St. Anthony, St. Jude, The Little Flower, but they gave me a great safety. *I* used the missal my father had given me for Confirmation. *I,* like him, followed the Latin of the Mass. At that time, my father was deeply involved in a movement called the *Missa Recitata,* a movement to educate the congregation so that it, as a body, could make the responses in Latin. He wrote scornful letters to *The Tablet* about pastors who encouraged the faithful to say the Rosary during Mass. The Mass, he said, was the Single Most Important Act in History. The Consecration, the Transubstantiation, was the central drama of Salvation. One of my purest moments of happiness occurred when Margaret hinted that she would like a missal for Christmas so she could become familiar with the Latin. My father told her she was best off doing what she had always done, what she was used to. Then triumph was mine; then I was carried on a palanquin through a crowd that cheered me.

I sat at the table across from Margaret, next to my father, who was reading the *Journal-American.* He would not take the *Times* because he said it was Communistic, although he freely acknowledged it to be a better newspaper. Margaret always slipped the rubber bands that held her prayer books together over her wrist. That sight roused in me a pure hatred; I was sure she did it to assault me, that thin, dry wrist, those rubber bands that looked as though she'd kept them hidden during the war. I wanted to rip them off her wrist, possibly breaking that easily breakable-looking arm in the process. But I wanted those rubber bands to go on forever. They told me who I was.

At the table I knew I had to get rid of her. Even the way she boiled water was offensive, and the way she offered to make another cup of coffee for my father. I decided to speak then. My mind was utterly clear, a hard, transparent membrane that no hesitation could violate.

"Margaret," I said, "there's something my father and I have wanted to talk to you about."

My father looked up at me with some alarm. He knew what I was talking about. It had been two months since we had gone to see *The Swan*. But he looked down at his newspaper quickly. He was going to let me handle it; he was going to give me my own way. Margaret, unable to make him look at her, looked at me. Had she been cannier, her eyes might have made a mute appeal. But she looked at me like a galley slave afraid that he has been discovered in the plans for mutiny that he will not yet abandon. That mistaken look freed me to go on.

"It has occurred to us—to my father and me—that we really don't need you any more. There are other people who need you. But we don't."

Her response dropped any pretense of humility.

"What's she talking about?" she said to my father.

But it was I whom my father looked at when he spoke.

"I think Isabel knows best," he said.

"About what? She's a child. What does she know about anything?"

She had made a grave tactical error. I went over to her chair. Even at thirteen, I was much taller than she was.

"What we mean is, you'd better look for some other job."

She panicked, like a rat looking for an open door in an experimenter's cage. First she went for me. I could tell that she wanted to do me some physical damage. I walked to the other side of the room. It was absurd. She should never have attempted to strike me; I was larger and quicker. I left her flailing. Her flat hand, poised for a slap on hard flesh, beat only air. My father did nothing to defend me. But he was right in his stasis; I did not need him. My power was so obvious that it would have been ridiculous for him to offer me protection.

Her panic made her desperate. She fell on her knees in front of my father. She began kissing the hem of his jacket.

"But you," she said, "I always loved you."

My father put his hand to his mouth. He picked up his coat and went out the back door. He left me alone with her.

She knelt on the floor, sobbing. Never have I felt less pity. I moved over to her. I stood above her.

"I think you'd better leave now," I said.

And the miracle is that she did. She could as easily have killed me. And until the day of my father's funeral, I never saw her again.

How did I become, at thirteen, such a monster of certainty? My sureness was imperial; at thirteen I could have led armies. I have lost that now. I am not, at thirty, the person I was. So that when I saw Margaret in my living room, I could not entirely stand up to her. I took her arm. It required all my courage to do so.

"He wrote to me every week," she said. "He sent me money every week. Ever since I left him."

Disgust and something else, something not as thick but meaner—was it jealousy?—sat in the center of my chest. I had not known this. How had my father kept it from me all those years?

"Even when he couldn't write, the lawyers sent my check," she whined. "He never forgot."

"He was a good man," I said. More than anything, I wanted to say, "How I loathe you; how I have always loathed you." My father had deceived me for this woman.

"I loved him. Whatever happened I always loved him," Margaret said, screwing her damp face up to cry.

"You mustn't say that. Not to me. Not now."

"Now I'm all alone. What will I do?"

She had used up my small reserve of pity.

"If you are in need, you must get in touch with me," I said.

I walked away. I could walk away easily. Many people wanted to speak to me. But I was not interested in what they were saying; I was interested in Margaret, and in my father's betrayal. We did not have that much money, he knew I was worried about money. And every week he had given money, *my* money, to Margaret.

Priests kissed me, priests shook my hand. They were beginning to leave the house. It was beginning to be over.

"We've both lost our best friend," said Father Mulcahy, weeping.

After the priests left, the house emptied quickly. Finally, there was no one there but women. It was odd, being in my father's house without men. Usually I had been the only woman. Liz left with her mother. Eleanor was drying glasses in the kitchen. And there was Margaret, sitting on the couch in her coat, holding her pocketbook.

"I missed my train," she said. "I have nowhere to go until tomorrow."

I looked at Eleanor. Her look said, "You are drowning now and I can do nothing to save you."

"You must stay here then," I said.

"I can't sleep on the couch, I have a bad back."

"You must take my bed."

"Shall I stay, Isabel?" asked Eleanor.

I did not want to expose her to the contamination of Margaret.

"I'll be all right."

"I'll call you tomorrow."

Margaret had taken her coat off and hung it in the living-room closet.

"The place certainly has gone down since I left it," she said.

"Things happen in seventeen years."

"You never did appreciate the work I had to put in to keep this house up. You thought you could do everything. You always did."

She was right. At thirteen, I imagined myself to be capable of everything. But the truth was I could not even begin to manage the house. There were things that I didn't know how to do that were so simple that I would have had to be extraordinarily intimate with someone to ask about them. And I knew no one well but my father. He seemed to take a pride in the curious degradation of our surroundings, as if the mess, the pileup, was an index to the richness of our interior lives. I did not take the same pride. It was with despair that I went into the homes of my friends, homes cared for by mothers who knew what they were doing, who understood what had to be done with old magazines, with the smell at the bottom of the sink. I could not ask the mothers of my friends for help or advice, not only because I thought they were on Margaret's side, not only because I feared their saying, "Don't you think you'd be better off with Margaret there to help you?" but because their identities seemed so utterly unlikely. I would never look like them: my hair curled back, my hard white stomach corseted, covered in a linen apron. I could not possibly follow their example, their advice, because we were so radically different. They only made me feel more hopeless.

So I would go home to my cheerless house and the prospect of straightening out the broom closet. It was a trick to open the door without everything falling out into the kitchen. Do not imagine some jovial, Fibber McGee untidiness. It was a disorder that vanquished me in private and in public mortified me. What was on the bottom of that closet? Rags, old newspapers, ancient brushes whose function I did not understand, desiccating like malicious emigrés in the darkness. Why could I never clear that closet out? Because I could not understand how to do it. And at thirteen, at fourteen, I should not have had to. But I had chosen the disorder, the sense of drowning in an ignorance that ought to have been escapable through some knowledge not difficult to acquire. I had chosen it but had not known what I was choosing. I persisted because all of it—the linoleum that stained black and came up on the bottoms of shoes, the drawers full of old birthday cards and lost bills—was better than having Margaret around, was better than giving my father up to her. And here she was now, alone in the house with me. Preparing to spend the night.

"You never kept this table up. Look at the scratches on it."

"I was very busy. Taking care of my father was extremely time-consuming."

"That man never had a sick day while I was with him."

I felt panic where I always felt it: in the soles of my feet, where I had felt it when I came home to see the ambulance at the door. She had said what for years I had most feared hearing, what I had stopped myself saying to myself. Arthritis had twisted her hands and her spine so that she looked half animal. Was she one of those magical creatures who had been given vision as a payment for ugliness? Was she the only one to know the truth?

I could no longer be in the same room with her. I said I was tired and needed to go to bed. Then I remembered: I would have to sleep on the couch. I showed Margaret to my room.

She put her suitcase on my bed. Why had she brought a suitcase? Of course, she expected that someone would ask her to stay.

"Will you want a bath?" I asked.

"Are there clean towels?"

"Of course," I said, knowing there were two.

Her presence in the bathroom was like escaping gas. I could feel it in the air, bluish but invisible. I had forgotten to get my nightgown from my room, so I slept on the couch in all my clothes. But I felt safer that way, with Margaret so near. It was a sour, exhausted sleep that spun with faces and the memories they had

demanded of me all day. I awoke several times. The
light in the living room was unfamiliar. I kept thinking, trying to identify the furniture, This is no longer
my father's house.

II

I could hear Margaret in the kitchen before I opened my eyes. The noise brought me back to my childhood rages, so that my first thoughts were not of my father's absence from the house, but of that woman's intrusion into it. But I refused to open my eyes until I could no longer not acknowledge Margaret standing above me.

"Do you always sleep in your clothes? That dress will be ruined. And it's expensive. Do you have to take it to the cleaners?"

"I didn't want to disturb you," I said.

"Disturb me? I couldn't sleep a wink all night. I was crying my eyes out for your father."

"What time is your train?"

"In an hour."

"Penn Station?"

"Grand Central."

"That's easier. You just take the Flushing line."

"I don't know if I can take the subway. With all the muggings."

"It's early in the morning."

"And all those stairs. With my arthritis. God knows it's a day's work just to climb a flight of stairs for me."

"Perhaps you could take a taxi."

"Me? *I* have to watch my pennies. I wasn't born with a silver spoon in my mouth."

"I'll pay for it," I said, leaning back on my elbows.

My stockings and my underwear felt as if I had traveled from Teheran to Amsterdam in them. I greeted the cab at the door with an extravagance that did not escape Margaret.

"You can't wait to get rid of me, can you?" she said.

"I'll be in touch with you," I said, giving her my hand to shake. I would have preferred any human action to an embrace.

"People always say that and they don't. Out of sight, out of mind."

"You know where to find me."

"Who knows what you'll get it in your head to do now. You can afford it," she said, getting into the taxi.

The day seemed excessively open; it was only seven o'clock. I felt neither sorrow nor relief, but only a vague agoraphobia: life was space, the borders seemed so far away from the vast airy center that there was no help and I remembered my childhood dream of falling out of bed, through the floor, and simply falling.

I went into my father's room, partly from habit, but also because in that great airiness habit was a border. And from habit I rubbed some Dermassage on my hands. There it was again: that feeling of accumulation, of the pileup of things and days and lives. What I had was either too much, things that would smother me, or nothing at all, nothing to break my fall. I wondered if it would be possible to walk through some moderate landscape, populated yet expansive, and blessedly to scale.

Catholic Charities had come and taken my father's hospital bed; with a kind of desperate efficiency I had called them about it an hour after I learned of his death. They had taken part of the other equipment away, too, so the place had lost something of its sickroom aspect, but the smell of sickness and medication still hung in the air like smoke in a barroom. And there was still the sheepskin that was supposed to help with bedsores, the suction machine for when my father was choking on his own phlegm, the huge jars

of Vaseline, the thousands of feet of gauze. The room
without a bed in the middle of it was denuded. Most
rooms have something in them of comfort; it is the
function of furniture to comfort the juts of the body
against the hard limits of floor and wall. But now there
was only one corner of the room that was inhabited or
habitable. My father's old desk, the hard oak with
grains of black like pencil lines in it, so that when I
was a little girl I had colored in the lines with a pencil, stood where it always had, although for five years
my father had been unable to sit up for long and it
had become what everything else in the room had become: a place to put medicine. How my father had resented that, and I had resented it for him, but we
had both allowed it to happen, for the room, with its
added accretion of wheelchair, commode and suction
machinery, could not have supported another table. It
was difficult enough as it was for me to maneuver
around the room's accumulations, all of them necessary, some of them making a real difference to actual
suffering, but none of them beautiful.

Above my father's desk were pictures that had
hung there as long as I could remember: a print of
Holbein's Thomas More, a Dürer engraving of St.
Jerome and the lion. Despite its usurpation by medical
artifacts, the top of my father's desk still smelled of
carbon paper and cigars. I thought of the fretful strain
of his shoulders as he typed on his huge black machine. And the image filled me with what, through all
the years of my father's illness I had not finally lost:
admiration for his fierceness, for his absoluteness and
the consequent ironies of his considerable tenderness.
For my father was sure: he had faith, he had truth;
they had wired his muscles and made his bones like
steel. And if his faith and his truth had made him arro-
gant and filled him more with hate than with love (although he *said* it was the love of God that stirred
him) and if his arguments were spurious and even
sometimes wicked, his life had the grandeur of a great

struggle, his mind the endurance of great Renaissance sculpture.

I cannot dismiss his faith, no one could, for it had been fiercely stripped of any pietism or sentimentality. Even my father kneeling with a rosary in his hands was not a pious sight. His faith had the appeal of war, and the horror. It was a force: manly, gladiatorial. No woman could have approached anything like it, for his relations with God had nothing of the lover about them, as a woman's inevitably have. He and God were fellow soldiers. Because he knew what he wanted, he felt entitled to do anything, and was capable of it.

The appeal of his fire and the appeal of his love were connected; they did not crumble as his body grew distorted and inept. For he raged at his body, which he had never thought kindly of, with a fine, useless passion. And when he could not speak, he wrote, and when he could not write, he wept and prayed to die. And I was devoted to his anger and his sorrow and my days were used up for the comfort of his body, which I could effect, and his mind, which I could not touch. And if I went to bed weeping for the absurd and utterly needless suffering of my father's body, I awoke in the morning to relieve it. And if those years were lost to me in ways that are impossible to calculate and impossible to regain, I knew why. I did this for the person I most loved, with the passion of mind and soul that he reserved for God.

And yet the day of his funeral I had not begun to miss him, or if I missed him, it was the habit of him that I missed. There had been one brief spasm of grief when the hospital called about his death, but the grief was as much a sense of having been cheated; after all those years of care and watchfulness, my father died alone, in his sleep.

When I tried to imagine him after death, I could imagine nothing; I could only hope that all his beliefs had won him something; that all his anger had bought him a place in an orthodox heaven.

I opened one of the desk drawers and took out a

folder of his articles. On the top was one that had been published in a magazine he had been part of in the forties called *Catholic Word*. As I turned the pages, they began to crumble into flakes. I came to my father's piece: "The Catholic Temper." Protestants, it said, thought about moral issues, drank water and ate crackers, took care to exercise and had a notion that charity was synonymous with good works. Catholics, on the other hand, thought about eternity, drank wine and smoked cigars, were sometimes extravagant, but knew that charity was a fire in the heart of God and never confused it with that Protestant invention, philanthropy.

What was the point of these cleverly malicious exercises? Who would read them? What would they do but convince the already convinced of their obvious superiority? What an exhausting occupation, constantly supporting the hierarchy from the bottom, constantly buttressing it by seizing on the rest of the world like a great cruel bird taking its prey home to tear apart and examine the contents of its stomach. I put all the articles in a carton marked Cinzano Bianco, taped it shut and labeled it on the top. I packed his magazines in another carton, and for the rest of the afternoon I piled the cartons up against the wall: gray and brown and solid, they were lunar mountains in the room's wide neutrality.

I had done all this before even thinking about breakfast. I looked in the refrigerator. I hadn't shopped for days, since before the wake, and I had hardly been home enough even to open the refrigerator door. When I did, I was greeted by the defeating stench of rotting food. I tried to find the source of the odor; I smelt the milk and looked carefully at the hardening block of yellow Cheddar. Then I bent down and opened the vegetable bin. The sight of broccoli liquefying at the bottom made me want to run away and set a match to the whole house. I lifted up the cold slime of the vegetable; I could barely endure the horror against my hands. I began shaking the cloggy leaves into the garbage bin frantically, but I could not get them off my fingers. I began to cry.

The phone rang. I wiped my hands on a paper towel and answered it.

"Isabel? It's Liz."

"Hi, Liz."

"What's wrong, dear? Is it your father?"

"No, it's a broccoli," I said, and then I began to laugh. I could hear Liz laugh in relief on the other end.

"There was this broccoli in the vegetable bin, rotting. You have no idea how it defeated me."

"I do," said Liz, "of course I do."

We chatted for a while about the news of Liz's family. Alexander had been exposed to chicken pox; John would be away. I drank in the domestic details of Liz's life. The ordinariness, the predictability of that life made me feel, even at this remove, more human.

"The main reason I called is," Liz said, pausing in midsentence as she always did, *"Top Hat*'s going to be on the late movie."

"Thank you. You've saved my life for tonight. I'm going to Bloomingdale's tomorrow. With Eleanor, to buy clothes."

"Don't come back looking like something out of *The Faerie Queene.*"

I was momentarily stung by Liz's peremptory jealousy of Eleanor, which was, by now, instinctive. But I realized that she was right; it would be all too easy for me, having learned no style of my own, to ape the wardrobe Eleanor had created for herself over the last five years. And Liz was right in another way: on Eleanor, such clothes looked poetic; on me, they would be absurd.

"I'm going to get a copy of *Vogue* this afternoon," I said.

"You don't have to do it like a term paper."

"But I'm so out of things. I've hardly been on the street for eleven years. I haven't been into the city since 1965."

"You'll be smashing," said Liz, half-heartedly.

"You don't sound convinced."

"I'll see what you look like."

I wanted to tell her what Margaret had told me, about my father's having sent her money every week for all those years. But I did not want to give it importance by speaking about it so soon after I had learned the truth. And yet I wanted to betray my father, as he had betrayed me, by opening the circle of our honor, by letting secrets out.

"Do you know what Margaret just told me?" I said. "What?"

I hesitated a moment. "My father's been sending her money every goddamn week. For seventeen years."

"Oh, Jesus, isn't that typical."

"Typical what?"

"Typical Catholic blood money. You starve your family to keep alive some lunatic in Canada who thinks he has the stigmata. How much did he give her?"

"I don't know. I'll have to find out from Delaney."

"You won't go on giving her money now, of course?"

I was embarrassed that the idea had not occurred to me.

"No," I said. "No, I don't have that much money. There's the house, but I think that's it."

"Did your father have any kind of pension from St. Aloysius?"

"Nothing. He thought that it showed a lack of faith to contribute to pension plans. He was very opposed to Social Security. He said it was socialist. He said it was against the spirit of the Gospel. I guess he thought it was going along with the spirit of the Gospel to let John Delaney invest his money for him."

"I don't understand it," said Liz. "How could you put your child's future in jeopardy for such an abstract idea? It's a kind of brutality."

"Oh, Christ, Liz, of course you understand it. 'What doth it profit a man, if he gain the whole world and suffer the loss of his own soul.' They were always tell-

FINAL PAYMENTS

ing us that. My father took it more literally than most."

Liz laughed, a public laugh, a Catholic school laugh.

"I would have loved to have seen my husband trying to talk to your father. That's his big thing: government responsibility for the aged. I would've loved it.
Your father could've slashed him to ribbons."

So Liz was unhappily married. How had I not
known it? Because she would not have told me while
my father was still alive. Clearly, even this soon after
his death, I had become to her a different person.

"I have to go to Delaney," I said. "I'm late."

"You know what I'd love more than anything? To
catch John Delaney *in flagrante delicto.*"

"I'll keep my eyes open."

John Delaney's office had been on the second floor
of 1235 Meadowbrook Parkway since 1932 when he
had begun his practice. John had handled all my father's legal affairs, as he had handled those of the parish and the nuns at Anastasia Hall. He took a not
inconsiderable pride in being a worldly man who handled the business of the otherworldly, who left them
free for the pure business of the mind and the spirit. It
was a peculiarly Irish pride; it made him the kind of
lawyer that he was, and it made him able to act, if not
unscrupulously, at least shrewdly, with considerable
depth and charm.

John had been wearing the same kind of suits for
forty years, huge dark tents of suits that made it impossible to imagine the contours of his body. His age
had always been professionally indeterminate, but
never more so than now, when the suits he had always
worn were beginning to come back into fashion. He
was an old Tammany Hall Democrat whose thinking
had not changed for fifty years, an unselfconscious
racist, who thought it was perfectly within the spirit of
the Gospel to refuse to defend a black man in court as
long as he performed extraordinary acts of anonymous
generosity. This queer amalgam of cutthroat expan-
siveness alternately enraged and drew me. That day I
was in the mood to be taken into his florid atmosphere.

His secretary buzzed him, and he came into the outer office to meet me. He put his arm around my shoulders and half lifted me off the ground with his embrace.

"Ya see this girl, Miss Templeton? Ya see her? She's a saint. I swerta God, an honest-to-God saint. She took care of her father like a little saint, God rest his soul."

I felt acutely the impossibility of the situation, and I smiled anemically at Miss Templeton. What could I say? I simply walked into the office with John, his arm still around me in a way that made it impossible to walk naturally. I sat across from him at a distance that forced me to take in his lunchtime whiskey breath.

"I've paid all the bills for you, honey. It's the least I could do, my God, after all you've been through. And there'll be no bill from me. Wait till those doctors get through with you, you poor little kid. It's a good thing I've looked out for you all these years or you'd be in some trouble."

"Exactly what is left, John?" I thought if I spoke with dryness and restraint it might serve as a blotter for his extravagance.

"Well, sweetheart, you've got the house free and clear. I should be able to get you twenty-five grand for it at least. But everything else is gone."

"That's very good, isn't it? That's a lot more than a lot of people get."

"You're a saint Isabel, a saint of God. I always said it. I'm assuming you'll want to sell."

"Yes. As soon as I get cleared out."

"No rush, honey, you take your time."

"I'd like it to be done as quickly as possible."

"You've got plans, honey?"

"I'll think of something."

"Can you type, honey? A refined girl like you can always get a good typing job. Why not take some shorthand? You'd make a damn fine secretary."

"I can type, but I don't intend to make a living at it."

"You're going back to school? Teaching, that's a good profession for a woman."

"I don't know, John, I haven't thought it all out yet."

"How about nursing? With your experience."

"No. I don't want to do it. I'm not really very good at it. I couldn't do it for strangers."

"You know what, I'll talk to some of the priests I know. They always have some good leads. People need paid companions, that sort of thing. I remember when your mother died, God rest her soul, Father Mulcahy and I put Margaret Casey in with your family."

A blot of nausea bubbled at the back of my lips. So this was how they perceived me and my life, as they had Margaret's, as they had the interminable history of good daughters who cared for their parents. What happened to the daughters when the object of all that sacrifice was gone? It was this enmeshing network of clergy and professional men that surrounded them, finding them places, among their *own kind* where they could feel needed and of use. Where, with God's help, they would say, they would end up one of the family.

I thought of Margaret. She was probably not too much older than I when she came to our house twenty-eight years ago. At that moment, I felt for John Delaney a pure hatred. He went on talking, about my money, about the house. I understood nothing he said. The histories of those women fell unheeded around me. It was, perhaps, inevitable. One was born and certain things happened and one responded. Cause and chance and the slow, inexorable accretion of events, and one looked to the past, to people who had lived through the same kinds of events for the outcome. And what was the outcome of these women? How did they move from Sunday to Sunday or Christmas to Christmas? Charity is tedious, and sacrifice is not, as Christ deceived us into thinking, anything so dramatic as a crucifixion. Most of the time it is profoundly boring.

On the way home, I bought a copy of *Vogue,* which I read with my lunch. It took courage for someone like

me, who had worn clothes for decency and warmth
during the years of life when women find clothes the
center of their lives, to look at clothes as adornment,
as fashion, to consider how I looked. All those years,
I watched old movies on television with a determination not to forget that part of life—beauty, and glam-
our, and audacity and chic. I remembered being
nineteen, or rather I had not forgotten, had worked at
not forgetting, the lift in my stomach, the pull, like a
diver's arc, when a perfectly strange man would give
me a look or a nod, acknowledging our complicity, telling me he had observed me and I had pleased him.
And I wanted this for myself again.

But as I looked at *Vogue,* I began to think it was
all quite impossible. Young and tall, with hips and
breasts like boys' and cheeks dyed the color of a Bosc
pear, with hats over one eye, and scarves six feet long
and slacks as wide as cassocks, these models seemed
entirely foreign—they might have been another spe-
cies. Did they walk in these clothes on ordinary
streets? I had never seen them. I had never seen anything like them even in movies. Advertisements for
lipstick and eyeshadow, pictures of mascara and eye-
brow pencils took up whole pages. I had never thought
of buying anything like them. In 1962, when my fashion sense had stopped, I was wearing a light-pink lipstick and a touch of pressed powder. Now there were
greens and purples and browns to contend with. And I
did not know how to begin.

When I got on the subway to meet Eleanor, I was
on the lookout for women who might serve as more
realistic models. I thought of Liz's accusing me of going at the thing like a term paper, and I laughed, but
only for good luck. For, having waited so long for this
almost Copernican reversal of my way of looking at
myself, it had to be right.

Although it was astonishingly hot outside, Bloomingdale's was autumnal, not only in its air-conditioned
iciness, but in the russets and deep-green wools the

mannequins wore. I panicked; I saw nothing that I could possibly wear until mid-October.

I could not move until Eleanor walked through the revolving door, her smooth hair on the top of her head like a Gibson girl. She was wearing a violet skirt, a thin pink T-shirt and the kind of wedge sandals that we used to make fun of people's mothers for wearing. In my navy-blue cotton skirt and yellow sleeveless blouse, I felt a fierce determination to buy something that I could wear *today*.

"Let's look at the tops first," Eleanor suggested, "and then we can build skirts and pants around them."

"Yes, I read that in *Vogue*. An article called 'Tops You Can Build Your Fall Around.'"

"They make it sound so easy to change your life," said Eleanor. "They say things like, 'New eye-shadow colors make a whole new You.' If only it were that easy."

"The trouble is, I partly believe them," I said. "That's why I'm here."

It was with immense relief that I found on the third floor summer clothes still available. But I felt inferior to the other women who were not creating a wardrobe with my catch-as-catch-can urgency, who had the leisure to try on tweeds in August.

"We'll just buy a few things," I said. I was beginning to feel dazed. And Eleanor, knowing me so well, realized what had happened.

"Let me pick something first, Isabel. For good luck."

"What frightens me is that there are so few things I can *do* any more. Perfectly normal things that children can do. The smallest thing now makes me feel ruined. Maybe I left it too long."

"Left what, dear?" Eleanor said, gazing at me with that pure, almost dumb look of understanding that could inspire such love.

"My life," I said.

"Come now," said Eleanor, like a nun. "It's exciting. It's like being Robinson Crusoe. Or an astronaut. Just think, you have no past to embarrass you. You have nothing you've done to anyone that you'll never recover from."

Not having told Eleanor about David Lowe, I had withheld from my best friend some of the central information of my life.

"Eleanor," I said, "do you think it was crazy? What I did all those years. What I did for my father."

Eleanor circled my wrist with her left hand. "He was a compelling man, Isabel. Not like anyone I've ever known. Not like anyone in our age. So things made a kind of sense in regard to him that they didn't with anyone else."

I felt, through Eleanor's understanding, the removal of a great weight. She had almost offhandedly been selecting clothes as we walked through the racks. She steered me toward the dressing room. I climbed awkwardly out of my sweaty clothes and looked at myself in my white pants and bra. My breasts were full and high; they were all right, and my waist tapered—there was nothing to worry about. But when I looked at the loose flesh of my thighs, I was embarrassed for Eleanor to see them.

"I have to lose some weight," I said.

"Nonsense," said Eleanor, "don't get into that trap."

"I don't think my figure's in fashion any more, if it ever was."

"Don't worry, men are always fond of breasts. Whatever *Vogue* says. Try these on now, Isabel. It's dispiriting to look at yourself so closely in the mirror."

I tried on a blouse first. It was too small. Tears came to my eyes.

"Just wait here, Isabel. I'll get another size," said Eleanor, leaving me alone in a tiny enclosure that was mirrors on all four sides. She came back with the same blouse in a larger size and a brown-paper package.

"Before you try anything on, I've bought you some underpants. You can't buy anything new in those."

I opened the bag and took out a pair of nylon bikini underpants: dark green with ivory lace. They were delightful even to hold in my hand. But I didn't know if I could take my underpants off in front of Eleanor. It was one thing to talk in underwear: that was girlish and friendly and bespoke an athletic-minded informality. But to stand in front of a friend with a bare crotch was an affront and an embarrassment. But it would have been even worse to ask Eleanor to leave. Quickly, I pulled off my heavy underpants and slipped on the silky new ones. The effect was immediate and delicious. I laughed, in embarrassment, in pleasure.

The blouse, to my impossible delight, fit, and with trepidation I tried on a pair of green linen slacks. They were light and roomy and their feel on my legs was totally unexpected.

I saw myself tall and cool, my lines definite and spare. It was a success, and success had always made me greedy.

"Now," I said, "I want another top, and a long, light skirt, and a pair of black high-heeled sandals." I embraced Eleanor. "It's working. I think I can do it."

When we had paid for the clothes, I said, "What about makeup? I'm entirely in your hands."

"Let's go home to my house," Eleanor said, "and I'll let you experiment, and then you can buy what works."

On the bus to Eleanor's apartment, I looked over at her with a pang of love that was like hunger. How rare Eleanor was, to have kept up with me all those years, to have taken me through this day. I took her hand and squeezed it.

"In many ways," I said, "you've kept me alive."

"You've never seen my place," said Eleanor, blushing, looking out the bus window. "I'm afraid since Justin and I split, I've come down in the world. You should've seen that apartment."

It was unbelievably tiny, and the walls were stark white. It was a new sensation for me, to be in the home of a friend that was not a parent's home. I felt pleasurably illicit as I sat on the couch and kicked off my new sandals.

"I thought we'd make dinner here," Eleanor said. "How about an enormous salad and some cheese and a lot of cool wine? And you can stay over tonight. As a matter of fact, you *must* stay over tonight. It's an age since you've slept anywhere but Dover Road."

It suddenly struck me with real alarm that I had no one to ask permission of, no one to report back to. I felt myself looking down at my life from a height, in a thin layer of ozone where nothing bred.

"I'd like that," I said to Eleanor, using all my courage. "I'd like that very much."

I wanted to say, "Now I am alone again, and frightened. Even your presence cannot bring me back."

"Come and help me chop things," said Eleanor. "Or come and talk to me while I chop."

Once more, Eleanor had understood me, had sensed my fear.

"Look at these lovely creatures," Eleanor said, taking things out of the refrigerator.

Eleanor bent down, took out onions, tomatoes, two heads of lettuce and a peach. Seeing her like that I was no longer frightened. I said, "I am at this moment completely happy." I put my arms around my friend, and we embraced in the promising heat of the August evening.

"I can't tell you how beautiful those vegetables are," I said. "We ought to take a picture of them."

"Let's," Eleanor said. "I'll get my Instamatic."

We peeled and chopped and mixed everything up in the light wooden bowl that was almost half the size of the table. Eleanor would start a song and I would finish it. Then I would begin one for her.

Looking not at me but at the sink, Eleanor said, "You were saying how grateful you are to me. I'm terribly grateful to you. You've been important to me, too. It's been important to me that we've kept up."

"I don't understand."

"You're the only thing I have to go back to that I like. When I moved in with Justin, my family cut me off. And then I didn't want to admit to them that the whole thing hadn't worked after all. So my mother sort of calls me on the sly and cries and my sister and I talk, but there's nothing really."

"Tell me about Justin. I feel terrible that I've never talked to you about him."

"No, it was exactly right. You were the only person I could go to that hadn't been touched by him—who was completely free of any trace of him. It was a real comfort. He was so overpowering. I think he still overpowers me."

"In what sense?"

"Well, for one thing, professionally. He's a very big art historian. I quit graduate school to keep house for him—or rather, to play house with him. And it worked. I was amazingly happy for three years. I'd spend all morning shopping, then I'd meet him for lunch and I'd come home and make these incredibly elaborate dinners. All out of the Julia Child cookbook."

"I never even asked why you weren't going to graduate school any more. I didn't even think of it. Was I really that self-absorbed?"

"No. I didn't make much of it. It didn't seem much at the time. Well, Justin and I went out every night—to his friends—I had no friends. I mean, the people I knew at St. Aloysius, it was unthinkable that Justin would get on with them. So that was how it was for three years. And then—I don't know—I was sort of in a daze for a year. All I wanted to do was sleep. I slept fifteen hours a day. No more great dinners. No more adorable lunches. Then I decided to get the job in the gallery. And Justin got sort of berserk. He started sleeping around with everyone. He gave me gonorrhea. This went on for two years. And then he found someone else and sort of threw me out."

"How did you go on like that? For two years! It must have been hell."

"It was. As if there were splintered glass all over the place, tiny cuts all over my hands and feet. But I kept believing it would all work out. I'd probably still be there if he hadn't got rid of me."

"It's impossible to imagine that anyone would want to get rid of you."

"I understand it. First of all, I'm not very good in bed. I sort of drift away. And sometimes I sort of drift away in general. Much less so, now. I'm better now. I fantasize much less. I suppose that's a good sign."

"You know, all those years with my father, I kept alive these enormously complicated fantasies. About me, and how I'd look and men with nice backs and terrific voices."

"I guess it's partly what kept you going. It's what holds me back. I could never do what you've done, get hold of my life as you have after all that. I can't get hold of my life now. It sort of swims above me."

I said, with a false curtness, "Eleanor, I never told you. I went to bed with David Lowe. And I liked it. And I want to go to bed with someone again soon."

"It's funny," said Eleanor, as if she were not impressed with the enormity of my confession, "I don't want to go to bed with anyone for the next thirty years. I guess I feel it muddles things. I feel much clearer when I'm chaste, much more capable of loving well. Sex is so self-interested, in some way."

"The only time in my life I ever felt totally at the center of things, totally myself, was when I was having sex with David. I'll never forget it, even if I never have sex again. So much of me drifts above my life."

"Speaking of fantasizing, for years I had elaborate sexual fantasies about your father."

I sat up, as if the train I had been peaceably riding in, looking through the window of, had jerked to a painful halt. I realized then that we were both slightly drunk.

Eleanor went on, unaware of my displeasure. "I'd have this fantasy conversation in which I'd tell you that even though I was your stepmother, we'd still be friends." She laughed. Foolishly, I thought.

"You probably could have had him, if you'd really

wanted him. It would have been the sort of thing he'd have loved: a beautiful and devoted young wife at his feet."

I was conscious once more of my jealousy of Eleanor, of the dirty pebbles in the stream of our love, of my jealousy of her beauty, her fragility, of her dreaminess, of her long, light hair.

"I think I got involved with Justin because he was like your father in a way."

"What way?"

"Oh, they wore the same kind of shoes, and their voices were the same, and they were authoritative and sure and capable of extraordinary rudeness. I don't know. It's crazy, isn't it?"

I wanted to say, "Then you do understand, you do understand, why I did what I did, why I stayed with him. And how awful it was to see him deteriorate." But I wanted more to punish Eleanor, to deny her this intimacy, to make her pay for the crime of having loved my father, too, and for the even greater offense of being potentially more attractive to him than I was.

"You've got a lot of hang-ups about men, don't you?" I said.

Eleanor was clearly hurt; she was clearly sensible of the deprivation I had intended for her.

"I never thought I'd hear you use a word like 'hang-up.' You were always so sensitive to jargon."

We cleared the plates and washed them, but there was a strain between us; the air in the kitchen, which had seemed welcoming as we prepared the meal, began to seem stifling.

"Do you want to try the make-up now?" asked Eleanor.

I thought it would be unbearable now to see myself in the same mirror as Eleanor, or to be close to anything that was connected to her beauty. I faked a yawn.

"What I'd really like is a nice cool bath and bed."

Eleanor was not taken in; she recognized my Catholic-school *politesse*.

"It *is* hot. And shopping is tiring. I have some lovely bath oil. It's by the tub."

I hated myself, sitting on the edge of Eleanor's tub, for having a heart that contracted at the beauty of one I loved. But jealousy stuck in my heart like a sharp chip of ice and would not melt.

Eleanor had made the couch into a bed for me. Her face had the pure look of pain of a child who knows she has been unjustly punished. I could not go on with it; her beauty, her perfectly simple kindness, bending over the couch, lifting the cushions, made me see myself a monster. But it made me love her again as well.

"You see how terrible I can be," I said.

"I was tactless. You see, I just drift off and forget about everything. It's a kind of cruelty."

"Let's sleep. Our background makes these orgies of self-abnegation entirely too seductive for the both of us."

Eleanor laughed. We both had a sense of great freedom; we had come to the portage and had carried each other across. We had survived our first fight. We would go on.

But as I lay in the dark, the street lights illuminating the unfamiliar furniture, making it look preternatural, I thought how my father had affected Eleanor, too. And despite my love for Eleanor, which was deep and poignant and satisfying, I would never quite forgive her.

III

I awoke in Eleanor's apartment, my head resting uncomfortably against the arm of the couch in a way that warned me that my neck would ache for the rest of the day. It was only six-thirty, but the thin curtains, which had not kept out the queer light of the street the night before, now let in the morning sun. I resigned myself, in a churlish way, to taking up the day, but once again I was startled by its openness, its emptiness; it was like an unused warehouse that I would have to fill.

"Hi," I heard Eleanor say, sleepily from her bed. "What time is it?"

"Six-thirty. I'm a brute, I know. But I couldn't sleep. You rest though, I'm all right."

"No, I like to get up and read before I go to work. Except I hardly ever manage to do it."

I brought a cup of instant coffee to her bed, and she moved over so that I could sit beside her. The early hour and the whiteness of the sunlight gave everything a fragility. And Eleanor, still partly asleep, one arm over her head, soothed me by her solidity and delicacy. The pink tint of her throat and arms cloaked my fear and made me feel attached and occupied.

"I've got wonderful things for breakfast," she said. "Melons and croissants and Kenyan coffee. Or do you want eggs?"

"Who would want eggs?"

"Thank God. If you'd wanted eggs, I would've been so disappointed."

"Then why did you ask? You needn't even have brought it up. You could have used your leverage as a hostess."

"I've always thought leverage was horrifying. Whenever I think I have any I try to get rid of it."

"How do you get what you want?"

"I suppose I still think that if I'm very good things will come."

"Do they?"

"No, that's the problem. But I'm so frightened of my own unfair advantages that in the end I think things are right as they are."

"Eleanor, I was thinking. When I sell the house, I'll have money. Do you want to go back to graduate school?"

"Thank you. You're the only one I *would* take money from. But I've blown it in academics, and you don't just fail out of one place and start in another."

"Why?"

"You just don't. And besides, it's too tied up with Justin."

"What do you want, then, from your life?"

"I don't know. I'd like to do something I was entirely sure of."

"Like we used to be about the Church. It's so unfair. There's nothing like it, nothing takes its place. Only, when you stop believing, even it doesn't work."

"Do you miss it?"

"I miss that sureness. But I don't miss the people, and what it does to them."

"Yes," said Eleanor, "it ought to make them happy, but it doesn't."

"They keep saying they're not after happiness, but they are. It's unfair to them, really. They do give up rather a lot. And they're still miserable. Except the stupid ones who'd be happy anywhere."

"How can you call people stupid?"

"How can you not?"

"I'm afraid to."

"I can't help it."

"By the way, did you ever find out about Margaret and the money?"

"Delaney didn't say anything about it, and there was nothing in the will. So I guess she didn't get anything more."

"Thank God. If she had, I was planning to burn her house down. With her in it."

"Do you know, Margaret haunts me. I have a great fear of turning into her."

"That's crazy. You're nothing like her."

"But how do we know what she was like when she was young?"

"We know she wasn't good-looking. Or smart. Both of which you are."

"Those unfair advantages you believe we'll have to pay for in the end."

"I didn't say we'd have to pay for them."

"But you believe we will."

Eleanor looked worried. "Yes," she said. "I do."

"So do I."

She looked at her watch. "I have to get ready for work. Do you want to try some of the make-up?"

She had on top of her dresser a startling variety of cosmetics. I felt a twinge, remembering why we didn't experiment with them last night. To punish myself for my failure of generosity, I declined Eleanor's offer, although the seduction of the cosmetics settled in the back of my throat like the imagination of a great dessert.

I left Eleanor at the bus and walked the three blocks to the subway. As I walked down the subway steps, a man, who had slung his jacket over his shoulders, looked up at me, nodded and smiled. I nodded back. We both went on walking in opposite directions. I walked into the hot underground, my eyes bright, my face flushed and foolishly smiling, sure of myself as an athlete or a well-fed dog.

I had forgotten that I was supposed to have supper

with Father Mulcahy. I knew his habit of calling the morning before any evening engagement; it was the insecure discipline of a man who has never lived with a woman. I hoped that he would not be worried. He was used to finding me always at home. In the home of an invalid, someone is always there to answer the telephone. I knew that his first thoughts would be imaginations of disaster. As soon as I got in the house, I telephoned the rectory.

"I thought you'd be worried about me," I said when he came to the phone.

"Worried! I've been over to your house twice this morning. Where've you been?"

"I've been with Eleanor. I spent the night."

"Ah, Eleanor," he said. I knew he was mentally praying for Eleanor's return. If he were Protestant, it would have been her return to righteousness he would have prayed for: the word would have been sharpened by the implications of punishment and a fine moral outrage. Being the kind of priest he was, he was praying for Eleanor's return to the True Faith; it was a homecoming rather than a change in behavior that those words implied.

"I had a wonderful time," I said. "I bought some new clothes."

Father Mulcahy would, I knew, be interested in my new clothes in a way my father would not have been. My father preferred women to be beautiful, fashionable even, but he preferred to think that the finished product was spontaneous. If he believed the final effect to have been studied or even casually planned, it was spoiled for him.

"Well, I hope you'll be wearing them tonight," said Father Mulcahy. "I'm taking you to Tarrantino's."

He considered going to an Italian restaurant the height of epicurean adventurism.

When Father Mulcahy rang the bell at six o'clock, my first thought was of the dilemmas of hospitality he caused. Did you offer him a drink or not? If you did, you were encouraging him to drink. If you didn't, was the point painful in its obviousness? I decided to play it girlish; all priests liked girlishness; it was their feminine ideal.

"Look, I'm starved. Can we go there absolutely *immediately?*" I said.

"You're always the same, aren't you? An appetite like a horse. God, I remember you and the cotton candy at Coney Island. When you started on your third, I began to get worried."

"I never got sick, though. Kids would probably never get sick if their parents didn't tell them they were going to."

"Come on, then, in the car with you before you start eating my hat."

Father Mulcahy was clean as a piglet bathed in milk. His black hat was brushed as smooth as the skin of a fruit; his white hair, so thin that the hard, pink skull showed beneath it like a flagstone floor, looked as though the color had been taken out of it purposefully, through a series of savage washings. He gave off the odor of an impossibly chaste talcum powder; they all did. I'm sure they buy it where they buy their vestments. But over it all, like a tropical storm over Norway, was the secular smell of his Old Spice.

Mr. Tarrantino embraced Father Mulcahy when he entered the restaurant, and his wife came out of the kitchen, clapping her hands. I guessed that this meal would not be paid for. I was impressed by the sheer amount of genuine love Father Mulcahy had inspired in so many people. They had come to him in periods of astounding grief, in turmoil, in sickness, in unhappiness, in madness even. And he had understood the violence of their lives and their sorrows. He had sat with them for endless hours listening to them weep, listening to the catalogue of human suffering that is surprisingly varied, surprisingly limited. And, in their moments of success, at their daughters' weddings, the births of their grandchildren, their fiftieth wedding anniversaries, he was there, carrying his shy festiveness around like a valise.

I had gone to school with Marie Tarrantino, so Mr. Tarrantino kissed me after he had seated us at the table.

"You must miss your papa, Isabel. So you have another papa here," he said, pointing to Father Mulcahy.

I wanted to say, "That's not it at all; that's not it at all. I don't miss him yet, and Father Mulcahy is quite different." I wondered if I would ever get over that desire to tell everything about myself to people like Mr. Tarrantino, whom I liked and would not see again for another ten years. I smiled and nodded and was silent, the mixture Mr. Tarrantino wanted of mourning and shy affectionateness. Above all, I did not want him to think me eccentric. Men like Mr. Tarrantino were in some ways frightened of unmarried women, especially when their daughters were expecting their fourth or fifth child.

"Now, Isabel, you order whatever you like," said Father Mulcahy, "and don't hold back."

"I have to hold back a little bit. If I'm going out into the great world, I can't knock it over if I'm a big tub of lard."

"All the girls today look like matchsticks. I'm sure the young men don't like it."

"I'm not doing it for young men, Father."

"Well, I want you to think about getting married. You're still a young girl, and you've a sweet disposition and a heart of gold. You ought to be married."

"And you ought to be trying out for *Going My Way*. You'd make a great Barry Fitzgerald."

He slapped my hand. "You always were the freshest kid in the parish."

"I'm going to try to sell the house, Father."

He looked up at me with an expression of fear that made his light eyes look the color of a chemical.

"Will you be going away, then?"

"I don't know. But I'll be out of money soon if I don't sell the house."

"Are you looking for a job?"

"I will, but I don't want to do just anything. And the problem is that at age thirty I have no experience and no qualifications. If it were the nineteenth century, I'd have to become a governess."

"Old Mrs. Healey is looking for a live-in companion. She's a grand soul, Isabel, a beautiful soul, and she hasn't anyone in the world."

I felt the same brown bubble of fear I had felt at John Delaney's office, but I was incapable now of anger. I took Father Mulcahy's pink hand.

"Father," I said, "I want more than that. I don't want to end up like Margaret Casey and all those other women. Please see that."

"Margaret Casey is a good soul, though."

"How can you say that after what she did to you?"

I thought back to the time when I had arranged to get rid of Margaret. When she found out that Father Mulcahy had been involved, she reportedly became hysterical and threatening. A week later, the pastor received a series of anonymous letters saying that the parishioners could smell whiskey on Father Mulcahy's breath in the confessional, that Father Mulcahy staggered at the six-thirty Mass. The pastor had advised that Father Mulcahy take a "rest," had arranged for him to be put in a home for alcoholics at Spring Valley, where he wrote my father and me letters of excruciating cheer. I remembered going to visit him, seeing old men in bathrobes, their hands shaking, walking around the solarium. When we left, my father told me they were all priests. I remembered my terror, driving home.

"How can you forgive her?" I said.

"We don't know if it was her that did it, Isabel. Our Lord said judge not. And if it was her, she was very upset at the time. That was my fault. I'd no idea she'd be so upset. I had another place for her, I thought it would be all right. Poor soul, she never had anything."

Sitting across from me, his expression was one of genuine sorrow. He loved Margaret Casey. After all that, he loved her, and it was not a neutral love, it was an engaged love for one of God's poor.

We had taken a long time after dinner, so that Father Mulcahy's drinks had been absorbed by the heaviness of the meal's many courses. It was ten o'clock.

"I have the six-thirty in the morning," he said. "So I'll drop you off if you don't mind."

"I'm having lunch with Eleanor tomorrow."

"Eleanor," he said, thinking, I was sure, of her dreaminess. "She was a lovely girl. What made her go wrong, do you think?"

"Eleanor's the best person I know, except for you. Don't worry about her. I'm sure she'll get into Heaven."

"I pray for her every day in my Mass, that she'll come back."

I thought that Eleanor would be pleased to know that Father Mulcahy prayed for her, even if he were praying for the wrong things. I kissed him good night as he left me at the door.

"Will you come in a minute, Father, for a last cup of coffee?"

I could feel him retreat from me; it was like a sudden cold wind.

"No, honey," he said. "I'll be off."

I had forgotten; priests were never in houses alone with a woman. Even if the priest were in his seventies and he had known the woman all her life. I felt an inconsolable sense of loss, of having been cheated, and I was angry at this perfectly unnecessary and obtrusive reminder of my sex that the Church was always introducing.

In the dark house the dust smelt like menace, and I rushed to turn on the living-room light. It was tenthirty, the hour holding up things left undone. The air itself discouraged me; it hinted of futile lives. I began to look at the job advertisements in the *Times*: keypunch operators, clerks, cocktail waitresses, Gal Fridays (I imagined Robinson Crusoe; I wouldn't be good as the assistant survivor). Which of these jobs could I possibly do? I imagined myself at a job interview. Experience? None. What have you been doing all these years? Taking care of my father. Puzzled looks. Does anyone do that any more. Or puzzled neo-Freudian arched eyebrows. Your father, do you say? I could lie; I could say I'd been married and was getting a divorce. People would feel much more comfortable with that these days. But I looked at the jobs again; there were none that even deserved a lie.

I considered different possibilities. I could sell the house and go back to school. To train for what? What job could I get that could involve me in discussions of contemporary manners and the nineteenth-century novel? The idea of teaching made my palms sticky with anxiety and distaste. I did not want to spend the next six or seven years, or until I was nearly forty, studying to teach literature like my father.

I tried to determine my qualifications. Loyalty. I loved my father deeply; I was devoted to him. What a nineteenth-century phrase, "that young woman was devoted to her father." In the nineteenth century, it would have had a resonance; now, devotion was something dogs had.

What I wanted was what Eleanor had said she wanted: something I was sure of. But I wanted something outside myself, and larger. Perhaps I could go to Italy and save ruined churches. Perhaps I could become a scientist. I thought of a book I had had as a child. It began, "Look, look and you will see all the things I want to be." The first page was a little girl's body on top of which was a hole for the head. As you turned the pages, the empty hole was filled with women's heads wearing the hats of their various careers. It reminded me of myself: the perfectly empty circle of the child's head and the sickening expanse of potential.

All these years I had dreamed that when it was all over I would simply take up my life. And now, perhaps, I had spent it.

Out of habit, I started to pray. "Dear God," I began, but no longer believing a face behind the name,

I stopped. Having given up the rigors and duties of belief, I had no right to its comforts. I believed that if God were there, He would love me for my courage, as He would love Father Mulcahy for his simplicity, and Eleanor for her good nature, and Liz for her irony and my father for his anger.

I decided to call Liz and to invite myself to Ringkill for the weekend. It was summer; I would swim with her in the lake that was near their house as I had when we were girls and I went on vacation with Liz and her family to Cranberry Lake. I dialed Liz's number. Her little girl answered the phone.

"May I speak to your mother," I said, thinking it was late for the child to be awake, thinking how odd it was to be referring to Liz as "your mother."

"Who's calling, please?" said Sonia, with extreme formality.

"Isabel."

"One moment, please," said Sonia, like a butler.

Liz got on the phone, "We work in the formal mode here. Sonia is planning on being impeccable by the time she's ten."

"Lizzie, can I come up this weekend?"

"God. Yes. Wonderful," said Liz, giving each sentence equal weight, "I'd like you to meet my horse."

"I didn't know you had one. I didn't know you could ride."

"I couldn't. I bought the horse so I would learn to ride. Now I'm building a barn for her."

"By yourself?"

"Yes. I'm glad you can be here to see my summer muscles. They're very impressive. And I'm almost completely flat-chested: no vulnerable abutments."

"Maybe I'd better go into training for a day or two."

"I'm planning on staying up all night to talk to you."

I lay in bed thinking of Father Mulcahy and my father and Liz. How adult Liz had sounded: she was building a barn; she was somebody's mother. She was capable of a fine malice; she had a cutting edge like a good French knife. And Father Mulcahy, perfectly good, could not believe that anyone was wicked, could forgive anyone of anything. And hence was vulnerable to everyone and needed to be protected, to be kept from things like a child. But thinking of Sonia, I felt that at five she was more canny, more resilient than Father Mulcahy. There was no need to lie to Sonia, or to Liz, or to Eleanor. They had not made a world of impossible goodness that was fragile as snow. How had they made a world of impossible dangers inside which good had to be guarded as if it could be damaged by the human breath? Both Father Mulcahy and my father were children, and their love made the exhausting demands of a child's. Perhaps it was because they were used to loving God, Who found nothing exhausting.

I closed my eyes and imagined another kind of man, with a hard brown back and hands that were short and broad. He was touching me in clever, surprising ways, and making my mouth water. I kissed him and his mouth tasted of celery; it was as cool as a pear. And he wanted me so much that he could not stay away from me. Even for a moment. He could not speak, that was how he wanted me. And he lay above me and it was like swimming and drowning and he wanted me again and again. I will buy a suitcase in the morning, I thought, drifting into sleep.

IV

The train to Liz's followed a route directly up the Hudson. The mountains were dark as yew trees and the water was gray-blue, clear, like the water in a Dutch landscape. The air outside was vague and gray: soothing little clouds smoked away and left the sky gradually bluer. The colors were cool against my eyes, relieving, as if I had just wept.

On top of my clothes in my new brown suitcase was a box of Barricini chocolates. It had been so long since I had visited anyone that I wasn't sure if people still brought chocolates. That was the sort of thing that Liz would register if it were no longer done: I could see her glance flicking up and down in the quick, ticking silence that marked her disapproval. This was frightening, and I wanted to ask the woman behind the counter if it was still appropriate to bring chocolates, but then the woman would think me odd. I felt again that new unsureness, as if I were walking on ice of uncertain thickness, brown water and mud just below the surface, bubbling at the pressure of my step. I thought of my father and his sureness, his body in the bed at the center of the room, and I wanted to cry out, "I am terribly alone," in the midst of the summer travelers in Grand Central Station. But on the train, the sun still not at the center of the sky, I was both calm and excited. I was going to see my friend, who was someone's mother, someone's wife. I thought of John Ryan: his blond, thickly muscled body, his perfectly secure blue eyes, which showed plainly that he never questioned the rightness of his life and its success. I remembered asking Liz why she decided to marry him. Liz had said, "Because he could beat me at tennis and none of the other men I knew could. And I thought he would leave me alone more than any of the others. And he seemed like he was going to make it, and if I didn't marry him, he'd never let me forget it."

He had made it: the top of his class at law school, opportune involvement in Washington during the Johnson years, and now he held some big position in Ryder County—something to do with social services. Because I didn't like him, I resented the good he did. When Liz would tell me about some change John had effected for welfare mothers or children on a free-lunch program, my first thought was that he didn't deserve to have done it. For I was sure he felt nothing for his people. What he did was a kind of reflex legacy from Catholic high school, when the coolest boys, the basketball and football stars, were also members of the Catholic Big Brothers, taking slum children out for picnics, an impulse from the Kennedy years, when the most glamorous men in the country were seeming to care for the poor. I knew of nothing that moved John Ryan, neither pain nor grace, and I thought it miserably unfair that his actions should have such a profound effect on people whose lives had no effect on his.

He was proud of Liz as Liz was proud of her horse. I had seen him run his hands over Liz's lean hips with a proprietorial pleasure that had made me want to strike him. And I had seen dislike flick across Liz's clear brown eyes—not hatred, but the knowing look of a wife who has put her foot through the sham of her husband's character and has decided to keep on walking. The children, Alexander and Sonia, had Liz's dark looks, her alert impatience, her quick refusals and acknowledgments.

Liz was standing on the platform as if she just hap-

pened to be there, as if her being there had nothing to
do with the incoming train. She walked toward the
train but did not greet me. In her heavy jeans and
blue work shirt and tan cowboy boots, she looked
spare and effective and purposeful: her refusal of
ornament was a cunning trick. The children walked
behind her in their skimpy summer clothes like colorful chicks behind a stern hen. Liz took my suitcase as
if we had been on the train together and had only
stopped talking a moment ago.

"Are you hot? We can be in the water in ten minutes. Unless you want lunch?"

"No. Yes. *Will* you say hello to me, Elizabeth."

Liz embraced me seriously: no mere convention or
show of manners at a train. The delay of that embrace
made it seem a matter of choice, a decision rather than
a gesture. The children hung back, uncertain of their
behavior. They had not seen me since they had been
two and three. At five and six they probably considered themselves different persons; they might never
have met me.

I decided, meeting Sonia's serious stare, to shake
hands with the children. It would make them realize
that I took them seriously. Their pleasure in the hand-
shake was obvious and, by adult standards, dispro-
portionate.

"You come from New York City, from Queens,
where our mother was born. We went to your house
once, but I don't remember. We were quite small at
the time," said Sonia.

"But we still had the same dog then," said Alexander, gesturing to the ancient beagle who was strug-
gling to hang his head out the window. "You know,
Susie was my mother's dog before *we* were her
babies."

"I think Alex is afraid that gives Susie some kind of
priorities on the lifeboat," Liz said. "He's always planning procedures for the impending disaster."

"Your father just died," said Sonia. "Are you extremely lonely?"

I turned around to look at the child, to address my remarks to her. I remember how it would annoy me when I would ask questions and people would answer my father.

"I am not as lonely as I thought I'd be, although I miss him in some ways. I think I'm not as lonely as I'm supposed to be."

"Are you afraid you're not suffering enough?" said Liz. "Don't worry, you have a lifetime. They'll get you in the end."

"That's what I'm afraid of. The surprise attack," I said.

"Umm," Liz said. "Who knows, maybe you'll be immune, like the people who survived the plague."

"What's the plague?" said Alex.

"It's when a lot of people get sick and die," said Liz. "It's spelt P-L-A-G-U-E. They don't have them much any more."

"Our horse is pregnant," said Alex. "We'll take you to see her."

"Do you know how long it's been since I've seen a mountain?" I said.

Liz looked at me fishily, as if to say "no more of that kind of talk, please," and in that look I could see my excesses, what was by now a habit of unstated pleas for sympathy. I wondered, with a deep embarrassment, how long I had been saying things like that, sentences that began with "Do you know how long it's been since . . ." I was grateful for Liz's rigor and impatience; the word for it came from the nineteenth century: "salutary."

"The house is, of course, a wreck," said Liz. "John keeps wanting me to hire someone to come in and clean, one of his huddled masses yearning to breathe free, and I keep insisting I don't need help, I can do it. Which of course I could, if I considered it important. I'm going to take a course in real estate. Don't you think I could make a lot selling houses?"

"A million. Do you need it?"

"The money? No, I need to be able to make it. Do

you know what it's like never to have earned any money?"

"Yes. That's the problem. Perhaps I ought to go into real estate, too."

"You'd be terrible at it. You're awfully good at implications. You'd be telling people the moral implications of owning property, or of your commission, and you'd end up buying their house for them."

"What am I good at, then? There's not a big market for implications."

"We'll think of something," said Liz.

I believed her, as if she had just said she'd find a place for us to have a clubhouse.

Liz's house was on a road with a number of working farms. The swings on her front lawn were a nice relief from the intense serviceability of the silos and earnest-looking barns that surrounded them.

Liz stooped into the back of the station wagon to pull out a bag of groceries. Turning my ankle on the uneven ground, I knew that I had worn the wrong shoes. With a sense of helplessness, I teetered over to the front porch behind Liz. I felt like a caricature of an Italian movie star walking the *campagna* in high heels.

As she struggled to open the door, Liz said, "I'm sorry John's not home. He's spending the day with his mistress."

When I laughed, Liz looked at me with a perfectly clear stare.

"I'm quite serious."

"I'm sorry," I said.

"Oh, there's nothing to be sorry about. She's perfect for him. She has enormous breasts; she's smart enough to laugh at his jokes but not smart enough to make her own. It's what he's always had in mind. Especially the breasts."

"Oh, come on, how much do breasts mean? Not as much as you think, Lizzie. They couldn't possibly."

"I'm convinced that breast size is determinative of an incredible amount. For instance, if you'd been flat-chested you'd probably have sent your father to a nursing home. And if I hadn't been, I'd never have married John."

"Liz, that's silly," I said, remembering that I had imagined Liz perfectly happy.

"Anyway, it all works out very well for everyone," said Liz, putting groceries into the cupboards. "He leaves me alone, which is fine because I never liked him much anyway. But I do like the kids and this house, and he likes Marlene and she likes him."

"Who is she?"

"I'm embarrassed to tell you," said Liz. "She's his secretary. John has always lacked imagination."

"Does he want to marry her?"

"Yes, I suppose, but it would be political suicide, so he never will. John is remarkably discreet and so is she. I actually rather like her, except that she keeps giving me these *stricken* looks when we meet, like a sheep who's just raided the cookie jar."

"I think you're mixing your metaphors."

"Similes," said Liz. "But I'm very active. I ride. I can beat the local pro at tennis. I spend a lot of time with the kids. I read eighteenth-century history; I'm very fond of the eighteenth century. I like my life. It's just difficult enough to suit me."

"You've always liked that best, behaving well in difficult situations."

"Come and look at the horse," said Liz. "She's going to foal in April. I'm building a barn for the winter."

We walked out to the pasture where the horse ran in a grassy area behind a redwood fence. Liz climbed into the paddock and pulled the horse to the edge of the fence. She was stroking the horse on the sides of its distended belly.

"I take her maternity very seriously," said Liz. "All maternity, I guess, is serious. I can never understand how people can go through the experience and be trivial afterwards. People seem to have an enormous will to be trivial against all odds."

Liz stepped through the fence and lifted up a post that was six feet long.

"First I dig the holes for the posts," she said, "and then I hammer them into the ground with a sledge hammer. That's the first step. Do you want to see me do one?"

"Do I have a choice?"

Liz laughed. "No. This is the boy in me I buried prematurely." She took off her blouse and underneath was wearing a green tee shirt. Her arms were brown and muscular; she might not have had any breasts. And yet the word that came to mind was "womanly."

Liz's face was red and almost agonized with effort. She picked up a sledge hammer and hammered the post into the hole she had already dug. I could see the strain in her back and I longed to stop her. But finally, the post was hammered in. For no reason I could explain, I began to cry.

"It's very difficult," I said to Liz.

But Liz was grinning at me like a winning child about to claim a prize. "Yes," she said. "It's very difficult. Shall we have a swim?"

When I unpacked my suitcase I could not find my bathing suit.

"I must have forgotten to pack my bathing suit," I said to Liz. "Stupid."

"You can wear one of mine."

"It will be dreadfully small."

"Oh, I'm bigger than I look," said Liz. "Except on top where I'm smaller than I look. Besides, it's only us, and it's only the pond in the back. We could swim naked, but neither of us is hip enough for that, are we? At least with each other."

She handed me a brown bikini.

The bottom stretched so that it was decent, but just barely. The fit of the top was impossible. By pulling the top down to cover the undercurve of my breast, I left the nipple nearly exposed. If I pulled the top so that my nipple was comfortably protected, the bottom half of my breast, like a half-peeled peach, was painfully naked. I decided to pull the suit down and hope that my nipples would behave discreetly. Fearfully, I stepped over to the mirror.

The effect of the suit took my breath away with disappointment. The prominence of my breasts in the skimpy suit made me look as if I was making a wrongheaded attempt at piquancy, like the hippopotamuses in ballet costumes in cartoons. The loose rippling of flesh at the back of my thighs looked like mountains of cottage cheese. I could scarcely bear to confront Liz, who was standing at the other side of the door, her body brown and taut as an Indian boy's. But there was nothing for it but to go outside and endure the dark ticking of Liz's silent assessment.

"Do you have a shirt or something?" I said, walking through the door.

Liz looked at me with unguarded attention.

"Not a very good fit," she said.

"I look like an idiot in this suit."

"Yes," said Liz. "We'll have to get another in town. But you can cool off in the pond, and we'll have lunch on the grass."

She had not stopped looking at my body.

"Your body has changed so," she said. "I think of Isabel's body at Cranberry Lake, and here is the same Isabel, in the same body I suppose, but utterly different. Very peculiar."

"Do you feel you've begun to age yet?" I said.

"No. My body seems the same to me as when I was fourteen. And yet I still keep making mistakes. I wish I could see myself aging; it would give me a sense of accomplishment. The children seem to age, to move forward, and you have, but I seem to stand still, except for a growing meanness. That's what I'm afraid of."

"What I'm afraid of," I said, "is being, at thirty, absolutely empty, except for a load of baggage I can't wait to unload and am terrified of unloading."

"You can be whatever you want," said Liz. "You're lucky."

"Can I? It seems like one of those tricks you have to be clever for."

"I keep tricking myself through my life," said Liz. "Children are a trick, and a house, and work, and our friends. We have to keep tricking ourselves."

She dove into the greenish water. I followed her slowly, gradually, until I had slid into the pond horizontally.

"I've always understood why Ophelia wanted to lie down in the water," I said.

"It was better than lying down with Hamlet," said Liz.

"And so much more private," I said, looking at the mountains and the grass. "All this is yours. Imagine my having a friend in the landed gentry."

"Sometimes in the morning, very early when no one is up, I put on my boots and pace the boundaries of the property. There's usually a kind of damp chill in the air, and things seem rather unclear, and I say, 'This is mine.' You've no idea how wonderful that kind of attachment is."

"You ought to've been born on an estate your family lived on for generations."

"Except, being a woman, it probably would have gone to one of my brothers, or some crazy cousin from the city. Then I probably would've gone berserk and broken all the windows in the conservatory."

"That never happened in Jane Austen," I said.

"Many things never happened in Jane Austen."

"Nothing really important, I think."

"Isabel, even you don't believe that."

"No," I said, "but I'd like to."

In the kitchen, Liz made peanut butter-and-jelly sandwiches on white bread for the children and ham on pumpernickel for us. There was a small pot of French mustard on the table, and next to it a silver knife with an enamel handle.

"I was trying to make the children gourmets, but it was too exhausting and they were starving to death," said Liz. She poured wine into thin crystal glasses.

"We'll take you to buy a bathing suit," she said, "and then we'll go to the lake and drink gin and tonic out of a thermos. What do you say?"

I thought how odd it was that I was doing something so adult, so middle-aged, something that people's mothers did. Or people in movies.

I bought a black tank suit at the sporting goods store in town. I tried it on very quickly, simply to see that it fit. It was hot and the children were waiting in the car. I did not want to open myself up to Liz's scrutiny, either real or imagined, by taking a long time to decide on a suit.

When we got to the lake, the children split off from their mother and me like torpedoes. The other mothers looked up at Liz, and she passed through them with vague, benevolent acknowledgments, like visiting royalty. There was no bond between Liz and the other mothers, as I had imagined there would be, their shared estate linking them by small understandings. The eyes of the other mothers were waiting for Liz to make a mistake; her quick, almost stiff progress disappointed them. She led me to the furthest point of the lake where there was a little shack for dressing and depositing baggage. She brought out blankets and cigarettes, the thermos and two, considering the occasion, surprisingly thin glasses. The mothers from across the expanse watched Liz take off her shorts and shirt and put them on top of the basket.

"I'll just go in there and change," I said.

"You see why I wanted you to get a decent bathing suit," Liz said when I emerged from the hut. She cocked her head in the direction of the mothers. "Vultures," she said, "they eat human flesh."

"Do they eat yours?" I asked.

"I'm too quick for them," said Liz. "They can't catch me for my cleverness."

The blankets made the backs of my legs itch as the blankets I had lain on with Liz always had. I thought of all the blankets we had lain on, and all the water—lakes, oceans, ponds—we had been in together, and now Liz, envied and wished ill by a score of women, lay next to me here.

"Are you lonely, Liz?" I asked, as if the memory of all those blankets, all that water, had given me the right to certain quick intimacies.

Liz turned onto her stomach.

"I think people make far too much of loneliness. It's not anything you die of, like hunger or thirst. It can be endured. I almost think it's childish to think it can be avoided."

"You don't mind, then?"

"I used to think of myself as a pilot on an Arctic flight. But then I got bored with that and I've stopped thinking of myself as having missed something. I try not to look at my life as a biography. One day at a time it's very satisfying."

"And John?"

"It's much better now. When I expected something of him—conversation, or companionship, or whatever they vulgarly call it nowadays, I despised him. I used to think he was a hypocrite. Now I see that he's not; he has no solidity, so he's not being false to anything. And I'm grateful to him. It's because of him I have the children, the house, the horse, all those nice books about the eighteenth century. I think I owe him something for that."

"Affection?"

"Certainly not."

"And you don't want other men?"

"No, I'm not very interested in that kind of sex. I'm not active enough. I'll probably never go to bed with a man again in my life."

"That's what Eleanor says."

Liz stiffened. *"She'll* never be able to stick to it, though."

I lay on my back. "I seem to want it. Is that odd?"

"You always did. More than any of us. I hope you get it. I hope it doesn't hurt you."

I closed my eyes and saw purple rings projected on the lids.

"It's worth a try, don't you think?"

Liz patted me on the stomach. "You ought to have hundreds of lovers. You were born for it."

"Please allow me my singular modesty."

"You see," said Liz, "if I were going to do it, I'd have either none or hundreds."

"My father always said you had an extravagant nature. Even your abstention is extravagant."

"I think I was the only woman who wasn't afraid of your father. I think I could enjoy him in a particular way that none of the rest of you could because I wasn't."

"Did you think him absurd?"

"Absurd?"

"Full of sound and fury, signifying nothing."

"Oh no. Jesus Christ, he signified. He signified all over the place."

"Like a boy who writes his name on the sidewalk and on the sides of bridges. Leaving his mark."

"He had authority. I remember when I was a teenager he was the only person who really seemed like an adult to me, the only one whom my perspective didn't change on. The others seemed as if they were pretending something, or imitating something. I liked him because he didn't give an inch, and he could make me look foolish."

"You liked that?"

"Yes, he could maneuver me into a corner with words, even though I knew all the time that what he was saying was perfectly crackpot. But he would set such elegant traps. And then I would spring myself with a joke, and he always enjoyed that. It was like a very elaborate and formal game, or a dance."

I felt again the flash of jealousy I had felt with Eleanor. But with Liz I was not afraid to speak, perhaps because I felt that Liz was not vulnerable to me.

"I never had those kinds of games with my father. Not like you and Eleanor did."

Liz looked at me as Sonia had earlier; her mouth

in a perfectly relaxed, perfectly composed line, her eyes unblinking, as if she were looking into a desert.

"But, my God, how he loved you. I've still never seen anything like it. How I used to envy you. I still do. No one will ever love you like that again, you know."

I remembered the tightness of my father's hand on my shoulder, and the choke of his great, inarticulate love, when his eyes would cloud over and he could not speak.

"It'll be hard for you, Isabel. You can't help but expect that kind of love again and you'll never get it. You've had your great love, and you can't expect another. I don't think people get two per lifetime."

"Most people don't even get one. Liz," I said, "you understand why I did it, then? All those years with him. You don't think I was crazy?"

"Of course I do. Everything I know of psychology and human experience says you were crazy. Masochistic. Acting out of guilt. But I envy you for having done it."

I closed my eyes and let myself slide into sleep, horizontally, as I had slid into Liz's pond. When Liz's voice came to me, I had difficulty placing it.

"What I said before, that I wasn't interested in sex, that's not true. I have a lover."

I tried not to sit upright, knowing that that would display, almost in caricature, the intense and, I felt, unseemly interest that Liz's sentence had created. I opened one eye slowly, in a pretense of languor.

"She's a woman," Liz said.

A thrill of fear needled in between my ribs. I leaned my head on my hand and tried to make my glance large-minded and neutral.

"Don't give me that Catholic-school *tout comprendre, c'est tout pardonner* look," she said.

"Are you happy with her, Liz?"

"What a seventies question, Isabel, and utterly inappropriate to you, I might add."

"What shall I ask, then? Is it satisfying? Is it splendid? Is that the kind of question you expect from me?"

"Yes. It is satisfying. It is splendid. I adore her. She's magnificent. She's like your father, she doesn't give an inch."

"I wonder what my father would say to being compared to your female lover. Tell me about her."

"You see," said Liz, "when I married John, I was attracted to his discipline, to his ambition, to his precision about things. Then I found that there was no moral basis to any of them. They were entirely show. Erica has all those kinds of—for lack of a better word —male qualities that I admired, and that loneliness that men never have."

"You love her very much?"

"Would you like to meet her?"

"Of course I want to meet the person you love."

Like a child who has thought of a better diversion, Liz sat up and began to collect her things.

"Let's go there now," she said.

"All right."

"Unless you want to stay."

"I was about to say it was getting a bit chilly."

"Isabel," said Liz, "it is for your perfect manners I have always loved you."

Liz had to re-enter the net of mothers in order to collect Sonia and Alex. But now she did not even acknowledge them. She was businesslike; she clapped her hands like a nun. The children came with what was, I thought, a remarkable lack of fuss. I wondered if Liz would take the children to see this woman, whose name I could not call to mind.

"We're going to see Erica," said Liz, "so move it."

"Erica has a stable full of horses, you see," said Liz. "She's very wealthy."

"What does she do?"

"She's perfect."

"For money?"

"No, duck. Independently wealthy. You see, like most Irish Catholics, I'm drawn to the smell of untainted cash."

Looking at Liz as she drove to her lover's house, I thought I had never seen her so light-hearted, so girlish. I reflected on my own lack of astonishment at what was, objectively, an astonishing revelation. Liz loved women; she did not love men. The word "lesbian," with its unpleasant, swampy sound, its connotations of a certain damp furtiveness, seemed to have nothing to do with the matter. Liz loved a woman: we were driving to see her at four o'clock on an August afternoon with the children sitting in the back of the car, their heads stuck out the window, their dark hair blowing into their open mouths.

We drove up a long country lane with a thick, improbable growth of pines on either side of it.

"Her property begins here," Liz said in a tone of quiet pride.

Once out of the pine copse, I could see a large fenced-in meadow. Two horses, whose hides gleamed like polished nuts, were cropping the grass, ruminative, deliberate. One looked up as the car drove past and then went back to eating.

I saw a woman on a horse galloping out from under the trees. As she came closer, I could see that she was wearing a large denim cap with a hard peak. She got off the horse, took off her cap and shook out the long auburn hair that had been piled inside it. The gesture was so perfectly engaging that I was sure it must have been studied: an acknowledgment of her lover, or a tribute. Or was it possible, I wondered, looking at the girl's slim hips, her black boots that were delectable as candy, the tight jeans tucked into them, that the gesture was unconsidered, and it was for this that Liz loved her.

When she approached us, I could see that the girl was only about eighteen. Her face was dark brown, the color of stain, and her light-blue eyes were both cold and frightened, as if a natural arrogance and a natural shyness fought in them for mastery. She and Liz did not, as if by some previous arrangement, greet one another. Clearly, this was by now habitual; something they could later tease each other for, compliment each other over.

"This is Isabel," said Liz. "I've often spoken about her to you."

"Are you interested in horses?" said Erica.

"I haven't thought much about them," I said. "They're very beautiful." I decided to underscore my urbanness rather than to make any pretense of rural expertise.

"You don't ride then," said the girl, getting to the heart of the matter.

"No."

I could see relief sinking into those light eyes.

"Give her a chance, baby," said Liz.

Silently, Erica led Liz and me around the paddock. She climbed the fence, and whistled; the two horses walked toward her with ill-concealed regret.

"This is Sundance," she said, as one of them tossed its head. Its eye was huge and clear, all dark color, a perfect organ of pure vision. It seemed, on account of its size and clarity, to be able to take in the whole phenomenon of the world with a steady magnetism.

"How's Punch?" said Erica.

"Fine," said Liz. "She seems to be thriving."

"Sundance is Punch's sister," Erica said to Isabel, "and their sire is the sire of Punch's foal."

"All very inverted, these horses," said Liz, putting her arm across Erica's shoulders.

Erica looked around. "Where are the kids?"

"In the barn," said Liz.

Erica relaxed.

"Erica is much more worried than I am about the corruption of my children. I of course consider them incorruptible. I brought them up to touch pitch and not be defiled."

"Thank you very much," said Erica.

"That was irony, love," said Liz.

"I can never be sure," Erica said, "about what you say is irony."

"Why don't you offer us some tea?" Liz said.

"My parents are away," said Erica. "I tend to be naturally rude," she added, as if that observation were connected to the first.

The kitchen was large and open, with dark exposed beams and walls the color of leather. One of the walls was entirely taken up by a picture window. The valley spread out from the kitchen like a lap.

"This is a wonderful room," I said, not having got rid of my discomfort.

"I'm hardly ever in it, except to eat," Erica said.

I wondered if this was a joke, but decided it was safer not to laugh.

Erica put the water on to boil. "I got this banana cake. Liz said you liked banana cake."

I was touched by Erica's uneasy domesticity. Obviously, she wanted very much to please, and I wanted to show that I was pleased.

"God," I said, "Liz and I used to sit down and eat a whole one of them after school. I'm surprised we're not dead the way we ate."

Erica obviously enjoyed this glimpse of Liz as a fallible adolescent, so I went on. "In our senior year of high school, the fashion was potato-salad sandwiches. Can you believe that human beings would eat that?"

Erica laughed, and I could see the eagerness that made her lovable.

"I'm lousy at tea," said Erica, "the leaves always come through."

"Well, we can always get a gypsy in to read them," Liz said.

"Jesus," said Erica, "I can't think of anything worse than knowing my own future."

"Nor can I," I said. "Nothing."

We drank our tea, making comfortable, inconsequential conversation. I was trying to say, by my eyes, by the posture of my body, I like you, please know that I like you. Suddenly, our civilized ease was broken by the sound of a child crying. Liz was on her feet and out the door before I realized that the sound was coming from Sonia.

Erica got up and brought the teacups to the sink.

"Something like this always happens," she said, bending over the teapot.

I could see that the girl was crying.

"But the children would have to be—most important," I said.

Erica nodded.

"That must be very difficult. I know I would find it difficult."

Erica stopped her tears and stood up abruptly, but I was surprised to see that she did not seem embarrassed, or to regret her weeping.

"I'll give you part of this cake to take home," she said, "if you like it."

The girl's tense muteness made her seem very vulnerable; it was the pressure, like my father's, of all that could not be said.

"I'd love it," I said, "you're very kind."

"That's what Liz says about you. She says you're very kind."

"That's because she hasn't seen much of me lately."

"But we will now, won't we? We'll see you again soon."

I embraced Erica and was shocked at the hardness of her body.

"Yes," I said, "I hope so."

Liz came in with Alex, who looked as if he had expected the worst and it had happened.

"Sonia's cut her knee," said Liz. "I'll have to take her home."

Erica nodded. "I'm giving you the rest of the cake."

Liz's mind was obviously on the child in the car. "Good," she said. "I'll see you on Monday," with an absentmindedness that I thought must have caused Erica real pain.

Erica walked to the door and watched us pull out of the driveway. I could see her leaning against the door frame; she waited there until we had driven down the road.

In the back of the car, Sonia was being irritable in response to Alex's solicitous ministrations.

"She likes to be left alone, Alex. I know it's hard, but that's the way she is," said Liz.

She turned to me. "Well," she said, "what do you think?"

"I like her," I said. "She's very young."

"Not that young," said Liz. "You mustn't think of us at nineteen. She's nothing like that."

I thought of myself at nineteen; it was when my father had his first stroke. How would Erica have dealt with that? Was she really so different from what I was then? The difference between Erica and me now made the space of those years seem huge. I had that sense again, the one that had begun at Father's funeral, of looking down at my life from a height.

Liz took Sonia into the bathroom and bandaged her knee. Then the children sat down in front of the television and regarded it with a rapt, unquestioning contemplation I had not imagined them, being Liz's children, capable of.

Liz was taking things out of the refrigerator. "I don't want you to think of me as some kind of Sister George," she said. "She was the one who seduced me."

"How?"

"Very simple. She kissed me on the mouth. And I went crazy. It had never happened before."

"But you've never had anyone but John."

"I never wanted anyone. But I want her, Isabel. Dear God. Love among the roses."

"She liked you," Liz went on. "It's very rare. You're the only one of my friends she likes. I guess that makes you indispensable."

"If there's anything I'm tired of it's being indispensable," I said, relishing the compliment. Who wouldn't rather be told that than almost anything, I thought.

"Cut up carrots, then. And mix yourself a drink."

"Will John be home for supper?"

"Oh yes," said Liz. "Gracing the head of our table."

"Does he know about Erica?"

"Of course, I wouldn't keep it a secret. That's the difficult part. I wouldn't shy away from that."

"How does he respond?"

"He wants her himself," she said, "and he can't keep his hands off me either. What he would really like is the two of us in bed with him. Plus Marlene, probably."

"And this is the marriage half the mothers in Queens hold up to their daughters' downhearted gazes."

I heard a car come up the driveway. I knew that John's entry would change everything: the look of the room, the position of the bodies, the children, Liz. He was fair and everyone else in the house was dark; he was taller and larger than any of us. I saw his size and his coloring as an intrusion. I began to be frightened of his entrance.

He was wearing tennis whites; his legs had been burnt a salmon pink, and the reddish hairs gleamed against them. Around his wrist was an unfamiliar-looking elastic bracelet; he had a towel around his neck. He walked into the kitchen as if he were expecting to be photographed. I sat up straight and smiled what I knew was a perfectly false, perfectly ingratiating smile. I did not get out of my chair.

"*Is*abel," John said, "how super to see you." He bent over to embrace me and I could smell his expensive soap. I imagined it in a cardboard box: light brown, the shape of a tongue, with a rope attached to the end of it. We had not seen each other in eight years.

"God, you women, you never change. You and Liz look like you just got out of Anastasia Hall."

"That's because when we were in Anastasia Hall we looked as if we were forty. It was the uniforms," said Liz.

John went over to his wife and embraced her from the rear.

"What about this one, though," he said, patting Liz's behind. "She still has the figure of a sixteen-year-old, even though I knocked her up twice."

"John has always had a way with language," Liz said. She had not stopped cutting the beef into strips.

John took a beer from the refrigerator and sat down next to me. He held my hand. It was the first time in years that a man under sixty had deliberately touched me. I was chagrined at the pleasure it brought.

"Isabel, Isabel, you've got your whole life ahead of you, don't you? A big clean slate, and you can write all over it in great big goddamn letters. God, I envy you."

He continued to hold my hand and now began to chafe it. Despite my dislike of John, I did not withdraw my hand. The smell of his good soap drew me, and the heat that his body seemed to transmit like a coil. I felt the air grow bright with sexual charge. I imagined silver-blue pluses shooting out of John's skull and reddish minuses out of my own. I almost laughed out loud, imagining us in a cartoon, but even my laughter did not neutralize the pull of John's blatant sex. Liz had continued to chop and slice in the corner. Had the charge hit her over by the stove? Was she repelled by her husband's performance, or merely bored by its expectedness?

"I didn't think you'd envy anyone, John," I said, feeling that the silence had to be broken or the charge would become palpable.

"Knock wood," said John. "In politics you could be out on your ass any time."

"You can always make a movie with John Lindsay if things get rough," said Liz.

John got up and began to nuzzle Liz's neck. "Ya want me to take you to Hollywood, baby? You want me to make you a star?"

Liz stirred the pot on the stove as if she were alone in the kitchen.

"I'd like you to change for dinner now," she said, "so you can spend some time with the kids."

He slapped Liz loudly on the behind. "Where are they," he shouted, "where are the little stinkers?" He slammed the back door.

Alex and Sonia ran to his call and began jumping and climbing on him. He carried Sonia into the living room, and dragged Alex, who hung onto his leg. He got down on the floor and played with his children. John Ryan. Down on the floor with the children. John had vulgarized a concept I had always liked, and I resented him for it, as I resented him for his sex, and for his success with people. I was surprised that the children seemed genuinely to enjoy their father. I thought they would see through him. But he was their father. My father had nothing to do with *that*, I thought, looking at John's behind, which jutted into the air as he crawled on the floor with his kids. I wondered what Sonia would make of her father as an adult, if his animal vigor would be able to sustain her love.

"He's a six-foot walking penis with a social conscience," said Liz, looking into the living room, "but they're crazy about him. He ought to spend more *time* with them," she said, and I noticed for the first time triangular lines where Liz's eyebrows began.

"Can I do something?" I asked, moving toward the stove.

"Yes," said Liz, "you can help me make sense of my life. You can help me understand it."

"You expect me to be some kind of sibyl, Liz. I don't even understand my own."

"*I* don't understand yours, either. Jesus God almighty."

I laughed at the fifties expletive.

"John's great luxury," said Liz, "is that he never tries to understand anything. It's what makes him so effective."

"What have we got that he hasn't got?"

"Elegant perceptions like heroic couplets," said Liz. "Not much of a bargain, is it?"

"Would you like to be him, though?"

"I'd rather be Alexander Pope."

"He was awfully short."

"Yes, but I heard he was a great dancer."

Liz's dishes were heavy and blue-black. Her cutlery had dark wooden handles. The table gave the impression of solidity and seriousness, and John sat at the head of it like a stranger.

I looked around at the others at the table; they were a family, a unit. Liz cut the children's meat; John joked with his son and laughed at Alex's new riddle. I had slipped out of their circle. I shivered for a moment, as if I had just walked out of the moonlight into a dark clump of trees. And I felt that distance, distance from Liz and her family, from the food, which someone else seemed to be eating; a distance from myself, a distinct sense of how easily the business of the world could be carried on without me. I had never felt that with my father; even before he became ill, his life was unthinkable without mine. I thought of Margaret, sitting at the edge of so many tables, nervously picking at her food and cutting her meat into small pieces to make it last longer, so she would not have to leave.

"Lizzie, you're a genius," said John. His overripe, good-fellow voice forced me back to the table.

"More?" said Liz, the candles softening her demands. "I'll bring out the dessert," she said, when everyone seemed to be finished.

"Now," said John, leaning back in his chair, as if nothing untoward had ever happened or could ever happen to anyone connected to him. "I have the announcement of the evening. Daddy has got a job for Mommy."

"What?" said Liz, looking at him for the first time all evening with real attention.

"You know that project I started, the one on home care for the aged? Well, the state people are very interested. And they want a detailed report. I've hired you to head the team."

Liz's quick eyes considered her husband.

"I think you should give the job to Isabel," she said.

"What?" John and I said in unison.

"For Christ's sake, Liz. You've been bitching for two years about how you want to get a job, and I break my ass to get one for you and you give it away to a complete stranger. That's typical, you perverse bitch," he said, banging his wineglass on the table. Some of the wine splashed onto the table top.

Liz wiped the spilled wine with her napkin. I wanted only to be as far away as possible. I was thinking that this must be happening to someone else. I did not get involved in this kind of drama.

Liz's voice was unnaturally calm. "First, Isabel is hardly a stranger, she's my oldest friend. Second, she God knows has experience in home care for the sick and the aged. Third, it would look pretty fishy if the report on *your* program were written by *your* wife. How do you think that would go in Albany?"

The last argument seemed to strike John; his body relaxed in his chair.

"But Isabel doesn't have a degree," he said.

"Neither did Judy Michaels when she wrote your report on welfare mothers."

"That's different," he said.

"Yes, you're not sleeping with Isabel."

I was surprised that John didn't answer; his silence hung over us like a tent. I looked at the children; they glanced from their mother to their father with absorption but, surprisingly, no anxiety.

John rubbed his eyes with his right hand. He looked at his wife with genuine regret. "You always give away everything I give you," he said.

"Don't be mawkish," said Liz, with a delicious slice of injustice that snapped her husband back to attention.

"You sure you don't want it then?"

"The horse is going to foal."

John took my hand and held it over his head like a prize fighter.

"Isabel," he said, "you've got yourself a job."

"No one's asked her if she wants it," Liz said. "We've talked as if she weren't here."

"Do you want it?" said John, lighting a cigarette.

I felt the necessity of making a quick decision.

"Yes," I said, looking at John's eyes for the first time.

"You got it, then," he said.

"Just like that?" I asked.

"Just like that," said John.

"My husband," said Liz, in a perfectly flat tone, "is a very powerful man."

V

For the rest of the evening, I was certain that John would change his mind. Surely he would come into the room and tell me that he had only given me the job in anger, to spite his wife and her gladiatorial ingratitude. It would not have been impossible to understand; he was a man used, above all, to gratitude; his work and the public direction of his life had been born of a taste for it. And it would have been an apt punishment. If Liz refused the job he would give it to the first person who came along, diminishing its value and the sting of the rejection, diminishing the importance of Liz and her talents. So a man who is rejected by a beautiful and intelligent woman will marry a plain and stupid one, as though the loss of the first choice had spoiled the idea of choice itself.

"Six months, at the most," John had said. Would it be foolish, then, to leave everything, to sell everything, to move from the house I had been born in for a job whose end was entirely visible? I thought of the clump of white chrysanthemums in the corner of the garden, and the forsythia that came out at the end of March. I was interested in them, not because I was interested in flowers but because they had always grown, quite spontaneously, near the house, because they could be expected every year: a gratuitous beauty that required no effort. Had I planted them myself they would have ceased to interest me. It occurred to me that I could be gone by the time the chrysanthemums were up. I was unable to discern whether I was glad that I would not see them again, but I knew I would move away; not to take this chance would have been ingratitude, not to John, for whom I cared less than nothing, but to chance, against which breaches were clear and punishable.

John came over to me at the table. He took my hand and chafed it in the distressing way I was by now sure was calculated.

"You'll have to have an interview, babe. But it's just a formality. I'm the captain of the team, and I say you're on the team."

"Everyone in the office wears football helmets," said Liz. "Except the secretaries. They wear little cheerleading skirts. It's all such a great deal of *fun*. And it's not winning or losing, it's how you play the *game*."

I wanted to laugh, but John pressed my hand in such a threatening way, in a way that had so clearly to do with my future, that I turned my back on Liz. Pretending to want a cigarette, I pulled my hand away from John's. He patted my knee. "I'm going off to the office," he said. "Got to get that report for the county legislature on Tuesday."

"But it's nine o'clock," I said.

"Baby, when you're dealing with the people, there're no time clocks," said John, walking out of the room.

"Is he really going to *work?*" I asked Liz.

"Yes. He *does* work very hard. I give him that. And he's on the right side of things: individual freedom, justice for the poor, all that. He really does a lot of good around here."

"But?"

"No buts. It's all very simple for him. He's hoping Robert Redford will star in his life story."

Liz's tone was distant; she was performing her Catholic high school girl trick of comedy instead of intimacy, the endlessly entertaining routine that can deflect sexual advances, declarations of love or hatred, talk of death, fear of aging.

"Liz," I said, "did you want that job?"

"Yes. So?"

"So why did you give it to me?"

"Because I wanted to. Because the horse is going to foal."

My throat constricted at the impossibility of expressing gratitude to someone like Liz. I wanted to say to her, "You're giving me my life. I have always loved you." But what was the possible response? An embrace that would be awkward for us and difficult to break away from. And then what would we do with our faces, with the position of our bodies? How do people who are not lovers break from one another and arrange themselves in the room in a way that can express the ease of their affection and regard? Perhaps it was possible, but not with Liz, who was sitting on the counter like Annie Oakley.

"I suppose I'll live in Ringkill," I said.

"You could live here."

"No. Thanks, but no."

"It'd be swell," said Liz. "You could be an aunt to the kids, a sister to me, a confidante to John in his brief domestic hours. Just like a Jane Austen novel."

"That's what everyone in Jane Austen gets married to escape, you jerk."

"Do you want to get married?"

"I want a terrific pair of high-heeled shoes, and a lipstick, so I can make noise on the sidewalk with my heels and put on lipstick like Rosalind Russell. Then I want a very small apartment, and I want people to refer to me as a bachelorette."

"I think the term is swinging single now," said Liz.

"And they call that progress."

"It *is* important," said Liz, violently changing the subject. "This idea of John's. It really can change people's lives, get them out of those ghastly nursing homes into people's houses. It's very exciting."

"What about the people who take care of them?"

"That's what you'll have to find out."

"You mean I have to go into people's homes and look around and ask questions?"

"Why don't you dress up like a nun. Nuns were always doing things like that and everyone thought it was terrific."

"I feel frightened."

"This could help people. You could do a lot of good."

How funny, I thought, despite all the breaches between them she still believes in his work, like a good wife. I was struck by the real loyalty that it is the instinctive privilege of a marriage, even a bad marriage, to command.

I thought of what Liz had said, "You could help people. You could do a lot of good." It made me think of life as an endless, exhausting circle: the unfortunate, helped by the fortunate, who will one day be unfortunate, unless they die young. Bodies using their own strength to make sure that other bodies can go on. And no one asks, "Go on to what, go on for what?" Love? Love of other bodies that will one day be lost to them, to keep back loneliness, to keep back death? But those were the choices: life—keeping the body, keeping the bodies of others—or death.

If I chose life, it was clearly best to do something to alleviate suffering. I thought that what I would most like to be was an anesthetist, and I imagined myself in a white mask, and the patient's grateful look as he closed his eyes for a long, a very long time. I did that for my father. I was able to relieve the pain of his body. I could assure him he would never be alone. I would try to do that again, I thought. Only now I wanted walks by myself on summer evenings, and good meals with wine, and the touch of hands on my body that would bring tears to my eyes and make my mouth fill with water.

What was the connection between all that and asking questions, going into people's houses? John's plan was to give a stipend to people who cared for the aged in their homes, whether or not they were relatives. It was a good plan, a humane plan; once more I was surprised that John had thought of it. Where did his caring spring from? Or perhaps he just had good ideas.

I sat in Liz's kitchen, and thought of what my father would have said to John's program: monstrous, he would have said, to think of paying someone for an act of charity. But the demands of charity are extraordinary. If one is charitable, if one does extraordinary things for others, out of love, one expects extraordinary things from others and the same love. But the problem is that whereas people don't mind loving others for the love of God or humanity, no one wants to be loved only because of a general, undiscriminating love. Hence Margaret and the yellow look around her eyes of having been cheated.

Liz was putting the children to bed. They came down, in their pajamas, decorated with baseballs or flowers, their hair smelling sweet and wet and dirty. I embraced the children and felt the thin bones of their backs. They are as frail as birds, I thought, children. But when I looked at them, brown and sleepy, I thought they were not frail at all but flexible and full of tensile strength.

"I'm glad you'll be living near us and working for our father. We can show you the country in the fall. The leaves are very nice," said Sonia, as formally as a Victorian hostess.

"I'm glad, too," I said.

In the morning on the train, I looked at the matte green of the hills and the clear, reflective river. There were houses in the landscape, with clothes on their lines: little snatches of bright, human color. I would come up next week for an interview; I would sell the house.

I thought of having to meet with John Delaney. He would think me foolish; he would advise me not to sell. We would argue; he would call me ungrateful, for the price of his favors was never to disagree with him. Even thinking his advice over was a breach, like

Moses striking the rock twice. Well, it was possible
that I could cut off relations with John Delaney, except for a yearly Christmas card. But Father Mulcahy,
what would he say? It had certainly never occurred
to him that I would go away. He would miss me, and
he would not come to see me; he never drove his car
through Manhattan, and so it had circumscribed a
perimeter of thirty miles. And Eleanor, would she resent the connection of Liz to all this? No. I would, but
Eleanor would not.

It would not be difficult to tie up the ends, and the
simplicity of it made me see my life as a desert landscape, with a desert landscape's sparse appeal. I
would fill it up now, with people, with work. I thought
of the winter clothes I would buy.

Since it was only noon and Sunday, I decided to
stop by at Eleanor's. I called her from one of the
rows of glass telephone booths in Grand Central Station. In the booth next to me was a woman, asleep.
Her legs were completely wrapped in bandages; she
was obese and nearly bald. She gave off an appalling
odor, the distillation of all I feared. But I would not
move to another booth. I wanted the discipline of enduring that odor. If I were still in the Church I would
have called it a penance.

I had obviously awakened Eleanor. "I was taking a
nap," she said. The image came: Eleanor sleepy in
her pink wrapper on a late August Sunday. Pinks and
silvers, a silvery gold.

"Please come," said Eleanor. "It's one of those terribly empty Sundays when I take three or four baths."

"I have a marvelous surprise. I have a job."

"Isabel," said Eleanor. "How wonderful. Will you
be going away?"

"I'll come and tell you," I said. When I hung up
the phone, the woman in the next booth had gone.

"It's terribly hot," said Eleanor, opening the door.
"Do you want a bath? Am I getting obsessive about
baths?"

"No, it's a marvelous sort of twenties idea, a bath after the train."

I bathed and dried myself with one of Eleanor's opulent blue towels. I felt cool and relaxed, on the edge of a delicate indolence.

"Do you have another wrapper? I can't bear the thought of getting into my clothes."

"I have this Chinese thing," said Eleanor. "It would be wonderful on you."

She gave me a red kimono made of crinkly material with gold borders on the sleeves. It was as light as rice paper.

I told her about the job. Tears came to her eyes.

"I'm really impossible," said Eleanor. "I had worked out an elaborate fantasy that you'd get an apartment near here, and we'd meet for lunch, and go to concerts and take walks. Forgive me. I'd no right to plant you so firmly in my fantasy; Justin always said he felt I was stealing his life from him when I did that."

"It's a lovely idea," I said, half regretting my decision.

"No. We'd start taking a lot of baths and sitting around in housecoats."

"It wouldn't hurt for a day, though. Let's have that kind of day. Let's not get dressed till tonight, and then we'll go to dinner someplace that has tables on the sidewalk."

"I have the *Times*," said Eleanor. "I'll make lemonade."

She went into the kitchen and came back with a tray of cookies and a cut-glass pitcher of lemonade. The lemons fell to the bottom of the pitcher like plump, cheerful swimmers.

"Liz has a lover," I said. "A woman."

"Oh," said Eleanor, in a way that indicated that she wished I had not told her. It made me wish it, too; it was the sort of thing Liz would consider a betrayal. I would try to pass it over.

"John is the same as he was in Fordham," I said. "The distressing thing is, he's effective."

"Well, he would be, wouldn't he."

I was wondering how I could explain to Eleanor what John Ryan had made me feel, my tremendous resentment of his consciously forceful sexuality, my revulsion at its obviousness, at the sheer bulk of his maleness that intruded upon my vision like a truck on an empty road. And at the same time, if I were honest I would have to say that something in me had moved, something had lifted, some wing had brushed inside me so that my resentment was not only against the sheer mass of him and his effects and his connections, but also against the fact that all of it had not left me unmoved. I could not explain this to Eleanor, who looked like Christina Rossetti in her thin pink gown. But it reminded me of something I wanted to ask her.

"Eleanor, do you know a good gynecologist?"

"Oh, yes, Dr. Mintz. He's great."

"Will you make an appointment for me?"

"Why?"

"I've never been."

"You should have a yearly Pap smear, Isabel."

"Yes," I said, wondering what kind of contraceptive I would ask for. My ignorance on the subject was vast. It was too vast even to ask Eleanor about. And the kind of preparedness I had in mind would trouble the delicacy of Eleanor's ideas about sex. Whatever she had gone through, she would always be more innocent than I, for she believed in the impromptu, the chance encounter, the happy ending. Being beautiful, I suppose, she counted on something in the universe to come to her rescue. And of course it would; it was impossible to believe that something would not act, even extravagantly, at the sight of such beauty in peril. But believing myself more physically ordinary, I believed that the physical world needed my constant attention. I have always wanted to be ready for whatever happens; I have always hated surprises.

"Is Liz happy, and the children?" said Eleanor.

"Yes. They've all worked out an odd life that suits them. Liz reads a lot of eighteenth-century history and she's building a barn."

"And I take baths and read *The New York Times*. Liz always made me feel insubstantial."

"You're perfect," I said. I wanted to say, I can tell you about Liz. I could never tell her about you; that means something. But I said nothing, because I did not know what, exactly, it meant.

"Perhaps I'll look for a new job myself," said Eleanor, as if what I had said meant nothing to her.

We dined at a small French restaurant that had put a few tables outside in almost caricatured homage to the American image of Paris. We walked back through the cool streets of the Upper East Side. White lunar street lamps shone through the leaves of trees that had fences around their trunks to protect them. From what, I wondered? Erring dogs and the importunate hands of children? The warm, regretful end of summer threw Eleanor and me together in a pleasurable melancholy. Next week, perhaps, there would be a touch of cold in the air, and we would be thinking of the beginnings of things: an old legacy from childhood when September meant a return to real life. But now we walked with the sense of something coming to a close, with the sense that we would remember what we were doing, walking like this, terribly slowly, on the last Sunday in August.

"Perhaps when we're old we'll get a house together," I said.

"Yes," said Eleanor. "If we're still alone."

The house, when I entered it, had the old smell of accumulation, but it was no longer dangerous. I looked at the living-room couch, which had faded to the color of the inside of a plum, and wondered if I would feel sad to leave it. I knew I should be feeling sadder. I remembered my high heels digging into the grass at the edge of my father's grave.

If I told Father Mulcahy that John Ryan had given me the job, he would be much less sad at my leaving. He thought of John and Liz as a perfect couple, with their success at sports and politics, their children, their fine white teeth and firm healthy flesh. Even Liz's irreverence was part of the charm of the picture; it was an Irish tradition, a lightning rod that channeled the energy of doubt to a safe grounding. If I emphasized John's part in the adventure, it would seem to Father Mulcahy that I was going to my own kind. And that was important; the charmed circle of fortune and benefice would not be broken by strangers. Even so, his look of pure loss (why were Father Mulcahy's eyes always so much one thing or another? The lack of a mix made everything infinitely more difficult) was a surprise and an anguish to me when I went to see him the next morning.

"Well, it's the work of the Holy Spirit, isn't it, you up there just as a job opened up in John's office."

"It's only six months."

"You won't sell the house, then?"

The desperation in his voice made me hedge.

"I don't know," I said, although until that moment I had been sure I would sell the house as quickly as possible.

"Well, you'll leave that all to John Delaney."

"I guess," I said, not wishing to argue.

"He's a good man," said Father Mulcahy. "He just goes to show you can serve God and Mammon."

"Perhaps they have to take turns."

"I don't know where you get this critical streak in your nature, Isabel," said the priest.

"Don't you now," I said, in a mock Irish brogue. "Did you remember a fellow name of Moore? His tongue had a rough side to it, I hear."

Father Mulcahy lapped up teasing like a hungry cat; it was one more proof of his loneliness.

"I'll miss you, pal," he said, holding my hand.

"I'll miss you, too," I said, wanting to say, I love you. You are perfectly good. There is no one like you.

But old Mrs. Keeney hovered in the background, as if to protect Father Mulcahy from my blandishments.

"I'm not going to China," I said.

"You might as well be. How many times a year does Liz come and visit her mother?"

"But she doesn't like her mother. You know that, they've never gotten along."

"Grace O'Brien is a hard woman. Doesn't give an inch. And Liz has a stubborn streak."

"I'll come and see you, Father. Please don't worry."

"It'll be different. You won't be here."

"Different doesn't mean bad."

"It does at my age."

"Nonsense, you've been the same age for thirty years. You never change."

"Everything changes," said Father Mulcahy, in a meditative tone that was so different from his usual ruminative purr that it made me sit up straighter in my chair.

"Look at the Church," he said. "I can't get used to it."

"The people seem to like it."

"Not the old ones. They feel like someone's broken into their home and stolen all the furniture. I feel that way myself."

I felt like saying, I agree. It was dreadfully wrong of them, but I did not wish to encourage his regret by making him appear to have allies in another generation.

"It's still the same God," I said.

"Yes," said Father Mulcahy, "He never changes."

Which, I thought, is the secret of His great appeal.

I decided to go to John Delaney's on the way home from the rectory, as if some of the aura of clerical protection would still be clinging to my clothing. I tried to imitate Liz's ticking-off glance so that I could cut through John's meaty effusiveness.

"I want to put the house up for sale," I said.

Delaney didn't move in his chair.

"Now, you don't want to rush into anything, honey."

"I'm not rushing into anything. I've thought it over quite carefully."

"You don't know the market, honey. Why don't you leave all that to me. There's an Irish couple in the parish just over from the other side. You could rent it to them."

"I don't want to rent it. I want to sell it. If you won't put it on the market, I'll find another lawyer who will."

I was shaking with anger and pleasure at my own daring.

Delaney did not lose his temper. He brought his bulk to a standing position and loomed above me like a wounded hippopotamus.

"I don't know what your father would think of this ingratitude. After all I've done for your family. And the man not even cold in his grave."

Funeral baked meats, I thought, standing up so that John and I were more equal in height.

"If my father had wanted the disposition of the property to be your decision, he would have left it to you. As it is, it is entirely my affair. I am moving to another city. I wish to sell the house. It is an extremely straightforward matter."

I stared at him as if we were wrestling. I could see the color of his eyes diminish in defeat.

"Well, honey, I just wanted to make sure you knew what you wanted. Of course I'll handle it."

I resented his desire to control even my victory, but nevertheless I complied with his tone.

"It's awfully big for one person."

"We'll put it on the market at MacDermott's. He'll have a buyer in no time. And the right color, too."

"I'd sell to a black family if they wanted to buy."

"Luckily, none of them deal with MacDermott," said Delaney, making notes on a pad.

I felt a cave of cowardice hollow out in the bottom of my stomach. But I did not want the breach with

John Delaney to be final. All night long I upbraided myself for not pressing the issue of his bigotry. In a similar situation, but with the opposite political cast, my father would not have given in. And I hated my own uncertainty, my lack of authority, my concern for what people thought and felt about me.

I thought how far the house had gotten away from me. Books lay on the floor in desiccating piles; it had been fifteen years since my father and I had gone through the books, and at least that long that the shelves had been filled to double-layer capacity. Arranging for the installation of new bookshelves was the sort of thing my father didn't think of and I was baffled by. Whom did you call? What did you say? As for getting rid of the books themselves, I had tried, but the dust made me sneeze; it clung to my hands in a way that made me feel insane; an ache would settle in the muscles of my haunches and I would give it up. And then, so many of the books were my father's, and it would have been an affront to have packed them away as he lay in his bed with nothing to do but read.

But now I put on my shorts, tied my hair in a bandana, and surrounded myself with empty cartons from the liquor store. The books on literature I would keep for myself; the religious ones I would give to Father Mulcahy; the political ones I would send to the local Conservative Club; the ephemeral, to the Veterans' Hospital. My eyes watered, the way my hands felt made me want to cry out, but I kept on. As I filled each carton, I carried it down to the basement.

Eleanor had promised she would bring the car and help me. But it was dispiriting work; it was two weeks before the piles on the floor began to disappear, and I had not, even then, got to the shelves. And the piles being gone did not change the look of the room as I had hoped it would; it did not seem bigger or more full of light. But at least with the books off the floor I could have the rug shampooed. Why had I not thought of it before? One looked in the telephone book under rugs: shampooing. And by one of those elevating do-

mestic coincidences, the man who shampooed the rugs
would shampoo the sofa also.

But the look of the house did not change. I moved
on to the kitchen. I took down the crystal and the
china that had been my mother's, that my father and
I had not used except at Christmas. In the last years
we didn't use them at all. Dust had become so permanently a part of their texture that if I ran my finger
across the surface of a plate or glass it made no difference: there was no clear streak parting a gray sea.
I left them to soak in a solution of ammonia so strong
it made my head ache. I polished the glasses till they
sparkled and I stacked the shiny dishes with their
sweet, understated pattern of roses in the cabinet I
had lined with yellow paper. I wondered if it were
foolish to do this just before I was ready to move out.
But something had changed. I had broken through
something; my kitchen looked like the kitchens that
had been cared for by my friends' mothers. But I had
done it myself. I had even taken care of the books.

Eleanor had made an appointment for me with her
gynecologist. She apologized that it was on a Wednesday morning, the one day that she would not be able
to get off. Was I relieved that I would be going to the
doctor alone? Not immediately. My first sense was of
pure inadequacy. I was sure that there was some procedure that everyone my age knew that I did not
know, something so obvious that I could not even begin to formulate the first question about it.

I had never been to a gynecologist's office; I had
never been in any doctor's office except the one I had
gone to since childhood, the office of Dr. MacCauley
with the picture, next to his diploma from Notre
Dame, of Jesus and the children. It occurred to me
that this was my first encounter with a professional
man who had not known me since the day of my
birth.

Dr. Mintz's office was so different from Dr. Mac-
Cauley's that it surprised me that they were even pe-
ripherally in the same business. First there was the

matter of nurses. Dr. MacCauley had, of course, his wife, whom he may have married for that express reason. Mrs. MacCauley sat behind her desk typing on a machine that looked as if it had something to do with the Manhattan Project. Every inch of her was starched; her white cap, almost as big as a Sister of Charity's, had aggressive black stripes that seemed to say, *Don't think you can get away with anything here.* She had to assume that identity because Dr. MacCauley was so vague.

Dr. Mintz's nurses had bouncy, coppery hairdos and wore jump suits. On the wall were Picasso prints of nursing mothers and the Muzak played soothing, rhythmic tunes that had, I was sure, something to do with advanced notions of parturition. I wished that the whole motif of the office were not so heavily geared toward maternity; in its way it made the atmosphere as antisexual as Dr. MacCauley's. When I walked in, the pregnant women (there were four of them, spread out, looking decidedly uncomfortable on Dr. Mintz's Danish couches) looked at me with suspicion. I could see in their eyes what they were thinking. *We know what you're here for.* They all thought of themselves as more adult than I, which was certainly not helpful of them. I tried to look wicked and as if I thought birth was messy and beside the point as I sat in the one hard chair that none of them had wanted.

One of the bouncy nurses gave me a form to fill out. I was sure that the panic in my eyes made the nurse suspect that I was there about venereal disease. But there seemed so many questions on the form that were inappropriate to me, perfectly sensible questions like how many pregnancies have you had, what methods of birth control have you used, what is your health plan. Health plan? I thought I ought to leave. It was one thing never to have had any pregnancies but never to have used birth control and never to have had health insurance betrayed the radical emptiness of my life to strangers, strangers in jump suits, in a way I would have preferred to avoid.

One of the nurses showed me into a room. I had expected that behind that door would be an examining table and a stand for dangerous-looking instruments. But this was the only room I have ever seen that I could possibly think of describing as a parlor. There was a delicate-looking settee and what appeared to be a writing table with chairs around it that I was afraid to sit on. It would have been a perfect setting for *Pride and Prejudice*. I stood at the door, trying to remember why I'd come.

Suddenly, the opposite door whipped open and in walked Dr. Mintz with a force and an energy entirely inappropriate to the room. If Dr. MacCauley's mien indicated vagueness and subservience, Dr. Mintz's suggested business and science. He would treat, cure and charge you. He indicated that I sit in the chair nearest the door. He sat across the table from me, already reading my form.

"Now, Miss Moore, what can we do for you?" he asked, looking directly at my belt buckle.

"I'd like some kind of birth control," I said, feeling keenly the inexpertise of my diction.

"What have you been using?"

"Nothing."

"Nothing whatever?"

"No."

He didn't even look up. I liked him for trying to act as though this were something he came across every day.

"You have had sexual intercourse?" he said, making little marks on my form, which I was sure were gibberish, something to do so he wouldn't have to look at me.

"A long time ago. Eleven years ago," I said, beginning, to my horror, to blush.

"That's all right," said Dr. Mintz, furiously writing.

"What?"

"I said that's all right."

"Oh, thank you."

"Not at all," he said, opening the drawer in front of him.

"The three choices you have, Miss Moore, are the diaphragm, the pill and the IUD."

I knew about the diaphragm: I had read Mary McCarthy. I could all too easily imagine myself on all fours chasing the thing around the bedroom. It was not what I had in mind.

"I don't think I want a diaphragm," I said.

He shrugged. It saddened me to think that he didn't care that much about which method I used. I was hoping he would have more of a stake in something.

"The pill has certain side effects that you should know about. It can cause blood clotting, depression, and weight gain. It can increase the size of the breasts."

"What about the IUD?" I said quickly. If there was one thing I didn't want it was larger breasts.

Dr. Mintz pushed toward me what looked like a primitive charm, something white and plastic in the shape of a crab.

"This is called the Dalkon shield. We find it the most effective method for women with no previous pregnancies."

"How does it work?"

"We're not exactly sure. When it is inserted in the uterus, it has a 97-percent success rate. That's better than anything else except the pill, which is 99."

"I think I'd like to try the IUD," I said, as if I were selecting a hat.

"Good," said Dr. Mintz, putting his samples back into the drawer. "I must warn you that insertion can be quite painful. But once it's done, you can forget about it."

"That sounds fine," I said.

"You can go inside now," he said, opening the door to a room that was more like what I had imagined. I was immensely relieved; I had been afraid he was going to ask me to lie down on that chintz sofa.

The less bouncy of the nurses came in and stood beside me.

"If you'll just take everything off and slip into this dressing gown."

She held up a garment that looked as if it were made of paper towels. I knew it would fall apart the instant it touched my skin. But I dutifully changed behind the curtain. The dressing gown barely covered my buttocks. I have never felt so spuriously clothed.

"Just hop right up here on the table," she said.

"Put your feet here, right here in these stirrups." She indicated steel half-cups at the sides of the table. Whoever thought of calling them stirrups?

Never in my life have I felt so thoroughly exposed. I was stretched open so far I could imagine someone walking into me. It was worse when the nurse left the room; at least when she was in the room she was taking up some space; there was something that could not disappear into me.

"Doctor will be with you in just a moment. Just lie back and relax."

I wondered how anyone could relax in the position I was in. Added to my physical discomfort was the distress that someone was going to touch me in a place that no one had touched me for eleven years. I reminded myself that he was a doctor, a man of science. Nevertheless he was a man. Would it have been better if the doctor were a woman? No, I have always felt more exposed to women than to men; the additional exposure would have made the situation even less modest.

Doctor Mintz walked in as if he had never seen me. He put on a plastic glove. Only one. I wondered if the naked hand had a special significance.

"We'll just do a pelvic on you first," he said. I noticed that he and his nurses had a tendency to say "just" a lot. Did they feel some particular need for diminution?

I lay back trying to decide whether or not to tell him that I had never done anything like this before. But it

sounded so virginal an admission that I could not bear
to make it. I saw him reach for what looked like a
rather advanced corkscrew. Was he going to put that
in me? He was. I felt my pelvis expand. He twisted a
screw and I felt a sudden sharpness in a place so deep,
so tender, that I could not believe it had always existed in my body without my knowledge. It was an unpleasant sensation, not the kind that makes you cry
out, but the kind that makes you want to cough, as if
some bad air had just come into the room.

"This will be somewhat painful, though less in your
case than in others."

What did he mean by that? I felt gifted by his observation of my specialness, however false. But I was
not prepared for the shock of what followed. He was
stretching my bones; he was invading the deep, the
tender center of my body. His eyes were the eyes of
an astronaut, entirely abstract.

Never had I felt such pain, and there was an added
sense of outrage in knowing that I had invited it.
Tears came to my eyes, but they seemed a perfectly
physical phenomenon, as if it were impossible to think
that I would ever be able to stop them. I lay perfectly
still, weeping with a calm that seemed utterly foreign.
The nurse patted my leg. I wondered if she had trained
with a veterinarian.

"It'll be all over in a minute," she said. "And then
you won't have to worry about anything. And think
how glad your boyfriend will be."

My boyfriend. Whom had I been thinking of when
I planned all this? The only man I had been in contact with was John Ryan. I thought of his pink,
burnt-looking thighs, the color of salmon. He was the
last man in the world I wanted to touch me. But lying
on that table, exposed and calmly weeping, I could not
imagine that any touch would stir in me anything but a
terrible tenderness, the tenderness of the wound that I
was sure Dr. Mintz was permanently inflicting to my
misguided order.

"That's it, Miss Moore," he said, patting my leg. I knew where the nurse had learned the gesture.

"Just lie back here for a moment. We'll give you some Darvon for the pain," said Dr. Mintz.

I was in some discomfort, but that was nothing to my desire to get out of that room. I became obsessed with the need to be in my own house. It seemed to me terribly bad manners to be in pain in some stranger's office. As soon as the doctor and nurse left the room, I started to get dressed.

When I appeared in the outer office, the nurse looked surprised.

"Don't you just want to rest a little bit?" she said.

"No, I'm fine," I said, as brightly as possible. I tried to make myself look Protestant. I gave a cheerful little wave as I walked out the door. The second I got out of the office I had to vomit. I made it to the tin ashtray which was blessedly beside the elevator. I ran out of the building like a criminal. I hailed a cab with some frenzy. The taxi driver was surprised when I gave him my Queens address.

"It will cost you a bundle," he said, tentatively starting the meter.

"It's all right," I said, closing my eyes in the back seat. "I'm planning to sell my house."

I would have done anything to avoid taking the subway. By the time I got home, the pain had subsided to a dull ache. It was a comfort, that ache; it made me feel something definite had happened; it made me feel both adventurous and safe, as if I had set out on a journey with the best and most expensive equipment.

By the time Gerry MacDermott, the real estate agent, called to say he would bring the first couple around to look at the house, I was ready for them. The house looked as though anybody might have lived in it. Anybody but us.

The Murphys were a very small couple. Mrs. Murphy was probably younger than I. Her neat little feet were nipped into their sling-back sandals; her legs were shiny and tan beneath her whitish stockings.

They had two children. Mr. Murphy was an accountant for Sunoco. He had gone to St. Aloysius; he knew my father. He had never taken a course from him because, he said, he wasn't that kind of brain. Professor Moore, he said, made guys like him afraid.

"To think I could be living in Professor Moore's house," he said.

Mrs. Murphy loved the garden, the way you had to step down to it. And the cunning window seat; she could imagine little Crissy and little Joey sitting on it reading. Will the house be big enough for them? I asked. They are used to an apartment, said Mrs. Murphy. I thought that was beside the point. But I was trying to sell my house. Nonetheless, I did not want to do anything that would mar the sheen of the Murphys' perfectly deserved happiness.

"It's not a very light house," I said. "I'd say that was its biggest drawback."

"We could cut down some of the old maples," said Mrs. Murphy.

So, that was why the house was so dark: the trees. I could have had them cut down any time. It had never occurred to me that the house's darkness came from a natural, correctible source.

"The trees must make it cooler in the summer, though," said Mr. Murphy.

I would not like you to cut down the old maples, I thought, but if I sell you this house I have no claim on it; it is out of my hands. I began to think how odd it was that if I sold the house I would never come back to it. You could not come into someone's house and say, "This used to be mine." You could not knock at the door and say, "What have you done with it, now I'm gone?" No, everyone wants to think their house has always been theirs, to pretend that they will never move out and that they were born there. It would be brutal to remind people of one's former occupancy, to remind them that nothing is permanent, that we move from house to house, losing, each time, part of our lives. So if I sell them this house, I thought, that is the end of it.

"So nice to have such a big bathroom. And such a solid tub," said Mrs. Murphy.

I thought of myself in the tub, thought of my father bathing me as a child, washing my hair and lifting me up in my big green towel. And later me, lying in the water, discovering my growing breasts and the hair on my legs and my vagina. It was in the bathtub that I had first seen my own menstrual blood, spinning out from between my legs like a spirit.

"How old are your children?" I said.

"Are there children that age in the neighborhood?" asked Mr. Murphy.

I was embarrassed, "I don't know," I said.

Gerry MacDermott rushed in. "Isabel, Miss Moore, I mean, has been very absorbed by her father's illness."

Absorbed, that was a good word for it, I thought.

"I'm sorry," said Mrs. Murphy, making her eyes look dim as she had doubtless been taught by an Irish mother.

"It's all over now," I said. "I'm starting a new life now."

Mr. Murphy giggled tensely. I realized I must have sounded heartless.

Gerry MacDermott called me that night and said that the Murphys were interested; they would pay, he said, twenty-seven-five. But he added, "Don't let them have it, though."

"Why?"

"I think you can get more. Just keep them on the line, in case."

But I didn't want to go through it again, showing my house to strangers. Opening it up and giving it out like that.

"I want them to have it. She said she liked the garden."

"OK, it's your funeral. I mean," he said nervously, "it's up to you."

"Let's get it over as quickly as possible. Tell Delaney to get moving."

The house, now that I was about to leave it, seemed newly precious. It was here that my mother had come as a twenty-two-year-old bride, here that she had brought her baby daughter. It was in front of this house that she had been killed and here that my father had suffered his stroke and lain, for years, with his window looking out on the garden. It was here that we had eaten meals, mostly with priests sitting jovially around the heavy dining-room table. I could see that it was a fine house. I felt remorse for my own blindness, for my own neglect of the house and its considerable spaces. Mrs. Murphy would not neglect it, I knew, and there would be children. All this I am leaving, I thought, as I sat in the middle of the floor, weeping. I wept for my failure of love for the house that had kept me since childhood.

Why, I wondered, didn't I care for the house, when certainly I could have? I had done more in a month than I did in ten years. Why did I let it go?

There was the lack of time and the demands of my father's body. But sometimes time had frightened me by its expanse: I would wake in the morning, frightened, wondering how I would fill the hours until it was time to go to sleep again.

How did I spend my time? I tried to call it back. I remembered the tasks I did for my father: bathing him and shaving him, the medications, the dressings. I would do the laundry in the basement; sometimes if it were a fine day I would plan to hang it on the line, but I never had, not once; I had always put it in the dryer. And I cooked, did the dishes; there was the same blue enamel basin I had always used. Objects were a help to the terrible abstractness of memory. I had read: there were all those books, and I had gone to St. Aloysius library for my father. I watched movies on television. I visited with Eleanor and Father Mulcahy. I ate; I shopped; I remembered waltzing down the aisles of the Safeway to the Muzak, which I enjoyed, knowing I ought not to enjoy it, stunned by the plenitude before me: fruits and lively green and yellow vegetables, eggplants purple and polished, little foreign-looking boxes of cookies, red forthright meats under lights like movie stars. And I slept. I slept in the late morning when my father slept, and in the afternoon, and if there were no late movie I wanted to see I would sometimes, exhausted after getting my father ready for sleep, go to bed at ten o'clock. It horrified me now, only a month later, to think how important food and sleep had been to me, like a primitive, like a child with a damaged brain.

I could have taken care of the house. I could have learned a language or knitting. I could have kept a journal or written a history. For all those years I was a servant to bodies, my father's body and my own, which had spread and softened from languor and neglect. I was always terribly tired.

But now I would give the house to Mrs. Murphy, who never slept, who never brooded or lost houses in stolid dreams. Mrs. Murphy was quick; instead of bones she had wires, and a bright little eye like a bird's. She would care for her own body and for the bodies of her husband and her children; I could see Mrs. Murphy doing calisthenics in the bedroom, splashing her breasts with cold water. She would care for the house.

I had sold the house to strangers, so now I tried to make up to it for what I had not done for it, could never do for it. I could not love it until it was no longer mine.

The air was sharp, the apples grew red, the days were frighteningly shorter. Eleanor had come and helped me take the books away. The men from the veterans' hospital had collected theirs and the rest were put into storage with the furniture, in a warehouse that belonged to a friend of John Delaney's, who had agreed to store my property without charge.

It was October when the Murphys moved into the empty house. Father Mulcahy and Eleanor stood next to me and watched the men carrying in the unfamiliar furniture, the strange boxes with their descriptive tags. Mrs. O'Hare kissed me; Mr. O'Hare shook my hand. Bobby did not appear. I imagined him doing something unspeakable in his room, enraged at my abdication. Mrs. Murphy flitted about; Mr. Murphy watched the movers with a fine suspicion. All the papers had been signed, so there was nothing for it but to drive away in Eleanor's car, with a large suitcase, my only property, in the back seat. Father Mulcahy stood outside the house, waving us off. Eleanor and I wept until our faces felt fragile as balloons. We would go on to Ringkill, we agreed, that same evening.

VI

Considering all things, my gratitude to Eleanor and my fears for her, I thought we should stay in a motel while I looked for an apartment. I knew how Eleanor would fade under Liz's sharp eye, fade to the color of white flowers in water. The vagueness that I loved in Eleanor had always irritated Liz. I could imagine Eleanor disappearing against the dark wood of Liz's kitchen.

This was Eleanor's vacation. Vacation: the word spun around in my brain like a close-up of a spinning record in one of those fifties movies about rock-'n'-roll stars. For eleven years I had had no vacation.

"Let's go someplace warm for Christmas," I said.

"I know this person who knows this island where no one lives except some people who bring you fish and breadfruit, which, by the way, is supposed to be terrible. Such a nice name, too," said Eleanor. "Breadfruit. It's supposed to taste like wet bread."

"I still want to go. We should make plans now."

"It's only October."

"If you don't pin things down they slip away."

"Mm," said Eleanor. "Let's go for a swim."

The blue of the chlorinated water was unnatural as a jewel. I dove in. It was night, and the light bulbs under the water gave it a transcendental look, but the definite edges of the pool kept it all quite safe. I swam under the water, sure of my body as a fish. When I came up, I could see Eleanor lying on her back looking at the ceiling.

"This motel is huge," she said. "It's sort of a monstrosity but I like it. Imagine all those rooms and a swimming pool in October."

"It's utterly comfortable. I could live here forever."

"It's probably very bad for us," said Eleanor. "I'm sure it's very bad for us."

"Yes, but we don't do it *all* the time. It might be bad if we did it a lot, but just this once."

"That's what they used to say about sin," said Eleanor. "Do it once and you're hooked on it."

"They were right, too."

"It's funny, I don't think I commit any sins. Sometimes just for practice I examine my conscience and I can't find any sins. The only one I used to commit was having sexual relations out of wedlock. The sixth commandment. And that's out now, I guess."

"I still commit sins against charity," I said, "the way I always did."

"Who don't you love?"

"Margaret Casey. I really hate her. Sometimes I think about her and it makes my spine ache. Father Mulcahy used to say if I could truly love her I would have conquered myself."

"But she's completely unlovable. She's worthy of hate. She's a hateful person."

"That's why I feel I ought to love her. It would be one of those pure acts."

"Why do you want to *conquer* yourself? And why pure *acts*? Freud tells us there are no pure acts."

"And no jokes."

"What?"

"Freud says there are no jokes."

"And no accidents."

"God, what a life. Who wants all that control?"

"I suppose once you know about it, it's cowardly not to take it."

"Yes, but we have to *pretend* there are jokes and accidents, or life is unbearable."

"And pure acts of love?"

"Yes," I said, diving under the water.

Our motel beds were firm and springy as trampolines. We sat smoking cigarettes, looking in the newspaper for apartments. Landlords tended not to want tenants who would stay for only six months.

"You see, if we were connected to the Church, we'd just go up to the parish priest; he'd be sure to know of something," I said.

"Yeah, he'd put you up with someone like Margaret."

"Just look in the papers," I said, thinking how pleasant it was to go at something straightforwardly, to take one's place with, and if necessary behind, the others, to get something with no special privileges or connections, no leverage but one's own almost accidental suitability.

I didn't want to call Liz until I had found an apartment. For Liz, with her political connections through John, the strands that tied her, willy-nilly, to the community through her children, would doubtless "know of something," would be able to "put in a good word," so that once more I would be ahead of people, would have advantages. Or at least Liz would know some efficient way of going about looking for an apartment; she would have some sort of plan that would cut through time and effort like an expensive knife. But I wanted to go through all the red tape like everyone else. Eleanor and I would not be clever enough to avoid it, and as I looked over at her dangerously and sleepily smoking a cigarette, I thought how I would enjoy it all.

A landlord named Mr. Cohen said he would show us an apartment that was really the top floor of a house. It was full of furniture that looked insubstantial as twigs. But the rooms were large and light, and it had a back porch that was all windows. There was a gray rug on the living-room floor that disturbed me so much that I realized I had already decided to take the apartment.

"You verk for the county. You're a politician," said Mr. Cohen in a heavy Yiddish accent.

"Not exactly," I said, thinking how odd it was that someone would refer to me in those terms.

"For my money, there's only one politician. Franklin Roosevelt. After him, they're all, you should pardon the expression, hot air."

"Didn't you like Kennedy?" said Eleanor.

"He was too good lookin'. I got my first job on the WPA. The post office here, they got a WPA mural. You should see it some time. It's a work of art. He woulda changed the country, but they wouldn't let him."

"Who?" I said.

"The bankers. Roosevelt had a lot of Jewish advisers. Are you Jewish?"

"No, but I'd like to be," I said, trying to be mannerly.

"There's no like about it, if you're not you're not. So you want the apartment?"

"Very much," I said.

"You take it then. You have trouble, you call me. I'm a plumber. I have a daughter your age, she's an actress in Paris. She calls me up, 'Pop, I need some money, Pop.' So I send it. They put those telephone calls under the ocean. When she calls up all I can hear is the waves going over the line. I can't even hear my daughter. It's terrible. What's terrible? She's happy, God bless her."

"It's very good of you to take that attitude," I said.

"What attitude? I want she should be happy. If she breaks her mother's heart, that's her mother's headache. If my daughter's happy, I'm happy. So. You get a leak, or a fire, you call. Give me a deposit. I give you the key."

"And that's it? That's all there is to it?"

"You want me to make it harder for you? If it

makes you happy I could create already some difficulties."

"When can I move in?"

"You're moved in. It's yours. Enjoy it in good health."

He closed the door.

I was glad that my new bed was double. "But I'll have to get new curtains," I said to Eleanor.

"Perhaps the two Persian rugs from Dover Street," said Eleanor. "You could cover this gray thing with them. Or would that be bad luck?"

"We can't go on thinking of the past as a kind of bad luck."

We walked around the neighborhood and bought food for dinner at the corner store. The sky was purple and the dangerously weaving branches promised a cold rain. The dry leaves blew low to the ground against the cuffs of my corduroys. The tops of the celery in the brown paper bag I carried tickled my cheek. It is autumn, I thought. I will cook for the first time in a house that is only mine. I will make a meal there for my oldest friend, who floats beside me; no storm can hurt her. This is life, this is life and life is good.

"I'll have to eat all my meals on this little table in the living room," I said.

"Everyone does," said Eleanor. "Nobody's kitchen is big enough these days."

"That's true, unless you get married. Nobody who's single has kitchens that are big enough. That's very stupid," I said, with sudden vexation.

Eleanor turned on the radio, which was one of the few things we had unpacked. We decided, with some solemnity, that it would go on the small table next to the telephone.

"Damn," I said. "I'll have to get the phone hooked up tomorrow, and the gas. These heaters run on gas."

I spoke, I felt I ought to speak, as if this were a trouble, but I thought it was exciting to call large companies who would send their men, competent and uniformed, to connect me up to the rest of the world. It made me feel protected and attached to large, benevolent forces.

The radio crackled with static; suddenly melody broke through. Beethoven was ours, and the painful sweetness of the C sharp minor quartet invaded the room.

"I ought to call Liz," I said to Eleanor, "and tell her where I am and that I'm settled. I ought to have called her before."

I knew that Liz was alive, always, to possible breaches of manners. I would lie; I would say I arrived today, had had phenomenal good luck in finding the apartment immediately. For it would hurt Liz to think that her friend Isabel had been too absorbed by practical matters to contact her. It would hurt any of us, I thought. We all like to think we are the center of each life we meet.

"Will I have to see Liz?" said Eleanor, already a little smaller in her chair.

"You saw her at the funeral."

"But people always behave well at funerals."

"Liz always behaves well."

"Yes, but what is she thinking?"

"What are you afraid of?"

"I'm afraid of thinking that my life is empty and inactive."

"You're still imagining Liz as a senior at Anastasia Hall, captain of the basketball team, president of Sodality with the desk the nuns used to show the sloppy girls as an example. She's lost her adolescent perfection. She has two children, for one thing; that's bound to be softening. And her life has irregularities now."

"But she still has those frightening eyes. They haven't softened."

I thought how Liz's brown eyes were a comfort to me, how I loved them for their rigor, their very unforgivingness. But then I had been immune from the censure, and it is always pleasurable to watch the censure of others, no matter how one loves them, and to feel oneself preferred and safe.

"You'll like her children. They're very serious. And don't you want to see John Ryan? Just for curiosity?"

"I'll go if you want me to, Isabel."

"I think you must."

"I suppose it's probably that we're jealous of you."

"How foolish," I said. I liked the idea. It had never occurred to me that I would be real enough in a woman's life to cause jealousy. In my father's life, yes, but that was because he could not always distinguish his life from mine. But Eleanor, who had given me so much and asked for so little, did Eleanor need, as my father had needed, my particular affection and regard? Then we are connected, I thought. I am not entirely alone.

Liz said we should come for lunch. Eleanor spent the morning putting on eyeliner, taking it off, putting on jeans, taking them off, changing her blouse four times and frowning at herself in my spotty greenish mirror. I watched her with great interest: Eleanor had placed her fears of Liz, her fears about herself, almost literally on her own shoulders, as if she had made her body the beast carrying the burden of her inner life. I stood next to Eleanor in front of the mirror and imagined us in one of those Victorian photographs that are lit in such a way that everyone looks beautiful. How I loomed above Eleanor, although we were the same height! Eleanor looked fragile beside me, but that day I liked the strong bones of my face, my clear green eyes, my heavy, springy hair that I had promised my father I would not cut.

Eleanor drove badly in the country. She was, surprisingly, an aggressive driver; her slim foot pushed the gas pedal to the floor the second the light turned green. She had a terrible tendency to tailgate. Her nervousness made her reckless, and, once or twice, I gripped the hand rest and was seriously alarmed.

As we pulled into Liz's driveway, I could see Eleanor crouching into her body like a bird. When she said, "It's lovely here," I had to say, "What? I can't hear you," twice, so inaudible were her comments.

Liz stood on her front porch like a matriarch; she might have been holding a rifle instead of a wooden spoon. She nodded her head, moving no other part of her body. She kissed me stiffly, kissed Eleanor like a mechanical doll. Dear God, I thought, what atrocities I commit in the name of good manners.

Eleanor was getting smaller and smaller. Liz asked her if she would like to see the horse.

"What horse?" said Eleanor, with perfect imbecility.

I stamped my foot involuntarily; I had told Eleanor about Liz's horse and how it was going to foal. We had had a long conversation about it.

"I'm afraid I only have one," said Liz, with unnecessary edge.

Eleanor cooed at the horse as if it were a duck.

"I'm building a barn for her," said Liz.

Jesus, God, I thought, as Liz began to swing her sledge hammer dangerously, she's going to hammer in a post to show off and Eleanor will simply disappear under the ground like Rumpelstiltskin. They are both at their absolute worst.

"Aren't the hills lovely," I said, trying to reclaim Eleanor. But she did not even hear me. Liz gave me a look that said, "You have betrayed me to a fool."

"Liz has built all this by herself," I said.

Eleanor gave me a look that said, "I am drowning. Save me."

I wanted to put my hands on my hips and shout, You are both being impossible. I am going away. You can do what you like to each other. But I felt the full weight of my responsibility. I had brought these two together: something must be salvaged of the day. And they were both so marvelous. Why were they like this with each other? Neither was like this alone with me.

The past, I thought. We all share a past. I must fish up something of the past, something brilliant, something glittering, or the day will be ruined. Eleanor was standing behind me like a child behind its mother in a crowded department store. It was ridiculous of her to be standing that way. And Liz was leaning on the sledge hammer like a Visigoth. It was completely unnecessary of her to look so menacing. Why was she doing it? Did she like to terrify? And Eleanor, did she like being terrified? Still, I had to do it; I had to bring them together because they were in the same city and had shared a past.

"Sister Adolphus is supposed to have a radio program on Sundays called 'Sister Says.' Can you believe it? That jerk. She has debates with rabbis about situation ethics," I said.

Liz's body relaxed; she took one hand off the sledge hammer.

"I saw her on TV. Can you imagine, that idiot on TV and here I am moldering in obscurity. She was saying, 'I am a *nun*. My business is *love*.' And she was carrying this terrible pocketbook."

Eleanor stepped out from behind me.

"They all have terrible pocketbooks. And terrible shoes. I don't know where they get them."

"They probably have this boutique, except instead of rock music they have Gregorian chant and instead of strobe lights they have vigil candles," said Liz.

"Actually, that sounds like it would catch on on the Upper East Side," said Eleanor.

Liz laughed; it wasn't funny. None of it was that funny, but we laughed. She put down her sledge hammer. The three of us walked into the house. I breathed normally for the first time in twenty minutes. They would not be friends, but Eleanor would not hide and Liz would not menace. It was possible to go on living.

At two-thirty, Liz had to pick the children up from school. She got up and slung on her brown suede jacket like a cowboy. She kissed Eleanor and me quite naturally. Perhaps, in Eleanor's case, it was only a kind of homage to the past, but her body bent to the shape of the past and did not, as it had before, stiffen against it.

"I'll go home tomorrow," said Eleanor, as we got out onto the highway.

"Yes," I said. "I don't want you to go at all, of course, but I have to get at things by myself."

By things, I knew Eleanor understood me to mean: my life. And Eleanor in my apartment protected me from my life like a veil or a curtain of flowers. Now I had simply to get on with it: I thought of my life now: austere, a lunar color, whites and grays, the temperature of the moon.

Still, when I stood at the door of Eleanor's car, and Eleanor rolled down the window to kiss me good-by, I felt the dampness of fear, as if at the center of my chest, right at the sternum, there was a small cold pool that was about to spread, ruining warmth, ruining safety with its greenish chill. Eleanor saw the look in my eye.

"Don't be frightened. You'll meet all your new people tomorrow."

"That's what I'm frightened of."

"Is it?"

"No. Of course not. I'm frightened to begin my life."

"But you've been living it for thirty years," said Eleanor.

"Not this one."

"But our lives are only the one thing. We're always only the one person."

"You see, I don't believe that," I said. I was not the person who lived with my father's body in the center of my life, in my father's house, with his bed at the center of it. I stood on pavements now; I leaned on cars. And then I was terribly tired.

I stuck my whole torso through the window, and Eleanor and I laughed as we extricated ourselves from the awkward posture that the shape of the car demanded.

"God bless you, Isabel," said Eleanor. "I'll come up in two weekends."

"I'll call you when my phone's hooked up. You'll be my first call."

Eleanor's Saab drove down the street whose trees were vivid red. The morning light made the car seem at once terribly dream-like and terribly solid. I would speak to my friend, would see her. If my life became too difficult, at least I could hold on to that.

I had left the apartment door open, so that the air in the rooms seemed thick with cold. The gas man had not connected the heaters yet, so I shivered and put on my new green cardigan. It will be winter, and then it will be spring, I thought. I had to say that to myself because seasonal change always surprised me. When it was autumn I expected it would be autumn forever; when it was too cold it was impossible for me to believe that I would ever be too hot. But this I had always liked: the first serious chill of autumn, the need for bundling into heavy clothes for the first time.

I sat down among the dirty breakfast plates. The light from the largest window in the living room looked as though it had been blown through a tube. I thought that one day perhaps this furniture would be as familiar to me as the furniture in the house I had lived in all my life. And that was queer, too, how quickly things became familiar, how quickly the present became the present, and expected, how quickly the past became the past, and odd.

And now I would have to go into other people's houses, new ones, every day, each one with a bed at the center of it, and age, and death, and ask of people, what do you eat, what do you do between the times you are sleeping, what would it take to make you happy?

I thought it would be impossible to ask these questions of strangers. One had the right to ask them of someone one loved, but not of strangers. But there was the possibility that I could make someone's life better. Someone would have more time and someone else, perhaps, more company because they had talked to me. And these things mattered, these small possible things.

I decided to scrub the apartment until the walls

were white and shining. I would shop for the things I needed for the house. All this made me foolishly happy. I made a list. I was singing; I wrote down: thumbtacks, dish drainer, rubber gloves.

VII

It was my first day of work; I awoke thinking of my father. Always there had been a little note of panic in my awakenings, for there was always the chance that I would go into my father's room and find him not breathing. But that had not happened; he had died, after all, in the hospital, which had made me feel both cheated and delivered. I had not had that from my father: his death, which he might have given me, a perfect presentation in the shape of a white, solid disc. But then I had always seen him breathing, and which gift was the more lovable?

I wondered when I would no longer wake thinking of my father. I sat on my bed drinking a cup of coffee from the big French cup Eleanor had given me. It was white and blue, and in the center was a dark-red shape—a bird or a heart. Eleanor could not decide which, but she bought it, she said, because either shape is hopeful.

I was thinking of how, when my father lost the use of his hands, I would shave him every morning. And I had enjoyed it; it was almost the only physical ministration I had enjoyed. I would make jokes; I would pretend to be an Italian barber and would sing made-up songs in made-up Italian. And it would make my father laugh, almost in the old way; I could feel his body shaking in the old way, although his face could no longer produce the semblance, the signals of laughter.

When I got to the County Office Building I could see that I was much too early. The secretaries were buzzing around in sleepy, tentative ways, trying to organize coffee and little trays of pastries; there were no men in sight and I did not want to be tangled up in that compliant buzz. I walked around outside the building looking for a coffee shop. The office building and its workers were surrounded by four square blocks of restaurants, cafés, and shops, in a kind of desperate effort to keep people amused on their hour of freedom from twelve to one. But just outside this corral was an area near the railroad station. Black men walked restlessly on the streets, looking ill and unhappy; pregnant white mothers smoked cigarettes and slapped their children, who were not even surprised. They shopped in the five-and-ten for socks or make-up. I went into the L&P store; it had the cheap, cottony smell of fish that always made me feel there was no sense going on with life. I bought a roll of Scotch tape as a kind of reparation, to make up to the store for the hatred it had inspired.

When I walked back to the County Office Building, the autumn air, after the air in the store, was almost too clear. I took the elevator to John Ryan's office. It was on the top floor in the County Executive's suite. There was a huge window and a planned view of the mountains.

The secretaries huddled around John like attentive little planets. I stood in front of the desk while John distracted the secretaries' attention with jokes that were all about sex, although it was never mentioned.

One of the secretaries turned away from John to me with obvious annoyance at being interrupted. This stopped the mechanical rhythm of John's attentions: joke, laugh, joke, laugh, pat, joke, laugh.

"Isabel," he said, and put his arms around me, kissing me (quite unnecessarily, I thought) on the mouth.

"This just shows, friends, I have nothing to hide. This broad here is from my old neighborhood. And she's my wife's oldest friend, and I'm bringing her in to let it all hang out."

The secretaries laughed but had decided as a unit that they did not like me.

"I'll take you in to meet the boss," said John, walking me toward the County Executive's office. His arm was still around me.

I was surprised that Dominic Napoli looked like someone I could have gone to grammar school with. I thought I must be getting old, if politicians were beginning to look my age.

Dominic Napoli was working hard on not appearing Italian. He dressed like an English don; I admired his tweed suit and his brown, hard-looking shoes. He shook my hand as if he had made an art of it. But I liked him; his light-brown eyes were not amused by John.

John sat down and immediately put his feet up on the County Executive's desk. He took his tie off.

"Jesus Christ," he said, "once I get out of politics I'm never going to wear another frigging tie in my life."

Dominic sat so straight in his chair that I felt compelled to sit straight in mine.

"You understand the project?" he said, with such formality that I wondered how he had ever got elected. It obviously had something to do with John.

"I think so," I said. "You've given stipends to people who care for the aged in their homes, and I'm supposed to check up on how things are actually going."

Dominic nodded.

"You see, Dom," said John, "the terrific thing about this whole project is that it's so goddamn human. Isabel's not some kind of tight-ass social worker or professional do-gooder, and the kids who'll be helping her are all from the community college. I mean that's what's so goddamn beautiful about it; it's a real community thing. I swear to God, this'll put you in Albany."

"I'm not really from the community," I said.

John looked at me as if I were a subject who had just questioned the propriety of monarchy.

"You live in this town now. You're part of the community. Besides, who has more experience than you in this? You'll really understand these folks' problems. And besides, you're a good-looking chick with brains, and they're not easy to come by."

I was embarrassed, but I was helped by Dominic's embarrassment.

"Now," said John, "the people over in Social Services have made out this basic form. Every house you go into you ask these basic-type questions. And then there's space for your own remarks, of course, if you want to do any freewheeling."

I looked at the form. There were questions about square feet of space and medical equipment, about the patient's age, the state of his health and the frequency and kind of medication. Nothing was said about how people felt and what they wanted. It said nothing about being tired or lonely or in despair. But I would stick to the form.

"Now we're going to have a meeting this afternoon with the kids from the college. Great bunch of kids. They'll be doing some of the interviewing, but you'll have to roll the whole ball of wax together."

"I'm in *charge,* then?" I said. "But I don't actually know what I'm doing."

"Nobody does," said John. "That's the terrific thing about it. We're doing something completely new. It might be as big as Medicare."

Dominic and John simultaneously bowed their heads, as if someone had spoken the name of God.

The students who were there to help me made me feel totally helpless. I had always been put off by the heartiness of young people with a social conscience. It reminded me of people I knew who joined the Peace Corps in the early sixties. They were always having things called beer blasts and hootenannies.

They always seemed to work very hard at having a good time; I had always suspected the loudness of their laughter, their good-natured, deliberate, but finally asexual fumblings after buttocks; their groaning recital of the things they had to do (wash the car, sit through High Mass) with terrible hangovers. It had always made me want to pull down the shades in my bedroom and read *Piers Ploughman,* or pretend to have the vapors.

The students' adulation of John made me more uneasy. I thought that it would only be a matter of minutes before he began tossing around a football. But I had to remember his effectiveness. Exquisite taste and a perfectly modulated spirit can do nothing to relieve the sufferings of strangers. And practically all the world are strangers.

"OK, gang," said John, "this terrific-looking broad who can give you all the poop on me as a kid when we're all smashed tonight happens to be one of my oldest friends. But not only does she have a body, she has a head—she wouldn't even talk to me in high school. I was only a jock on the basketball team."

I wasn't even aware of him in high school. He was five years ahead of us. Why lie like that, what good would it do any of us? But he was right. If I had been aware of him, I wouldn't have talked to him.

"Seriously," he said (had he been joking?), "she's someone who's had real experience with home care and she'll know what to ask. Now I want Isabel to talk, and we'll all just freewheel a little and get a feel for each other."

Everyone looked up at me with perfect expectation, as if they had never been disappointed in life, or considered the possibilities of pride, or pettiness, or evil.

I cleared my throat, knowing even as I did it that it was a great mistake. They would know that I had not been thinking about this at all yet.

"Well," I said, "I don't know what to say. This is a very complex issue. I suppose the most important thing is not to make people feel as though they're being invaded. After all, it's their lives we're going into. We mustn't make them feel as if we were stealing something from them, or that we thought our lives were more important than theirs."

"Point number one," said John. "Sensitivity. Awareness. The old third eye. Is that what you're driving at?"

"Yes, I suppose so."

"Only let me add a little piece of advice," said John. "Sure, you don't want to come over as Mrs. Bureaucrat—or *Miz* Bureaucrat as the case may be (the students laughed at this, particularly one of the smaller girls)—but you're there to get information, not to make friends. You've gotta break some eggs if you wanna make an omelet. Go on, Belle."

I wondered if he had any idea how homicidal I felt when someone called me Belle. But he was right, I supposed, about friendship and information and omelets.

"I think what we ought to do among ourselves," I said, ideas coming to me like little windfalls as I talked, "is to try to figure out what seems to make these people happy and what doesn't. Perhaps if we can understand the good things that people do we can tell other people about them. It's easier for people if they don't feel so alone in these things."

"Point number two. Efficiency Analysis. Information Dissemination. *Communication,* that's the name of the game, right, baby?"

"Yes," I said, not really listening, anxious to go on. "I think what we should all do is to listen to the way people talk; find out if they have private jokes with the people they're taking care of. Jokes are very important."

"Back to the magic word *communication*. I swear to God, it's everything."

"And you ought to see if the people taking care of the old ones look tired or unhappy. Or if the old people seem to be bored."

"Of course, first you've got to make sure they're being properly fed and are getting competent medical care. You don't want to go off the rails," said John, looking at me with suspicion. "First things first."

"Of course," I said, feeling foolish, not agreeing with John, but knowing that was a quirk of my own soul, that I thought jokes were more important than medicine. Or at least I preferred talking about them.

"Of course," I said. "We must consider bodily welfare first. But people can hide things. Try to talk to the old people alone. Maybe we could make up some incredibly complicated form for the younger people to fill out so they'd be kept busy while we talked to the old people."

The students laughed; John slapped me on the back.

"You're not a tricky Mick for nothing," he said.

I was thinking, Perhaps this will be possible. I looked at the students sitting around the table. Like John, they still had suntans. They must all have been lifeguards over the summer, I thought. I imagined that they probably thought me peculiar. But there were some things I wanted to stop them from doing.

"Any questions, gang?" said John.

There were no questions.

"Wait till they get a little booze into them. We'll all go off to the community center for a beer blast to celebrate the inauguration of Project Caretaker."

I had an impulse toward hysteria. Thank God Liz isn't here, I thought. But then, this was Liz's husband.

John came up to me, rubbed his hands together and slapped me on the behind. More than anything I wanted to slap him back, but I thought how all the students liked him. I thought that this was probably the sort of thing that men did to their women colleagues. It was probably all under the heading of fun at the office. It was probably what people called horseplay.

But John kept his hand on my behind and was ruminatively stroking it.

"Did anyone ever tell you you have a delicious little ass?" he said.

I felt again that annoying heat, that reprehensible flip beginning in my stomach. But I despised John Ryan; I forbade my body to respond to him.

"It's hardly little," I said, remembering from Catholic school that laughter and irony are the great anaphrodisiacs. Only I wasn't very funny. And he did not take his hand away.

Boys were cooking hamburgers in the kitchen of the Community Center as they always had for the church bazaars in the Parish Hall. But instead of the pastor and the curates walking around talking to the parishioners with one eye on the teenagers in the kitchen, John Ryan and the other politicians walked around, their expensive shirts unbuttoned as the priests I had known would never have unbuttoned their cassocks. Didn't they ever get hot? I had never seen them sweat, except outdoors on very hot days when they were wearing cotton shirts. Nuns never sweated. It probably had something to do with not wanting sex.

People handed me hamburgers; people handed me beer. A serious-looking girl wanted to talk to me about the state's record on the aging.

"The old are the invisible minority," she said. "They have no power; they're worse than blacks or women."

"But they do have the power to menace us with our own inevitable futures. White people aren't afraid of becoming black or men of becoming women. Many people act as they do to old people because they're afraid of being like them, or because they want someone to treat them the same way when they're in the same condition."

The girl looked at me very oddly. I reminded myself that I could not talk like that to these students. I thought that before they began this project they should all be required to read *King Lear*. Then we could have interesting conversations.

There was a jukebox in the Community Center and

some of the students began dancing. I moved my hips slowly, holding beer pleasurably in my mouth. Then I remembered that I had not danced in eleven years, and that the last dance I had done was the twist. I could not possibly do that here; I imagined myself dancing with one of these boys and the rest looking on in pained embarrassment. I felt myself beginning to cry, and I ran to the ladies' room.

I closed the door of the booth and sat on the toilet, sobbing. No one must see me. What could I say? "I'm crying because I don't know any of the dances"? It was absurd. I sobbed into my cold hands. I couldn't do it; it was wrong to believe that I could. I should give it up now, give up my apartment and go back— where? I had sold the house; I could not go to Liz. I could not hang onto Eleanor. Perhaps I could become the housekeeper in the rectory so I could be near Father Mulcahy. I shuddered, thinking of Mrs. Keeney, thinking of Margaret Casey who had lived their lives so that they would not have to sit on toilets in strange cities, holding beer in a paper cup. Once more I was looking down at my life from that height. And I wanted to jump down on it, swoop it up, carry it away in my mouth like a bird. I washed my face and put on mascara so that I would not cry again. Liz was right; life was a matter of tricking yourself: you sold your house so that you could not go back to it; you wore mascara so that you would not cry.

I would look among the faces of the students for a face that I could love. I would look for something original, something arresting in the shape of the chin or in the eyes, something that suggested the belief that there was residual pain that could not be touched by legislation. But they all looked so relentlessly happy and healthy that they did not interest me. I realized that I was looking for someone who was sad, and I was angry at myself for making the equation, my father's equation, the Church's equation, between suffering and value. I would have more beer; I would enjoy myself. Perhaps I would ask one of them to teach me to dance. No, that was too embarrassing. They so obviously had their own kind of solidity that it was impossible to break into it. I knew nothing about Ringkill politics; of course I had always voted Democratic, but that was not enough; I could not break into the circle and say, "I've always voted Democratic." I could not say, "I made phone calls for McCarthy and McGovern." And they did not seem to want to talk to me.

I didn't like the look of myself, straggly, outside the warm solid circle. I decided (realizing that if I had had real moral courage I would not do this) to speak to John Ryan. Most stupid things are done for fear of having no one to talk to.

John offered me a sip of his beer. It was foolish; it was a public gesture, not of desire but of a lax determination to possess. Beer, which I did not like, was a perfect drink for John Ryan. Its gold was a male color; no woman's hair ever shone like that. And its structure was right for men, too: clouded on top, then clear to the bottom. For women, it would have to be the opposite arrangement.

Go on, said something inside me, friendly, poking me in the ribs, laughing but not unkindly. Whatever it is you will get away with it, it was saying. You can't go on like this, it was saying. You don't want to be alone; you don't want to be lonely.

One of the students gave me another beer. They were asking me about John Kennedy, and I was saying no, I was not old enough to have voted for him, but yes, I had worked for him. I told them I had worn a straw hat with a bumper sticker around the hatband; we all believed, I said, that he could change the world. And when he died, I was thinking, I had already been taking care of my father for a year, so it was not so shocking. I had already stopped believing that life was full of promise.

"Do you remember what you were doing when you heard Kennedy was shot? I read somewhere that that's the only memory all Americans have in common," I said.

"Which one?" said one of the boys.

"Which one what?" I said.

"Which Kennedy?" he said.

It was a perfectly sensible, perfectly callous question, and it underscored the difference in our ages. Probably they had grown up knowing that the world was not full of promise. Did that make it easier, I wondered, or more difficult?

"John Kennedy, she means," said a girl with very dark, very untidy hair. "I remember I was playing. I was in the second grade, and everything stopped, and some of the children started crying."

I looked at the girl, wanting to say, Thank God, you at least have a lovable face. The girl's eyes were very dark, with a pure seriousness she would doubtless lose along with her virginity. Only now they lose it very early, I thought, and still manage to look serious.

"Jesus Christ, you're getting morbid," said John. "Let's all have some more beer."

The inside of my head was turning golden, the color of beer or toffee, and spinning, swimming in that pleasant way that was saying, It doesn't matter. It doesn't matter. I was eating hamburgers and spilling ketchup on my blouse, but I could see the students liked me for that, liked me for rubbing the ketchup into my blouse with my thumb.

Suddenly a group of black children appeared in the room, bouncing basketballs. I had drunk enough so that this confused but did not worry me. We were talking about Kennedy, and now here were these children with basketballs. How interesting it all is, I thought, ideas floating through my brain like charming balloons.

"Hey," said John, "we've got to clear out. Can I trust you guys to clear up? I've got to take Miss Moore home."

"Some guys get all the breaks," said one of the boys, extraordinarily pleasantly, I thought. Extraordinarily pleasant it all is, I was thinking, all these nice young people asking about Kennedy, and immensely pleasant leaning against John as I walk, and the way he smells of beer and soap, that terribly expensive soap, the color of honey.

I swung my legs into the car as if they belonged to someone else, and I looked up at John through a cloud of kittenishness. I had never looked at anyone like that. And how he seemed to like it, and how kind it was of him, with his hand on my knee, stroking the silk of my stockings, and how charming the color of the hair on his hands, golden and shining, the color of beer.

"I'm going to take you to see the sunset on the river," he was saying, with his tongue in my ear.

"I think that would be lovely," I said, moving my head, exposing my neck so he would kiss me there. He would like my neck, I thought, having to move my hair to get to it. It was so soft, so warm, he was saying.

The friendly voice that had poked me in the ribs was smaller and colder now. It was saying, This is Liz's husband. This is a man you can't bear. But then it was also saying, It's not like that. Liz doesn't want him. Liz likes women. And it was saying, how marvelous he is to be near, moving his hands so cleverly.

He was unbuttoning my new blouse and saying, "Look at the sun on the river." But he was not looking, he was diving and landing, his mouth on my breast, and I was crying out in pleasure and surprise at what his mouth was doing.

"Beautiful tits, beautiful tits, just the way I like them, big and firm."

You don't have to listen to what he says, said the voice inside me now. Just let him go on.

He was breathing, chewing, I could feel myself bucking, a horse, a fish. He was breathing as if he were going to die, that was how much he wanted me.

He lifted up my skirt and took down my panty hose. I was moving, and then he was inside me and I was crying out, in pleasure, in surprise, and he was crying out a moment later.

He gave me a handkerchief.

"We don't want to stain the upholstery. It's a county car," he said.

It was over and wrong. I was suddenly sober. I looked at myself. Ridiculous, my panty hose around my knees, my hair impossibly tangled, and I groaned. He thought I was groaning with pleasure.

He handled my breast as if he were making a meatball.

"You were really dying for it, weren't you? I'll bet you haven't had any in years. I was afraid I was going to have to pop your cherry, but no such luck, somebody beat me to it. You got a great future ahead of you, honey, the way you need it and those terrific tits."

He started the car. I was soaking wet between my legs; it felt like the symptoms of a terrible illness.

Dear God, I said to myself, desperately careful to remain silent. I wanted to weep; I wanted to bathe. The sky was alive and orange.

I got out of the car and tried to smile at John. What would I say to Liz? My legs were impossibly heavy as I climbed the stairs to my strange apartment. I had enjoyed it while it was happening; I must never lie to myself about that. I had, as a man would say (but not a woman), asked for it. And that was what Liz would despise me for most: enjoying it, wanting it, feeling what I felt. And now, feeling wet and dirty, I wondered whom I could tell, how much I would have to tell. At least when you confessed, you knew you had to tell everything. It was not a question of kindness, it had nothing to do with human feelings. You unburdened; you did not hurt.

I bathed myself in the dark. I was thinking as I fell asleep: I must do something about curtains.

I thought that if I dressed very carefully and looked very smart perhaps no one would think the worse of me. I tried to make breakfast for myself, but the kitchen smelled bad and the little particles of green pepper and onion in the drain and the film of what looked like rust on the frying pan made it impossible. My head ached and my eyes felt small and prominent and fragile.

I walked to the bus, beating out with my heels on the pavement, "Everybody knows, everybody knows." But they liked John, and they liked people who drank, maybe they would like me, maybe they would think I was a good sport, maybe it would make me seem human. I thought people only used the word human in that sense when one had done something particularly degrading.

Lavinia Hartman was the kind of woman I wanted to be: I knew that when I had first seen her, talking to students a week before. Her hair was gray and very thick and she wore it in a low bun at the back of her neck. It was held with hairpins that were probably plastic, but that looked like bone. She could have been a dancer or an abbess, so straight was her spine. Her hands were a tawny color; the tips of her fingers were spatulate and the nails arched competently over them. She was the social worker who had worked on the project since the beginning.

Lavinia was a widow. I will never be like that, I thought, with that hair and those fingers, because of what John Ryan could make me feel. I would never be capable of that staunch widowhood. If John Ryan ever touched Lavinia, a dark light would come over her eyes like a shadow and he would be rebuked. I shook her hand, thinking it is best to have been born Protestant, for Lavinia had all those Protestant virtues that my father never talked about: discipline, and quiet, and a deep unstated sympathy. And wonderful bones that Catholics never have.

I thought it was tremendously kind of Lavinia to say nothing about my bloodshot eyes. She brought forward a huge stack of folders. She was wearing as a necklace a dull silver disc, absolutely plain, that hung between her thin breasts on a thong of leather. She lit a cigarette. I thought the yellow stains between her middle fingers were cunning, an apt finish, like varnish on a light wood.

"I hope you'll call me Lavinia," she said, as if she were imparting some terribly sad news. It was wonderful manners, I thought, to say, "I hope you'll call me Lavinia," instead of "May I call you Isabel?"

"My sister's name was Isabel," said Lavinia. "Still is, really." She laughed a dry, smoker's laugh that ended in a cough.

"Do you know I've never met anyone else called Isabel? Isn't that queer? Have you ever met anyone called Lavinia?"

"Practically everyone in my family is called Lavinia. But I suppose that doesn't count."

"No. Not a random sampling," I said.

Lavinia began opening the folders, smoothing them with the flat of her hand.

"The people you'll be interviewing are not a random sampling either. The only people you'll be speaking to are people we've already screened. That is, people who fulfill minimum standards of home care. You won't be seeing any of the real horrors. I hope you're not disappointed."

"Not at all. I have a rather low tolerance for horrors, actually."

"Me too. It doesn't get any better. I advise you not to go into social work. Or maybe I advise you to go into it. Not that you've asked for my advice."

"Oh, but I do. I'm in the queer position of being thirty and never having held a job, and having no training. I feel sort of like a spaceman."

"Just divorced?"

"What?"

"Were you married? Is that why you're feeling so unsure?"

"It was my father. He was an invalid. I took care of him."

Lavinia gave me a slow, dark look—a look that said, what a peculiar thing, but since you did it, it's quite all right. She had the facility—maybe it was only an accident of her looks—of making you feel you were the most important person in the room.

She told me what she wanted the investigation to accomplish.

"The politicians are trying to make political capital out of this, but it's not a political issue. What we want to find out is what kinds of situations seem to be workable and applicable to community care. It's all very tricky because you're going into people's homes."

She had said what I had tried to say to the students, only how high-flown and florid it had been as I said it. I thought that from her, perhaps, I could learn to be simpler.

Lavinia did a sample interview with me. She showed me names and folders. They meant something to Lavinia, but to me they were only a blur.

I asked Lavinia if she would have lunch with me.

"I always have lunch with my daughter. She comes home from school and fixes it for us. It's my one unbreakable date."

I felt foolish and rebuked, as if I ought to have known. It made me feel unconnected; I was sure everyone else knew that Lavinia always went home for lunch. I had been too forward; I should have gone more slowly with a woman like Lavinia, who would resent the assumption of instant intimacy. It was partly for her coldness that I liked her, and liking her, I thought with some regret that we would never be friends.

I had been given a desk a little way from the secretaries. I realized how much of my time would be taken up with paper, but that was all right; it might be a relief from the suffocating presence of people. I opened my desk and looked at the supplies: pads and clips and delicious new pencils and erasers.

I could hear John coming into the office. I had

forgotten that part of it; I would have to see him every day. What could I do? Would he continue wanting sex with me, or in some kind of perverse chivalry would he let the matter drop?

He came over to my desk and threw some keys at me. "I got you a county car. Not everybody gets a county car. Only my very special people."

The leer in his voice made all the secretaries look up.

"Come to lunch," he said.

"I'm just getting started, John. I want to keep at it for a while."

I thought if I could do tricks with my voice, achieve Lavinia's timbre, Lavinia's diction, he would neither resent nor want me.

"I hope you're not going to be a pain in the ass about this job. You've gotta live, too, if you get my drift."

I wanted to say, If I get your drift. You're not exactly Dante, you fool. But I said nothing.

"Liz wants you to have supper out there tonight. I'm not going to be there, so there'll be no awkward triangles."

He had not lowered his voice at all; the secretaries were simulating busyness with their first real energy of the day.

"Thank you, I'll call her," I said, trying to smile like somebody's little sister. I looked up and saw Lavinia in the background.

"Sorry to interrupt," she said. (She heard everything, knows everything, I thought.) "Would you have supper at my house Friday, Isabel?"

"I'd like to very much, very much."

"Good, I'll give you a time and directions."

She smiled at John coldly, politely, as I knew she would. I thought, This is someone who doesn't know about me, who thinks I'm like anyone else. The idea was novel. Everyone else I had come in contact with had known my history. I wondered how much I would explain to Lavinia, how much I would have to explain, or want to.

John was still looming above me. "Watch out for her. She's dangerous."

"To whom?"

"Nice little girls like you who need someone to look after them."

"Please, John," I said, "try to behave decently."

The look in his eyes was pure menace. This is the danger, I thought. I knew I would have to go on with him or he would destroy me, perfectly simply, perfectly straightforwardly.

"What I mean is, I told you never to call me here." I giggled in a simpering way that turned my stomach. I was very frightened.

"Call Liz," he said, over his shoulder, "and maybe you can squeeze me in this weekend, if you get my drift."

How had it started so badly? How had it got so out of control? I thought of my father's house, and the books all over the floor.

And now I would have to call Liz. And do what? Tell her I had slept with her husband? Avoid the issue and face the almost atomic tick of Liz's glances? Miraculously, Liz sounded herself on the telephone. I would go there for dinner this evening.

I turned my ankle as I got out of the car, and I was limping as I came up to Liz's back door.

"My husband often has that effect on women," said Liz. "He lacks a certain finesse."

Slap, slap, went Liz's words on my cheeks. I turned my face as if from a blow.

"I turned my ankle," I said stupidly.

Liz was not alone. A man was sitting at the round kitchen table. His face was a mixture of sadness and puzzlement, as if it surprised him that anyone could speak anything but kindly. He picked up his glass of wine. I thought he had the most beautiful wrists I had ever seen. He leaned over the table, making a hollow with his body, as if he were used to protecting something, as if he were saying, "I will keep you safe."

"Isabel, this is Hugh Slade, my vet, or rather my horse's vet. Hugh, this is Isabel Moore, my oldest friend and, I believe, my husband's current mistress."

I felt the slaps again, harder now, and a cold wire thrumming inside my skull, which felt unnaturally high and light and empty. This is no more than you deserve, it was saying. Liz, who was so staunch and so demanding, Liz would not forgive. The foyer behind the kitchen was dark as a tunnel. I could feel myself backing into it, making myself smaller, wetter, until I could imagine myself disappearing entirely out the back door and into the dampening night air.

"That's enough, Liz," said the man. "You're making your friend extremely unhappy. You can see that."

How did that man manage it, a rebuke that sounded so loving, that conveyed not, I have never seen you act worse, but I have seen you act so much better? But no one could talk to Liz like that: she would resent that kindness as an invalid would resent the offer of a wrap on a summer afternoon. Surely Hugh Slade was aware of this. And yet his body was not poised for the slap.

The position of Liz's body suddenly shifted; it lowered so that her spine seemed a natural spine and not a monument. And now she merely looked disappointed and oddly aged.

"I'm sorry," she said. "I'm sorry. I can be so hateful."

And to my intense astonishment, she began to weep. Did she want someone to go to her, did she require, what almost anyone else would have required at this moment, an embrace? But this was Liz and the risk of the force of her reproaches kept me where I was, half in and half out of the dark foyer.

"I'm sorry, Liz. I'm terribly sorry," I said.

"It's just that it's so stupid, Isabel. Why him of all people? You don't even like him."

"I know. I have nothing to say for myself."

"And you didn't even use birth control, I'll bet, did you?"

Suddenly I didn't want to tell Liz that I had prepared for just such a situation. Instead I said brightly, "It's all right, I'm getting my period. I'm getting it right this moment."

Hugh Slade leaned his head back and laughed.

"You said that like a girl scout talking about a merit badge," he said.

His laugh was warm and hard and forgiving. It covered us, as women, in a male, foreign envelope.

"No, Hugh," said Liz, "that was not a Girl Scout talking about merit badges. It was a sodalist talking about spiritual bouquets."

"What the hell is a sodalist?" he asked. "And what the hell are spiritual bouquets?"

Once more, Liz and I were drawn together. Once more, the past had rescued us. But one day, I thought, that may not be enough.

We told Hugh Catholic-school stories. Hugh's family, he told me, were Quakers. They had wanted him to be a lawyer, but he became a veterinarian instead. They found it, he said, rather embarrassing.

"But why?" I said. "It's not like running a bordello."

"It's animals, not ideas," he said. "I'm afraid it's very complicated."

Liz said, "I don't feel like cooking. Let's order a pizza and have some beer."

Hugh looked at his watch. For the first time, his perfectly smooth countenance foundered. That trouble touched me as if someone, quite suddenly, had lit a match beneath one of my ribs.

"Okay," Hugh said. "Why not."

The three of us ate and told jokes and then sat back and smoked long cigarettes that were delicious as dessert. I watched Hugh walk to the sink. He was not a young man; his hair was graying and he was beginning to go bald. There was less of the child about

him than any man I had ever seen. That was what I
liked about him. Every man I had known was always
saying, in one way or another, "Give me something.
There is something of yours I need." With John Ryan,
it was sex. With Father Mulcahy, it was lies, and with
my father, it was my life. But as Hugh Slade walked
to the sink, he asked for nothing. He demanded nothing. He was the only man I had ever known whose
walk had nothing in it of compulsion. When he leaves
here, I was thinking, It is possible I will never see him
again. This made me feel such despair that I spoke to
him more directly than I had ever spoken to a man.

"Perhaps we could have lunch some time," I said,
trembling at my great, my incandescent courage.

"I'd like that. I come to town on Thursdays."

It was as though I had passed out of a dark cold
road into the moonlight, which was somehow unex-
pectedly warm.

"I'll call you Thursday morning," he said.

"Yes," I said. "Yes, that would be wonderful."

He kissed Liz and shook my hand. His palm was
very flat, very dry.

"I'll see you this week, then," he said, letting my
hand go.

Liz walked him to his car. Alone in the kitchen, I
was thinking, What will happen? Meaning, This is a
man I could love, meaning, when we are alone will Liz
be hateful? And then what will I do?

Liz came back into the room and for a moment I
flinched at her possible conduct.

"I think you and Hugh are the only two adults I
really like," she said. "Only you mustn't fall in love
with him. He has a terrible wife. She'll tear you to
pieces."

I was very cold again. The tips of my fingers felt
like lost little fish.

"He's married?"

"Of course," said Liz, as if I were a child or an imbecile. "Why would anyone like Hugh not be married?"

I nodded. Still, I would see him again. We would talk. I thought of his wrists, of his light, rather puzzled eyes. I would see him again. There were many things that could happen.

VIII

I hated the Kerners' house. They were my first case, and I thought it was unfair of them to live there. I hoped I wouldn't get to calling the people cases, as even Lavinia did, implying that they were ill and that I could cure them. For the moment I could not think of another noun, entrapping and yet neutral, that would serve, but I promised myself I would think of one. That, at least, I owed to my father—making the effort to find the proper words for things.

The house was very clean. Mrs. Kerner was exceptionally clean; the pictures of her grandchildren on the piano sparkled like little monuments to cleanliness. Mrs. Kerner was very satisfied, as if she had got this house, this colored television that dominated the living room like a sullen, not particularly discriminating god, despite the predictions of her teachers and her family. The plastic doilies under the plastic fruit on her light dining-room table shone with a false sympathy that was really hatred for the poor, the halt, the slow, and the messy.

The fat that hung off the bones of Mrs. Kerner's upper arms had odd little dents in it, as if someone, in a mistaken attempt at ornament, had pressed small diamond-shaped cookie cutters into the flesh before it had cooled. She wore a great deal of perfume, which for a woman of her age and build did not have even the redemptive appeal of a sexual gesture.

"I guess you wanta see the patient. That's what they all come for," she said.

"Actually," I said, "I just want to get a general sense of things first."

"Ya mean ya wanna case the joint," laughed Mrs. Kerner.

"Yes, in a manner of speaking," I said. I knew that I shouldn't say "in a manner of speaking" to Mrs. Kerner, who would imitate me to her friends on the phone the minute I walked out the door.

Mrs. Kerner offered me a cigarette from a pink plastic pack. "I'll make coffee later," she said, "when you're finished with Granny. I call her Granny. It makes her feel more at home."

I wondered who could feel at home here.

"It's a laugh," said Mrs. Kerner, "because she's black as the ace of spades. But she's a good little girl, aren't ya, Granny?"

There was a silence from the area over Mrs. Kerner's left shoulder.

"She musta dropped off. I swear she sleeps an awful lot, but it's supposeda be good for them at that age."

"Mrs. Johnson is eighty-seven?"

"Yeah, and she'll bury all of us," said Mrs. Kerner, snorting.

"She's generally in good health, then?"

"Well, she's practically blind, and she don't walk too good and sometimes she becomes"—Mrs. Kerner paused momentously—"incontinent, but the doctor says she could go on for years."

"Would you say that you are satisfied with the provisions for home care that the county has arranged?"

"She has everything she needs."

"And the presence of this person in your home has not placed a burden, physically, emotionally, financially, on your family?" I read from the form.

"Nah, it's only me and my husband. My daughter, she lives around the corner and she comes every day to have coffee. Half the time I throw her out to make lunch for her own kids. I swear she'd move in here if

she got the chance. We're like that." Mrs. Kerner
crossed her two middle fingers.

"Yes," I said. I had always disliked the kind of girl
who was "close to her mother." At least one couldn't
be close to one's father in quite that annoying way.

"Are there any community activities in which you
and this person participate?"

"Well, I used to take her to bingo, but now she
can't see nothing at all, hardly."

"Are there any community activities which you
would like to see the county inaugurate that would be
helpful to you and the patient?"

"Listen, honey, she can't hear, she can't see, and
she can't walk. She ain't about to take up croquet."

Mrs. Kerner laughed at what she considered her
very good joke. I smiled. If only I were a nun, they
wouldn't expect me to laugh. I could pretend I didn't
get it.

"There are tapes of books that have been recorded
for the blind that are available from the county library system," I said.

"Listen, Mrs. Johnson likes the radio, which she's
got, and her food, which I give her the way she likes it,
and her ice cream in the afternoon and her graham
crackers at night. She's got what she wants. Don't go
making trouble."

"I was only suggesting . . ."

"Ya think it's easy taking care of a person like that?"

"I know it's not," I said. "I've done it." I thought
that would mean something to Mrs. Kerner, but it did
not even make her pause.

"Well, then, ya know that practically anything
makes them happy. They're like kids. Practically anything makes them happy."

Nothing had made my father happy. I thought of
his rages and his tears and his forced, resentful silences.
How nice it would have been if ice cream had made
him happy.

I walked around the house and made notes on space
and light and noted especially Mrs. Kerner's hygiene,

which, I was sure, she would want prominently mentioned in the report.

Mrs. Kerner showed me into Mrs. Johnson's bedroom. It was pink and white; there were pictures of little girls in pink dresses and white fur hats holding rabbits or white fur muffs. If I were Mrs. Johnson, I would have been insulted by this room, its childishness, its colors, but Mrs. Johnson was sitting up in her bed like a bright little bird, wearing a pink bed jacket.

When she smiled, showing a great deal of dark, toothless gum, she was as cheerful as a baby. I didn't like thinking that about a woman who, in another kind of world, would have been venerated for her great age.

"Granny's been a bad girl and took her teeth out," said Mrs. Kerner.

"It don't matter," said Mrs. Johnson. "The lady don't mind. Sit over on my bed so I can see you. And hold my hand. I like people to hold my hand. I can read palms."

Mrs. Kerner raised her eyes upward to suggest complicity between her and me against the world of the old and the foolish.

"I'd like you to read my palm, Mrs. Johnson. I'd like you to tell me my future," I said.

"I can't tell you what *will* happen. I can tell you what *can* happen," she laughed.

"Ya get her started on that, she'll be goin' for hours; there'll be no livin' with her," said Mrs. Kerner.

"Now, honey," said Mrs. Johnson. "This is a new person. She don't know nothin' about me." She waved the clawlike fingers that seemed too large for her body and yet, with their startlingly white fingernails, oddly attractive.

"You just met a man, a nice man, blue eyes. He like you. He think you're sweet."

Hugh Slade, I thought. It must be Hugh Slade. Maybe she knew something about it.

"Yes?" I said eagerly.

Mrs. Kerner snorted.

"He gonna marry you. You gonna have blue-eyed babies." Mrs. Johnson sat back on her pillows and giggled.

"She says the same thing to everybody. Marriage and babies, marriage and babies, the same thing," said Mrs. Kerner.

"I had ten babies. Three died," said Mrs. Johnson. "And the rest, they're out in the wide world now."

"And how many husbands, Snowflake? Tell the lady," said Mrs. Kerner.

I bridled, but Mrs. Johnson did not seem to mind.

"Five husbands. I was a pretty little thing," said Mrs. Johnson.

"Mrs. Kerner, I wonder if you could go outside and fill out this form while I have a word with Mrs. Johnson," I said.

Mrs. Kerner looked suspicious. "Don't believe half of what this one tells you. She's got a real imagination."

"I tell her you been kind to me, Adelaide. I tell her you always treat me good and get the doctor for me."

"You mind your manners, Granny," said Mrs. Johnson, feeling now that it was safe to leave the room.

"Mrs. Johnson, do you feel that it's good for you, living here like this, with the Kerners?"

"You got nice hands. You be happy with that blue-eyed man."

I squeezed the woman's hand. I wanted to say, Thank you, thank you, and make something happen. But I had to get Mrs. Johnson to answer the questions.

"You like living with the Kerners?"

"They treat me good. Get me that little bird. My Pete. He don't talk though," said Mrs. Johnson, pointing to a bored-looking parakeet in a cage near the window.

"Do you like living here or in the nursing home better?" I asked, trying to simplify what I now realized was the ridiculous language of the questionnaire.

"I like it here. I got my room. My radio. I liked it

there. I had my friends, but they died. People stole, though. Someone stole my eau de Cologne. I like it here."

"Would you like to meet more people your own age, go to things where you'd see people your own age?"

"I had my friends, but they died," said Mrs. Johnson.

The woman was happy here; what Mrs. Kerner had said was right, although her reasons were wrong. It took very little to make Mrs. Johnson happy: warmth and privacy, the most obvious color, a bird who did nothing but sit there. Mrs. Kerner could provide all that. And if Mrs. Johnson was lonely, she expected to be lonely: she was an old woman, her friends had died, her children had scattered, but that was what she expected. It was useless to tell her that Mrs. Kerner condescended to her, that Mrs. Kerner was a racist, for she was happy here.

It was not fair that Mrs. Kerner could make someone happy with her cleanliness and her ignorance, while the whole force of my love had not been able to lift one inch the burden of my father's profound misery. Nevertheless, I knew I must write a favorable report. I must write: this woman is happy.

But I wished Mrs. Johnson could live with someone nicer, who would let her read their palms, every day if she wanted, who would let her go on saying the same thing: babies and marriage, marriage and babies, every day until she died.

As I dressed to go to Lavinia's for dinner, I wondered what one did with the past. Did one present it to one's hostess on a perfect white plate, a rare, tropical fruit for her delectation? My past was the most interesting thing about me. What I came from was far more compelling than what I was. Would it be cheating to use the past as a kind of touchstone? I could test people by their response to my odd, uniquely arresting experience. People might think of my past as they did the Rosenberg case, distasteful but, despite themselves, riveting. I was beginning to think of my past, my personal past, as history, so different was it from the present and from the experience of the people I would now be meeting. One couldn't present oneself as a monument, that was clear. But how could I describe my father in less than monumental proportions, his bigotry and his learning, his harsh, provocative authority, his rages and his weeping, and his body, broken like a soldier's, gone helpless in his bed?

It was because I felt the present to be so fragile that I thought I must present the past. As with the students at the Community Center (don't think of that night, I said to myself as the image of John came into my mind, pungent as vomit), I was afraid that Lavinia would find me archaic and removed; I was afraid I had no conversation. I thought of businessmen who memorized jokes.

What did people talk about if they did not have the past to build on? We could talk about Mrs. Kerner and Mrs. Johnson, but my response to them was built on my past and would have to be explained in terms of it. Did most people find the present insufficient?

No one I had ever known had a house like Lavinia's. It was a postwar conception; I could imagine Lavinia a new bride with a husband who had fought in the war, gone to college on the G.I. bill, and settled here, expecting life to go on as she had planned it. It was a one-story house and the rooms were large and open. When I walked into the living room, I could see all the way out the kitchen window, and I thought how marvelous it was to have a straightforward house like that: no corners to collect grime or secret griefs, but everything visible, everything explainable and the light coming in that front window all day, as if there were nothing to hide.

Lavinia wore green pants and a striped top with wide, triangular sleeves. She was wearing sandals, and I was surprised to see that her feet had nothing of the grace of their hands: they were rather broad, and her big toe was round and serviceable. I sat on the edge of the couch, thinking, I have nothing to say.

"I'm sort of a lousy cook," said Lavinia. "If you want something good to eat, you'd have to come some night when my daughter's in charge. She's infinitely better than I am at cooking, at many things as a matter of fact. It's a funny feeling. Suddenly your child passes you. It's like the day when they're about thirteen when they suddenly discover they can lift you up."

"How old is she?"

"Seventeen. She'll be off to college next year."

"You'll miss her."

"Yes, and the peculiar thing is, she won't miss me in the least."

"I can't imagine that."

"No, I was perfectly elated when I left home. I didn't write my parents for a month. But then I hated my mother. She was quite awful. She never liked me either. Until I had Karen. Then she felt safe with me, I think."

Here is Lavinia offering me the past, I thought. Is that the way everyone operates, then? Do you sit on their couches, eat peanuts and hear "My mother always hated me"? But Lavinia, although revealing details that were potentially intimate, was not offering intimacy. She stood behind the smoke screen of details she had constructed, perhaps less reachable than before.

"How was your first case?" Lavinia asked.

"Queer. I really liked the old woman, really hated the woman who took care of her. But they got along fine. I had to admit everyone was very happy with the arrangement."

"Except you."

"Yes, but then I always hate to admit that anyone I don't like is good at anything. I realize that's quite irrelevant."

"But you can't help hating some and loving some. You just keep it out of the reports."

Yes, I thought, Lavinia can do that, hate a person but write a good report. And then forget about it. I could hate and write but could not forget. I carried my hate of Mrs. Kerner with me. Was it possible that, after all, I did not have a generous nature?

Lavinia's food was remarkably bad. I tried to determine the cause of the badness, but the food was too simple for the matter to be clear. The chops tasted as if they had been boiled before Lavinia gave in and fried them. The peas were canned and yellowy. The salad was lettuce and tomatoes and mostly mayonnaise. It was the sort of meal Margaret Casey would have made, I thought, shivering, the idea of Margaret entering, as it always did, like the terror of an unexpected cold patch in a lake. But there was no one who could be more unlike Margaret than Lavinia, sitting across the Danish glass table from me with her high, Indian bones.

For dessert there were canned peaches and heavy cream. Lavinia had put the cream in a dark-blue pitcher that made it seem at once rich, a luxury, and safe to eat. It wiped away the memory of the dinner's failure. We drank instant coffee in the living room. For a person of Lavinia's breeding, such a dinner was a deliberate gesture of contempt, of defiance, like having your head shaved or getting a tattoo. It was its deliberateness that saved it; it did not ask for pity, as Margaret's would have done. It said, "There are things I could do that I will not do." Was it an insult or a sign of affection? Lavinia held her mug of coffee between her knees to light another cigarette.

"I'm sort of fascinated by those years off you had," she said. "I didn't think that people like you took care of their parents any more."

"What do you mean by people like me?" I asked flippantly, flirtatiously even, thinking with great excitement, She will tell me what I am like. For I had never been judged this way before, by someone so obviously different from me, someone who knew about my background only what I chose to tell her.

"I suppose I mean someone intelligent and articulate and not particularly downtrodden. It must have been damned hard."

Lavinia said "damned" like a Protestant, like an American. I felt put on the spot. I felt that I had been called on to explain my life to someone who had no natural sympathy with it by reason of birth or a shared series of overcome prejudices. I would have to win Lavinia to my life as you have to introduce someone to eating artichokes, slowly, and with a combination of tact and salesmanship. I would have to explain about my father to someone to whom the word "orthodoxy," for example, might be utterly foreign, for whom the concept of authority was either public or menacing.

"I loved my father very much," I began, but I could see the suspicious Freudian cast of Lavinia's mind in the shifting colors of her eyes. Love means hate, devotion was another way of killing, that was what Lavinia was thinking. I would have to avoid that sort of pitfall: sentences like "I loved my father very much" were loaded with words like hidden land mines. I would have to choose words for practicality, as if I were buying a raincoat.

"When he became ill at first, when the strokes led to paralysis, he was very embarrassed for anyone to see him. He was a very proud man. I suppose I didn't have the heart or the will to oppose him, but it seemed natural, after a while, to go on, once I'd started taking care of him. I felt that he'd been through so much physically I didn't want to fight him."

"So you had him all to yourself, then," said Lavinia, as if we had been talking about a date with a movie star. Something in her tone frightened me. Whatever I said would be greeted by this probing incomprehension.

"There wasn't really anyone else," I went on. "My mother died when I was a baby."

"And no professional help?"

"You have to understand, Lavinia, that for my father, the parish was the community. There weren't social workers and psychologists. There were priests."

"And what did they tell you?"

"I didn't ask. I didn't have to. It was simply assumed that I would step in."

"And you didn't think of going outside for professional help or advice?"

It suddenly occurred to me that Lavinia probably thought me a lunatic or an imbecile. I asked myself the question that Lavinia had just asked me, but my only answer was the stupidest possible one: no, I hadn't thought there was a choice in the matter. It had all seemed exceedingly straightforward. My father was helpless. I would care for him. He wanted me, and I was there. It had all rolled out before me inevitable as a road. I would say to Lavinia that I was very young when he first became ill.

"And you never thought of it all that time?"

"Let's just say that as time went on, even if I thought of it, it didn't seem possible. It would have upset my father terribly. He came from a tradition where the people you loved took care of you."

"You mean immolated themselves for you."

"I'm still intact, Lavinia," I said, sitting up straighter on the couch, resenting Lavinia's taking my life in her shapely, interesting hands and squeezing the moisture out of it until it was as flat and dry and sickly as seaweed.

Lavinia looked at me very slowly, as if she were making a final check on something. "Surprisingly enough, I believe you are, on the whole. Why is that?"

I wanted to say there were days when sleep was all I wanted. There were days when I hated my father, when I could taste his death in my mouth, that was how much I wanted it. And he would cry in my arms, he wanted it so deeply. And both of us waiting, waiting for his death. And I wanted to say, When he died, I did not even weep.

But what I said was, "I guess there are scars that will disappear in time."

I knew now that Lavinia thought me peculiar. Perhaps she wanted me to ask about her husband's death. But I felt that now it would be a kind of revenge, probe for probe, unraveling for unraveling, or a kind of competition, the worst kind, the kind that Margaret Casey and Mrs. Keeney engaged in in my father's kitchen: whom has life dealt more badly by, which of us has suffered more?

In an oval frame on one of the window sills was a picture of a patriarch. This was a past that was more like history, round and distant and free from harm. The man in the photograph was a person of whom one could only be proud.

"Who is that marvelous-looking man?" I said.

"My grandfather," said Lavinia, moving to show me the photograph, and displacing, by the movement of her body, the air of challenge and disapproval and difficulty that had hung over us.

"Actually he was one of the guiding lights behind Prohibition. His father died a drunk, you see, and our family has always run to zealots."

The way Lavinia said "our family" meant money and formality, people who dressed for dinner, and quiet, choking griefs that led to suicides in the attics. It meant a life that had a clear sense of "us" and "them"; it explained Lavinia's terrible dinner.

I leaned back and said with perfect ease, "Tell me about your family. Were they all politicians?"

Lavinia crossed her legs, getting ready to tell good stories. They would be clear stories, stories of people who had been startlingly beautiful or startlingly ugly, who had been temperate or extravagant in large, original ways. We laughed; we drank the rather sour Beaujolais; we examined at the beautiful photographs of Lavinia's family who looked as though they had been born to be ancestors. When I looked at my watch it was midnight. We stood up, satisfied, as if the evening had been a good piece of work.

"I enjoyed it," I said.

"So did I," said Lavinia, as if she were surprised.

When Hugh Slade called me on Thursday, I had difficulty remembering who he was. Not that I had forgotten him; I had thought of him in those days with a constancy it embarrassed me to acknowledge. I had thought of his hands and his walk that was not always saying "give me something," and his eyes, and his back in his light-blue shirt. I had thought of having those arms around me, of the shape of his shoulder, how I would run my dry, closed mouth over it. And because of all that and because I had fought against it, knowing it to be dangerous (he was married; I had only met him once), I had trouble connecting the sound of his name, Hugh Slade, with all that thought.

"Do you have a regular lunch hour? Do you have to be back at a particular time?"

"No, it's all rather flexible," I said, looking at the folders and the students' reports I had to summarize. "I have a day of reckoning in about six months. Other than that, they only like to see my face. It makes it all much more tangible. They're a very tangible bunch."

My voice is stupid and fluttering, I thought. He will know instantly that I have been thinking of him; it will be for him only an embarrassment. He will know what men must always know: I need him more than he could possibly need me.

"I'll meet you at the Old Hat," he said. It was a bar that was supposed to serve huge sandwiches.

The click of the phone sobered me. Thinking of John, I resolved to be more austere. I could not start wanting this sort of thing. Or if I did want it, I must learn to say no from habit. I would not fall in love with Hugh. I would not go to bed with him. I would not even let him touch me. That would be the first thing, because once I let him touch me I would be tempted to make mistakes. And I did not want to make any more mistakes. I had lived too much of my life for that, to ruin the rest with mistakes that would leave small destructive holes in the regular surface of my new life. Hugh was married. Had Liz said anything about his having children? Of course he would have children.

Yet the frightening thing about him was that he would never *make* you do anything. Never had I seen less of an air of compulsion. If Hugh had a kind of natural power, he was aware of its implications and would use it seriously, wisely. It would be quiet and careful; he would want me, if possible, to be happy.

I looked moony and ridiculous in the mirror, like one of those girls in church everyone knew were going to be nuns. I stiffened, prepared to fight my low Oriental inclinations to luxury and languor. I thought of Sister Scholastica, who always said to the debating team before we went to another school: Remember who you are and what you represent. I no longer knew whom or what I represented, and I became absorbed in the word itself. What did it mean, to represent? It meant you were not yourself but something larger. Only you were not the thing itself; you were the parts of you that were like the thing you represented. It meant being connected to something so strongly that people could not think of you without thinking of that thing. What if you represented nothing but were only yourself?

The secretaries began walking into the ladies' room, talking to each other loudly as they urinated, taking out make-up from plastic cases the size of small mammals. I would be late, but then I had not wanted to be early. It was better to prepare your face while walking into a restaurant than to sit at a table with it prepared. But when I got to the Old Hat, I could not see Hugh in the gaggle of robust lunchers.

I was thinking as I rubbed single grains of salt into the dark wood of the table that this was the sort of bar my father would have liked. He would have liked the clock and the sawdust on the floor and the bartender who did not wear his teeth, but he would not have liked the people, the smart, tall women leaning against the well-dressed men.

Hugh was wearing a jacket and tie, and looked uncomfortable in them.

"I'm sorry to be late," he said. "I had my arm halfway up a cow's rear end all morning."

"Have you seen Liz?" I said, thinking that was our only and possibly our safest link.

"You ought to call her, Isabel. She thinks she's treated you badly and may never forgive you for it, unless you do something quickly."

"I've always loved that unforgivingness about Liz; it never occurred to me she would use it against *me.* But I deserve it. I did a very stupid thing."

"I was thinking of writing a book called *Sex Can Make You Stupid,*" said Hugh.

"It would have tremendous sales; it's the one thing nobody mentions about sex—stupidity."

Clearly he did not think of me sexually, if he could talk that way.

"You made a real impression on Erica," said Hugh. "But Liz had set us both up for you. I think that's why she was so angry at you; she thought you were immune from the sins and errors of the flesh."

"I think Liz has a more highly developed sense of sin than anyone I know."

"What a barbarous background you all had. It's as strange to me as if you'd been brought up in the Fiji Islands."

Interesting, I thought, that he uses a word like "barbarous." He spends the morning fooling around with cows' guts and uses a word like "barbarous." It was an apt word for what we had come from: it caught the rigor and the cruelty and the adventure. But it did not catch the cloying, trapping closeness that bred people like Margaret. You had to be raised in it to know that.

"How were you brought up?" I asked. "No, don't tell me. I can guess: with great rationality."

"Well, my father believed that religion was superstitious wickedness. I remember when my grandmother took me to church once he came in and dragged me out."

"I'm surprised you're not an archbishop in rebellion."

"No, they were quite admirable, my parents; you had to go along with them. My mother was so much fun, and so loving—except that during the McCarthy years she hit our next-door neighbor over the head with a frying pan and knocked him unconscious."

"My father picked up extra money polishing Joe McCarthy's speeches," I said. "He had a picture of him in his bedroom. It said, 'To one of my favorite eggheads from Joe McCarthy.' " I shivered. "It's not something I like to think about. There are particular nights when I can't think of anything but the Rosenbergs and air-raid drills in my grammar school. We all had metal tags with our names on them so they'd be able to identify our skeletons after the holocaust."

"America is so odd," said Hugh. "My parents practically financed Norman Thomas's campaigns; your father wrote speeches for Joe McCarthy, and we sit here talking about it, contemplating our sandwiches."

"Our potential sandwiches you mean. We haven't got them yet."

"I'll fight my way through," he said, after we had decided on ham sandwiches and dark beer.

I watched him making his way through the knot of people at the bar, not pushing ahead, not lagging behind, but doing everything at exactly the right tempo, with exactly the right degree of force. Like my father he had authority, but it was not an authority supported, like my father's, with the certainty of his rightness and the wrongness of everyone who was not like him. What was the source of Hugh's authority? Was it connected to his work, did it have something to do with animals? Or was it what he was: entirely himself, a man of kindness and ability? Seeing him move toward my table brought tears to my eyes. We talked about my work, and Lavinia, Mrs. Kerner, Mrs. Johnson. He didn't ask about my father; he did not say, "What were you doing all those years. Why did you do that?" Perhaps I would tell him later. With him I could use words like "devoted" and "duty" and he would understand. He would take those words and polish them like stones.

He looked at his watch; it was nearly three o'clock. He said, "I have to get my children now," as if it were something he had been looking forward to. I felt a little stitch of fear. I knew it now—he had children.

He walked me to the car, and I gave him my hand to shake. He lifted my hand and kissed it, but it was not a continental gesture or an act of urban manners. He kissed my hand as if it were oddly valuable, squeezing the fingers into a fist.

"Can we do this again next Thursday?" he said.

"Of course," I said. "Of course, if you'd like to."

"I'd like it more than anything I can imagine."

The words were extravagant. But he was not an extravagant man. He looked at me as if what he was about to say surprised him.

"You're very lovely," he said.

I felt tears in my eyes. I kissed his fingers. I said, "I'll see you," meaning, "I am falling in love with you."

He walked away. The sight of his back was so beautiful that I felt a kind of despair. If he wanted me, my life would be full of separations. He would always be going away, back to his children, to his wife. It was possible that today I was doing something that would cause pain to strangers, but I did not care. I felt I had finally joined the company of other, ordinary humans. It was the first time I had wanted anything in adulthood: I wanted him. I felt I was capable of extraordinary selfishness. I was saying over and over, "I am the beloved; the beloved is mine."

And I thought of the depths of selfishness in those words.

IX

When Eleanor called, I could think only of the things I ought to tell her but didn't want to. All the things we don't want to tell people are about sex. Sex separates us from everyone but our partner.

Within two weeks, I had done two things I was embarrassed to speak of. For eleven years I had done nothing that needed to be kept secret. I could even say to Eleanor, "All day I wanted my father to die," because it had the freshness, the thrill of the unexpected: life in death, hate in love; it spoke of a complex mind capable of ironies. But to say, "Within two weeks I had sex with a man I hate and have fallen in love with a married man, the father of children," spoke only of someone at once vulnerable and out of control. What was it about sex that I was most ashamed of: the vulnerability it introduced, or the selfishness?

Eleanor was taking a yoga class, she said. She had decided to be vigilant about additives in food. Would I like to go away with her this summer to one of those places where you fasted for a whole week, drinking spring water and herb teas? It purified your body, Eleanor said. It got rid of all the poison.

I was thinking, I don't want my body to be pure. I want red meat and liquor and cakes made with cream and butter. I was thinking, What I want is Hugh; what I want is pleasure. My body wanted to be warmed and filled and rested. I decided I would tell Eleanor part of what had happened, but not about John Ryan. That was only the body; that was not really interesting. I would tell Eleanor about Hugh's mother and the frying pan, and about how he got the sandwiches at the bar.

"You're opening yourself up for a lot of heartbreak," Eleanor said.

"I know. But I've never wanted anything like this before."

"I hope you get it."

"You've never really wanted a man, have you?" I said, with a certain edge.

"Not unless I was about to lose him."

All this wanting, this absorption, this infant's mode of living made me feel cut off from Eleanor, precisely because she would never want anything or anyone as I wanted Hugh, as my body wanted his body, as I wanted to be simply in his presence.

"Go slowly, Isabel," said Eleanor. "Just go a little more slowly."

"I'll try," I said, thinking, My best friend no longer understands me.

Wanting Hugh had even altered my relations with my own new rooms. I bought curtains: a white background with yellow and red tropical flowers that caught the sun at the right hour of the morning. On the wall I hung postcards from the Metropolitan Museum: a heavy Renoir woman combing her hair with her greenish, monumental arms above her head, a Persian on a black horse, a clump of Dürer's violets. I put down the rugs on the faded carpets, so that the eye fell on them first. I had read once that the knots in the carpets were tied by five-year-old children who were paid slave's wages so that people in the West could have these things. An awareness of the immensity of human suffering came to me, and of its cleverness— all those guises, all those paths to unhappiness. I had questioned my father about it as a child; he had said that suffering brought us close to God, that we were making up for the sufferings of Christ. Even then I could not love a God with such a wide imagination, who could trap people into devotion when they were too lonely or hungry or tired to resist. It all came back to the body—people loved God because their bodies had not done well by them, had not given them sufficient pleasure. Pleasure. I held the word in my mouth like a plum. Is it enough then just to live and die, to eat good food, to love and be beloved, to read only the novels you liked in your comfortable bed? Hugh, I thought, would say there is more than that. He believed in work and nature. My father always said that Catholics did not believe in nature, they believed in revelation.

There was a knock. I thought for a moment that the intensity of my desire had brought Hugh to me, but when I opened the door I saw John Ryan.

His large blonde presence dwarfed the rooms I had been so proud of a moment ago. It made them seem shabby and finicky and dark and genteel, as if he had only to open a window to make everything fly out and disappear. I knew what he was there for: the certainty of his desire landed in the bottom of my stomach like a flatiron. My mouth tasted metallic, as if I had been sucking coins. I was frightened to refuse him, but to have sex with him again, when possibly I could have Hugh for a lover, was like a combination of sacrilege and a bad investment. In any case it would be *wrong,* the first clear act of wrong I had perhaps ever committed.

Power was his as he walked by me, not authority, which Hugh had, which my father had, but power. He was stronger than I; it would be possible for him to hurt me. How did the weak overcome the strong as they sometimes did? By cunning, I supposed, but he was far more cunning than I. All my intelligence, all my refined perceptions had not equipped me to survive him. He noticed nothing, would respond to nothing except the coarsest of stimuli. But in the car, watching the sun go down over the river, I had responded to him. And because I had done that he had the right to me. I had wanted him once, and so he deserved to be here; he was perfectly right to be sitting on my faded pur-

ple couch with his legs open, taking up half the space
of my living room.

He had brought a six-pack of beer. Probably he
would bring beer every time he wanted to sleep with
me, on the principle that what had worked once would
have a good chance of working again. I wanted to
kneel before him like the woman in the holy card I
used to carry in my Missal—St. Agnes, was it?—beg-
ging deliverance from the Roman emperor. And then
I thought, I will close my mind off and let it go on.
I looked at his shoes. They were the brown lace-up
kind with little pin holes in the toes. I was angry at
John for having worn them, as I had been angry
at him for playing on the floor with his children. By
acting in a particular way he removed the luster of that
particular action, so that by observing him fewer and
fewer male acts and objects would be left intact for
me.

I brought a glass for his beer but he had already begun drinking it from the can.

"I hear from the grapevine you had quite a chummy
lunch with Hugh Slade."

He had invaded that now. I wanted to slap him and
say, I will not allow you to talk about it. But I said,
"How did you find out?"

"I'll give you a hint. It was a woman."

"Liz?" I said, wondering at the curious tendency of
my friend to confide in a husband she affected to despise.

John didn't answer; it must be Liz, then.

"I don't care what you do on your own time, baby,
as long as there's enough left over for me."

He grabbed my buttocks in two discrete handfuls. I
felt myself fly away from myself. A mist rose over my
brain. I thought, This is not happening to me. I am
not doing this. I let him go on.

His kiss was like the blow of a fist. I was conscious
of swallowing his saliva. He held my breast in his hand
as if it had no connection to my body. "Let's go to
bed," he said. His voice was wet with beer. I lay on

top of the spread, quite still, as he took off first my clothes and then his and lowered his enormous body onto me.

I kept my eyes on the damp stain on the ceiling, imagining it a camel, imagining it a snail. I was aware of the separate force of each stroke of his penis. I began counting them and I noticed, with a certain detached interest, that I had counted to sixteen before he finished.

Since I had wanted him once, he deserved me now. If that was what he wanted, to labor and sweat over me like that, it was only what he deserved. By wanting him once I had forfeited the right ever to deny him. And when I was with Hugh (but Hugh would never want me now) I would be different. I would be so much with him that it would be as though this with John had happened to someone else, another very different kind of woman. But I did not deserve Hugh now.

John took a shower and left with his hair still wet. After he was gone I could smell semen on the towel he had dried himself with, and when I bathed I could see a little flow of semen between my legs, thicker and darker than the scented water of my bath, the blood of a colorless fish.

Sally Beckett's looks were startling, and they hit me as the force of an unexpected wave hits a swimmer. They seemed entirely out of context. I had prepared myself only for an interview, had braced my body as if for something painful that must be kept at a distance, and here was beauty demanding to be brought close. She stood at the door in jeans and a man's white shirt; her hair was down below her waist, her cheekbones were high with disappointment, her eyes full of reproach, her mouth of sadness. I expected her to speak with a foreign accent, so strange, so pointed was her beauty. I was surprised to hear the lockjaw tone of the Eastern seaboard. What was she doing taking stipends from the county for the care of two old women?

The Becketts' house was on a dirt road a mile from the highway. It was an old house, and it had been self-consciously restored. Couples who were in *Newsweek* for doing something trendy had houses like this. There would be small, dark photographs of them, their babies, named Cassandra, or Maude, or Oliver, crawling on the furry rugs among their legs, the caption reading, "So and so take time off from videotaping to play with their children in their country house." And yet I did not dislike Sally Beckett. It was probably impossible for me to dislike anyone who looked so unhappy. And her babies crawled around the floor with more desperation than inventiveness, more boredom than triumph.

The kitchen walls were covered with well-stocked shelves, Mason jars full of dark, rich-looking fruit and vegetables, tall European-style bottles filled with macaroni or herbs. Children's paintings were hung all over the kitchen walls: colorful eggs or trees or mothers or fathers with stringy, elongated bodies.

"How many children do you have?" I asked.

"Four. And you needn't say it's too many. I know it's too many."

Her stiffness was the stiffness of a child. I found it strangely engaging.

"I wasn't thinking of saying it. I was thinking it must be fun having all these children."

"It isn't fun," Sally said, "but thank you for saying it, for even thinking it."

I turned to my pink form; I would not enter into this stranger's grief. I could not and then just leave. It always seemed that there was a great problem with sympathy: if you really cared for the person, or even for the extremities of their situation, you ought to do something, or you ought to give up the luxury of caring. Either you should move in with Sally Beckett and help her with whatever it was that was worrying her —children, or money, or boredom—or you should admit that whatever it was you were feeling was simply a trick of the liver, as transitory and insignificant as indigestion.

I was thinking of St. Paul on charity as I drank the coffee that Sally had ground herself. "Charity suffereth long and is kind," I was thinking. That was it, unless you were willing to suffer in your kindness, you were nothing. Barbarous, Hugh would have said. He would have said that most people feel nothing, that you can be kind in simpler ways. But with me I carried the baggage of the idea. Love and charity. One was that feeling below the breast, and the other was doing something, anything, to take people's pain away. I remembered the lettering on a bulletin board at Anastasia Hall: LOVE IS MEASURED BY SACRIFICE. And I remembered thinking how wrong that was, because the minute I gave up something for someone I liked them less.

"Ah," Sister Fidelis had said when I asked her, "you don't have to like someone to love them in God."

But who wants to be loved in God? I had thought then, and still thought. We want to be loved for our singularity, not for what we share with the rest of the human race. We would rather be loved for the color of our hair or the shape of our ankle than because God loves us. I looked at my pink form; I would not ask Sally Beckett, no matter how beautiful she was, why she was so unhappy.

"Have you found this system of home care satisfactory?" I asked.

"For whom?"

That was something I had thought of, but that none of the people who had been interviewed had brought up. It was entirely possible that this kind of care made life better for the old people but infinitely worse for those who were taking care of them. I had known the tyranny of the sick and the dying, the anxiety, the resentment, the impossibility of the healthy person's ever saying, "What *I* want is more important."

I wanted to say, I know what you mean. We understand each other. But I said, in my new, public voice, "Perhaps you could clarify what you mean."

"Well, I suppose the system works fine for Mrs. Claddack and Mrs. Brown. They're sisters, you see, and haven't lived more than a block away from each other at any time in their lives. So they can be together in their old age; so it's good for them. It's even good for my kids. Mrs. Claddack tells them stories and teaches them to knit. Mrs. Brown is so senile she seems about their age, and they wheel her around outside and show her things. They have a devastating amount in common, the children and the two old ladies. But I don't like them. I think they're boring and cruel."

"Boring and cruel?"

"You see, Mrs. Claddack has a limited number of stories and after fourteen months I've heard them all too many times and I'm bored with them. With the kids it's different. My son Jason asks the same riddle —'What's black and white and red all over?'—about fifteen times a day and laughs hilariously every time. So does Mrs. Brown. And Mrs. Claddack tells the kids stories fifteen times and they're ready for them another fifteen."

"Why cruel? I can see that they're boring, but why cruel?"

"Mrs. Claddack has always resented her sister. Mrs. Brown is younger, and Mrs. Claddack is clearly delighted that her sister became senile before she did. And she says the most terrible things to her. Makes the most terrible accusations, brings up crimes that are seventy years old. She's never forgiven her sister for a thing. I can't bear it. And Mrs. Brown insists on taking her teeth out when she's not eating, so that makes it all much worse. Are you going to put this all down?"

"No, I leave out anything having to do with emotion or personality."

Sally smiled. Her teeth were as white as a cat's.

"May I ask you, not for the record, just for ourselves, why you decided to do this? Quite frankly, you're not a typical person for it."

"Okay. My husband was headmaster at an experimental school and he was thrown out. He's been looking for a job for three years. At the moment, he tutors some private pupils and works as a night watchman. I have four children, aged eight to two and a half. I quit college after two years to get married—no skills, but I can read Russian. When everything was going well, my mother used to say, 'Sally can diaper a baby and cook a meal and read Dostoevsky all at once.' It was true. I had everything under control. But you can't control things without money. And David can't find a job and I don't want to leave my kids every day so I can go out and work as a waitress. So I thought this would be a good plan when I read about it. I thought it would expose the kids to old age. Their grandparents are only in their fifties and they play tennis every day. I tried selling magazines over the phone, and baking bread and cakes for the local store, and hiring myself out as a caterer, but I couldn't sell magazines and I spent more on butter and eggs than I could make. So here we are. I take good care of them. They eat well. They have company. I take them to the doctors. The only thing I can't do is love them, and they don't care about that. Only I care."

I took Sally's hand. "I don't know what to say. Sometimes I think people like us aren't good for anything."

"It doesn't matter," said Sally, standing, not wanting me as at first I had not wanted her. "I'll take you in to see the two women."

I walked in, feeling unreasonably depressed, feeling it was unfair. Sally Beckett was trying to be good. She was a good and a caring person; she ought to be happy. Goodness ought to make people happy as it did in other ages. But now goodness was a private, esoteric hobby, like painting miniatures, or putting ships in bottles.

Mrs. Claddack and Mrs. Brown sat in the light,

high bedroom on their dark-blue chairs. Mrs. Claddack was very thin and had her hair in a net. Mrs.
Brown was as round and as bland as a pudding; her
toothless mouth opened with an unlovable kind of
wonder. Her childishness was an affront. There was no
hardness about her, no sense that age was partly a
joke, partly an insult. Only the round open mouth demanding to be fed. She wore a cap to hide her nearly
bald head, but it was tilted to the side and the bow tied
not under her chin, but below her ear. She kept working on the ribbon, but it was obviously beyond her
abilities.

"Sit up, Bess, and tie that ribbon right," said Mrs.
Claddack. "She can do it any time she wants. She just
does this to provoke me. It was like the time when she
was a little girl and wet her pants and I had to take
her home from school. She's always been like this."

"I just want to ask a few questions," I said.

I asked about the frequency of meals and the ad-
ministering of medicines, how often they were taken
to the doctor's.

"Oh, that one does everything by the book. She
doesn't miss a trick," said Mrs. Claddack. "She knows
if she slipped up they wouldn't pay her."

Mrs. Brown began giggling and her sister hit her
hard on the upper arm.

"Very lah-de-dah. A real lady. Only her husband's a
night watchman and she can't be proud. So she stoops
to taking us in. A real comedown for her. She only
takes us for the money. She thinks she's better than
us, and she don't let us forget it."

She put her finger under her nose and lifted it.

"But you have no complaints about the actual care
you're receiving," I said, thinking, She's right if she
thinks she's better than you are. She is. You're a mean
old woman and deserve nothing.

Mrs. Brown poked me with her damp, fat fingers.

"What's black and white and red all over?" she
said.

"A newspaper. Everybody knows that," said Mrs. Claddack.

Mrs. Brown ignored her sister and tapped me again. "What's black and white and red all over?" she repeated.

"I don't know," I said, in politeness.

"A newspaper," she said, the loose tops of her arms shaking with her laughter.

I stood up, going to the windows, noting their distance from the bed and the distance from the bed to the bathroom. Facts were wonderful, facts were a relief from the steamy life these old women wanted to absorb me in, to smother me in. I wrote numbers on the pink form with my black pen. They were cool and spare and beautifully dry. I said good-by to the women and closed the door.

Sally Beckett stood by her front door as if she wanted me to leave as quickly as possible.

"I'll give you a good report," I said. "But I think you should give it up."

"Thank you," said Sally, "but I can't right now."

We shook each other's hands. We did not look at each other. I thought that if I were my father I would have written a bad report to make happen what I knew to be right.

Hugh said on the telephone, "Can you get away for supper tonight?" As if I had something to get away from. But I wouldn't say that, it would be like lifting the lid of the evening and introducing a small mold into it. I had decided that I wanted him, and so I must root out those little molds, must not think of him as a rich philanthropist with connections (his wife, his children) that allowed him certain charities: me, the orphan, smelling of disinfectant and reproach.

I had a dress made of light-green wool with a thick leather belt that showed off my waist. I tried to remember the things I had seen Eleanor do, had heard Eleanor speak of doing. I put perfume in my bath water, behind my ears, between my breasts.

I could smell my perfume in the living room where I had walked half an hour ago to get my pocketbook. I sat on the couch. The living room was too cold and too dark, but to turn on the heat or the light now would be bad luck: it would mean I expected him not to come.

He had said six-thirty, and it was nearly seven. His wife had found out; perhaps he was involved in some terrible scene. Accusations, recriminations and I, the unknown woman at the center of it.

He gave three knocks.

"I had the wrong address. Forgive me."

He held my long, new gray wool cape and I slipped into it. He went down the stairs in front of me, not touching me, not saying I was beautiful, not even saying, I like your new cape. But he had no way of knowing it was new; I remembered I hardly knew him.

As we drove, the sky a November gray that offered no comfort, I could see that he was nervous, and it touched me. But I was nervous, too; I didn't want to tell him about Sally Beckett: it was dangerous to talk about beautiful women, and I wanted to have something to give him over dinner, when we were warmer, when we were away from this inhuman sky.

"My friend Eleanor is coming in two weeks," I said. "She grew up with Liz and me."

"But Liz doesn't particularly like her."

"They're as different from one another as . . ."

"As chalk from cheese," said Hugh.

It was a beautiful phrase, chalk and cheese. It meant you had listened to your grandmother as a child and remembered, or you had sat at someone's kitchen table while she made pastry, with her back to you, talking over her shoulder.

"Yes. Except chalk and cheese aren't really that different."

"They are, you know."

"There are many things that are more different."

"Like what?"

"I don't know. Chalk and cantaloupe."

"All right then, from now on I'll say 'they're as different as chalk from cantaloupe.' But only to please you."

He wanted to please me. I cupped my hand under his chin and held it for a moment. Then I let it go; he had done nothing in response. I felt frightened and stupid, as if someone had asked me to do a dance I didn't know but ought to have known. And he did not take my hand. He was concentrating on the traffic, looking at the road as if the light were bad.

We sat in a dark booth at the back of the restaurant. I was so happy to be sitting across from him that I couldn't think what to eat, and I said to him, "Order for the both of us." That was something I never thought I would get to say; people in movies said it or in cheap novels, and now I had said it. It made me laugh.

He looked up and laughed with me but did not ask what we were laughing at.

I ate Wiener schnitzel in a haze. My mouth was dry. I was afraid I smelt bad, was afraid he could smell desire on me. In the middle of dinner, I went into the ladies' room and put perfume between my legs. Then, on the way back to the table, I was afraid he would smell my perfume and know what I had done. I ate only half my dinner.

As we drove through the city, which had put on lights while we were in the restaurant, lights around which the new November cold circled in moist circumferences, I wondered what I should do. I was sitting very far away from him; I could feel the door handle cold against my hip. I had said nothing to him all evening, nothing that would say what I wanted him to know, that what happened to my life had not flawed me entirely, that I could make him happy.

"Good night," I said quickly, feeling the full weight of my failure.

He put his arms around me as if he were putting on a raincoat.

"Please don't be frightened. Nothing has to be decided instantly."

I had my mouth against his cheek; it was chill against my lips, which were sore with distress.

"But you see I want you very much," I said.

It was very simple; I had said it, and now he was kissing me. He was kissing the ends of my hair, holding the ends of my hair in his squarish fingers.

"Oh, my dear," he said over and over. It was old-fashioned and oddly formal, and it took away my fear.

We walked up the stairs to my apartment in the darkness. We were both terribly thirsty. I got glasses of water, and we would kiss and drink, drink and kiss. He touched my breast; all the life in my body collected there so that I must cry out.

"Come to bed," I said, as if we had been children together.

The flesh of his buttocks was solid, not like marble, but like the flesh of a pear. His mouth and his hands were over me, never making errors; my mouth and my hands were over him as if they always had been. We were crying and flinching; we were swimming over and under each other. When he entered my body, my body that was now entirely open, I closed around him like a cat. And one part of my brain, cool and green, the color of celery, was saying: This is happening to me.

X

He slept for two hours holding my head down on his chest with one hand to keep me there. I couldn't sleep. My eyes were wide in the dark; I could pick out the yellow flowers in my curtains, but the red ones had disappeared. I felt joy and fear, breathing in the dark hairs of his chest and then remembering that when he woke he would be leaving. I had to lie perfectly still; the moment he awoke he would already have left me.

He woke slowly and yawned, and I could see the inside of his mouth, dark red, darker than his lips. I wanted to put my fingers in his mouth and have it begin all over again. He had liked that; he had sucked each of my fingers slowly, separately, and then closed my hand into a fist.

"When will I see you again?" I asked.

"I'll see you tomorrow."

"How?"

"Somehow. Wait for me."

When he left, the apartment was emptier than it had ever been. I had been used to living alone in it, but now all the furniture that wasn't mine seemed sad, the way I had read that hotel rooms could be sad, although I had never stayed in a hotel except with my father. I turned the radio on and hummed tunes in a frantic, quiet way, a spinsterish way. I didn't like my voice.

It had happened to me. Not the way it had with
David Lowe, where I had been (the only words I
had ever been able to use, a nun's words) *in charge,*
or with John Ryan, where I had to be drunk or dazed,
but with a man who had held me and made me close
around him like a cat, who had held my head in his
sleep. And who had gone, who would always be going.

When I tried to think of him, I knew so little about
him that I had to play the same scenes over and over,
like a projectionist in a ghost town with only one
movie. He was married; he was the father of daughters. His wife's name (he had said it once as if he
expected me to know it) was Cynthia. And then there
had been all that love-making, all that business with
our bodies, all that feeling if one of his fingers happened to brush somewhere after having been somewhere else, and then some words, foolish words, not
even memorable, and then the sleeping.

I thought of the two of us, perfectly alone in the
world, making each other feel so much and hardly
knowing each other.

I had written a letter to Margaret Casey, out of
courtesy and guilt and the accident of geography, for
Margaret happened to be living sixty miles to the
west. I had given Margaret my new address and had
said in the letter, "I will be here if you should need
to contact me." I remembered Margaret crying in her
boxy coat at my father's grave. But for my will and
cleverness Margaret might have been a married
woman, might at least have had that, might have had
some legal rights, as a wife, might for the first time
not have had to behave like a beggar.

Margaret's spidery handwriting had become even
more shaky. Her address on the envelope was barely
legible, and reading the letter on lined paper that
looked like toilet paper was like reading a foreign
language. At the top of the page was a cross and the
words "To Jesus through Mary." In grammar school
everyone headed their pages like that, but even the
nuns in Anastasia Hall didn't insist on it; it was one

of those detachable pieties it was permissible to grow
out of. But Margaret had kept it up until now, in her
seventies, it was again appropriate. The dampish,
hanging image of Margaret still made me feel slightly
sick. I forced myself to read the letter.

Dear Isabel,
    I all ready knew where you were because Fa-
ther Mulcahey told me. My arthritis is very bad
now. I thank God I can still take care of myself.
My sister Edith died last year, not long before
your father. You didn't know her so there was no
reason for you to send anything, but your father
knew her and I'm sure they are angels together
in heaven.

(He's not with your family, I thought, hoping there
were some arrangements for first-class compartments
in eternity so that people like Margaret would be kept
out, separated by an implacable conductor with no
pity and no ear for excuses. It mattered to me that if
there were life after death it should be in good taste.
I went on with the letter.)

    I don't know for how long I can go on for I
may have to go to the Dominican home after all
there's no one to take care of me. I always thought
I'd die in your father's house after all I was like a
wife to him all those years.
    Your lucky to have a job and a good job. It
pays to have friends. I have no friends and nobody but Our Blessed Lord but I don't complain
but I have no pension. I could of had but working
for your father all those years.
    After all you don't owe me anything. Nobody
owes anybody anything these days and a just God
will give everyone a just reward when He comes
in glory at the Last Judgment. Then He will separate the sheep from the goats.

I still pray for you I always have Please pray
for me. We all need prayers. God bless you.

                                        Margaret

I crumpled the letter and put it in the sink. There
was a knock at the door.

Liz walked in before I got there.

"You ought to lock that door. Any pervert could be
raiding your refrigerator."

I was so glad to see Liz after reading Margaret's
letter that I forgot there had been trouble between
us. Liz's presence, with its sharp edges and clearness,
could protect me from Margaret's, sticky and clinging.

"You'll never guess who I got a letter from. Margaret Casey."

"Jesus God. Didn't she die yet? Let me see the letter. I want to see her handwriting."

Liz's rapid glance flicked down the page in seconds.

"Isabel, if you answer this letter I'll tie you to a
tree."

"But my father . . . I tricked her out of my father."

"You mean you rescued him from her. Imagine
going to bed with her." Liz shuddered.

"They wouldn't have gone to bed. They would have
had one of those Josephite marriages, like that couple
came and talked to us about in high school."

"Oh, yeah, you live together but you don't screw,
and you get to say the family rosary. Wonderful set-
up. Only Margaret would have insisted on her con-
jugal rights. You know how they are about getting
everything that's coming to them."

"I'll have to answer the letter. It's bad manners not
to."

Liz was silent. She thought manners were important.
She could never argue against them. I knew they were
the one thing she could not be flippant about.

"Have you seen Hugh?" said Liz.

I blushed. "He was here last night. How did you
know?"

"I didn't. My husband is the one with spies. By the

way, his secretary saw you with Hugh in the Old Hat and rushed to tell him. By God, that girl is loyal. She spies on her lover's lovers."

"You mean you didn't tell him?" I said, immensely relieved.

"Of course not. You and Hugh are much too important to me to talk to John about."

"He tried to make me believe you'd told him."

"Bastard," said Liz. "That crummy little bastard."

It was the first time that Liz seemed affected by her husband's behavior.

"The reason I came over, besides wanting coffee, which, by the way no one's offered me yet, is to tell you that I'm behind you both. I'll do anything to help."

"What's his wife like?"

"A harridan. She's got this enormous bust and skinny little legs, and she shouts at him from across the room. They obviously hate each other."

"The children?"

"Two girls, fifteen and thirteen. Needless to say they're terrific and crazy about Hugh."

I was thinking, He'll never leave them for me.

"Listen," said Liz, "either don't fall in love with him or leave him instantly because you'll never get him away from his family."

"I can't leave him and I'm already in love with him," I said, running the top of Margaret's envelope under my fingernail.

"You could leave him. Can't is for things that no one can do. You can say, 'I can't fly,' not 'I can't leave him.' "

"I won't, then."

"You're going to be hurt."

"I don't care."

"There's nothing I can say. Only I'll do whatever you want me to."

"Tell me if you think it's worth it."

"Of course," she said. "Don't be trivial. What does it matter what I think?"

"It matters because you're the only one who knew my father who knows Hugh."

"Keep your father out of it. It's bad manners to bring him in."

"All right then, from the past."

"The past is a bad investment," said Liz.

"But the past just ended for me four months ago, and what I'm doing seems to have nothing to do with it."

"It never does," said Liz.

I nodded. I did not believe her.

"I want you and Hugh to come for a hike with Erica and me."

"Okay, I'd like that."

"Get a good pair of shoes," said Liz sternly, "not that nonsense you usually wear."

I laughed. "What would I do without you, Liz."

"Turn your goddamn ankle and have to be carried home. Now get me some coffee."

That was wonderful, that sternness, that bantering. Liz was mine again. I made her coffee. It was possible to go on.

Rose Gerardi was wearing white high heels in the middle of November. She teetered into the kitchen in a worrisome way for a woman of her age. The house smelled of polish but was cluttered with racing forms. Everywhere I looked there were pages of newspaper, either spread out or crumpled, with firm, decisive-looking circles around horses' names in different-colored inks. A very elegant-looking old man sat in front of the television in the living room. A large woman with purplish hair sat next to him and said in cultivated tones, "I told you he was a sleeper, and Rose told you he was a sleeper, but you went ahead and you've only yourself to blame, my dear."

"The track was muddy. I had forgotten that," said the old gentleman.

Rose shouted from the living room into the kitchen with great volume, "Ruth, put on some coffee for us."

She cleared some newspapers off a black leather chair for me.

"Sit down, honey. You must be dead tired."

Four children ran through the living room, scattering papers and furniture. They were all thin and dark and nervous, and they made straight for the kitchen. There was a loud crash. One of the dark children came into the living room.

"Ruth dropped a pitcher," he said.

"So," said their mother, "it's the last pitcher in the world. Clean it up."

I was surprised to hear an old woman's voice say from the kitchen, "The frigging thing slipped right out of my hand."

The old woman with the purplish hair said to me, "Ruth never spoke like that before she moved here."

"But I always wanted to, Alice," said the voice in the kitchen. "That's what you've never known, my dear."

"She picks it up from my kids," said Rose. "They all talk like sailors."

"Yes, but they're wonderful children," said the woman named Alice with some concern, as if she were afraid I might misunderstand. "We never had so much fun in our lives, did we, Richard?" she said, turning to the old man.

He bowed toward Rose with extreme courtesy. "No, my dear. I believe Browning was talking about Rose when he said, 'the last for which the first was made.' "

Rose accepted the compliment with an aristocrat's deference. She had not changed her position in the chair.

"I'm dead," she said to me. "It's the first time I've been off my feet since this morning. I had to clean up the house because you were coming."

That made me laugh. If you were going to try to deceive someone about the conditions of your house, you completely undid it by telling them you were trying to deceive them. I liked Rose for her sloppiness and her languor, for running out of energy in the middle of a lie.

The phone rang. The old man got up to answer it and came back in a few seconds. I thought his cravat particularly beautiful; it was a blue paisley pattern and was held by a diamond pin.

"It appears that Alice's long shot has paid off," he said.

The woman with the purplish hair said, "Well done me. We shall all celebrate. Rose will have a new dress and will go out and tell us all about it."

Rose said, "Maybe I'll find a handsome man to get us all a house in the country."

The three of them laughed as though it were a very old joke that they never tired of hearing.

A tiny woman came out of the kitchen. She was wearing a velvet dress that looked as if it had come out of Blanche Du Bois's trunk.

"Miss Moore, we hope you don't have to report this particular aspect of our lives to the county as we are aware that it is quite illegal. We rely on your discretion. We've found, however, that it is an excellent way of supplementing our pensions as well as keeping our minds alert."

"You must excuse my sister," said the old man. "She was a schoolteacher and she tends to talk to one as if she were teaching the three-times table."

"Nonsense, Richard," said his sister. "The young lady and I were merely having a conversation."

Rose poured the tea that Miss Ruth Blake had brought in. She crossed her legs so that I could see the dark tops of her stockings. It was usually a sight that I hated, but it was not unattractive on Rose.

One of the children ran through the living room. Rose caught him by the waist of his pants. "Did you rip your jacket again, you hooligan? Didn't Alice just sew it for you yesterday? Change it so you don't look like you live in a slum, and put it on top of Alice's sewing pile."

"Try to be careful in the future," said Alice.

"Yes, Alice," said the boy, hugging her roughly. "Thank God you're around or we'd all be bare-assed."

No one had addressed any remarks to me in some minutes. They were obviously absorbed in each other, and their absorption shielded them from the consciousness of a stranger. This is love, I thought, this is happiness: going on, ignoring the one who has come to judge you. It struck me that this was the nature of my work; it was this that I was paid for, to judge these people and their happiness (welfare, the county called it, but it was happiness they meant), to make general statements about the nature of happiness. I who knew nothing ordinary, who had learned nothing in the orderly, gradual way of other people, people who went from one thing to another as if there were a line in life that went from A to L, from middle C to high C in a series of connected if dissimilar components.

I gave the old people, whom the record told me were husband, wife and husband's sister, the forms to fill out. As a matter of habit I asked Rose to fill her form out in the other room, but I knew the Blakes would tell me nothing that they would not tell Rose. They would gather round her to protect her from any malice, real or suspected, of the official world that I represented.

Mrs. Blake, the medical report said, had cancer of the colon; within a year she would be dead. She had been told. Her caseworker reported that she had no religious preference. She had a colostomy that required daily changing by Rose; she had refused cobalt treatments. There was a queer time-bomb effect about the old woman, sewing and betting and waiting to die. Coloring her hair in that mistaken way.

When I went into the kitchen, Rose was crying. She rubbed her wet cheeks with the heels of her hands.

"It's Alice," she said. "I can't stand it, you know what I mean, knowing she's not going to be around."

I looked out the door at the three old people, who were arguing about whether to put a comma or a semicolon somewhere in their report. To care about punctuation with death about to go off like that was a way of saying life is good, life is valuable. I sat across from Rose and began crying myself. The two of us cried in silence. Rose said, "Come over some night and see us. Have a beer." I said yes, I would, I would love to. But I would never come back to this house again, because you simply didn't. You didn't walk into people's lives carrying a briefcase, carrying forms, and then go back again as if you were just another person, as if your meeting had been an accident on a bus or in a tea shop, instead of an official investigation, a politically motivated probe.

That old woman was dying, and I sat across from someone whom I ought not to have liked, who probably took money from these people and gave them the housework she didn't want to do. Whose house was certainly the least clean, the least well appointed for the care of the aged of any I had visited. Yet I would have liked to talk to Rose about Hugh. But I would not go back there. I thought that Lavinia Hartman would have thought that I had acted badly.

I bought a good pair of shoes. They had thick rubber soles that looked as if they would protect me from everything.

There was a problem with words again, for when Hugh and Liz said, "We'll go for a long walk," what did they mean? The last time I had taken a long walk that was not on pavement I was sixteen years old. I felt a thrill of discomfort wondering what they would expect of me: dexterity, endurance, silence, balance—and they would think they were asking nothing.

Hugh came for me at six in the morning. What had he told his wife? The sky was gray. My breasts were cold when Hugh touched them, but he said they were lovely and cool and he put his cheeks against them, lying beside me in all his clothes.

We sang in the car together. He sang, "I'll Be Seeing You," and I sang, "I'll Take You Home Again, Kathleen," because he said it was his favorite song.

He told me about a little pond and how it was beginning to freeze over; we could see the ice coming together on the edge, he said.

I told him I had not been out of a city in more than ten years. I thought he would sympathize, but his frown was angry.

"So you don't like the country," he said, disappointed.

"I have no experience of it," I said, like a slum child.

He took my hand and kissed the inside of it.

"Never mind," he said, as if he had already forgiven me for something.

"My father said Catholics didn't need nature," I said, trying to make a joke, hoping he would know it wasn't really funny.

"But he was brought up in the country, you said?"

"Yes."

"I've seen it happen hundreds of times. People with that kind of brutal rural background always want to get as far away from it as possible."

So that was it. My father wouldn't take me to the mountains, to the ocean, but it had nothing to do with Catholicism or revealed truth. It had to do with his own father. There was nothing mysterious about it; it followed some kind of law to which human beings, weak and predictable as they were, seemed to be susceptible. Where I had seen a compelling mix of tradition and original thought, Hugh had seen the slow damage of family relations. It made it so much simpler—and less interesting—this being able to understand things.

I put my head on his shoulder. "Of course," I said, "I never thought of that."

"Of course," he said, kissing me.

We seemed to be driving into the sun. The sky was gradually absorbing light and changing it to color so that it was now the sharp reproachful blue of a December morning.

We drove uphill to where there was snow on the

ground. There had been snow on Thanksgiving, but nothing had come of it. I remembered that I had not celebrated Thanksgiving, that my father had never celebrated it. It was a Protestant holiday, an American holiday, my father had said, and we were Catholics, with a tradition that was rich and ancient and had nothing to do with cold, thin-blooded Puritans sitting down somewhere in New England.

The stern light came through the tall pines soft and dreamy, coated us as we got out of the car to walk, feeling the cold for the first time that year in the small veins of our noses. Hugh put his arm, slippery in his ski jacket, on my shoulder. The weight of it was as pleasurable as the green light. His shoes were brown and huge and serious with red laces twisted around small metal hooks, foreign and endearing.

Liz and Erica were sitting on a gate. Liz was smoking. Erica wore a red wool cap that made her skin brown and her eyes darker. Her face was shy again and challenging. Hugh put a hand on her shoulder, and they gave each other short, rough kisses.

"Come on, then," said Liz. "We've been waiting ten minutes. Did you ever notice how heterosexuals have no sense of time?"

The three of them walked together, talking about horses and feeds and protein and exercise. I hung back. Everything was wet and light; nothing would stick or press against a body here. At the ends of branches were distinct drops of water. I felt a queer sense of fright.

I wanted to lie down, not on the ground but floating a little above it, and there they were, walking faster than I would have wished, using words like "farrier." I was stopping to look at the thin white skeletons of the winter flowers. They were walking on ahead of me; I could see their breath.

Hugh came back to me. I was looking at water running through a ditch. Everything was new to me; everything was beautiful. Even water in a ditch was a miracle. I was light and sleepy.

Hugh said, "I guess you're not used to the pace we set."

Something hard had formed and fallen. What he had really said was, You can't keep up, turning my fluid center into a fist.

"I thought this was a walk in the woods. I was not aware that we were involved in the Olympics. Had I known that, I would have gone into training."

His eyes changed color. They were grayer, smaller than I had known them. "We always get to the Iroquois trail before ten," he said.

"Well then, by all means go without me, if that's what you want."

"You don't know the way. You'll get lost." He had turned his back to me so that I could see the white circle his words made in the air, but not his face.

"Why is it so important to get there by ten o'clock?"

"The view is spectacular," he said. "It's the right time of morning for the light on the mountain."

"So you can't take the time to enjoy anything on the way."

"If you can't keep up, say so, and I'll stay behind with you."

I was a huge bird now, crouched over the dark egg of my anger. And he was inflexible. He had said, "We always get there at ten o'clock." And he would go on getting there at ten o'clock. I could not imagine why I had felt anything for him. But I would not let him beat me. I would walk at their pace.

"We'll all go together," I said.

We walked on opposite sides of the road, disliking each other. When we caught up with Liz and Erica, I kept a few paces behind, but only a few, so they would not keep looking at me with expressions of enduring exasperation.

The muscles in my thighs thrummed with effort. The center of my chest was hot and stretched; my physical discomfort turned my anger into hatred. I thought, If they fall off the mountain, I will be happy.

"We'll rest a moment," said Hugh, with perfunctory

chivalry. He had heard me puffing; neither he nor the other two needed any break.

I took deep, painful breaths. I hoped I would never have to see any of them again. My father was right to keep away from this sort of thing. After today, I would do as he had done.

At the top of Iroquois Pass was a sheer face of rock with little shelves that a goat might have found possible but that seemed out of the question for a tender human foot (my foot). Erica sprang to the top like a chamois. Liz scrambled after her. Hugh was looking around as if to say, I could be up and down four times in the time it will take you.

"Give me your hand," he said.

"No, thank you," I said, thinking, How did I ever allow this tyrant to touch me? I thought of young blond Nazis being trained to climb the Jungfrau: I could see him at the head of them.

I pulled myself up the rocks he was jumping.

At the top Erica called down, "I'll show you a real good exercise for balance."

Murder was in my heart as I scraped more skin off my hands with every inch.

Hugh said, "If you'd just jump, it would be a great deal easier."

"I don't want to spend Christmas in traction."

"Nonsense."

"Do shut up," I said. "That's all I ask."

I distinctly heard him say "imbecile."

"Come on, Erica," said Liz, trailing scorn. They were running across the top of the cliff.

Hugh was standing with his back to me when I finally made it to the top.

"Who the hell do you think you are, Moses?" I said angrily.

"No," he said, "just a reasonably fit adult and not a bad-tempered child."

I struck him hard between the shoulder blades, meaning to hurt him. He did the same thing to me.

There was a silence and then I began to cry.

"Don't ever do that to me again," he said.

"You deserved it."

Suddenly I saw in surprise that what we were looking at was astonishingly beautiful. Now I was crying because it was beautiful, because I had never seen anything like it.

"Forgive me," I said, embracing his coat. It was cool to my cheeks and smooth and full of stiff, synthetic fibers that would not absorb tears.

He rubbed my face with his hands. He said, "You see, I love you."

"Yes," I said.

"Come and lie down in the sun."

He found a place where it was wonderfully warm. He collected dead leaves and piled them over pine needles. We lay in each other's arms.

And I said to myself, This is love. It is saying, You are the only one, it could not possibly be any other. It is saying, Without you my life will be immensely impoverished. And I thought of the poverty of my life before this moment of impossible richness, lying in the sun in the middle of December, and I thought of all I would lose when I lost him. There was in me now the new sense of the inevitable and for the first time, of the particular, and in the center of it all, even in the sun, in all this beauty, the first fear of loss, the first foreboding that what I valued was at once irreplaceable and impossible to guarantee. I closed my fingers tightly around his wrist.

XI

Mrs. Regan was a professional, and she was clear in her thinking about people like me.

"What are your qualifications?" she asked, closing her front door.

I felt like a carny barker whom the police had finally caught up with, proving to the crowd that there was no pea, had never been a pea, under the quickly moving walnut shells.

"I'm a county employee," I said. I could hardly have made a worse answer.

"I'm an Elpie-enne," said Mrs. Regan.

"Pardon?" I said, thinking that the woman had suddenly begun talking about mountaineering.

"An L.P.*N.*," she said, with real exasperation, "a licensed practical nurse. And you can tell whoever it is you work for that I could get three times the money. I only get by because I have a pension. And you know, I saved the old woman's life. She had a piece of meat stuck in her trachea and I forced her to expel it."

I wanted to say, Suppose she didn't want to expel it?

"The old woman's loony. Loony."

"I believe there's a medical term for that. I believe it's called senility."

Mrs. Regan ignored me.

"Well, this one thinks she's in a rock-'n'-roll band. Where she got that idea I don't know. The family says it's because one of her grandchildren ran away to join something like that. Well, you can imagine what it's like all day."

The great thing about being attached to a large organization was that you could mask fear by being official. I told Mrs. Regan to fill out the form while I saw Mrs. Mooney. I was terrified of Mrs. Regan, but she would do whatever I said if I ordered her to do it in the proper voice and handed her the proper pieces of paper.

Mrs. Mooney was strapped into her bed. She appeared to be only a skull with little tufts of hair. Her exceptionally long fingers kept playing an imaginary keyboard on her bedclothes.

"Oh, you must be the new agent," she said to me in a voice that was shockingly robust.

I sat down on a chair next to the bed.

"No, Mrs. Mooney, I just want to ask you a few questions."

"Oh, then you must be from one of the magazines. We don't give interviews."

"Well, if you'll just give this one," I said. The idea of this tiny, ancient-looking person being involved in a rock-'n'-roll band was irresistible.

"Are you treated well here?" I asked.

"All the hotels have the same pictures. The last one, the food sucked. But luckily, we're on one-night stands."

I started at the woman's profanity. Like her fantasy it was incongruous, given the reality of her body.

"You're in good health?"

"Everyone takes drugs but me," she said. "I got a new organ."

She went on playing the top of her blankets. I decided I would not get much more out of Mrs. Mooney. She seemed perfectly happy. She made me feel unreasonably cheerful.

Mrs. Regan walked in the door. "I want to ask you something about question twelve."

"There's the new manager," said Mrs. Mooney.

"That bitch doesn't care about music, she's just in it for the money."

Mrs. Regan began tucking the old woman's blankets in.

"I don't know how she became so foul-mouthed," said Mrs. Regan. "She was a very religious woman. Her family said they have no idea where she learned this language. They assured me she was a real lady." She took Mrs. Mooney's pulse.

"Blow it out your ass," said Mrs. Mooney.

"Mrs. Mooney!" said Mrs. Regan, dropping the old woman's hand in horror.

"And you," she said, pointing to me with one of her long fingers. "I want to see everything you write before it's printed."

"I'll send you a copy," I said.

"It does no good to encourage this sort of thing, Miss Moore," said Mrs. Regan.

"Shut up, you bitch," said Mrs. Mooney. "You're just jealous because you'll never be a star."

It was around Christmas that Hugh first spoke of his children. He said, "It's very hard for a father to know what his daughters want." He meant Christmas presents; he meant it was hard for a man to go into a store and buy what they had told him to buy. But I could tell from the way he said it that he liked even that part of his fatherhood; that he liked it when he came home with the wrong thing and they said, "That's not it at all; that's not it *at all*." It was the distance that was so pleasurable between fathers and daughters, that made love not only possible but always interesting.

His older daughter, he said, was very serious, very passionate. He was afraid she would suffer. Even at fifteen, he said, she suffered unimaginably. And she went into rages, slammed doors, broke things. Once she had put her hand through a window; he had come in to see her covered in blood. But he loved her for that, I could see; and she was very beautiful, he said, and men would treat her badly. But she would treat men badly too, he added. He was afraid she would always be testing, always be measuring, and no one would ever measure up.

"And the other one, the younger one?" I said, wanting to hear now so that I would no longer have to fear hearing about them.

"Sara is a golden child. Everybody loves Sara. She enjoys life immensely; anything interests her; the way a vacuum cleaner works, clouds moving across the sky, bob-sledding. Everything but school. That bores her to tears. Her latest phrase is 'That bores the ass off me.' It drives her mother wild, of course."

That was it. He had spoken about her, even though he had only called her "her mother," it had been done. But the idea of her seemed seated everywhere; on all the furniture was a fierce woman, accusing.

"I wonder if you ever have a large enough family to protect you from people's generosity at Christmas," I said. "People were always asking my father and me places for Christmas and thinking we were terribly brave and terribly sad to refuse, when all we wanted was to be by ourselves. We had a terrific time as long as nobody happened by."

"Just the two of you. This will be your first Christmas without him."

It hadn't occurred to me. Because he still seemed near, because he was so far away for so long.

"Oh, but when he was sick, we never had Christmas. My friend Eleanor would come out on Christmas Eve and we'd put up a tree and have eggnog, but after my father was sick, it was only sad. Yet I felt we had to do it. If we'd ignored it, it would mean we'd given up any hope of anything."

I was thinking, I'd given up any hope of his dying while I was young enough to start my life. But I was also thinking how I had feared his dying, as if he might take my life with him. It sometimes surprised me that he was dead and I was still alive, that I had gone

on with my life so rapidly, so easily. I was thinking of
Margaret.

"When Margaret was with us, she'd always hint
around to spend Christmas with us, but my father
would never let her."

"You say that with such triumph," said Hugh, "after
all this time."

"You don't understand. She's a terrible woman."

"Then why think of her?"

"Because she haunts me."

"Only if you let her."

That was Hugh: life was simple, life was livable,
you could do things with it, could prevent things happening. I didn't believe that, of course, but I loved him
for believing it. I thought of him at the head of his
table, carving his turkey, a father, a husband, and I
was jealous, not for him but of him, having all those
connections, all those perfectly straightforward, perfectly lovable things to do.

"What will you do at Christmas?" he said, looking
worried.

"I'm going down to Eleanor's and I'll visit Father
Mulcahy."

"You'll like that?" he said, still worried.

"Eleanor is an angel. We'll spend the whole day
cooking. She has this *tiny* apartment. You always feel
like you're in Paris."

Hugh kissed the top of my head. "I make your life
difficult," he said.

"Ssh," I said, putting his hand on my breast.

John Ryan had asked me several times in the past
weeks when he could see me again, and I had always
managed to put him off. Luckily he was busy. Luckily
he had other girl friends, so I could get away from him
with jokes and promises. But I was not entirely surprised to see him at my door that evening. Even though
I was ready for him, he frightened me. I had decided
I would not let him have me again.

I turned my face from him when he went to kiss me

and stiffened at his approach. But he didn't stop. It was as if he didn't notice my closed mouth and my posture of refusal. I hated him for making me say something.

"It's no good," I said, trying to pull away from him.

"Don't say that, baby, don't say that."

He was trying to undo the buttons of my blouse. His voice sounded younger than I had ever known it and at the same time more dangerous. He had his arms very tightly around me. I could feel his thigh between my two legs. It was the bulk of that thigh that made me panic; I felt as if I were drowning and I began to flail like a drowning person. I hit him in the eye and he cried out; a surprising cry of real pain. He backed away from me, holding his eye.

"You cunt," he said, "I'll make you pay for this. You and your friend, too."

Then he was gone. I felt a queer elation and a fear. There was no one I could go to. And I didn't know when he would do it, or how he would do it, only that he would do something, that it would be clever and effective and full of hurt. It was snowing. I thought of boys who put nails inside snowballs.

Mrs. Rosenfeld made me very nervous. She was the smallest woman I had ever seen. I was afraid her house was going to fall around her; it looked so insubstantial I wondered if it had been made of ice-cream sticks. Everything in the house looked light and temporary, as if it could be dismantled and made to disappear on the shortest possible notice. What was there in Mrs. Rosenfeld's life that made her dream of a quick getaway? She was divorced; she had one son, she told me, who was living in a commune. It seemed clear that she had taken an old person into her house because she was lonely. I tried to determine her age, but her dun-colored, almost bloodless skin, not in its way unappealing, made it hard to pin down. She showed me into, as she called it, the gentleman's room.

Mr. Spenser was clearly a gentleman. He was reading the *Memoirs of Casanova*. He had no teeth and he said to me, "If you would prefer, I will put my teeth in." He made it sound like an extreme courtesy.

I said he needn't; I wouldn't be staying long. He seemed rather disappointed at my diffidence.

"I wish you would stay longer. I rarely get to see a beautiful woman nowadays. Although she is kind, Mrs. Rosenfeld has no complexion and no bosom."

I slipped quickly into my official tone; I asked the old man questions about diet and doctor's visits and bathroom facilities, all of which he answered perfunctorily, as if he had something more important on his mind.

"What has surprised me most in my old age is that at eighty-three my interest in sex has not diminished one iota. The last time I had sexual intercourse was eight years ago. It didn't occur to me it would be the last time or I would have been more conscious of detail. For my memoirs."

"Yes," I said. "You feel then that the program provides you with real benefits?"

"I always had a woman to care for me, but they seemed to get older and older, and the last one died six years ago. I was in a nursing home, but there were entirely the wrong sort of people there. A very ignorant lot. Of course, Mrs. Rosenfeld is exceedingly ignorant, but at least I have privacy. I no longer think of being happy. I didn't live the sort of youth that would buy a happy old age—grandchildren asking for stories, that sort of thing. Many of my relations tended to be ephemeral. One can only *collect* in old age; people are only good to old people out of guilt, and I had never done enough for anyone for long enough that I could make them feel guilty."

"Then you don't believe in acts of pure generosity?" I said. I was thinking of my father.

"I find the concept of purity rather a jejune one."

"You sound like a friend of mine," I said. "I always lived in a world where people asked the impossible. Anything else has always seemed mediocre."

"Tell me about your friend," he said.

I told him about what I felt when I saw Hugh walking in the distance, how I felt myself pulled to him, how new it was, all that love-making, as if it were the most natural thing in the world.

"It is," said Mr. Spenser.

"Not always," I said.

"Go on about your friend," he said. I understood why women had loved him. It was the way he listened to you with his head tilted like that (it worked, even though he was eighty-three and toothless), as if he had always been waiting for precisely what you had to say, as if there were nothing in the world he would rather be doing. I told him about Hugh's wife and his daughters and the Christmas presents.

"You love him?"

"I'm afraid," I said, meaning, "I'm afraid so," and at the same time, "I'm frightened."

"You must try to keep him. I have confidence. Remember you have a great deal of power. A beautiful woman always has more power than she knows."

"But I'm not beautiful," I said.

"My dear, do not ask me to insult you by repeating the obvious."

I took his hand. "You've helped me so much. I'll come and visit you."

"Don't. That would be a mistake. Then you'll feel obligated to me when I am no longer able to be amusing. I will only ask you one thing."

"Name it."

"Let me see your breasts."

"What? I can't."

"Why?"

"Because they're *mine*."

"It's the only thing you can do for me that I want."

I tried to think of a good reason not to do it. It was something he wanted. I thought of the incident of a woman who went to Confession in *The Brothers Karamazov*. She told the priest she could not give up her adulterous affair because "it gives him so much pleasure and me so little pain." I began unbuttoning my blouse.

"Suppose Mrs. Regan comes in."

"Lock the door. The only good feature in this otherwise featureless room is its lock."

"I hope this will make you happy."

"It will mean more to me than you know."

"Will you take down the details for your memoirs?"

"Oh no, my life is effectively over."

I had trouble unhooking my bra. My breasts fell out of the cups like oranges out of a paper sack.

Mr. Spenser did not smile. He nodded his head and closed his eyes.

"You have done me a real kindness," he said. "You have given me what I wanted, not what you thought I wanted, or what you wanted me to want."

I dressed. We shook hands very formally. I wondered if what I had just done was quite insane. I would tell Hugh. Would he think me unfaithful? But Mr. Spenser had said wise things, had said interesting things, had given me what I most needed: conversation. He had listened to me about Hugh. I had no one else to talk to. And I had given him what he wanted and neither of us had suffered loss. That was rare. I had not believed it possible: giving and getting, as if no one had to suffer, as if it were possible not to feel cheated in the act of giving.

I realized that I had never cooked a meal for Hugh, and I wanted to do it before Christmas. Leaving Ringkill for the first time would mark the end of something, or perhaps coming back for the first time would mark the beginning of something else, and I wanted a meal with Hugh to give a shapely end to that time which had been so marked as the beginning of my new life.

I planned the meal for days. I took both volumes of *The Joy of Cooking,* in paperback, out of the library and read with an absorbed and utterly sensual disbelief the descriptions of the foods that all those steps and all those ingredients would turn into. I decided on coq au vin. I spoke flirtatiously to the butcher so he would cut up the chicken with particular tenderness. I shopped for wild rice in a gourmet store. I stood ruminatively in front of French wines, in love with labels. Never had a day given me more perfect happiness. I finished my shopping at eleven o'clock; I cleaned the apartment from twelve to two; by four o'clock I had sliced the mushrooms and peeled the onions; by five, everything was simmering on the stove. I had two hours to bathe and get ready for my lover. Everything was planned correctly. Never had I liked myself so much.

I let myself stay in the tub for forty minutes. I put lotion all over my body. I got into my black velvet caftan wearing nothing underneath. I felt cool and expert and utterly desirable, but what was more important, I felt that I had finally caught up with other people, that I had finally learned what other women my age knew; I felt that I was no longer a child. I flipped through the pages of the January *Vogue* and thought that if I could see myself I would think I was the person I always wanted to be; I was the kind of woman younger women would envy.

I could hear Hugh opening the front door, and I rushed down the stairs to meet him. His embrace was dry and restrained, as if he were thinking of something else. How can I describe what that embrace planted in me: a wedge-shaped shadow, a shadow only, but I had lost my enviable clarity.

"Did you have trouble getting away?" I asked, thinking perhaps that was the reason for his distraction.

"Not really," he said, looking around discontentedly. "Everything smells quite nice."

Quite nice.

"It's coq au vin."

"Oh. I bought white wine. I'll go and change it."

"Don't bother. I've got more of the red."

"Fine. You can save this for John Ryan, then."

His unfairness stung me because justice was the virtue I had thought most particularly his. Unfairness was

something my father had, that Catholics had, a quality
to which I believed Hugh with his even, secular gaze,
immune. And I had thought him miraculously free of
a trait I had associated with men who had been
brought up in the fear of an angry God: the habit of
drumming up crimes, of inventing sentences, always
when one was most unready, when one felt most safe
from the possibility of punishment. It distressed me to
realize that I would have to use ordinary words with
Hugh, make ordinary protestations that I might have
had to make to any man.

"You know that I won't see John Ryan again."

"So you've said."

"What is the matter with you tonight?"

"Nothing is the matter. Get on with what you were
doing."

I was sorry I had left so little to do. I boiled water
and watched Hugh looking around for something onto
which he could pin his dislike of me. That was it: he
disliked me tonight, the one night I had arranged for
his adoration. Where did it come from, that dislike? I
knew it was my fault; I was as sure of that as anything
I had ever known, although I could not precisely identify the cause.

He came into the kitchen carrying a coffee cup. I
wondered, with a flush of alarm, where he had got it.

"Isabel, I want you to look at this and explain it to
me if you think there is any possible explanation."

I looked at the cup. At the bottom was a quarter-
inch of congealed coffee in which green mold grew like
rings around the moon. Here was the man I loved
holding in his hands the proof of my defeat. How deceived I had been, sitting on my couch—was it only
half an hour ago—reading *Vogue,* thinking I could be
like other people. I thought of the terrible disorder of
the closets on Dover Road, of the shame and anguish
they had caused me, of my belief, held onto until I
sold the house to strangers, that there was nothing I
could do about them. I had thought of all that as behind me; I had thought I could be the kind of woman

I dreamed of being, but I was wrong. Always there would be some proof, undeniable as that cup, that I had failed, that I had missed out on some vital knowledge that ought to have been passed down to me by some woman, some knowledge that was crucially connected to sex. I felt as I stood near Hugh that I was not a woman; I felt the shame I would have felt had I discovered on my face the beginnings of a beard. I began to cry, but Hugh was paying no attention to me; he was washing the cup.

"It was right on the windowsill behind the curtain. In the middle of your living room where you sit every day of your life," he said, ignoring my distress.

"Please stop," I begged. "Please don't go on." It was such a simple, clear request; it did not occur to me that he could ignore it.

"I don't see how you could live in such filth. How could I even contemplate living with someone who could live in such filth?"

I ran into my bedroom. He didn't care how much he hurt me. He knew all my uneasiness on the subject of housework; we had talked about it, about Margaret, and what happened to the house when she left. He had taken the area of my life that was most tentative and had chosen it as the place to inflict the brand of his random malice. I remembered him on the mountain when, seconds before he said he loved me, he wanted to make me acknowledge my weakness and the superiority of his body and his courage and his training and his breath. I remembered his back to me as he stood looking over the landscape, an Old Testament back, a punishing back. That was it, that was something I must remember; there was in him the desire to punish. And I was perhaps the person in the world most guilty of the sins he considered the most grievous. I could not keep up with the demands of the physical world in my body, in my home.

I could hear him in the living room, switching the radio on, turning the pages of magazines. I would not go out to him; he had hurt me unforgivably, and I had

never been quick to forgive. I lay on my bed in the
darkness, smelling the perfume I had put on the pil-
lowcases for his pleasure, feeling hate thicken as the
sky darkened. Suddenly I remembered the wild rice.
It was on a very low flame, but it would have to be
checked. It was very expensive. I would not ruin it for
a third-rate gesture of pride.

I tasted a few grains and saw that it was ready. I
served the meal, not as I had imagined, in a haze of
sensual love, but in a thick blanket of righteousness.

"It's very good," he said, not looking at me. "Very
good indeed."

His staring down at his plate made him look very
young. I could see the stubborn boy in him, the boy
who had defied those perfectly kind parents.

"Hugh," I said, taking his hand, "what is it? Why
are you acting like this?"

He looked up at me with eyes that were so purely
unhappy that it was unbearable to look at them. It was
the pained look of a good man who cannot understand
how his life has become so complicated, how he has
put himself in such unexpected danger.

"It's you and Cynthia and the children. Christmas,"
he said, "makes everything more real somehow."

What he said did not move me, for I did not believe
that he seriously considered even for a moment the
possibility of leaving them.

"Let's give each other our presents," I said, feeling
suddenly rather tired, and wanting to be alone in my
own place. It exhausted me, that masculine indirect-
ness, that masculine pain. It made me want to get on
with some other kind of life.

He had bought me a copy of *Northanger Abbey*,
bound in green leather, with pages mottled like plover's
eggs. In the flyleaf was the name Jennie Walter and
the date 1913. Underneath he had written, "Isabel
from Hugh." But he had read it himself first; he
wanted to be sure, he said, of what he was giving me.
He told me I must look very carefully because he had
plucked hairs from the rims of his ears and stuck them

on the pages he liked. He said it was a nervous habit; he tweezed the hairs in his ears when he read, but this way it would remind me of him.

"I think there's a little skin on the end of them that makes a kind of adhesive," he said.

That made me love him again.

"What made you think of doing that, sticking hairs on pages?"

"I just thought of it."

"How did you know it would work?"

"I just did."

"For which I love you above other men," I said.

I had bought him a Swiss army knife. He opened the blades, each of them separately, and looked at them with a pure, material absorption that would not have been possible for me, or for my father, or for Father Mulcahy, or for anyone who had been brought up in the Catholic Church.

"I'll have to leave it here," he said. "I can't risk Cynthia finding it."

That was a grief that settled in my stomach, making the food seem heavy and false. He could not keep my gifts; he would have to leave them behind. For the first time, I acknowledged the illicit nature of my relationship to Hugh. I was his mistress. Adultery was the word for it. I did not want that word, with the ugly shape it made in the mouth, with the ugly images it conjured: motel rooms, detectives, ringing telephones next to unmade beds. But there was Hugh sitting across from me, holding the knife I had given him. The knife looked so perfect in his hand that there was nothing about it I could regret. For a moment I was glad that the knife would have to stay in my house, that I could keep it by me.

"Isabel, do you mind if we don't make love tonight? Somehow I feel too fragile."

Fragile—it was a beautiful word for a man to use about himself. It brought him back to me as the beloved.

"Of course," I said, standing up to embrace him.

We held each other for a few seconds. He left before ten o'clock. It was not the night I had planned. I would never quite forgive him; never again could I trust him as I had, for it was always possible that he could take my new, shaky womanhood and mock it.

But I had never loved him so much.

The sun shone through the path of windshield I had cut from the ice that morning. Mine was the only car on the road. I felt extraordinarily competent; adult, driving home like this at Christmas.

It was a queer thing, spending Christmas with only one other person and that person your own age. Hugh would be with his parents and his children. And his wife. He had got her a blender for Christmas. When he talked about her he shivered. They slept in separate beds, and when she made the beds in the morning she pushed them together so it would look like a double bed, so no one would think they were unhappy. I had never known anyone hate a body as he hated his wife's body, the literal flesh of it.

I wondered what Margaret was doing for Christmas, and then I remembered the Christmas card I had got from her a few days before. It was glossy and had a picture of a Madonna who looked as if she could be advertising Ivory Snow. My first thought was that my father would not have liked it. "Meretricious," he would have called it; that was one of the words he used quite easily in conversation. I would have to tell that to Hugh, who made me laugh with his occasional exotic words, foreign or old-fashioned; he sometimes used the language with the formality of an immigrant. But how awful it would have been if Margaret had sent, say, a reproduction of a Fra Angelico as her Christmas card. I had sent Dürer woodcuts; how unbearable it would have been had Margaret by some chance sent the same card. For that was my protection against Margaret: I sent Dürers, Margaret sent babyfaced blondes; I desired Mozart; Margaret desired Lawrence Welk.

There was a whine in Margaret's one-sentence message. She was eating Christmas supper in the parish basement at a special affair for Golden Agers. What was golden about Margaret's age? Or her youth, for that matter. She said she supposed I would have some place nice to go. I had sent her a basket of fruit. Margaret had thanked me but said that my father had always given her a case of port wine; she said that Father Mulcahy sent her fifty dollars.

How pleasant it would be to see Father Mulcahy. His cheeks were always very cold and very rosy in the winter; it was a pleasure to touch them with your lips if he came from the outside. Even his scalp showed rose through his beautiful white hair. But if I told him about Hugh he would not want to see me. Perhaps he would cry. Of course I would not tell him. It was the function of the Church to make you keep things from the people you loved. I would see him the day after Christmas. I had bought him a white silk scarf that I had seen in the Abercrombie & Fitch catalogue. He would like that; he would put it on to show me, like a woman, like a child.

Eleanor's apartment was shockingly cold.

"It's the landlord," she said. "He's trying to freeze me out."

"Can't you do anything about it?"

"What?"

"Complain."

Eleanor shrugged as if I were a novice in a convent she had lived in for years.

On a small dark table against one of Eleanor's white walls there was a silver bowl of holly. I touched the round sides with cold fingers. I bent down and put my cheek against the bowl; it was freezing and distinct and smelled of leaves. Never had anything in a room so delighted me. I stood back to look at it, then came close to it and walked back again.

"Eleanor, how perfect."

"Let me just refresh the leaves a moment." She walked over and sprayed the leaves with a pretty brass atomizer.

"What a wonderful expression, 'refresh the leaves.' Refreshing—that's a beautiful idea, like rest, like hospitality."

Eleanor was looking very sly.

"You like it then?" she said.

"I adore it."

"That's lucky. It's your Christmas present."

"But it's too good for me. I wouldn't know how to take care of it."

"It's not fragile. You just polish it occasionally. That's why I bought it for you."

"But I may have to be moving, soon. In two months."

"Well, then, it's perfect," said Eleanor, somewhat illogically. "I should have left it wrapped up, but I couldn't resist the holly."

I embraced her. "I'm beginning to think life can be immensely enjoyable," I said.

"On and off," said Eleanor.

I reached into my black canvas bag. "Since we're being bad about Christmas presents, here's yours. I want you to wear it instantly."

I had brought Eleanor a sea-green shawl the size of a blanket. Eleanor put it around her shoulders and over her head. It made her look like a widow, like someone who would go on watching for ships relentlessly, even though she had seen her husband's drowned body.

"I think this is going to be the only Christmas I've ever really enjoyed," said Eleanor. "Come and look at my beautiful food."

There were nuts, round and dull, oblong and polished in light wooden bowls. There were strings of plump, meaty figs and dark dates still shining in plastic. There were gold raisins and dark brownish-purple raisins. The whole table was covered with nuts and fruits.

"I have a quite insane recipe for stuffing. It involves nuts, raisins, apricots, cream, chestnuts. We won't be able to walk for a week."

"I never cook anything good for myself," I said.

"I don't either. You know, there was this woman that I truly admired, revered, I think, because she lived alone and made marvellous meals for herself every evening."

We drank red wine from Eleanor's goblets; we ate fruit instead of dinner. It was Christmas Eve. Eleanor said, "Do you remember two years ago on your birthday we made lemon meringue pie and the meringue just sat there, and how your father laughed at the way it looked? The three of us just sat on the bed, laughing about the meringue."

"I forgot," I said. "I forget. I forget my father laughing. I forget that he was still him after he got sick."

"One time, five years ago, when he had real trouble talking, I remember he asked me if you were unhappy. What could I say? I said no, I didn't think so, and he began to cry, and he said he would hear you at nights, crying yourself to sleep."

The tears were large in Eleanor's eyes. I said, "Help me to remember things like that."

Eleanor said, "I remember he always used to cut the ends off your hair, even when he was feeling bad he'd do it. And he'd say, 'If you cut your hair, don't come back to this house,' and you'd say, 'Who'd put up with you except me?' and he said, 'Queens is full of eager widows.' "

I looked at my hair. "Just before he went into the hospital, I sat next to him in the chair reading, and he scratched my head for about an hour. We always did that."

I turned to Eleanor. "Please help me remember," I said. "Please tell me I'm right, that it wasn't all unbearable. He didn't turn into a monster. He was still himself."

"Of course he was," said Eleanor, "only thank God it's over."

I was thinking how I was enjoying everything: figs, holly in a silver bowl, Hugh's hands, the hair on his forearms. And that is not possible when you are waiting for someone to die. It is impossible not to hate the dying.

"All these old people that I see and talk to, the only thing they really want is to be at the center of somebody's life. I mean, all that talk about charity. People don't want that kind of love. They want people to like them."

"Then it's all terribly random," said Eleanor.

"What else do you have? Affection. Personal regard. You see, I really *liked* my father. I really enjoyed his company."

"And Hugh? You like him, too."

"I like him immensely."

"That means you want to be with him."

"Yes. So?"

"So now what?" said Eleanor.

"I don't know," I said. I dropped raisins into my glass of wine.

"Will he leave his wife for you?" said Eleanor.

"Who?" I said.

"Hugh," Eleanor said, as if it were a normal thing for me to have forgotten my lover's name.

That was what no one had said aloud, not even Hugh, and I myself had never said it, certainly. I felt a thrill of fear, as if a dentist were just coming to a tooth I knew all the time was painful but had lived with so long I had forgotten.

"I don't know," I said.

"What do you want?" said Eleanor.

"I don't know. Hugh. But I'm afraid. If you make someone leave his wife, then what happens to you? And children. My God, Eleanor, he has two *daughters.*"

"What will you do, Isabel?" said Eleanor with some urgency. Anyone else's voice saying those words would have made me feel trapped.

"I don't know. I've just gone on enjoying things, thinking it was a miracle that all this was happening to me after all that time, after all that business with my father, that I had this love with this man. I felt, I still feel, a kind of generalized fear, but I didn't think of asking for anything more from him."

"But you'll have to. Or you'll have to give him back."

"As if he were a cup of sugar I'd borrowed?"

"And if he does leave his wife, you'll never have any money; he'll have to give her everything. You think it doesn't matter, but it does, eventually. I know, from Justin. And then there'll be those children, who don't want to know you but have to know you. And perfectly strange middle-aged women you've never seen before who look at you as if you were a thief."

"So you think I should give him up?"

"No," said Eleanor. "I only think you should realize what you may be in for."

"Let's not think about it on Christmas."

We turned on the television. Bing Crosby was singing "White Christmas" in a movie he had made thirty years before. We were falling asleep in front of the screen; it took all our discipline, all our will, to undress and to go properly to our beds.

Did everyone go on like that, doing things, and then being surprised that other people thought they had a meaning? It was odd that your life could have more significance to other people than to yourself; it was odd that other people understood what you did while you were simply going on and doing it.

After all my thinking about things, I had fallen, or rather run, into the important things in my life, the way a pilot, hypnotized, runs into a moving propeller, all the time believing he is acting with deliberation. But I would not think of myself like that, as someone mutilated, because I was there the day after Christmas, with my silver bowl in the back seat and my *Northanger Abbey* beside me. (I flipped the book open to one of the pages with hairs on the top; I knew where they all were by now; I could go to one instantly.) I was driving to see Father Mulcahy.

But I was thinking that something would have to

happen. Either I would lose Hugh, or he would come
to me, leaving his wife, leaving his children, leaving a
trail of hate and grief that would always go behind
him like that of a snail.

And what would I say to Father Mulcahy? We
would talk about my job. I would tell him funny
things. We would talk about Liz, but I would say nothing really true about Liz, nothing really important.
We would talk about Eleanor. I began to resent him
because I had nothing to say to him that I really
wanted to say. I could say nothing that would ease
my burdens; he could say nothing to help me. It had
always been like that: he was too good for my life,
too simple. And there was the Church, which knew
what was wrong, which said, "I will tell you what is
wrong and then you will not do it," which would,
could give sympathy only (and really, I understood
it) if you took its advice.

Father Mulcahy had been waiting for me, literally
waiting; he answered the door just as I began to ring
the bell. I was grateful. I had feared seeing Mrs.
Keeney with her dead eyes that were nearly Margaret's eyes, who would somehow know everything
that had happened to me, who would give me a look
that would make me feel that what I had done was
disgusting. But she did not answer the door. It was
Father Mulcahy, looking as he always did when he
saw me, as if I were the person in the world he
wanted most to see.

He loved his white scarf. He said he'd always
wanted one like it, where did I get it?

"From Paris," I said, "from Khartoum, from Tan-
gier."

"Where?" he said, puzzled.

I forgot: it was my father who liked things like that,
who laughed at them, who said, "Go on, go on." Of
course Father Mulcahy was puzzled; anyone would
be puzzled.

He had bought me an immense box of chocolates.
"My God," I said, "I thought these kinds of things

were for movie stars. I didn't think people like *me* got things like *this*." I fluttered my eyelids, imitating a starlet.

"By the way, I saw a picture of your friend Grace Kelly," he said. "She looks like the broad side of a barn."

"Don't tell me," I said, covering my ears. "I don't want to know."

"Facts is facts, girl. I hate to be the one to tell you."

So we joked like that, about candy, about movie stars, as if eating and getting fat and getting older were the most amusing things in the world. And I told him about my job, and that some people were happy and some people were terribly unhappy and I was trying to figure out why.

"The only thing I can say is that everybody wants to be the most important person in someone's life and most people don't get it."

"But we're all the most important people in the heart of God. Jesus Christ died for each one of us; He would have died for you or me if we were the only person in the world."

"But you see, that's not enough," I said, and then, realizing whom I was talking to, stepped back. "I mean people are still lonely; they're still unhappy."

"Happiness isn't everything," he said.

"What is, then?"

"Faith, girl, faith. All this stuff about happiness. Was Christ happy in the Garden? We weren't put on this earth to be happy *here*. We were put here so we could be happy in heaven. *For all eternity*," he said, as if he were in a pulpit. "What's sixty or seventy years, happy or unhappy, compared with that? My God, girl, you sound like you're losing your faith."

"Nonsense," I said, conscious of the danger and wishing to skate over it as if it were a dark patch of ice. "Everyone has doubts."

"Now your father, for all his brains, had the faith of a child," said Father Mulcahy. "It was beautiful. He was an edification to me."

And at the end of his life, I thought, he was full of bitterness and rage.

"It's hard to believe he's gone," said Father Mulcahy, beginning to weep.

I took his hand. My eyes were dry. I was conscious of their distinct coldness, as if they had been plated over with cold skin. I felt nothing for my father, nothing for Father Mulcahy; I was thinking how good it was that tonight I would be alone again in my apartment. And I was thinking, as I almost always was now, of Hugh.

XII

"It's becoming impossible to leave," Hugh said, holding my head as he always did, as if it were some immensely valuable treasure. How I loved his holding my head like that and making me feel that he knew exactly what was most beautiful about me, that it was precisely for *this* that he loved me.

"It's like losing a limb," he said, as we moved away from each other, standing beside the bed, naked in the dark. I turned the lights on, as I always did. The light hurt my eyes. I walked around still naked (once I had put on a robe and he said, "Why do you do that? Don't do that"), doing practical things, making instant coffee, brushing his clothes, all with a terrible ache because I was no longer holding him and a fear for the ache that would spread and settle when he closed the door behind him.

But that night when he held me before leaving he said, "I want to be with you all the time. I'm trying to make up my mind to leave her."

I said nothing.

"Would you have me then?" he said, with a kind of humility I had never seen before, certainly never in a man.

"Of course," I said. I could say it because I did not believe it would really happen.

"I can't go on leaving someone I love to go back to someone who disgusts me, someone I despise."

It would have been much less serious had he used the word "hate," but he had said "disgust" and "despise."

"But the girls?" I said.

He held me more tightly. "Can it do them any good to live in a house with people who can't bear the sight of one another?"

"No. I don't know. I don't know what to say. Whatever I say could be because I want you so much."

He kissed my forehead as if he were anointing me. "Be patient with me. I'll need your patience."

I called Liz. Why had we stayed away from one another? When we lived a hundred miles apart we were closer; we had had telephone calls that were like works of art, full of color and definite line. They had helped me. I wanted to tell Liz now, more than she could possibly know. I had been trying to remember what my life had been like, how I had got through it. Hugh had been helping me; it was terribly important, he said, that I remember. I seemed, Hugh said, to be wanting to let it all go. That was bad; dangerous was the word he had used. I was beginning to be able to see my father's face again; I could run him through my mind as I did the rest of the film of my past, and his face was beginning to come into focus, whereas before it had been a black spot, or the face of a younger man, a healthy man, not the face of my father dying.

I said to Liz, "What's wrong with us? Four months, five months practically of keeping away from each other."

"I've been busy, you've been busy."

"That's not the truth of it," I said. Once, I would have been afraid to challenge Liz like this. "That's not all of it. Come and spend a day with me."

Liz said, "Yes, I'll come," but was it fear or relief, that breathiness in her voice?

When Liz arrived, her stiffness made me feel exhausted. I wanted her to go home if it was going to be such hard work. And there would be all the tense preliminaries before we could get down to the heart of it: "What's happened to us, why are we afraid of one another?"

Liz was talking about her real-estate course; she imitated the other women. She was perfect in her imitations and I loved that, had always loved it. When we were teenagers we would ride the subways and pretend to be Southern tourists, or we would pretend to be girls from Brooklyn who worked in a dry cleaner's and were going into the city to pick up men. But even as I was enjoying what Liz was doing, I had a sense of some hollowness, some wrongness. Liz and I came together best when we were hooking onto the past, riding it as if it were a raft we were terrified to get off. Liz stopped. A palpable silence seemed to enter the room.

"Why do we do this, Liz? Why don't we talk to each other about now, or something real in the past that affects the present? It's always jokes about nuns or making fun of something."

Liz looked up at me with distressing clarity. "It's because I associate you with the past; it's because I think of you as immune."

"Immune from what?"

"The present."

"Change, you mean. You thought I would never change, that nothing would ever change me."

Liz had not moved her eyes, had not, it seemed, even blinked in all that time.

"You see, I thought it was all right, whatever I did, sexually or socially, but sexually really, as long as you were there, just going on as you did, as you always had, somehow outside of everything. Then it seemed as if there were some things I couldn't touch, some things I couldn't affect, and, I guess, hurt somehow."

"You liked me better as an icon. And then I went off and slept with your husband and got involved with Hugh and messed up that lovely calm exterior."

"Monstrous, to think of a friend like that," said Liz. "You must forgive me."

"There's nothing to forgive. Don't you think it frightens me?"

Up to that moment it had not frightened me, because it had not seemed real, it had not seemed like part of my life, which was my father dying, which was giving things up for my father. But now it was real, and from now on I would be frightened.

"It can be very soothing, being an icon," I said. "There's something very sure about it." Then, abruptly, I added, "Hugh is thinking of leaving his wife."

"God bless him," said Liz, and we both laughed. It was such a Catholic thing to say.

"He wants to be with me, that's what he says."

"You know it will be hell in some ways. Cynthia Slade won't let go easily."

"But they hate each other. Surely she'll be glad to be without *that*."

"But he'll have left her, and everyone will know it, and she'll never forgive him. Never." Liz shivered. "I'm afraid for you both."

I began to think again (it was Liz's shiver that made me) that Hugh would never be free of his wife. Anger filled me. Why had he said he would try? He would never leave her. And how I hated him for that.

"We'll have to see," I said.

"Speaking of fear, my husband is out gunning for you, so watch out."

"What can he do to me?" I said. "The job's over; that was his only angle."

"He'll think of something," said Liz. "I know him, he's not stupid. Or rather, he is stupid, so he'll do anything."

"And you, Liz, will you stay with him?"

"I more or less have to."

"And Erica?"

"She wants to have babies. I think she thinks it's

like a horse and foal, which it is in some ways. So she will probably leave me one day for a man who can give her babies."

"And that makes you feel . . ."

"Like hell," said Liz. "Most of my life makes me feel like hell. Only there are some parts of it I enjoy immensely. And I am on the whole proud of it. So there it is."

"I'm going to need your help. I'm going to need you to tell me I'm doing the right thing more or less incessantly. It may get to be a bit of a bore."

"You're doing the right thing," said Liz, embracing me.

I felt a sharp, nervous flush, remembering that Liz had embraced women as a man would. But it was only for an instant, and then it was Liz, whom I had loved since childhood, whom I would always love, and I embraced my friend in silence, with deep love for the past and for the friendship that we did not yet know of that I was sure now would go on until one of us died.

My feelings as I walked up the path to the Kileys, were violently mixed. This was the end of something, the end of the only thing that was certain in my life. After this there was only chance. My life became as random as other people's, only it was worse; I was too old for life to be so entirely random, and I had no past that would attach me to the future in any but the most tentative of ways. Most of what would happen was up to Hugh. I hated having my life so much in someone else's power once more; it was worse than waiting for my father to die, because then at least there was some solidity, there was something for me to do. Now it was like jumping into space: it was feeling like an astronaut, as I had at my father's funeral, but now it was like jumping from nothing to nothing.

This was, of course, not the work I wanted to do, going into strangers' houses, asking them questions, and then leaving, going on to someone else. But it had been tremendously interesting; it appealed to the voyeur in me.

The Kileys' house was exactly the kind of house I most hated, and I had to go into too many houses. It was the middle of February, and if the Kileys' house had any residual charm at all, this was the time of year when it was most impossible to perceive it. Cats had been in the garbage; all over the bluish-gray lawn were scraps of milk cartons, brownish knuckles of bone, slivers of plastic and white lumps of Styrofoam. One of the windows had been broken, and someone had tacked over it black plastic that billowed out like shiny cheeks in the wind. A kinder person than I— Eleanor perhaps, or Father Mulcahy—would have said that this house had once been quite attractive, but I was too absorbed in a hatred of its present to be gracious about a past that was perhaps only an invention.

As I came nearer, I became aware that the house stank: the smell of cats hung over it like a curse. I wanted to leave. I could tell Lavinia that she would have to send someone else. I could not possibly do my work with such a smell around me. But this was almost my last case; there was nothing for it but to keep on going.

Patricia Kiley, the daughter, was, according to my records, twenty-eight years old. She had no front teeth left; her mouth was the mouth of an old woman. The shape of her pendulous breasts was distressingly visible under her green T-shirt; the pores were dark around her nose and her nails were bitten to the quick. I hated the sight of her, and I thought that the girl *made* me hate her. I walked into the cat smell as one might walk into an enormous glove; it closed around me. Most of the windows had been covered over with black plastic like the one I had seen outside, making the house as dark as a movie theater. With every step I crunched kitty litter into gritty small pebbles that stuck to the bottoms of my shoes. All over the house were magazines in untidy piles. For a horrible moment, those magazines reminded me of the house in Dover Road. Did it matter that the magazines I had let pile up were old *New Yorker*'s and *Atlantic Monthly*'s, and the magazines here were *True Confessions* and *Modern Romances?* The difference was slight, distressingly slight. I understood how Patricia Kiley had let her life become like this, but I went on hating her. I understood perfectly, because it was only *luck* that I had never looked like that girl, and that I read different magazines. My father and I had had Duccio Madonnas and these people had pictures of Christ in a pink nightgown—but it was only a random difference.

Patricia Kiley bumped her mother, strapped into a wheelchair, lovelessly across the floor. The girl's eyes were perfectly dead, and the mother, who had multiple sclerosis, was twisted excruciatingly in the chair. She too had no teeth, and her face sagged on one side. But I remembered that my father's face had sagged, too; I remembered how frightened Liz's children had been to see him. So I asked the Kileys the questions on the form in a perfectly flat tone. The house smelt awful, but the plumbing worked and the kitty litter that the cats had kicked onto the floor was not, I supposed, a health hazard. Mrs. Kiley saw the doctor regularly; there was nothing much that could be done for her; she could die tomorrow or she could go on living for years. Patricia kept playing with a sore under her right ear.

And what, I wondered, ought I to say to the county: that this girl is already dead, has been turned into an imbecile, but if we put her mother somewhere else she may have a chance of a normal life? Looking at her, I did not believe that. If she had not been taking care of her mother she would be doing—simply nothing. Something is better than nothing; taking care of someone in a house like this is better than living in it by yourself. And the report said that Patricia's IQ was under ninety. But she ought to be given a chance to get out from under, to invent a new life. And what about her mother? Would it matter if she did her dying here or in a nursing home?

I asked Patricia if she had thought of putting her mother somewhere for a while. The girl looked at me with her dead eyes and said, "We like it here. We like it like this. She's my mother. I can take care of her. She belongs here. We're all right." She went on picking the scab below her ear.

I wanted to slap her very hard and say, You're not all right; you're not all right at all. But what could she be that was better? Lavinia Hartman had said she was not showing me any of the real horrors, but here was a horror and only I, perhaps, knew the full extent of it. Well, I would let Lavinia decide what was to be done with the Kileys, but I would recommend that things be left as they were.

I could not imagine that my last case could be worse than the Kileys. Miss Plover, who took care of Mrs. Riesert, was a thin, worried woman. Maiden lady, I thought, was the perfect term for her. She rubbed her hands nervously as she talked to me. She had a series of small rooms with pleasant, domestic furniture and clear, realistic paintings, which were not beautiful but which, in their unassuming faithfulness to whatever it was they were portraying—violets, or apples, or ducks—had a diffident appeal.

Miss Plover wrung her hands. "She's terribly unhappy. She cries most of the day. There's nothing I can do for her. I hope it's not my fault. I try very hard to please her."

"I'm sure you do, Miss Plover," I said.

Mrs. Riesert was lying in the dark. Before Miss Plover turned the lights on, I could hear her weeping. When I went in she sat up and looked in my direction.

"Thank you, Miss Plover," Mrs. Riesert said. The small woman left the room.

I said, "Can you tell me what it is that is causing you to be so distressed?"

The old woman did not hesitate. "I'm alone. I'm old and I'm dying. There's no one who loves me enough."

Her complaint had the awful simplicity of a child's. I could say nothing. Finally this woman had told the truth, what so many of those old people were thinking but were afraid to say.

"You have no family?"

"I had a son. He was killed in Korea. My husband died last year. And I go on living," said the woman, weeping quietly.

"Isn't there anything that interests you?" I asked, knowing my words were false. "The county has several programs."

"What I want is to be with someone who wants me. Wants *me*," she said. "Or else I want to die. I don't seem to be dying fast enough."

"You must occupy your mind with something," I said. "You're making yourself much more depressed than you need be."

"Why should I occupy myself?" the woman said, looking at me with clear gray eyes that were remarkably young, as if all those tears had done them some kind of good.

"Because you're making your life difficult."

"I'm eighty-seven years old, and all I want to do is die," she said. "Miss Plover is very kind so I don't want to do it in her house, it would be a terrible shock to her. But you could help me," she said, grabbing my wrist with desperation, hurting me with the force of her grasp. "You could get me sent to a nursing home and I could do it there. I've saved up all these pills," she said, producing a little box from under her pillow, "and if I did it in a nursing home no one would care. You can get someone else for Miss Plover. It wouldn't matter to her. Please," she said, looking at me with those strange young eyes. "You're the only one who can help me."

I disengaged my wrist.

"Yes. I'll do whatever I can," I said.

The woman began to weep, but it was tears of relief she wept now, and she kissed my hand.

That was charity, then. You let someone die if they
wanted to. I did not hesitate for a moment. I told Miss
Plover that I thought Mrs. Riesert needed psychiatric
care, that I would recommend she be transferred to
a nursing home.

"I think it's the best thing all around," I said.

"Yes," said Miss Plover nervously, "it seems the
best thing."

What Mrs. Riesert had said was the truth. If that
was what you wanted—someone to love you for
yourself more than anyone else (what I wanted from
Hugh)—there was nothing worth living for once you
lost it. Better to be like Margaret, who wanted only
generalized charity, as much as she could get of it,
like a cow who can thrive on any kind of grass. She
would go on forever, whereas Mrs. Riesert, with no
one left who loved her more than anyone else (that
was chance; it could have been otherwise) would, with
my help, finally put herself out of a life she found
unbearable.

The two visits of the afternoon hung over the evening like a menace. I kept thinking that I was possibly
going to be responsible for an old woman's death. I
was surprised that no uncertainties arose; I was sure
she was doing the right thing. All the important de-
cisions I have made have seemed inevitable, not as if
I'd made a choice, but as if they were something I
had no choice about. And it would be up to Hugh
now. How strange it is, I thought, that within a month
I will know what my life will be. If he told me he
could not be with me, then that would be my life, that
loss would be at the center of it. And if he said he
would be with me, then that would be my life. So
it was not as if I were making a choice; it would be
something that would have to happen, as my father's

illness had happened, as I had acted as I had had to.

It was this evening I was frightened of, this evening and not the rest of my life. There was a fundraising cocktail party for Dominic Napoli. I had to go; it was impossible for me not to: I was one of Dominic's investments and had to be displayed, like a new park or a statue in front of a building. And I rather liked Dominic. He had always been kind to me; he was a decent man (decent was a beautiful word, I thought, that had been spoiled) and I would have been sorry to see him lose an election. Not that it much mattered to people's lives whether he was elected or someone else was. That was what I had learned; that was what I wanted to write in my report: it didn't matter, there was no way of predicting what would make people happy, no way of controlling it. You saw that people had enough to eat and wear; you gave them medicine if they were ill, and that was all you could do. The rest was perfectly random. People were happy, people were unhappy, for reasons no one could see, no one could do much about. Probably, I thought, if you expected very little you were relatively happy; if you expected a great deal you would end up disappointed, wanting to die. Mrs. Riesert wanted to die because she had had *it*—love, value, whatever it was—and no longer having it, no longer wanted to go on living. But old Mrs. Johnson, the black woman who lived in that horrible house with that appalling woman, enjoyed her ice cream every night and wanted to go on living. She did not care if she were specially treasured, uniquely loved. And Margaret Casey wanted to go on living. But Mrs. Riesert I had helped to die. It was Mrs. Riesert I was thinking of, but it was myself I meant. If I let Hugh love me like that, if I said to life, "This is what I want, only this; I can make do with nothing else," then I was immensely vulnerable. It was he I wanted, and even if he wanted me in return, it could not go on forever. At best I would be an old woman like Mrs. Riesert, weeping in the dark, wanting to die. Or, because it was all a

matter of chance, I could die first, and it would be
Hugh who would be like that, alone in his old age.
There is something wrong with life if it is like that, I
thought, and I remembered the word my father would
have used for it: error. I remembered Auden's poem
(I had started memorizing poems in the beginning,
when my father was first ill, but had given it up).
"Sept 1, 1939" was the name of the poem I thought of
now as I thought of myself, and Hugh, and Mrs.
Riesert:

> The windiest militant trash
> Important Persons shout
> Is not so crude as our wish:
> What mad Nijinsky wrote
> About Diaghilev
> Is true of the normal heart;
> For the error bred in the bone
> Of each woman and each man
> Craves what it cannot have,
> Not universal love
> But to be loved alone.

It was Nijinsky I always thought of first, and his
impossible leaps. And then the last lines: how we will
all come to grief because it is love we want, love
for our differentness, love for our uniqueness, rather
than charity, universal love, love because we simply
are, as everyone else *is,* the kind of love that is plenti-
ful, that is possible. And so I was opening myself up
to danger. I remembered when I had first come to
Ringkill and had sat on the toilet in the community
center, crying because I had not known any of the
dances, crying because I was frightened, because I had
taken a great risk. And I had thought of Margaret
then as I thought of her now: Margaret who had
never taken any risks, who had been content to grow
white and small and safe, under the wet blanket of
charity, under the dark bell of the familiar. Margaret
had written me another letter; she had told me that

her arthritis had gotten much worse, that she would
have to go to the Dominican home. Did I think that
was the right thing to do, she asked. That had been
several days ago. I had not answered. How did I
know what Margaret should do; it had nothing to do
with me.

Lavinia Hartman was at the door: she had said that
she and I should go together to the party since we
both hated that sort of thing. I had told Lavinia
about Hugh. She had been silent and sympathetic.

"You're a very interesting person, Isabel," she had
said.

"Me?" I said. What Lavinia meant, I thought, was
that she found me peculiar. She had thought it peculiar
that I had stayed with my father all those years, and
now she thought the business with Hugh was peculiar.
I had not thought it peculiar, but inevitable. Things
happened, and then you acted in a particular way.

"You spent eleven years in a totally *medieval* situation and then you get a man that everybody's been
trying to get away from his wife for years. I call that
interesting."

A new taste was in my mouth. It was jealousy.
There had been other women; Hugh had told me
that, but now they became real. I could see them.
They were near me, and I hated Hugh for that. Everyone must know about these women, if they lived
here, and they would have to live here, Hugh's practice was here. Everyone would think of me as someone at the end of a long line, someone who happened
to be at the right place at the right time, like someone who is the millionth person to cross the George
Washington Bridge and wins a hundred dollars. I
hated Hugh for that, and because I would have to see
his wife this evening.

"I have an offer for you," said Lavinia.

"Yes?"

"They've given me a new job. I have to open an
office for the aging. Very big stuff. Lots of money.
Lots of publicity."

"Congratulations."

"I'd like to have you as my assistant. You've done a damn good job, although no one around here will ever tell you. So, if you decide to stay here, I'd like to have you with me. You write a clear sentence. No one else I work with writes a clear sentence."

"I'd like the job, Lavinia, if I decide to stay."

"Good."

I had said, "If I decide to stay," whereas what I meant was, "If Hugh decides we will be together." It was up to him; it was entirely up to him.

I found Hugh's casual acknowledgment of me surprisingly painful. Knowing that we would see each other at the party we had planned to act coolly but to speak to one another. But when he greeted me as he might have greeted anyone he knew only slightly, I felt giddy, as if I had come to the bottom of a staircase and found one more step than my feet expected.

Liz walked up to me; I could tell that she was interested in the evening as a piece of theater. But her expression changed when she saw my obvious fear.

"Do you know which one she is?" she asked, handing me a glass.

"No."

"It would be sort of wonderful if you weren't involved. There she is," Liz said, cocking her head.

I suppose no one ever assumes such a clear identity as "the other woman"; all the complications of existence coalesce in a devastating syllable: HER. Hugh's wife was sitting behind a table; I was unable to see the bottom half of her body and afraid to look too closely at her face, but I could see she was like any middle-aged woman, like any Protestant middle-aged woman, neither thin nor fat, her hair in a pinkish blonde muffin, a careful helmet on her head.

She was not at all extraordinary looking, but it seemed impossible that she should be married to Hugh. I have always worked very hard to believe that looks are not important; it is a part of my heritage to find any visual evidence of questionable value. But it seemed wrong to think that Hugh should be married to *her*. And, of course, her wrongness was a great relief; it was a comfort to think that, at least in the precinct of the visually appropriate, he was more mine than hers; she could not menace me with beauty. Her looks would not invade and inhabit my life.

I stared at Hugh's back as he talked to someone I had never seen before. The back I loved, the beautiful, classical back I had run my fingers down, my tongue, my flushed, loving cheek. His back to me made me infinitely lonely. I felt as if I were looking at myself from a great distance; it was the way I had felt at my father's funeral. I tried to imagine my father here, but of course my father would never have come here, to a fund-raising party for a liberal Democrat. It occurred to me that in everything important he would consider me the enemy now. If he had to choose between me and Hugh's wife, he would, of course, choose her. I could imagine his back turned to me, as Hugh's back was turned to me, in a clear physical gesture of refusal, if he knew me as I was now. It was all I could think of, my father's back, my father's back to *me*, as I stood in this room of political drinkers who shook each other's hands like peddlers, like thieves. I was radically alone, and my sense of solitariness made me stupid. I wanted to leave, but the mechanics of my transportation were beyond me. I could not even move from the spot where Lavinia had left me.

How ludicrous it seemed that Lavinia thought me capable of promoting myself here for the job she had offered me, when all I could think of was my father's back. And I saw the backs of the priests who were there to support, perhaps predictably, the Democratic candidate. Priests' backs, the back of my lover, the back of my father.

I saw John Ryan whisper something to Hugh's wife. I could hear her talking angrily. But her language was perfectly abstract, perfectly foreign. I could see that she was beginning to walk toward me. It did not occur to me that I could move in any way to avoid her; it did not seem possible that I could in any way prevent her reaching me, her doing whatever it was she wanted to do.

"You're the one," she said, but not very loudly. "You're the little bitch."

She stood only an inch from me. She was pointing her finger.

"You think you're the first, but you're not the first, and you're not even the best-looking. You think you'll get him, but you won't. Do you know how many affairs he's been through? Fifteen. Twenty. Do you think I'm going to let you take him from me now?"

She paused. I said nothing. Was there something she expected me to say?

"You're a good person. John Ryan says you'll understand. He's helping me; he says you'll help me. I'm forty-eight years old. You're a young woman. You can get any man. I'm not young any more. He's throwing me away like a worn-out shoe. You don't want to be involved with that. You're a good person."

Someone was hitting my head; they were rapid blows, ringing blows. It was something heavy they were hitting me with, a hammer was it, or a rock? And then Hugh came up behind me. He put his hand on my shoulder.

"Don't do this, Cynthia. Isabel has nothing to do with you and me."

"You're a fool," she said to her husband. "You always have been."

"I don't want to hurt anyone," I said. But no one heard me; in any case no one looked at me.

"Come, Isabel," said Hugh, looking at his wife. "I'll take you home."

I could see that we had finally interested people. People turned deliberately away as I left the room with Hugh.

"I'm sorry, darling," he said, breaking the silence

in the car. "I'm sorry that had to happen. It won't be easy if you want me."

"It's all right," I said, with the politeness I reserved for strangers.

"Shall I come up with you?"

"No, you'd better go home and see to her."

"Right," he said, taking my chin in his hand. "Courage, then."

"Right," I said. It was the first time since I had known him that I felt only relief at his leavetaking.

In remembering those days I am grateful for one thing: there was a clear division between the time of my happiness and the time of its end. Hugh's wife did not exist for me until I actually saw her. Or she existed for me faceless and voiceless, so that when I tried to imagine her I became absorbed by the effort to construct a face for her, and her identity was diluted in my efforts at creation. There were whole mornings when my sole occupation was inventing her a blonde, then afternoons of cutting her hair, adding pounds and inches, taking them away. I had tried to imagine her as having the face of some famous person: Lady Bird Johnson or Gertrude Stein. But it was not frightening to contemplate theft from one whose face I had invented.

I was happiest with Hugh when I did not believe him seriously mine. The idea of ownership has always frightened me; I have never been able to understand collectors. I have always preferred the idea of longing for a Matisse to the idea of owning a Matisse. I have always preferred a sense of deprivation to a fear of loss. Perhaps this is unnatural; perhaps it is because I am the daughter of a father who assumed from the moment of my birth that I would give him my life. Behold the handmaid of the Lord, said Mary to the angel; be it done unto me according to Thy word. As a reward for the loss of a normal life, she became the mother of God. As the daughter of my father, I thought my fate as inevitable as hers, as

forcefully imposed, as impossible to question. I could
no more refuse my father than Mary could have refused the angel coming upon her, a finger of light.

There had been a gradual darkening in the background of my life with Hugh since he had first suggested leaving his wife. But after she had publicly
accused me of theft I began to accept the identity of
a thief. I lived as though I had been forced into a
hideout. It was February; the light was bad, as I
imagined the light to have been bad in wartime Lon-
don. I was afraid to go out of the house. It took a
new kind of courage for me to go about the business
of my daily life. I drove around the supermarket several times before I went in, trying to calculate the
possibility of meeting anyone who had been at the
party. In the years that I lived as the daughter of my
father I had always been greeted with reverence
and delight by shopkeepers, by people carrying groceries. I was the good daughter. I took care of my
father. I had nothing to fear. Faces were open to me,
for mine, they believed, was the face of a saint. Now
faces would be closed to me, and I myself would
learn to close my face. As the daughter of my father
I was above reproach. Can I explain the perfect
luxury of that position, so rare in our age? As the
daughter of my father I walked in goodness. I was
clothed in the white garment of my goodness, visibly
a subject of the Kingdom of God. As Hugh's woman
—there was no satisfactory word for what I would be
to him, I could not imagine myself his wife—I would
have to calculate each new face I came upon: would
it be open to me, or would it see me as the thief, to
be cast out?

As the daughter of my father I lived always in
sanctuary. Think of the appeal of sanctuary, the
pure shelter. As a child, when I read about the Middle Ages I was fascinated by the idea that there was
one automatic safe place, the simple inhabitance of
which guaranteed safety from accusing mobs and
ravening bandits. I had won myself a place there as

the daughter of my father. I had won sanctuary by giving up my portion, by accepting as my share far less than my share. I had bought sanctuary by giving up youth and freedom, sex and life. How beautiful, the neighbors said, as I wheeled my father around the garden. I was covered in goodness as if with a tougher skin. And now I was about to give it up. For love? For pleasure? It was as though I had been in a fire; I was exposed to faces that would close when they saw me, as they would close at the sight of the victim of a fire.

It took all my courage to allow Hugh to touch me the next day. He was working so hard above me, trying to bring me to him. But I could not be open to him in sex because I was so exposed by my connection to him. For the first time in my life, I simulated pleasure with a man, as I had read about women doing when they wanted things to be over. Hugh did not notice. He said I was a joy to please.

I had to spend the next day at the County Office Building going over the students' forms. I had never been called upon to exhibit the kind of bravery that makes one walk looking straight ahead, conscious of whispers. I became deferential to people I had previously been able to ignore, secretaries, minor commissioners I found myself next to in the elevator. I could not tell who had heard about my encounter with Hugh's wife. I had to assume that everyone knew everything and that I did not care. But I felt exposed among them, and I hated Hugh for having put me to a kind of test I had never dreamed of preparing for.

I sat at my desk moving papers around. But I could not concentrate; I kept waiting for someone to accuse me. I saw myself as the public culprit, the woman carried naked through the town, head shaved, borne aloft in a parody of the processions in honor of the Virgin. I heard John Ryan's door open, but it was not he who walked out. It was Hugh's wife. She was holding a file in her hand. Was it information about me? I looked down at the papers on my desk, think-

ing, with the perfect stupidity great fear can engender,
that if I did not look up at her she would not see
me. But she was walking over to my desk.

"May I have a word with you, Miss Moore?"

I believed she had the right to whatever of me she
wanted. I indicated the chair across from my own.
But I would not meet her eyes.

"I suppose you believe you're going to take my
husband."

"That's up to him."

She grabbed my wrist. It had not occurred to me
that she would touch me.

"You're a very, very sick person," she said. "There
is something very wrong with you."

I looked up at her, ready for her interpretation as
if she had just put me through a series of tests: blood,
stool, urine, as if she had access to information I had
suspected but had never been able to pin down. Why
did I believe her as I did? She was sitting very close to
me; she would not let go of my wrist.

"It must be disgusting to be as selfish as you are,"
she said.

I looked at her eyes. There was nothing extraordinary about them, except that they were the eyes of
anger. They were rather small eyes really. But her
face seemed to me like a kind of crust, covering
something molten. I did not dream of stopping her; not
for one second did I believe it in my power.

"What would your father say if he knew what kind
of life you lead?"

I thought of my father's back turned to me, my
father's finger pointing me away from him, my father's lips forming the words "culprit," "enemy."

"You didn't know my father," I said, looking at her
hands. Her nails were cut square; she wore no rings,
not even a wedding ring. They were broad hands; they
were rather short. She would not let go of my wrist.

"I know all about girls like you. You and your
friend Mrs. Ryan. Catholic girls with holy pictures of
virgin martyrs. They make perverts out of you, don't

they? Your friend Mrs. Ryan is a filthy pervert,
and you're just as bad. You couldn't wait for your
father to die so you could get a man between your
legs. There's something very wrong with you. There's
something disgusting and unhealthy. People like you
aren't fit for normal life."

I was sinking lower and lower. She was perfectly
right about me; I could see that. I had wanted my
father to die. I could see myself standing by his bed-
side, praying that he would die. Before I was too old;
before it was too late. For what? What she had said
was right. She knew what I had dreamed of. A man
in my bed.

I had murdered my father, and she had exposed
me; I believed she was right to do so. She was telling
me the truth of my life. She had seen what no one
else had been able to see, what I had hidden, protected as I was in the sanctuary of my life as my
father's daughter. But my father was dead. Something
slipped in me then, some solid bone dislodged.

My father was dead. I knew what that meant now.
I was entirely unsafe, entirely alone.

Now pain was all around me; I was drowning in
pain. I remembered my father's face when he had
opened the door and found me in bed with David
Lowe. How absurdly my breasts had bobbed as I sat
up. How horrified my father had been to see them.
And it came to me, with perfect clarity, that my father
was dead; he was not with me; I would never see him
again. And I had wanted him to die.

She was still talking.

"You want to be a good person. I know you are a
good person at heart. Everything John Ryan has told
me about you leads me to believe that you are a good
person."

Yes, I had been a good person. No one had been
able to question it when I was the daughter of my father. It was my great treasure, my visible goodness.
And I had been about to give up my treasure. For

what? For a man in my bed. I had not understood
my life.

But this woman had given me back my life. Or she
would give it back to me if I would give her what she
wanted, if I would simply not steal her husband. I
thought of my father's favorite phrase from the *Chan-
son de Roland:* "*Chrétiens ont droit; païens ont tort.*"
That was my error. I had tried to live like a pagan. I
had been entirely selfish.

I was swimming in pain, but I would have to dive
down lower still. I had let go my treasure, and I must
go down to redeem it. I would go down as far as I
had to to have them say again, "You are a good person." Priests in rooms, and my father, and strangers.

"I'm sure you'll be much happier in the kind of life
you were brought up for," said Hugh's wife, rising
to leave.

"Thank you," I said. I was terribly far away. I
was sinking lower and lower. People walked around
me, but I had no connection with them.

I heard someone calling my name. It seemed impossible that anyone could call my name, that I should
hear them. I looked up; Liz was standing beside my
desk.

"Hello, Liz. What are you doing here?"

"John said you were in some kind of trouble."

"Oh, no, everything's fine."

"What have they done to you, Isabel? Don't sit
there like a zombie. Let's get out of here. Let's go
home."

I allowed Liz to lead me to her car. I sat in silence
as she drove. And then I turned to her, because I
had to say what I had not, to my almost incalculable
loss, yet sufficiently acknowledged.

"My father is dead."

"Yes," said Liz, "I know."

And then it broke, the terror. I was entirely alone.
I wept like an animal. My mouth was open. I rocked
and rocked.

"Isabel, you have to go inside," I heard Liz say.

She took me in and made me drink something. She laid me in my bed.

"I want to die. I only want to die," I kept saying. I rolled around, back and forth, from one side of my body to the other, as if the motion would make the pain stop.

Liz grabbed me very hard by the shoulders. "Well, goddamn it, I'm not going to let you," she said. She held me very tightly and began rocking me. I gave myself up. There was nothing left. I would sleep; I no longer cared enough to fight sleep.

"You're a good person."

"I don't want to hurt anyone."

That was what I heard when I swam up from sleep, and so I would fall back again: anything was better than that.

Hugh had opened me up to reproach. When I was with my father no one would have dared to speak to me as that woman had. I saw myself cruelly naked, my buttocks soft and white in the air, thrashing about the bed with him. Pleasure, we had called it. And now I dove into another sleep, into anything to get away from it. He had deceived me; I could not forgive him his deceit.

He was holding my hand when finally I acknowledged that I would have to waken.

"Darling," he said, when he saw I was awake. He held me; he held my head against his shoulder. I let my neck go limp as if it were broken. I drew my soft flesh in, inside my skeleton, so it would not be accessible to him. And myself I drew away, so that finally he laid me back down on the pillows, he too no longer wanting contact.

The inside of my mouth was so dry that I felt conscious of each distinct tooth, dry and thick against my lips, an elephant's teeth, enormous, yellow. I bit my lips; I could taste the skin of them, salty, bloody, almost cold.

"I'm terribly, terribly sorry that you had to go

through all that," he said, but not touching me. "I've left her. We'll be together now."

It was interesting, I thought, but it had nothing to do with me. It had been a mistake; it was unfortunate, I would tell him, but it was not too late. I didn't care what I said to him; I could say one thing; I could say another; it wouldn't matter. He had nothing to do with my life. His eyes were full of pain and expectation; that was a real look; I knew he was feeling something. But I felt nothing. I floated away from him, apart from him. I watched the look in his eyes as if I had never met him.

"You must go back to your wife," I said. "We've been very wrong to hurt her like that."

Now he was weeping; now he was holding me. I could feel him clinging to me, asking things of my body. But there was nothing I could give him.

"We are both good people," I said. "We mustn't hurt anyone. We mustn't be selfish."

He was weeping and holding me. I could feel his tears on my shoulder through the material of my nightgown, on the bone where his eyes were resting. His tears were angry now; they came like coughs. The coughs were painful, I could tell. I was very cold, but apart from that I felt nothing. Soon, I thought, he will go away.

"But I won't give you up," he said, holding my head in his hands.

"I've already given you up, though."

I said it straightforwardly; I said it slowly. That was the truth, and now it was over. I got up out of the bed, letting his head fall onto the pillows. He was still sobbing. I thought, with some interest, that his weeping had lasted longer than I had imagined it would.

"Isabel, you're just upset because of Cynthia. You mustn't let her do this to you. You have to understand her. She's thought of herself as someone who started out with nothing, who got things through hard work and planning, so she's always thought she could do anything because she had nothing originally to lose. She always thought she could act worse than anyone else because her life had no bottom to it. But darling, you mustn't let her do this to *you*."

"She was right. We were doing wrong. We were hurting people."

"And what about now? Don't you think you're hurting me? And yourself?"

"We're strong; we can take it. But Cynthia's not as strong as we are; she hasn't had those lucky accidents. She doesn't look like me; she hasn't read what I've read or made the same jokes. But she easily could have. And then you'd have loved her as much as you do me, so it wouldn't matter."

"You're not making sense," said Hugh, with dry anger.

"You see, we've been given these gifts—looks, intelligence, charm—and what did we do with them? Used them to snare each other, not to make people happy, people who don't have as much as we do."

"Isabel, you're very upset," he said, coming near me.

"I don't want you to touch me," I said, but only as information; there was no emotion in my voice.

"You mustn't make any decision now."

"I've made a decision," I said. "I don't want to go on being selfish. I'm going to try and make someone happy, as I did my father."

"But me," said Hugh, "you could make me happy."

I smiled, as if he had missed a simple point.

"But many people could make you happy. Many people want to, because you have gifts. If it's not me, it will be someone else. Even your wife. When I was with my father, you see, I was the only one who could make him happy, when he was so ill like that."

"But you are the only one who can make me happy. And your father's dead."

That was what I had learned in all those sleeps; my father was dead; I would never see him again. Shocks of pure pain ran over my shoulders. But I had

learned, too, that I did not want to be selfish; I was
a good person; I did not want to hurt anyone; I had
never hurt anyone before. I would take away someone's pain as I had done with my father's.

"You mustn't think like that, Hugh. It will only
make you unhappy. I'm going to live with Margaret
Casey now; we must stop seeing each other."

Hugh slapped me, twice. The force of the slaps
moved me across the floor.

"Your father's dead, you're not dead. You have a
life. Why do you want to take your life?"

"I'll call you before I leave," I said, handing him
his jacket.

He was silent as he left. Probably, I thought ab-
stractly, he is in a great deal of pain.

XIII

It only amused me that Liz brought me suppers every night, suppers in covered dishes as if I were an invalid. Domesticity was not automatic to Liz: each act was considered, dwelt upon, and then decided. I could see myself in the eye of Liz's mind, sleeping or reading magazines, eating yogurt and putting the containers under the bed. It made me laugh to see Liz try, in the course of one of her attempts at sprightly conversation (a throwback, I could tell, from the way nuns told you to behave at a sickbed), to get the yogurt containers out without seeming to reproach me. I did not like this side of Liz: apologetic, tactful, hinting. She had even called Eleanor. How I disliked the idea of Liz and Eleanor on the phone to each other, talking about me, united in their concern for me, asking each other, "What can we do?"

I wished they could see how far I was beyond them; I wished I could see them acknowledge there was nothing they could do. I wished they would not come near me. I ate the meals Liz cooked; sometimes when Liz left I took the whole dish into bed with me and ate it (beef stew, macaroni and cheese) with a teaspoon. But Liz needn't have bothered; I would have been just as happy with yogurt or cookies. I was eating a lot, and I no longer cared about the flesh on the back of my legs, about my waist and how to trim it. My body had caused me nothing but trouble:

wanting David Lowe, wanting John Ryan, wanting
Hugh. There had been a long trail of grief beginning
with my father's illness and stretching to Hugh's wife
pointing her finger an inch away from my face.

"You're a good person," she had said. Once I had
had that, I was good: I was making my father feel
better. Every act had meaning, every gesture signified.
Now I had nothing, and if I had gone with Hugh, I
would have had less than nothing. Moments of pleasure, flashes of surprise, days looking at views when it
was not scenery I wanted, or the touch of fingers, but
that knowledge: I am a good person; I am doing good.

Pleasure. In the last few months I had enjoyed
things immensely. But that was because I had been
in error about myself, about the nature of things. I
knew now that the truth of my life was that buzzing
pain, black, purple, at the back of my skull; I was
alone; my father was dead; I would never see him
again.

I had enjoyed things immensely, but that was in
error; it was something you went through, a town you
spent a night in because you had taken a wrong turning. But I was beyond pleasure now; beyond loss. I
had loved my father; I had loved Hugh, had said of
them both: only this person and no other. But I would
not live like that again. I would love whoever most
needed loving, and then go on, for there would always
be someone else, anyone else, if it was not pleasure
you cared for.

I could not explain this even to Eleanor, for Eleanor
had wanted pleasure. She had given me blue-and-
white cups, a silver bowl with holly. Tricks to make
your eyes look bigger, your cheekbones higher, your
breasts as firm as a teenager's. And postcards of
Matisses, painting the light in the south of France.
This is what Eleanor gave me; it was what Eleanor
lived by. Her life was soft, and warm, and luxurious.
If there were no avocados on the market that day, Eleanor was unhappy. And if there were one persimmon

left, that was a miracle. Why had I never perceived the shallowness of that life?

And Liz. I thought of Liz, pounding posts into the ground like a lumberjack, proud of her house, proud of her children, proud of her boyish body and her good manners. How could I explain to Liz what I knew would make me happy: the knowledge, as cooling and refreshing as slipping into a cave in the middle of the hottest day of summer, that I am a good person.

They had been kind to me; they would go on being infinitely kind to me. They would try to understand. I could see the sadness of Eleanor's face, the restraint on Liz's as she tried to hold back her sharp comments. "You're very tired; you're upset," Eleanor would say. Liz would have fancier words for it, longer words, but the meaning would be the same: there's something wrong with you, but you'll get over it.

That was not right. There was nothing wrong with me, and I knew with my old, childhood certainty that I would go on being like this. I was not going to change. I knew that it was Margaret I must go to; only there would I be safe from Hugh, from Liz and Eleanor and their talk about "life." They did not understand my life, and they had caused me to misunderstand it. It was not possible for me to be like other people; I was not like other people. I was not satisfied with what they called "life."

I would take care of Margaret; I would devote myself to the person I was least capable of loving. I would absorb myself in the suffering of someone I found unattractive. It would be a pure act, like the choice of a martyr's death which, we had been told in school, is the only inviolable guarantee of salvation. If you died for the faith you would be guaranteed salvation. And when Margaret died, I would simply go on to someone else. I would be the person I wanted to be, beyond loss, above reproach.

At least Liz and Eleanor would listen kindly to what I was saying. How brutal Hugh had been when

I tried to explain things to him the night he came over for a drink. How he had assaulted me with his emotions—anger, fear, sorrow, and then anger once again. He had picked me up by the shoulders; there were marks from his fingers where he had shaken me.

Did he think it would make me feel something if he kept saying, "You're taking everything I most love and killing it"? All his appeals were to our past, which we had spent, I reflected, mainly in bed. How wrong he was, how foolishly off the mark. He might have been speaking in a foreign language when he kept shaking me and telling me to remember things; it was like a frantic litany in some kind of gibberish: Remember putting perfume between your legs, remember the air on the top of the mountain, remember how the holly looked in the silver bowl. "You like all that," he kept saying, as if to convince himself that I was the same person. "I knew you, you loved those things," he said.

He was terribly slow, really; it was making me tired. With Eleanor or Liz you could talk about the danger of pleasure: St. Francis threw himself into a bed of roses to avoid looking at a beautiful woman; St. Thomas More wore a hair shirt because he was too fond of his wife. They had known what pleasure could lead to: putting yourself in the center of the universe, your own body blocking the vision of God like an eclipse, like the moon off its proper orbit.

I said to Hugh, "I liked those things disproportionately. I made mistakes. I made people unhappy. I made my father ill; I nearly ruined your marriage with my selfishness."

Always, he responded with facts, as if facts were the whole of it.

"You didn't *make* your father ill. People get strokes because they've been building up for a long time, not because of a sudden shock. That's only in the movies."

The man of science, I thought contemptuously. Nothing, there was nothing he could make me feel; it had been a mistake, a bout of madness, like what happened to those people in the Middle Ages who jumped out of windows because of something in the rye crop.

"And what about your children? I would have left them fatherless. For my own pleasure. Explain that in terms that are calculated *to make me feel good about myself*."

"I know that I love you, that you gave me my life back, that when I was with you life seemed possible and full of promise. I'm leaving Cynthia now, anyway. I could never forgive her for what she did to you. So don't think you're saving my marriage by leaving me. I've moved into a room on Salvo Avenue."

"You must go back to her," I said, like an abbess, like someone very old. "You must try to love her again. You must have loved her once."

"I didn't."

"You married her," I said, cold as coins, with logic.

"I married her because she told everyone I was going to, because everyone thought I'd asked her. She worked for my family, and I'd gone to bed with her and then she said the only reason I wouldn't marry her was because she wasn't pretty enough and I was a womanizer, because she wasn't rich enough and I was a snob. She made me feel I ought to make up to her for things. When she had the miscarriages, she said I only wanted to leave her because she couldn't have children; when we had the children she said I only wanted to leave her because she was getting old. I gave up fighting her; she was stronger than I was, with all those lacks. I was never any match for her, with all her deprivations."

"And now you've lived with her for years, so why leave her?"

"Because I know you. Because I know how happy it's possible to be."

"Happiness isn't everything."

"What is?" said Hugh. It was a stupid parody of

conversations I had had with Father Mulcahy, with my father.

"Being a good person. Not hurting people."

"But you're hurting me."

"You'll survive. Think what a wonderful thing it will be—you can love your wife, not in the way you've loved me or someone else (I was remembering even now that I had not been the first), but you'll be at peace. There'll be no one to reproach you; you'll never have to reproach yourself. And you'll never be afraid any more; there'll be no fear of losing anything."

He slapped me again. This was the second time, I noticed coolly, as if it had happened to someone else.

"You're a coward. That's all you are, with your Catholic school virtue, and your pat little heart, and your sense of morals like a gold watch you won in Catechism class."

I let him go on like that. I had made my decision. I had already written to Margaret to say that I would take care of her, that she would not have to go to the Dominican home. Let him go on or not. Just as he liked.

"What you want, what you've always wanted, is for everyone to say what a good girl you are. Taking care of your father, everyone must have said it. You walked on the street and everyone said it: Imagine what she's done for her poor father."

He was right; I had liked that, that people had said that about me in the street. Extraordinary, they had said, what I did for my father. But that was not it, that was not all of it. I thought of holding my father's foot, of having him scratch my head as we were reading.

"But I loved him," I said, angry that I had responded at all to Hugh.

"Yes," said Hugh, "you loved him and that was why I've always thought you did the right thing, because you loved him and still love him. But you don't love Margaret and I don't love Cynthia."

"That's the beauty of it," I said, thinking for a moment that I could make him understand. "If we can love the people we think are most unlovable, if we can get out of this ring of accident, of attraction, then it's a pure act, love; then we mean something, we stand for something."

He slapped me again. Force. I thought of martyrs, bullied for telling the truth. He was simply a bully. Why didn't I see it before in him?

"It's like tying a living man to a dead man and sending them out on a raft," he said.

"You don't understand, you will never understand," I said to him.

It was over. I could feel him move away from me, could feel him stop trying to win me.

"And you'll go back to the Church now?" he said.

"I'm going to see Father Mulcahy."

"What will he tell you? What's he ever been able to tell you?"

"Something."

"Bless me father for I have sinned. I have loved and been loved. For this I am heartily sorry."

"Don't be vulgar," I said. This ridicule of the Church by nonbelievers was always in bad taste. They always used the wrong words, put things in the wrong context, mocked at the obvious when it was the hidden that was vulnerable.

"Your father is dead. So you'll make yourself dead. To get back to him. I can't win against that."

"You'll never understand," I said, the pain, the buzzing starting, for I had forgotten and now remembered: my father was dead; I would never see him again. "I'll always love you," he had said, but he had left me.

"You'll find someone else. Someone who will suit you better," I said, feeling old, much older than Hugh, as if I were his teacher and he had confessed that he had, from the back of the classroom, loved me, and I had pointed out that sitting next to him was a pretty girl with blonde curls (a young girl, a silly girl) who

blushed when he passed her. It was delicious: that
relief, that lightness. It was over.

The fire whistle usually woke me. I thought of the
Angelus that morning, but I was too tired to remember it. That was one of my father's romances: peas-
ants stopping their work at noon in the fields to pray.
Yes, it was a nice idea, a pretty idea, but I was too
tired to let it move me. I opened the refrigerator.
There was nothing in it but half a lemon drying on a
plate. I had stopped getting milk: it soured. I used
powdered milk for my coffee now. Cups littered the
counter, stuck to the top so you had to jog them before they would let go. I opened a bag of cookies; I
sat down on the couch and ate until there were none
left. They made my mouth feel sore and sticky, heavy
and unclear. But I went on eating them because that
was what I wanted to do.

I went over to the desk and picked up the files on
the cases I had visited. I had to write that report: it
was due in two weeks. There was something I had
wanted to say, about the nature of love, about happiness, how it was transient, random. But it was too
much trouble now to bring the idea forward to the
clear front of my brain, to find the right words for it.
I no longer cared: people, governments, all looking
for happiness. I saw it would all come to grief in the
end. Grief and loss.

It would make no difference whether I said something about life, about happiness, or whether I said
nothing. I would do whatever was easiest, whatever
would be over soonest. But I was too tired to do it just
then. I had collected the data from ten young students, but that was before it happened. *It: it* meant
that woman pointing her finger, knowing in my body
that my father was dead, that I would never see him
again, that I was not a good person. I lay down in the
bed I had just got out of. My nightgown was beginning to smell fishy but I was too tired to change it.

I awoke again two hours later. I thought I would

brush my teeth. I ought to go out. I would call Father Mulcahy. I would drive down there and be there after supper.

"Your voice sounds funny, pal."

"I've not been feeling well. I've been awfully tired. I want to go to Confession."

"There's priests up there," he said quickly.

"But I want to go to you."

"It's the Sacrament that matters, not the celebrant."

"But I want to go to you."

He could never hold out against me. "OK, honey," he said, but I could tell I had frightened him. But it was he who had to forgive me: he was my father's best friend.

I was too tired to drive down; I would take the train, and it was so tiring to have to wait for a bus to the station, I would take a taxi. I looked forward to sleeping all the way down on the train; there was nothing that was worth seeing out the windows. I bought some bars of chocolate from the machines in the station.

If people would just leave me alone. What I needed was sleep; what I needed was privacy. I didn't tell Eleanor I was going to see Father Mulcahy. Eleanor would have wanted me to come into the city for dinner, would have cooked one of her interminable meals, one very like the other, really, all meals were. What I wanted was quick foods now, foods you did not have to wait for or work over. It was a great luxury: eating what you wanted, sleeping all day if you wanted. Those would be my pleasures. No one would be hurt by them; I was tired of hurting people. And when you were taking care of an invalid you could sleep when they slept; I had done it with my father; I would do it with Margaret. I had made my father happy, whom I loved, whom I would never see again (there was the pain: I closed my eyes); now I would make Margaret happy, whom I had never loved, whom I had hated. I would make myself love

her now. Hugh I had loved, but that was over; that
was one of the mistakes I had made. I would not hurt
people now. I would sleep.

It was dark when I got out of the subway; my
mouth was sore and metallic. I had known this stop;
this walk up the hill from the subway. I thought of
stopping at Milt's for an English muffin and some tea
(I was thinking how greasy the butter made my fingers, how I wanted to lick it off but didn't dare, never
dared), but there would be all that talk, all the questions: where what you been; what's happened to you.
Unbearable. I would just keep walking up the hill to
the rectory.

Mrs. Keeney answered the door this time. I had not
thought of her, had forgotten to fear her. There she
stood, yellowing, reproachful. All the years of her life
had done nothing to invent in her what she had not
been born with: generosity, understanding, beauty.
No, there were the same dead eyes as always, saying,
"I'll get what you haven't given me."

"He's very bad," Mrs. Keeney said.

"What do you mean?"

"The drink. He's been very bad the last months,
since you've been gone, but today he took on something terrible. The pastor's talking about sending him
away to that home where he was before."

Where Margaret sent him, I thought. I remembered old men shuffling around in pajamas, and the
shock of it when my father had told me they were
priests.

"I'd like to see him," I said, through a syrup of
hate. How I would have liked to hammer Mrs. Keeney
into the ground until her awful face was buried. It was
no more than she deserved. Margaret, too. But it's
only an accident, I remembered. I could as easily love
them if they'd looked different, said different things.

She showed me into Father Mulcahy's office. When
he saw me in the room, he began crying. It was a
drunk's crying, blubbery, wobbly, loose. It meant
nothing; it did nothing to me, it signified nothing of

the depths of his heart. I had wanted him to forgive me; I had come to him for help. Damn you, I thought, looking at the old man crouched over his desk, crying. Damn you, I came to you for help.

"How are you, pal? I'm not too good myself. You're looking good."

The old Irish. Flattery. Treachery. Sympathy. Lies.

"I want to go to Confession."

"I've told Father Dolan. He'll open up the church and hear your Confession. We have to keep it locked now; the colored kids steal everything. He'll do it for you, honey."

"But I want you."

"I'm not well tonight, pal. I can't do it for you to-night."

"But you have to."

He looked up weakly, finished.

"Are you in a state of grace?" he said, drunk, but still a priest.

"No."

"Then you must go to Confession. Your soul is in mortal danger."

"I'll only go to you."

He began sobbing, a child's sobs. His teeth were bluish in the artificial light.

"I can't," he said. "I don't want to know what you've done. God will forgive you. Don't be afraid! He is infinitely merciful. Take the Sacrament of Penance."

"I'll only go to you."

It did not move me, his tears, his weakness; I had to confess to him; only he could forgive me.

He was sobbing now, he was saying, "I failed you. I knew you were falling away, and I couldn't save you."

This was nothing, his sorrow, his regret. I would make him listen; he had to hear everything.

"If I get hit by a car, I'll go straight to hell; it will be on your conscience."

He couldn't lift his head up; he was crying out for

me to help him. But I would do nothing for him until
he gave me what I wanted.

Suddenly, all the color was gone from his face; he
was falling out of his chair. He looked fragile, but he
made an enormous noise falling. I hated him, and the
brown whiskey that spread on the carpet.

Mrs. Keeney opened the door. She must have been
listening.

"What in the name of God," she said. "He's done
for. The doctor said his heart couldn't stand much
more of this."

I didn't care. I wanted him to help me; he was a
priest; he was not supposed to care who the individual
sinner was; he was not supposed to say, "Don't tell
me." He was supposed to offer forgiveness to the
repentant. And I was full of repentance. And he was
my father's only friend. And he did nothing. Coward,
I thought, helping to pick the old man up as I might
have lifted an old tire out of the water. That was
what Hugh had called me. But I was not a coward: I
had chosen my penance before I had been given forgiveness. I would never refuse anyone who needed
me; I would not fail, as Father Mulcahy had failed,
passing out, collapsing in his chair when I had needed
him to help me. The last thing I was was a coward.

"I'm taking the next train home," I said to the
young priest who was carrying Father Mulcahy upstairs.

"Will you call an ambulance, Miss," he said, with
exasperation, his face red with the strain of carrying
the old man.

I called the operator; I gave the address. Then I
disappeared down the subway. I was falling through a
hole in my own body. I am completely alone, I kept
saying to myself. When I sat down on the train, I
closed my eyes.

I would finish the report at Margaret's. I could not
bear to see the people in the office again, after what
they had seen, that red face, gaping, fragile, and then
triumphant, that finger pointing. And John Ryan.

Hugh and Liz had said he was behind it all. He had put Cynthia up to it, for revenge, because I had refused him. It didn't matter; it was all for the best. It made me look at things; it made me face the truth. How foolish I seemed to myself now, enjoying Hugh, enjoying life, as if I were not who I were, as if life were not as it was. It was certainly better this way: this truth. But I could not bear to see John's grinning face, his coming over to me and punching me on the shoulder as if it were all a good joke, as if he had put a frog in my bed or let the air out of my tires. Liz said she would leave him now, but I did not believe her. It was all to the good. But I would never forgive him.

Margaret had written back almost immediately. Her handwriting was almost entirely unreadable now, but she had said, "I never want to be a burden, but if you need somewhere to go, I'm sure your father would have wanted me to take you in."

I would not even gain her gratitude; she would never even thank me. But that was the challenge: I would love someone outside the accidents of loving, the accidents of loss. I would go up there immediately. There was very little for me to pack. I put my clothes in two valises, hating the feel of them against my fingers. I called Liz and told her what I was doing; I called Eleanor. They both told me to wait. No, I said, I would not wait. I called the landlord, who said I would have to pay another month's rent; it was not fair, he said, to do things so abruptly. I agreed; I said I would pay.

XIV

I was the only one to get off the bus at Ramona. For five hours I had let a bus drive me from Ringkill with my two suitcases of clothes. The rest—the other, solider possessions, the Persian rugs from Dover Road, the silver bowl that Eleanor had given me—I had left in the attic of Mr. Cohen's house. I could have left them with Liz or with Lavinia. But I wanted to get away. I wanted to disappear. To connect myself by things I had cared for to people I had loved would be a great danger. Love and beauty: caring for those accidents as if they somehow mattered more than anything had brought me to this grief, this pain that buzzed at the back of my skull.

But I was away from that now; I had cut myself off from the danger. There would be no more talk or thought of love that could be gained or lost by accidents, by jokes or the angle of a shoulder. I would love Margaret now as God loved His creatures: impartially, impervious to their individual natures and thus incapable of being really hurt by them. My father had once looked at me and said, "I love you more than I love God. I love you more than God loves you." I was six; I was about to make my First Communion; I knew my Catechism as other children knew the exploits of cartoon characters. I had studied it with a pure, delectable absorption. That absorption gave me the right, at six, to turn to my father and say, "You mustn't say that. It's a sin." I had been right; it was wrong, what he had said, loving me more than God. I could not love with God's intensity. But I would choose His mode: the impartial, the invulnerable, removed from loss.

The Ramona bus station had television sets that could be activated for half an hour by a quarter. People sat in front of them as if they had no choice but to be where they were. The sets flickered and buzzed; the images rode on top of one another like slow, marred waves, but no one moved to correct the pictures. They sat before the buses, their eyes perfectly dead: drunk, drugged or merely aged. I saw them move from set to set although all the pictures seemed to me identical. They moved from set to set because they had nowhere else to go, and I hated them for that; I wanted to shoot into them as a crowd, to deprive them of their lives in some violent way. I wanted them to disappear under some confusing smoke cloud that would lift to disclose their vanishing. They had no sense of style; they had no manners. Margaret had no manners. But I would help Margaret now.

One old woman, whose hair had patches the color of egg yolks, sat in front of one of the television sets reading a book. Her eyes looked as though they had been cut from their moorings; they focused on nothing; they merely sat, two jellies in their confining sockets. She put the book down on the seat next to her. I looked at the cover; it was *Pride and Prejudice*. The old woman caught my eye and laughed like an animal.

I thought how easy it would be to kill a woman like that. You could lure her with coffee and doughnuts and then poison her or bash her skull in. To watch her die would be perfectly enjoyable. I called a cab.

It was the end of March, the middle of winter. Snow had lost all its appeal and was only a reproach or a stubborn threat; it would never leave: there would be no change of weather.

The cab driver pointed out Lancer's box factory. "It's the heart of the city," he said.

But what had that building to do with the heart? Liz and I used to make jokes about it. Margaret worked in a box factory; we had laughed at that. But the factory building loomed above the yellow car I sat in, blotting out humor or affection or regard. It was the first time I had looked carefully at a factory, as if it had something to do with me. Now it was part of my life. Perhaps one day I would work there. I had got twenty-five thousand dollars for the house. It would disappear one day; and I would work in a factory, like other people, faces I had seen in movies, lives I had read about. And why not? I was not different; I was not extraordinary. I could work at the manufacture of paper boxes as well as any other person. You could do anything if you gave up thinking that it mattered what you did, if you gave up caring for one thing more than any other.

"If Lancer's factory moved out, the town may as well close up shop," said the cab driver, going through streets where high Victorian trees looked down on houses that had once belonged to bankers, where dusty black children now played with forlorn, battered toys. I imagined the women who had lived in those houses, and the contempt they would have for the people living there now. As if they could stop life happening. I imagined women polishing dark furniture. As if they could hold back ruin. As if they could stop loss. My father is dead, I thought, I will never see him again. The driver turned a corner. Here the houses were smaller and less stable, but they were cared for with a fierce, unimaginative pride. Catholics, I thought, seeing a Virgin standing in half a bathtub on one of the lawns. The houses of servants. Frightened of grandeur, frightened of the banker around the corner. And they were right to be frightened; they were right to build their small, unimportant houses, risking very little in design. These houses had not changed; they looked the same as the day they had been built. And the big, beautiful houses had given themselves over.

The driver stopped in front of Margaret's house. Its façade was a faded, false-looking brick. The mortar had aged into a sullen gray; the roof too had grayed as if by conspiracy. The lawn had yellowed with the yellowing snow. A pink rubber mat in front of the gray door said Welcome in elaborate black script. I pressed the doorbell.

Margaret peeked out from behind the curtain as if she were expecting a murderer. She opened the door only halfway. Encumbered by my baggage, I had to walk in sideways, bumping my suitcases behind my knees. I would have to embrace Margaret now; I could not remember ever embracing her before. Margaret's skin had a dampish feel, even through her clothes; her hair gave off a sour, closed odor. And this was the person I would now love. I shivered, and then apologized to Margaret. I said the open door was causing a draught.

"I suppose you'll want a cup of tea," said Margaret, "although don't expect any cake. I can't afford cake. Some days I just live on bouillon."

"You won't have to worry about that now."

"Yes, and you'll buy the kinds of things *you* want. Suppose I want to eat different things? You never think about me."

"I'll buy whatever you want."

"I'll show you your room," said Margaret, leaning heavily on the bannister.

My room faced one in the house next door. I could see a woman watching television with a young child. When she saw me looking at her she snapped her shade down angrily.

There was a single bed. On the mattress were two white sheets, folded, two gray blankets and a striped pillow. There was a cardboard dresser with blue and yellow birds printed on its surface. It went badly with the pink roses of the wallpaper. This would be my room now. It didn't matter, the wallpaper and the dresser. These things ceased to matter if you no longer believed they mattered.

I came downstairs and sat across from Margaret at the unsteady kitchen table.

"I'll only charge you what I charged the woman who lived here before," said Margaret. "She was a nurse. Ninety dollars a month. I can't afford to keep you for charity."

Charity. That was what I thought I would do for Margaret; I would love her; I would save her. And Margaret thought I had come because I needed a room. I would let her think that. The greatest love is to love without wanting anything in return, even an acknowledgment of loving. And this is how I would love.

There was no food in Margaret's refrigerator, only a bottle of brown medicine and a quart of milk. That refrigerator was meant as a reproach. I understood and accepted it.

"Where's the grocery store?" I said.

"Well, there's one around the corner, but they're Jewish. We go to Farrel's. Farrel's are from the parish."

"Where is Farrel's?"

"About half a mile."

"It's a long walk with groceries."

"Don't think you can change everything just because you came to live here."

"I'm sorry. I didn't mean to imply that."

"Don't think you can have everything your own way."

"I don't."

I would say anything so long as Margaret would stop. Her words were mallet blows on top of my soft, breakable skull. This was the person I had decided to love.

"You always did. You always got your own way with your father. That was your problem. What you need is someone to cut you down to size. You always had big ideas about yourself."

"I'm sorry," I said. Margaret was right. Once I had thought I was the most important person in the world. Now I knew I was no more important than anyone else. You could lay down your life for your friend with ease if you did not believe your life to be any more important than his.

"I'll go to the store now. What do you want for dinner, Margaret?" I said. I only wanted to sleep.

"Chops and cabbage. Lamb chops. That's what I like. Get that. Don't start buying fancy stuff. And don't go to Baumgartner's because you're too lazy to go to Farrel's. I'll know where you went. Everyone will know."

Everyone will know. What did anyone know about me, in this town where I had never been? What did Margaret know about me? What had she been able to find out? David Lowe, John Ryan. Hugh: my sex had brought disaster with it. My sex was infecting; my sex was a disease. But now I could make up for it. All that sorrow had come about because I had been selfish, because I had wanted too much.

The woman in the grocery store had a face the color of egg whites. The air in the store was amnesiac; I could not remember why I was there or what I was doing. I circled the store several times before I could find the bottles of vinegar. But I did not ask for help. I would *make* my mind clear. This was my home now; this was the sort of thing I would be doing from now on.

I was the only customer in the store. The woman behind the counter watched every move I made, as if she expected me to slip a weapon from my handbag. But she let me stand in front of the meat counter for a full five minutes before she would come to the back of the store and acknowledge me.

"D'ya want something?" she said in her flat, upstate voice.

"Lamb chops."

The woman reached into the showcase and put two chops on the counter.

. "Fine," I said. "They're fine." I did not look at the meat.

The woman wrapped the meat in pinkish-brown paper and stared at me, tying the string as if she were trying to think of some way to cheat me.

The two bags of groceries I had bought made me want to sit on the sidewalk and weep. How could food be so heavy? The cans on the bottom of the bag cut ridges into my hips; they made my belly vulnerable and oversized. My forearms ached; my fingers felt as if they had been stitched together. I opened the bag of chocolate chip cookies and ate two, for pleasure, or the memory of pleasure. I didn't like the taste; it made my palate heavy and dull. But I went on eating. It was a way of getting through this difficult time, this difficult walk.

Margaret began unpacking the groceries as soon as I put them down on the counter.

"What's this? These cookies are half gone. What happened to them?"

I let shame cover me like a blanket of steam.

"I ate them on the way home," I said, in a soft, bad-child's voice.

"What?"

"I ate them on the way home."

"Mother of God, you can't even control your appetites to that degree."

My father's face flashed into my mind: his face at the door and my breasts, naked and exposed to his gaze when he found me that day with David Lowe. I was sure now that Margaret knew about that. That was what she meant by "appetites." In the plural . . . "appetites" was what she said. And John and Hugh: it was possible she had found out about them. What had my father told Margaret? All those years he had given her money. Conviction of his betrayal sat at the back of my neck, a bird's beak working between two bones.

"You were that way even as a child. You ate like a pig and your father let you get away with it," said

Margaret. "Well, I suppose you're paying for it now that you're getting older."

I looked at my thighs that bulged in the pants that had become too small for me.

"What time will you want dinner?" I asked. Margaret had defeated me, but I would go on loving her. Because Margaret was the person I found most difficult to love.

"Five o'clock. I always eat at five o'clock."

"I'll make supper, if you like," I said. I looked at Margaret's arthritic hands. They had grown into the shape of the claws at the base of the legs of the dining table at Dover Road.

"I'm sure you won't want dinner after all those cookies," Margaret said.

It had not occurred to me that I would not have a meal this evening. But Margaret was right; I really should not have one now.

"I'll cook for you, then," I said.

"Thank God, food never meant that much to me," said Margaret.

"No," I said. I saw myself cased in the pink, sweating flesh of a pig; I could imagine my eyes grown small and light like a pig's. I wanted to sleep.

"I'll take a rest for half an hour, if it's all right," I said.

"I'll say my afternoon prayers. I'll pray for your intentions."

"Thank you," I said, walking up the stairs. I took off my clothes and got into bed in my bra and underpants. I had kept two bars of candy in my handbag. I ate them now, under the gray blankets.

And then I heard Margaret's voice, lifting the cover of my sleep. The voice was mixed with the face of a woman, pointing her finger, saying, "You are a good person," but it was Margaret's voice calling my name, telling me to get up. The light hung in the room like a menace, letting itself in through the cracks in the green shade. The light made everything queer; I did not know where I was. I should not have been sleep-

ing. There was Margaret's voice, calling me from a
distance. I came to the top of the stairs. I looked
down at Margaret, standing at the bottom in the
queer, green light.

"You said you were going to cook my supper. It's
a quarter to five."

In that marginal light, Margaret's face was gray and
dangerous. But that was only an accident: Margaret's
face, her voice, the tinge of her skin. What had that to
do with loving? This was the person I had decided to
love.

"I'm sorry," I said. "I'll be right down."

I looked at myself in the bathroom mirror as I
splashed cold water on my eyes. In this light my face
too was gray. It was the color of Margaret's face.

Above the stove in Margaret's kitchen was a white
plaque that said in blue lettering, "God give me the
patience to accept what I cannot change, the grace to
change what I can, and the wisdom to know the difference." The dishtowel had come from Lourdes; it
was a calendar for 1968. The dates were surrounded
by a maroon rosary. The kitchen was poor, I thought,
a kitchen of poverty. There were three saucepans and
two frying pans in one cupboard, and plates and cutlery for three. The poverty of the kitchen touched
me; it made me feel I was right to be here. There
was only cinnamon and nutmeg on the spice shelf.

Margaret watched me cook as if she were alive to
the danger of poison. I put the two chops on the aqua
plastic plate. The cabbage water made a dank rill
beside them.

"Did you tell them the chops were for me?" Margaret asked.

"Who?"

"Farrel's."

"No, I didn't think of it."

"I can tell. They're tough. They'd never give me
anything like this. I know her from the Rosary Society. They deliver everything right to this door."

Margaret tapped the last words on the table with her hook-shaped index finger.

"You didn't say they delivered," I said.

"They probably won't now that you're here."

I watched Margaret eat. The juices in my stomach started like a car. I wanted that solid lamb chop. I believed at that moment that it could have changed my life. Margaret pecked at it, ruining the joy of food for me.

I did the dishes after I decided that Margaret had finished eating. It was a difficult point to determine, for Margaret gave no sign that the meal was over; she had eaten so unsteadily, so unevenly that there was no precise moment at which it could be said she was no longer eating.

I dried my hands on the towel from Lourdes. Margaret was standing beside me.

"You use too much hot water with the dishes. I'm not a millionaire."

"Yes," I said. "I can see you're right. I'm sorry."

That was precisely the kind of thing I had never thought of, and that not thinking was another part of my selfishness. Now I would think; I would remember these things for the rest of my life. These were the things that would make Margaret happy. It would not be like living with my father, who loved books, and jokes, and arguments, who loved my stories about impossible places when really I had just gone to the grocer's. No, what would make Margaret happy would be my remembering to rinse the dishes in cold water.

I bathed in Margaret's tan bathtub. I had left behind my lavender soap and the bath oil Eleanor had given me. There was no pleasure possible in this room. The maroon tiles, the cold beige linoleum with the brown rugs to cover it did not invite introspection or repose. I bathed quickly; quickly I washed my hair. I wrapped it in one of Margaret's thin brown towels, the same one I had used to dry my body. I did not want to make more laundry, more work.

When I opened the bathroom door, Margaret was standing behind it.

"I heard how long it took the water to go down the drain. There's no necessity for using so much water."

"I'm sorry. I washed my hair."

"How often do you do that?"

"About twice a week."

"What for? Who do you think's going to see you?"

"I don't know."

"What?"

"I don't know."

"All that hair. I don't know what you want to hold onto it for."

"I've always had it like this. I never thought of getting it cut, I guess."

"That's just it. You never *think*. At your age, it's time you thought about a lot of things."

"Yes."

That was the conclusion I had come to myself. I would be more thoughtful. Now I was very tired. It was only eight o'clock, but I would go to sleep.

"Good night," I said to Margaret, brushing past her. I could see Margaret looking at my breasts through my nightgown.

"I suppose you're too good to say the Rosary. My sister, God rest her soul, used to say it out loud with me every night."

"I'll say it with you," I said. I had promised to do whatever would make Margaret happy. Whom had I promised? I had promised.

Margaret kept her rosary beads under her pillow.

"I don't suppose you have any rosaries?"

"Not with me."

"Not with me," mocked Margaret. "I don't suppose you've had any for years. I don't suppose you ever said the Rosary with your poor father."

"He preferred to pray alone."

"That's what he told *you*."

My father had given Margaret money all those years. I would be silent; I would not say anything. I had cheated this woman of my father as I had almost cheated Hugh's wife of him. This was what I deserved. Margaret was right to speak to me as she did.

It took half an hour to say the Rosary, because Margaret had many additions to the basic combinations. The bones in my knees began to grow into the floor like roots; my back was stiff and painful with kneeling. And I could no longer imagine a face who would be interested in me above all others, who cared for the nature and the quality of my prayer. I said these prayers because it pleased Margaret. But they brought me no comfort: there was no face, wise, amused, and dangerously open, listening to the words I sent out like cigar-shaped missiles to the neutral, heated air.

Margaret kissed the cross of her rosary.

"How long since you've made your Easter duty?" Margaret said.

"I don't know. I'm not sure. Quite a while."

"I'll call Father Pilkowski in the morning. I'll not have you sleeping under my roof until you've been to Confession."

"All right."

But now, I would simply sleep. I walked across the hall to my room and got into bed without turning on the light.

It was eleven o'clock when I awoke the next morning. I had slept too late, I knew, but the dark green shade gave me no indication of the sun's intensity or its position. When I came downstairs, I saw a light-colored, puffy-looking priest sitting next to Margaret at the kitchen table. I was embarrassed that he should see me in my nightgown at this hour. I felt dirty and unkempt; I felt as if I looked untrustworthy.

"This is the person I was telling you about," Margaret said, filling the priest's cup with tea.

My eyes were still crusted with sleep.

"Nice to meet you, young lady," he said.

Never had I met a priest with less charm. Polish. Not Irish. Not even German. He would not charm you into salvation or argue you into it. He would simply tell you the facts.

"We have Confessions this afternoon for First Friday," he said, opening his hamlike fist. "We hope to see you there."

"I'll be there," I said, too tired to determine the proper expression for my voice.

"Good. That's what I stopped by to be sure of."

He did not even look pleased to have saved me. I would confess that it had been eleven years since I had been to Confession. I would confess my three lovers. But my worst sin I would not confess, for the Church had not thought of a confessable name for it: the hunger of my spirit, the utter selfishness of my heart. But I had devised my own repentance: I was here. It was a penance more difficult than the Church could have imagined exacting, and because of this the Church could never be of comfort to me. I would pay for my greed with my future. I had thought myself at the center of my own life, the universe, and for this error I would give my life. Christ was right; He had said, "You must lose your life in order to gain it." By insisting on my own life I was in danger of losing everything. I imagined the priests at my father's funeral. They would love me for my life now: they could not help but love me. Had I gone on as I had been, with Hugh, with my plan for an enjoyable future, they would not have spoken to me on the street. It was not the giving up of my life that involved me in loss; it was taking it on that was the danger. Here I had built myself a sanctuary, covered over with approval, safe from chance.

Margaret was cutting cheese near the sink.

"Do you want something to eat?" she said.

"I think so, maybe."

"Is it breakfast or lunch?"

"I don't know."

"If it's breakfast, what time do you think you'll be having lunch?"

"I don't know."

"Well, make up your mind. You can't just do things the way you want. You shouldn't need lunch, sleeping so late."

"I won't have it, then."

I would do whatever Margaret wanted; I would eat later, secretly in my room. I hid a box of crackers under my bathrobe and went upstairs. I did not lift up the dark green shade. I put crackers in my mouth whole, and ate them silently, as if I were in a fever, as if I were being watched.

At three o'clock, I dressed for Confession. My nails were ragged; they made a run in the only pair of panty hose I had left. I took my brown tweed skirt from the closet and slipped it over my head. Halfway up, the zipper resisted; I made dents in my fingers, bruising them, trying to pull the metal tag up to its proper closure. It closed, making pockets of my soft abdominal flesh. I understood now that I was fat from eating and sleeping. But this seemed as inevitable as the color of my hair. I would eat foods quickly, furtively, in this dark room. Then I would sleep here. Sleep was what I needed. And I would grow out of my clothes.

My stomach was round and emphasized, a soft, vulnerable globe under the tight, itchy fabric. My coat strained at the edges of my hips. But it did not matter. How mistaken I had been to think it mattered. I walked, carrying my stomach at the front of my bones. I felt myself begin to menstruate, but I was too tired to go back home. I would walk that way, with the wet thickness between my legs, with my stomach at the front. My thighs ached. I had walked only two blocks and my breath was coming quickly, punishingly. I turned the corner to the church. I wished I could go back to sleep.

St. Stanislaus's had been built in the early sixties; I recognized the architecture. These churches were built to look like firehouses, impromptu, unconsidered, American. There was a statue of the Virgin Mary near the altar, made of coffee-colored wood. The

Virgin's eyes were modestly closed; her amateurish
hands rested on her perfectly flat breasts. I could not
pray to that image; it was not skillfully enough constructed; it was as if it were invented yesterday.

I imagined how my father would have stormed
through this church. I imagined the letters he would
have written to the pastor. But I was past caring if the
hands of Virgins were skillfully conceived or beautiful or ugly.

I knelt at the altar, looking at nothing. I examined
my conscience. I knew what I had to tell. I knew
what they wanted me to acknowledge. I would say
what they wanted me to say—that I had committed
adultery, that I had been away from the sacraments.
But I would keep the most important thing, the only
important thing, to myself. I had been selfish. I could
have devoured the world with my greed. But this they
were not interested in hearing. And for this I had devised my own repentance.

The confessional felt insubstantial, as though it
had been made of plywood. I was expecting the darkness of my past confessions, but this cubicle was il-
lumined by a yellow light, the color of summer lights
on front porches, lights to keep insects back, away
from the family. I did not have to guess at the outline
of this priest's face behind the screen: it was visible.
I could see exactly who he was: the man who had sat
at the kitchen table with Margaret. And he could see
me.

"Bless me, Father, for I have sinned."

But he had already begun talking. He was saying
something about the peace of the Holy Spirit. Why
was he talking before I had begun? Perhaps he was
just praying aloud so I would know he was there. I
decided to try again. Perhaps he had not heard.

"Bless me, Father, for I have sinned."

I could see the priest's mouth tighten in exasperation.

"Do you mind not interrupting me during the
Blessing?" he said.

"I'm sorry," I said.

I was terribly confused. What was he saying? It was entirely unfamiliar to me. What was he saying about unburdening my heart? That was not the language of the sacrament. Now he was silent. What did he want me to do now? I counted the silence. Ten seconds. That silence had a social awkwardness. But I was in Confession. Was it possible, in the context of the sacrament, for there to be a social awkwardness?

"You can begin now," he said.

"Begin what?"

"Your Confession."

"Oh, yes."

I had forgotten where I was. I began again.

"Bless me, Father, for I have sinned."

I saw the line of exasperation set on his mouth again.

"We don't begin like that any more. How long has it been since your last Confession?"

"Eleven years."

"I see. What is the reason for your absence from the Sacraments?"

"I no longer believed in them."

"And you have recovered your faith?"

"I've changed my mind."

"What?"

"Yes, I have recovered my faith."

I would say that, if that was what they wanted me to say. I could not say I was here because they wanted me to be here.

"Can you tell me your mortal sins since your last Confession?"

"I have had sexual intercourse with three men. Two of whom were married."

"Go on."

"I think those are the only mortal sins I have committed." Except, I thought, the one I cannot tell, the one you are not interested in: that I put myself in the center of the universe.

"You missed the Sacraments all that time?"

"Yes."

"Don't you consider that sinful?"

I wanted to say that I didn't, because I no longer believed in them. If I had believed and had not gone, then it would have been sinful. But, I wanted to say, I cannot confess my loss of faith because it is still lost to me.

"Yes," I said. I was too tired to argue.

"Is that all?"

"I think so."

"You're not sure?"

"It has been a very long time."

I could see him lean back, as if he had finished eating. He seemed to have lost some kind of energy. Perhaps he had begun to be bored.

"One of the sins we are most prone to these days," he said, "are sins of the flesh. Try to fight against them now that you realize their seriousness. For your penance think carefully about your future and say the Lord's Prayer. Make an act of contrition."

I understood that I had bored him, and I understood his boredom. The whole exercise seemed to lack importance. Certainly, he had said nothing of importance to me, nothing that would indicate that he thought that what I had done was really serious. That was it, there was no sense of seriousness here, no sense of inevitability. I did not believe that anything had happened, and I did not believe that *he* believed it. I began my old prayer.

"O, my God, I am heartily sorry for having offended thee . . ."

"Wait," he interrupted. "That's not it. You'll have to read it from the card in front of you."

I looked down at the handrest. There was a plastic laminated card on it. The printing was green; it had a border of yellow daisies. Had a nun painted it? The flowers did not seem virginal enough. There were three acts of contrition. There was a space under the third and then, in larger type, *Remember: Tomorrow is the First Day of the Rest of Your Life.*

Confusion clouded my brain like milk.

"Which one do you want me to say?"

"The second one will be all right," he said, as if he did not care particularly.

I read from the card:

My God,
I am sorry for my sins with all my heart.
In choosing to do wrong
and failing to do good,
I have sinned against you
whom I should love.
I firmly intend, with your help,
to do penance,
to sin no more,
and to avoid what leads me to sin.

There was a taste in my mouth as if I had just eaten cardboard.

"God bless you," he said, turning his back to me.

"All right," I said, and then, realizing that this was not the appropriate response, I said, "Thank you."

I walked out of the confessional through the church to the altar. I remembered the adjustment my eyes used to have to make, from the darkness of the confessional to the comparative light of the church. But now there was no adjustment necessary: both lights were the same.

I remembered the clear, airy feeling I used to have walking from the confessional to the altar, as if I were a cat, high on its legs. But now my bra cut into the undersides of my breasts. I could feel the menstrual blood wetting my panties. The zipper of my skirt bit into the soft skin of my stomach; I could imagine the red marks it was leaving on my flesh, marks of small teeth, as if I had been pecked by a bird. I knelt at the altar and said the prayers that priest had told me to say. But I said them to no one; I could not believe that anyone was interested in what I was saying. They had forgiven me for the wrong things. The rest I would not tell. The rest was unforgivable.

XV

I slept too late every morning. And every morning I awoke as if there were a war outside, as if I had only to open my eyes to see the corpses and the shell-shocked wounded. That was what I feared when I lifted the dark-green shade: I feared a face outside the window, dead eyes looking in at me as I pulled out of sleep. It took all my courage to wake up now, to raise the shade, to look at myself in the mirror as I splashed cold water on my eyes. Every day, I could see my eyes get smaller, my face become more taken up with face, with flesh. The food I ate turned into flesh, and that was what I would think about, too, as I lay in my bed—food turning into flesh, my stomach growing softer and rounder in front of my bones, my breasts getting heavier and seeming to drop from my body, the insides of my thighs growing into one an-other, so that they chafed and rubbed together as I walked. I would think of this as I lay in bed, afraid to get up in the mornings. I would think: today I will stop it, today I will not eat all this food. But then I would remember that it didn't matter if the bones of my face stood out or disappeared under flesh, if my breasts dropped and my thighs grew into one another, if I could no longer close the zippers of my skirts and pants. I would remember that it mattered to no one, that my body was of interest to no one; no one would look at it now, or touch it. I would think of Hugh, but then I would think of his wife's round purple face and I could hear her saying, "You are a good person." And I could hear myself saying, as if I were someone else, "I don't want to hurt anyone." And I would remember that all that was what loving Hugh had exposed me to. I had decided I was going to stop hurting people, I was going to stop doing damage. That was why I was here. I kept a box of cookies on my night table. I would begin eating before I was out of bed.

Margaret would come up the stairs when she heard me in the bathroom. She would always be outside the bathroom door when I walked into the hall. And every morning she would say the same thing:

"Good afternoon. Get your beauty sleep?"

And every morning I would say, "I'm sorry, Margaret. You should wake me earlier."

"I suppose you need your rest. You wouldn't sleep like that if you didn't need it. After all, you're a growing girl." And she would laugh, a dry, gassy laugh that sounded like the symptom of some illness that would end in death. "And you are growing"—she would spread her wounded-looking hands—"horizontally."

Every morning Margaret told me that she hated my hair. She would pick it up and put her crooked fingers in it until they were stopped by the knots my sleeping had made.

"There," she would say, "a rat's nest."

She did it again that morning. I hunched my shoulders so that they made a cave around my breasts. Margaret picked up my hair. She drove her fingers into it until she came to the knot at the center. "A rat's nest," she said. She tried to pull her fingers out. They would not move. She tried to free her fingers with her other hand, but her ineffectual hands, growing into the shape of claws, could not disentangle themselves from my hair. I could not breathe. Someone was stealing my air; someone was sealing me into a cave. It was possible that we would never be separated; that they would have to cut off Margaret's

hand. I lifted my hands above my head and pulled
Margaret's hands out of my hair as if it were on fire.

Margaret began screaming. "Cut that rat's nest off.
It's disgusting. You're going to bring bugs into this
house. Bedbugs. Get that hair cut off. It's not healthy.
It's sick."

I was shaking. I could feel individual beads of
sweat, like visible corpuscles, break out on my upper
lip. I wanted my hair cut off, too. I wanted to do it
now. As long as my hair was on my head, I could
imagine Margaret's hand in it. I remembered my
father saying, "Don't cut your hair." But my father
was dead now. It was of no interest to anyone if I cut
my hair. And now I would have to cut it, to get rid
of Margaret's hand.

Margaret's dry, virgin freckles had grown purple
with rage. I was afraid to look in her eyes. I looked at
the floor; I looked at my own safe feet. I walked back
into the bathroom, leaned over the brown sink and
vomited. I watched my vomit circle down the drain:
the food I had eaten that would never be my flesh
now. Margaret called the beauty parlor and made an
appointment for me that afternoon. She made one for
herself at the same time.

Dorothy Kowalski's beauty shop was called *Chez
Elle*. It smelled of hairspray and dye and the strong,
destructive odor of permanent-wave lotion. I remembered that smell from the Tonettes that Liz and I had
secretly given each other one Saturday when we were
twelve. But who got that kind of permanent now? That
smell hung over the other smells like a wicked miasma.

The women in the shop were all overweight. Their
hair, when it was finished, stood up around their fat
angry faces like stiff Japanese boxes. The colors they
had chosen for it were also angry, brash red or gold
that gave them trumpet-colored crests, artificial and
aggressive. Their feet sat like tanks in their small shoes.
It was torture to hear them talking in their Western
New York drawl.

They fluttered over Margaret; they clucked around her; they knew what she had suffered. Dorothy Kowalski brooded over her in the chair.

"We'll doll you up, Miss Casey," she said. "You have such pretty hair."

Margaret cooed and smiled up at them. She had never smiled at me; not once in thirty years. But I knew why: I had stolen from Margaret what she had most desired. But I would make it up to her. I would do anything to make Margaret happy. I would give my life for it. I would cut my hair.

Margaret said that God would bless all the women for their kindness. She let me sit under an inactive dryer for half an hour before she pointed her finger and said to the beautician, "This is the girl who lives with me. She wants to get that mop cut off, thank God."

"Well, I should think *so,*" said Dorothy. All the women laughed, as if sex had been mentioned.

I knew that I ought to try and joke with them. There ought to be something in the world we could talk about: movies, movie stars, I knew you could talk to anyone in America about that. But I was dumb and heavy with tiredness. The pain buzzed in the back of my skull. My father would not want me to do this, would be unhappy that I was having my hair cut. But it didn't matter: my father was dead, I would never see him again. There was the pain, sharper now: my father was dead; now I would do what Margaret wanted.

I answered the women's questions with vague half-smiles, half-sentences. I tried to make my eyes look sweet. But I knew that was not what they liked; that was not what they wanted from me. They wanted jokes; they wanted me to laugh like them, as if we were the guardians of something, as if we were keeping something intact. They wanted me to laugh with them as soldiers laughed in movies, as if we were in a war that made distinctions foolish, as if we were in the business of keeping alive. But I could not do it. I lowered my eyes. They were not interested in me. Dorothy

Kowalski washed my hair and then dried it in a towel roughly, half-heartedly, as if she would rather be somewhere else.

She separated my hair with clips and began cutting. First she took large sections of hair from the bottom; they fell to the floor like wet, flat insects.

"What kinda style did you have in mind?" she said.

"It doesn't matter," I said. "Anything that's easiest."

"I'll just give you the regular bubble cut."

"Fine," I said.

But even I had heard of the bubble cut. This place had frozen around 1962. The pictures showed women with teased hair, lacquered hair (Jacqueline Kennedy had started this), velvet bows. None of the women in the photographs had the long, promiscuous hair of the sixties or the stylish recent cuts that made everyone look like Carole Lombard. Nothing had changed here. And why should it? What did it matter? No one wanted it to change. They were happy with things as they were. I had no right to ask that things be as *I* wanted. I had learned something: I was not, after all, particularly important.

Now Dorothy had cut almost all of my hair off. My hair was only a cap on my head. But still I felt nothing: what did it matter; all my hair was gone. I remembered Margaret's fingers stuck in the roots of my hair. I was relieved, now, to be free of it. This was the right thing for my life now: short hair, a little of it, close to my head. Dorothy sprayed something on my hair and separated the sections for rollers. I didn't want it, but all these women did.

My face looked heavy and white in its shell of plastic curlers. I looked like all those other women. I closed my eyes under the dryer. It was hot; the heat burned the back of my neck, but I said nothing. I was sure that the others were used to that heat; to complain of it would only be to mark myself as different. And I was not different; I had learned that; I was no better than these women. I would bear what they had borne; the heat of the dryer, the sickish smell of the hair spray. I would be like them; I had done damage by believing myself distinguished, by believing myself important.

"Come on, you're done," said Dorothy, leading me over to her chair. My hair out of the rollers curled on the top of my head in stiff, oblong coils. Dorothy brushed my hair out. She began teasing it until it stood out around my head like Einstein's. Then she brushed it down until it made a sticky helmet around my face. She told me to close my eyes; she sprayed my hair for (I counted) ninety seconds. She stood back and told me to look in the mirror. I did as I was told.

I wanted to weep; I would have wept, but everyone was looking at me. It was not that I looked ugly, even; that I could have borne, but I looked foolish. I looked ludicrous. I was a caricature of every woman in the shop. This was not my hair, could not be my hair, that stuck out inches from my skull. Never had I looked so bad.

"Well?" said Dorothy, with a menacing expectation.

"It's not exactly what I had in mind."

Dorothy stamped her heavy foot. She put her fist on my shoulder. It lay there like a hoof.

"She tells me anything and I tell her a bubble cut and she says fine and then she says it's not what she wants. There's no pleasin' some of them."

Margaret sat up in her chair. "She was always like that," she said. "Never satisfied. You gave her something, she wanted more, she wanted something else. Never satisfied."

"Not like you, you little sweetheart," said Dorothy, putting her arms around Margaret. "You're a little pleasure."

Margaret's new, brash hair crackled with joy. I paid at the cash register. I paid for me and for Margaret. I gave Dorothy a dollar tip. I paid for a taxi home. I fumbled for my keys in the five-o'clock dark that frightened me, that had always frightened me, by its anomaly. I reached in the mail box. There was a letter for me.

I could see Hugh's square, foreign-looking hand-writing. I thought of my hair. I wanted to weep, hold-ing his letter. Now he would never want me.

"Who's that?" Margaret asked, pointing to the letter.

"It's for me," I said, slipping it into my handbag.

"Who's it from?"

"You don't know them," I said. I was thinking that if I said his name in front of Margaret, Margaret would be able to take him away from me. It was true that I did not have him, but I would not like Margaret to take him. I walked upstairs, thinking of Hansel and Gretel, leaving trails of crumbs that would never help them.

My hands trembled. I wanted to keep from opening the envelope for as long as possible, but I could not bear to leave it unopened. Whatever he said I de-served. He would say I had hurt him. He would say he could never forgive me. He had a perfect right never to forgive me. The note was on a piece of paper that had an advertisement for liniment on the bottom. He had given me pads like that: I had loved those pads, with advertisements on the bottom, with pictures of dogs and horses. That made me remember him; that made me think he was someone I had known. It gave me courage to look at the letter.

My dearest:
I ache for you. I long for you. I am always
waiting for you.

Hugh

I touched my hair. He would not wait for me. If he saw me now, he would not want me; he would re-member that I was unforgivable. I would write and tell him not to get in touch with me again. But first I would sleep.

I lay down on my bed. But now I could not sleep. I was thinking of Hugh's back, of his hands, of his broad forearms covered with soft, delicious hair. It came again. Desire was the word for it. It made me close my eyes, as if someone were waving something in front of me, some fan delectable with feathers that I had to close my eyes to savor, that made some wind I had to be sightless to take in. There was a wave in my stomach that was like a wave of sickness. Only it was not sickness; it was desire. The words to express it were simple: to want and not to have. Longing made my rib cage light; the bones stretched from each other like the fingers of a hand; my muscles whistled with longing. To want and not to have. To have had. Not to have again. These were the only words I was capable of hearing. I wanted him so much that I could believe him in the next room. The strange thing was that my longing had not brought him here; the miracle was that he had not come to me.

I touched my breasts, pretending it was his hand on them. He had loved them once; his mouth had covered them, wet and desperate. He had moved over me; he had needed me more than I could imagine. I turned on my bed, remembering how I had turned underneath him. And I had arched up to close around him like a cat, apt, definite, and perfectly expert.

I could hear his voice now. All this time I had not wanted to hear it, I would not call it to mind. And his queer, old-fashioned vocabulary, words wrong in their context, and yet utterly expressive. Once he had said, "Your body is perfectly efficient. Every inch of it, every curve, is perfectly desirable. Everything is there to make me want you."

I had traced the high ledge of his hip bone with my mouth until I arrived at the center where he grew high and solid and rose-colored with the strain of wanting me. I had kissed him there; I had closed my mouth around him; my mouth, wet with longing, and he had turned beneath me and cried out. And then I could not bear to be without him. I would lower my body onto him; I would cover him over with the pulse of a hidden muscle. And then we would strain, until the tension, the unbearable tension broke, and we would land together, birds on the ground, coupled, weeping.

I wept now to think of it. I could never ask him to come back to me. I remembered now; it was dangerous; it was harmful. Yes, that was it, that was what I had forgotten, thinking only of my body and its longing. I had forgotten my father's face at the door, dark with horror as he saw my breasts, and the red, accusing face of the woman, pointing her finger, saying, "You are a good person." I had forgotten that, turning here on my bed, pretending I was turning. I must not forget again, I must lose my life to gain it; I would get more, far more, by giving up life than by embracing it.

I looked up at the light bulb above my bed. I heard Margaret in the bathroom. I heard her flush the toilet; I could hear her spit in the sink. Now I remembered. I had come here because I had done such damage, through what I should not have wanted, getting what should not have been my own. I was here to get away not only from Hugh but from Liz and Eleanor and what they thought should be my life, which would make me only unsafe, which would leave me only vulnerable.

But I had heard Hugh's voice now. That was a curse. When I had not been able to hear his voice I had been able to think of him as an old disease that I need not remember, of which I had believed myself cured. Now the mark of him was on me. He had written to me. I could not sleep, I could not have him. I lay on my back and wept.

I began to be unable to sleep in the middle of the day. And I sensed a new danger: I could feel myself growing bored. But I had promised to stay here; I would try to do things with Margaret that would give some kind of pleasure to her. I wanted to read to Margaret as I had read to my father. I asked Margaret what kind of books she liked. What Margaret liked, she said, were romances. What she meant, I discovered, were books in which nurses married doctors, stewardesses married pilots, cub reporters married city editors. She liked books by Regina Carey, books whose location was always Northumberland where orphans married lords who seemed wicked but who turned out to be brave, noble, protecting someone. If she liked that I thought perhaps she would like *Jane Eyre*. The idea of reading *Jane Eyre* aloud excited me; it was the first thing I had looked forward to in months.

In the middle of the fourth chapter, Margaret asked me to stop reading.

"All that stuff is old hat," she said. "You can tell the person who wrote that was one of those unsatisfied women. Unfulfilled. I hate that kind of writing. It has no life to it."

I threw the brown book on the floor. It was my book; my father had given it to me for my ninth birthday.

"Who are you to criticize Charlotte Brontë?" I said.

Rage lifted the top of my head, made it a roof above my brain. I tried to tell myself that I had learned that these things didn't matter: Charlotte Brontë, Regina Carey, whatever Margaret liked was best.

But I did not believe it. No, I felt that that was wrong. I had to make Margaret see that Charlotte Brontë was better. If I could make her see that Charlotte Brontë was better I could change her life; I could turn her into someone lovable. But Margaret sat hunched in her chair, waiting for a fight.

"I'm not as smart as you, I never was, I didn't have your advantages. I was always taking care of somebody. I had no time for education or reading."

"Try and see, Margaret," I said, with some desperation, "try and see."

"I hoped that age would improve your bad temper. I prayed that it would. You were a stubborn, willful child; you could wrap your father around your little finger. And where did it get you?"

Here, I thought. Exactly here. Perhaps Margaret was right. It was my stubbornness, my will, that made things so wrong, that made people unhappy. It was caring about things so strongly, whether Charlotte

Brontë was better than Regina Carey, that had caused my trouble. I had forgotten what I had decided; I would do anything to make Margaret happy.

"Let's play cards," I said. We played two-handed canasta. We began to play it every day. But at the end of the game, Margaret was never happy. If she lost, she thought I had taken advantage of her; if she won, she felt she hadn't won by enough. Yet it occupied her, it seemed to interest her, playing cards. I began to try and lose, by more and more points, so that Margaret would win by a large margin, so that she would be happy. For that was what I had decided, after all; I would do anything to make Margaret happy.

When I could no longer sleep in the afternoon, I began to walk around the neighborhood. The light had stopped turning its dangerous green at three or four o'clock. I began to look closely at the houses.

I had never answered the phone in Margaret's house. Once I had moved toward the ringing phone, and Margaret had cut in front of me and pushed me out of the way. The force of the push had surprised me, the force of Margaret's breakable-looking body.

"Don't think you're taking over," she had said.

I had never answered the phone again. Even when I was alone in the house, I let the phone ring. It had not been difficult; I expected no one. Now expectation lifted the back of my tongue like the taste of lemon. Once Liz had called. She had said, "Meet me in Albany. We'll have dinner and a movie."

I had refused. The sound of Liz's voice made my own voice sound sad, a slow, old woman's voice.

"As it is," I had said to Liz, "I'm terribly tired."

The air had crackled with Liz's chagrin.

"Call me when you wake up," she had said.

Since then, no one had called. Eleanor wrote letters in her round, precise handwriting, as if nothing had happened, as if everything were the same. I never answered the letters. I kept them in a shoe box.

Eleanor would say, "Please be in touch when you are ready. I miss your company."

Perhaps I would never be ready. I could not bear for Eleanor to see me as I was, with my weight, with my disaster of a haircut. Eleanor was something I would have to prepare for, and I was not ready to begin preparing. I wrote to Eleanor and said that my life was quiet. I said I hoped I was beginning to heal. I said nothing about Margaret; I said, "I will see you one day soon." But it was possible I would never see Eleanor again. I would keep her at a safe distance, writing letters. Eleanor would not come if I asked her to wait. It was part of the beauty of Eleanor's love that she would wait forever if you asked her. I thought of Eleanor's face; I thought of the texture of Eleanor's eyelids. No, it was impossible that I would not see her. I would see her someday again. Perhaps when we were old women, unrecognizable. But one day I would see her.

That day the phone went on ringing and ringing. Margaret was at the doctor's; Dorothy Kowalski had come by in her white Buick. She had helped Margaret to the car. I had stayed in my room. I could hear the women talking as they walked down the path.

"Ungrateful," I heard Dorothy say.

"Ungrateful," I could hear Margaret repeat.

They were talking about me. But what was I supposed to be grateful for? I made a fist and brought it down. It made an infantile impression on the line of soot along the window sill. How long had it been since I had made a fist? Years. I had not made a fist as an adult.

The phone kept ringing. Whoever it was would let it ring eleven times before he gave up trying. It was a penance to sit through those rings, imagining someone at the other end wanting me, trying to get through. I accepted it as penance for the way I had begun thinking about Hugh again, the way I could not stop thinking of him and hearing his voice. I was sure now he was on the other end. Eleven rings. Eleven was a number he would choose. Neither ten nor a conventional dozen. I would have to answer the phone. I would have to tell him not to call again.

My voice sounded heated and uncertain at the receiver. My "hello" was off—a drunk's, a convict's, someone ill-at-ease with the commonplace.

"Hello, pal," I heard at the other end.

"Father."

I began to cry jerkily, hiccoughing into the black receiver.

"What is it, little one? Are you so unhappy?"

That was the voice I loved, that I had always loved. I had nearly killed him, trying to force him to understand what he could not understand, what there was, after all, no reason for him to know or to acknowledge. But he had not died. He was here now, on the phone, talking to me. Of course he had forgiven me for asking him for what he could not give me. And I could forgive him now. I could cry on the phone and ask him to come to me.

"I'm all right," I said. "Only I wish you'd come. I wish I could see you."

"Well, that's why I'm calling you. I thought I'd take a spin up and see my girl."

"Drive up? All the way up here?"

"I suppose it's time I let the old jalopy stretch its legs."

"You're coming up here?"

I was thinking of Margaret. I was thinking of Father Mulcahy in the home for drunken priests, old men shuffling in pajamas on a sun roof in Westchester.

"You couldn't keep me away."

"When will you come?"

"Monday. Lunchtime Monday."

"That's Monday of Holy Week?"

"Right."

I began to cry again.

"I can't wait for you to come. I've been a little lonely."

He would be here in a week, in less than a week. He

loved me so much that he would drive his car ten times the furthest distance he had driven it. It was a miracle, that love. No one deserved it; no one could, so I did not have to worry about deserving it.

I heard Dorothy close the heavy door of her station wagon. I ran to meet the women halfway down the path.

"Margaret," I said, "wonderful news."

She leaned heavily on Dorothy's arm.

"Father Mulcahy's coming for a visit. Monday. He'll be here."

"Very nice of you. Thank you very much, inviting company behind my back without even asking me."

"And in her condition," said Dorothy. "The doctor said he doesn't know how she stands the pain in that condition."

"Can I go into my own house before we discuss it?" Margaret said. She turned to Dorothy. "She's invited a man who's a hopeless alcoholic. A hopeless alcoholic."

"He's nothing of the sort."

"You don't know the half of it, Miss Head-in-the Clouds."

Rage made my brow widen.

"I'll call him then and tell him not to come," I said.

"No, you won't. He's a priest of God, whatever else he is. I'll have to press the linen towels."

Dorothy moved her heavy body, smelling of forced, middle-aged sex, behind Margaret's chair. She put her arms around Margaret.

"You little angel, you always rise to the occasion."

Margaret put her crippled hand to her forehead like the heroine of a melodrama.

I turned and walked out of the room. Dorothy shouted after me: "You're not doing justice to that haircut. At least come in and let me set it if you don't know how to take care of it."

I made exaggerated noises, child's noises, going up the stairs, looking at my shoes. Whatever happened I would make him comfortable. I would protect him

from these women. I began looking through the clothes
in my closet. The ones I liked I didn't have to try on; I
knew they were now too small for me. But he didn't
care, he didn't care what I wore. No, that was wrong;
it was one of the things he loved me for, that I had always put on lipstick for him. It was one of the things
that had kept me alive: all those years he had cared
about how I looked. All those Thursday evenings I
had had to care as well about the food we ate, about
my hair and my complexion.

I needed a new dress. There was only one dress
shop in Ramona. I went down to it the morning of
Father Mulcahy's arrival. The store was dark; no one
seemed to be there. Finally a woman came out from
behind a curtain.

"Yes," she croaked, in a voice like a fortuneteller's.

I had heard of a word for this woman's figure but
had never used it myself, had never imagined using it:
well-corseted. The woman's body was invented by her
undergarments. The flesh, if indeed there was any
real flesh, was forced and molded by iron bone and
flexible steel and rigid cloth. I could imagine this
woman alone in her bedroom at night; I saw her opening those garments, flinging them on the floor with
impossible relief. I realized I had been staring at her.
I would have to say something.

"I'm looking for a dress."

"What size?"

"I don't know. I've put on a lot of weight."

The woman clucked and took a tape measure from
where it hung like a necklace around her neck.

"It's a shame," said the woman. "You'd better take
it off before it's too late. Every year after thirty it gets
harder."

"Yes," I said, lifting my arms so the woman could
measure my bust. Everything this woman said sounded
like advice from the sibyl.

"Sixteen," said the woman.

"What?"

"Sixteen. Size sixteen."

Tears came to my eyes.

"That's impossible. I was a ten."

The woman shrugged, monumental in her indifference.

"All I can tell you is here are the sixteens."

I looked through the dresses on the rack. Within ten seconds I had given up hope. Now I could only try to find something that would fit. I picked out a dress in cranberry wool. The woman showed me into the back of the store, to an alcove with a mirror. I tried on the dress; it slipped off my shoulders and sagged around my breasts. I would wear my dark green belt with it; I would make a new hole in it so it would fit me. At least this dress was not too small; at least it did not reproach me with the past of my own body.

The woman pulled the curtain back.

"You could probably get away with a fourteen. That particular item runs big."

"This is fine," I said.

The woman shrugged again.

"Suit yourself. It's not my headache."

I carried the package home and let it bump against my thigh. Size sixteen, I kept saying to myself. But what did it mean? Ten, sixteen, my body had caused only damage. There were crocuses beginning on the lawns I walked by; purples, yellows, whites pushed through the meanest soils. My thighs chafed against each other as I walked. I decided to go on a diet.

But tonight, for Father Mulcahy, I was making Irish stew. Margaret hovered over me in the kitchen.

"I don't like that heavy stuff," she said, poking at the meat as it simmered, beautifully I had thought until she poked at it. "It doesn't agree with me."

"I'll make you an egg."

"That's a fine supper for me to have. In my own home."

"What do you want then?" I said. Rage was starting behind my eyes; it bulked like a building in my skull.

"A chop."

"All right. I'll make you a chop."

I left the stew to simmer on the stove. I went upstairs to look at my cosmetics. There was nothing I could do to help my face with my hair like this. I put on my old lipstick, the one I wore when my father was living. I put some of Eleanor's green shadow on my eyelids. The new dress at least gave me some color. But I looked like someone's mother, like someone who has decided she is no longer beloved or desired.

I ran downstairs to answer the bell. There he was, his eyebrows working furiously, clever as a prawn's. I held him as I had held no one for months. Had he always been so small? I realized, for the first time, that I was taller than he by at least two inches. But I must have been for some time; it was fifteen years since I had reached my present height.

"How are you, my pal?" he said, touching the ends of my short hair.

"Fine. You're here."

I could feel that he saw Margaret over my shoulder. Our embrace stopped cold, as if someone had spoken of death. We moved away from each other into the living room.

"Hello, there, Margaret," he said, going over to her, extending his hand. A gentleman, I thought. A perfect gentleman. He goes on forgiving the unforgivable. He goes on loving. He shakes hands with the woman who had tried to destroy his life. He embraces the child who nearly killed him. He goes on loving, I thought, and his manners are impeccable.

He opened his briefcase and took out a bottle of wine.

"The doctor says I can have one glass a night. None of the hard stuff."

"I suppose he knows what he's doing," said Margaret.

"Of course he does," I said. "Of course we'll have wine with dinner."

"I'll stay at St. Stanislaus's tonight. The pastor knows I'm coming."

"We haven't even had dinner yet," I said.

Father Mulcahy and I laughed, as if I had made a very good, very old joke that we had both forgotten.

"I suppose you two want to be alone," said Margaret nastily.

"No," said Father Mulcahy.

"Yes," I said. "Come into the kitchen and talk to me while I make the noodles."

He sat down at the kitchen table like a farmer's wife.

"You've been all right here?"

"Yes," I said quickly, pouring salt into the boiling water.

"You wouldn't think of coming back to Queens?"

"Not right now," I said, sitting across from him.

"You've been well?"

"Better."

There was nothing more for us to say. But then there was nothing we needed to say to each other. It was a great pleasure simply to be in a room with him, talking about my childhood. This we could give each other; it could not be taken away from us now.

I put the stew on the table and on Margaret's plate a single chop. I poured wine into each of the glasses. Jelly glasses and Melmac plates embarrassed me in front of Father Mulcahy. I brought the wine bottle into the kitchen and hid it behind the toaster.

"I guess there's not enough stew for me," Margaret said, poking at her chop.

"You said you didn't want it."

"I was afraid there wouldn't be enough for Father."

"Of course there's enough," I said.

"Now that I have the chop, I'll just eat it."

"As you like," I said, turning toward Father Mulcahy. He was talking about people in Assumption parish whom Margaret would know. Her response was always the same. It commented on their luck and her misfortune, the preference that had been lavished on them, the discrimination she had suffered.

I poured myself another glass of wine in the kitchen. Even Margaret's voice began to be more bearable as it grew more distant. Father Mulcahy walked over to

the old piano. In the months I had lived here, I had
never lifted the cover, I had simply dusted the top.

"Did you know I used to play in the seminary?"

"Get out," I said, "I don't believe you."

"All right, then, doubting Thomasina," he said,
lifting the cover. "Do you mind, Margaret?"

"What difference does it make whether I mind or
not? Make yourself at home."

Even that response was enough for him. He flexed
his hands. His fine, cared-for fingers played chords.
He began singing in his high, boy's voice, "I'll Take
You Home Again, Kathleen."

I joined in. I could sing the harmony; I had sung it
with my father. And I had sung it with Hugh. I could
never tell Father Mulcahy the truth about Hugh. But
that was all right. I could not tell the truth, but we
could sing at the piano.

Margaret began coughing behind us.

"I'd better go," he said. "I have to leave at five-
thirty in the morning. I told the pastor I'd be back to
say the ten o'clock."

"Then I won't see you again," I said, panic rising in
my voice.

"Not until the next time."

We laughed. That was another joke we had heard
somewhere. We would always laugh at the same
things. No one could take that away from us. We had
what we had.

I brought him his brushed, perfect hat, his hairy
black coat, the white scarf I had given him.

"It's an awful long way for you to come for nothing,"
Margaret said.

"Not for nothing," he said, shaking Margaret's
hand. "Keep me in your prayers, Margaret."

"Will you give me your blessing, Father?" she said,
trying to kneel, but squatting as if she were sitting on
a toilet.

"Don't kneel, Margaret," he said, making a cross in
the air over her head, and then over mine.

I walked him to the car, holding his arm. The cold, dark air made me feel icy inside my nose.

"I think you should leave here," he said. "You could come home. I could always find something for you in the parish."

"I can't," I said. "I promised."

"Even God breaks promises."

"Only in the Old Testament when He's being awful."

"Here," he said, squeezing a crumpled bill into my hand. "Get your hair done on me."

"There's no place to get it done."

"Well, then, watch your weight, honey. God gave you beauty. If you waste it, that's a sin against the fifth commandment."

"Thou shalt not kill? What does that have to do with it?"

"It means slow deaths, too," he said.

I held him in the dark. I kissed the top of his head as if he were a child.

"See you soon," I said.

He put his thumb and index finger into the Ballantine beer OK sign.

"See you soon, pal," he said, and rolled up his window. He drove down the street as if he were driving off to comfort the dead.

When I walked back into the house, Margaret said from the seat I could see she had only recently got into, "What were you doing out there with him all that time?"

I ignored her. I went into the kitchen to clean up. But she followed me, hanging behind me as I stood at the sink.

"What were you doing out there with him all that time?"

I turned to her with a ferocity that made her back across the room.

"What do you think I was doing? What can I possibly have been doing?"

"He's capable of anything when he's had too much to drink."

I swept the glasses onto the floor with the palm of my hand. Their bounce on the linoleum was not as definitive as I would have liked, but finally they hit one another and broke with a muffled seriousness.

"You are a wicked, wicked woman," I said. "And what's worse, you are a fool."

She was crouched behind her rib cage. I had frightened her.

"You'll have to pay for those glasses."

"*You* never paid for them. You got them free when you bought the jelly."

"I'm a poor woman."

"The poor you have always with you," I shouted, slamming the kitchen door.

It is one of the marvels of a Catholic education that the impulse of a few words can bring whole narratives to light with an immediacy and a clarity that are utterly absorbing. "The poor you have always with you." I knew where Christ had said that: at the house of Martha and Mary. Mary had opened a jar of ointment over Christ's feet. Spikenard, I remembered. And she wiped his feet with her hair. Judas had rebuked her; he had said that the ointment ought to be sold for the poor. But, St. John had noted, Judas had said that only because he kept the purse and was a thief. And Christ had said to Judas, Mary at his feet, her hair spread out around him, "The poor you have always with you: but me you have not always."

And until that moment, climbing the dark stairs in a rage to my ugly room, it was a passage I had not understood. It seemed to justify to me the excesses of centuries of fat, tyrannical bankers. But now I understood. What Christ was saying, what he meant, was that the pleasures of that hair, that ointment, must be taken. Because the accidents of death would deprive us soon enough. We must not deprive ourselves, our loved ones, of the luxury of our extravagant affections. We must not try to second-guess death by refusing to love the ones we loved in favor of the anonymous poor.

And it came to me, fumbling in the hallway for the light, that I had been a thief. Like Judas, I had wanted to hide gold, to count it in the dead of night, to parlay it into some safe and murderous investment. It was Margaret's poverty I wanted to steal, the safety of her inability to inspire love. So that never again would I be found weeping, like Mary, at the tombstone at the break of dawn.

And I had cut my hair. I had wanted to give up all I loved so that I would never lose it. I had tried to kill all that had brought me pleasure so that I would not be susceptible. Why had I done it? For safety, certainty, for the priests, the faceless priests who blessed my father's coffin, who had sat at my table, who had never remembered my name. For them I would give up all I had most savored, those I had most treasured: Hugh and Liz and Eleanor, even Father Mulcahy, so that those faceless priests could say, when they thought of me, "She is a saint."

I knew now I must open the jar of ointment. I must open my life. I knew now that I must leave. But I was not ready. I would have to build my strength.

In the evenings, I closed the door of my room and read the prayers of Holy Week. Monday in Holy Week, Tuesday, Wednesday, three times when, as a child, I could expect to hear the Passion read before the evening of Maundy Thursday. It would approach like false dawn, like a sky emptied of color. As a child, I had waited for that evening, had imagined men, hidden away, eating with each other, waiting for death. Always I had imagined it fragrant, dangerous: men smelling of fish having their feet washed by another man. I had been able to feel the dust on their feet, the cool water, the comfort of having someone you revered kneel before you and hold your foot in a towel He had hung across His shoulders. The relief of that, the pure rest of it, and the inevitable menace in the warm dark. I could feel it now, although the

April of this year of Our Lord was snowy, and outside
was not the warm pre-summer of the Middle East but
the wet, late winter of Ramona, the air cold and dis-
concerting with no hint of reprieve.

I turned the pages in my old Missal, the Missal my
father had given me. There was a holy card with the
words of Juliana of Norwich printed on it in the slant,
liturgical script that had made its truth seem inevitable:

> He said not thou shalt not be tempted
> He said not thou shalt not be troubled
> He said thou shalt not be overcome.

I wrote a letter to Hugh. The memory of his body,
smooth in places, then rough, made of the juts and
hollows I had run my fingers and my mouth along,
was with me now, and his voice, and his hands, that
had seemed to me the hands of God—merciful and
healing, and perfectly just. I wrote: "Please wait for
me if you can. I long for you too, but am still troubled.
I don't know what my life will be."

I knew I could not possibly see him as I was now,
with my stomach hanging over the top of my underpants, with my thighs that chafed together because
they were beginning to grow into one another. I remembered how he had looked at the cup he had found
behind the curtain on the night I had made him dinner.
That is how he would look at my body now. He loved
things that had been cared for, things that looked as
if they had been polished or burnished. And he would
look at my breasts, pendulous, dropping from their
own weight, as he had looked at the coffee cup where
mold grew in the sticky film. I would have to do so
much before I could see him. For I knew, and in
knowing this, I hated him for a moment, that without
my beauty he would not love me.

I tried to imagine a love that would make no distinctions, that would not be tried by flesh that lost its

smooth surface, that would not be tested by ingratitude, or sadness, or betrayal or a simple coldness of the heart. But that was not a love possible to a man like Hugh, watchful and expectant, judging me with his eyes. Without that judgment he could not be the man I loved; he would be nothing like my father. And I needed a man whom I could love for his rigor, for the challenge, and the sense of having been carefully chosen after a consideration that was not hasty. It was impossible that he should see me now.

I had at that moment a flash of revelation about the body that had the simplicity, I thought, of great art. The body changed, went on changing, and could be changed. What I had done to myself was not final. It would take time, but I believed, with the unlikely faith of an early Christian, that I could make things happen to my body that would allow him to love it again. I sealed the letter to Hugh. I would lose weight. My hair would one day, I was sure, grow longer. I began that day. I ate no lunch. Margaret tried to urge me to eat. I denied her invitation.

I mailed the letter on my way to the Good Friday service.

"What's that?" Margaret said, as I slipped the letter down the chute.

"Nothing. A magazine subscription."

I had begun lying. More and more, I began to feel the need to lie to Margaret.

"What magazine?" she said.

"The *Atlantic Monthly*."

"I never heard of it. Would I like it?"

"You might."

"Anyway, I don't want a lot of magazines cluttering up the living room."

"I'll keep it in my room."

The church was dark with the number of the congregation. And the statues, covered in their purple cloth, stole what light there would have been available. A sense of unaccustomed shock hung in the air, as if

the people kneeling here this afternoon were waiting
for a storm. I too knelt and put my hands in front of
my face. I thought of Christ, of the death of Christ.
We were here to acknowledge the presence of death
among us. We were here to acknowledge our own inevitable deaths.

My father was dead; there was the pain. I had loved
him, but my love had not been able to help him. Even
my love had not made him immune. I had wanted to
inject him with love like a vaccine, to keep him from
loss as you might keep a town from cholera. But my
love had not kept him from death, had not even held
back the impulse of his brain that shattered and de-
stroyed his nerves even as I stood near him. Love had
kept nothing back; not even the smallest disasters. My
father had died, but I had not killed him, as I had not
been able to save him. I would die; everyone in this
church would die. Everyone I knew and loved would
die: Father Mulcahy, Liz, Eleanor. And Hugh. They
would be lost to me. I would, one day, never see them
again.

That was what we were kneeling to acknowledge, all
of us, on this dark afternoon. We were here to say that
we knew about death, we knew about loss, that it
would not surprise us. But of course it would surprise
us; it had surprised even Christ in the Garden.

The priests entered in a somber chain. No bells
were rung; the silence lay on the heads of the parishioners like a reproach. But then we were here to be
reproached. The priest, in the voice of God, read out:

My people, what have I done to you? Or in what
have I offended you, answer Me? I planted you my
most beautiful vineyard, and you have become to
Me exceedingly bitter, for you have given me vinegar when I was thirsty and with a spear have pierced
the side of your Savior.

For your sake I scourged Egypt with its first born

and you scourged Me and delivered me to My
enemies.

I opened the sea before you, and with a spear you
have opened My side.

I went before you in a pillar of a cloud and you
brought Me to the palace of Pilate.

I gave you a royal sceptre, and you have given Me
a crown of thorns.

Years of atrocities, monstrous ingratitude: who
could make up to God for the stupidity, the selfishness
of His people? And yet the people of God went on,
generation after generation, making the same mistakes.

I knelt to kiss the giant crucifix. That was vulgar, I
regretted the priests doing that, wiping the feet of
Christ with a tissue after the brush of every mouth. I
wished they wouldn't do that; it made me wish I hadn't
come today, to kneel and kiss and kiss and walk with
all the others, as if I were one of them.

But I had wanted to hear those words spoken, the
harsh Old Testament words and then the words of
John. I wanted to hear the story said aloud, and I
wanted to hear about His rest in the dark tomb. I
wanted to hear it in the presence of my kind.

For there was death; you had to know that, and
betrayal, and the negligence of friends at crucial moments, and their sleep. I wanted that acknowledged in
the presence of my kind also.

I walked home with Margaret, feeling my body
moving on its clever legs. Christ had suffered in the
body, and I too had a body. I knew it false but capable
of astonishing pleasures. Christ had been betrayed by
His friends, but my friends had stood by me in a
miracle of love when I had ceased to love them. Christ
had died, but it was not death I wanted. It was life,
and the body, which had been given to me for my

pleasure, and the love of those whom loving was a pleasure.

I knew what I wanted now. I told Margaret to go home. I walked into a drugstore, I entered the phone booth. My heart was painfully large, my mouth dry as an old woman's. I dialed Eleanor's number.

And the miracle was that Eleanor answered the phone. There was her voice: clear, and delicate, and full of love, as if she had been waiting.

"Isabel, it's wonderful to hear you."

"And you," I said, beginning to weep in the drugstore phone booth.

"Eleanor, I have to ask you what I have no right to ask you. Can you come up here now? Tonight. I need your help. I have to get out of here now. I'm afraid to wait; I'm afraid if I don't go now I'll die here."

Eleanor's response was instantaneous, as if she had been preparing for months to respond to what I had only just now known I wanted to say.

"I'll be there tonight."

I went on weeping.

"Eleanor," I said, "do you think it will be all right?"

"Yes," said Eleanor on the other end, weeping with me.

That night I thought of what I had come here to get away from. I had promised Margaret I would stay with her as an acknowledgment of my own dying. If I called Eleanor, if I wrote to Hugh, if I sang at the piano with Father Mulcahy, I was susceptible to all that loss. It came to me that life was monstrous: what you loved you were always in danger of losing. The greatest love meant only, finally, the greatest danger. That was life; life was monstrous.

But it was life I wanted. Not Margaret. Margaret's unlovableness rendered her incapable of inflicting permanent pain. She could decay the soul, but she could not destroy it. Only love could do that, and the accidents of love. So that at Margaret's death I would feel nothing: only relief. But it was life I wanted. Life and loss.

If I wanted I could have, perhaps, everything— love, work, friends. If I wanted, perhaps I could give reasonably without giving my life. And perhaps I would get, for my pains, refreshment, sustenance, and the rewards of a reasonable life.

I would work for a government, a dealer in charity without the weights of love. I had thought it unforgivable to imagine that you could dare to help someone whom you did not love personally. But Margaret, for example, needed help, and Margaret I could not love. Did that mean that I had no right to help her? Perhaps it meant only that I had no right to expect love in return.

Governments gave money and did not ask for love. Money was beautiful; if you could give money and not want love in return, you could change lives without giving up your own life. That would not change the sorrow of Mrs. Riesert, who wanted to die because there was no one who loved her more than anyone else living. But much sorrow money could change. For most people, it was a great gift to have the sufferings of the body, the worries of the body, lessened. Margaret's life would be more bearable if she did not have to worry about money. And I had money, money from the sale of the house. It occurred to me, simply, that I could give up my money; I did not have to give up my life.

I walked downstairs to Margaret as if I had given up my body. Margaret sat under the dim kitchen light. She was twisted and unhappy. But she was not near death. She seemed to me immortal, slowly moving to the rhythm of the body's enforced decay. I knew I must speak now.

"I've come to a decision, Margaret," I said, standing above her. I was a much larger woman than Margaret. She could have been pitiable, but she was Margaret, and it was in her power to make herself small, like a witch whose metamorphoses were her greatest danger.

Standing as I did above her, I wanted to give up my power. Sitting under that light, Margaret was not dangerous, she was simply perhaps what she had always been: exhausted, frightened. She needed some kind of help. I would give her help. But I would not give her my life.

"I realize," I said, judicious, an ancient Italian, the mother of sons, "that it is not good for either of us, my being here."

"What will happen to me then?" said Margaret, beginning to whimper.

"You won't have to worry. I'll give you what you deserve. You ought to have some kind of pension from us, from my father and me. You worked for eleven years for us. You deserve something for that. I'll give you what would be the equivalent of a pension. I'll give you the money I got for the house. You should be able to live in comfort, without fear."

"But who can I get to take care of me?"

"I don't know that," I said. "I don't know you well enough to answer that."

I left on the table in front of Margaret a check for $20,000. It was all the money I had in the world. But I was free of Margaret now, and I felt weightless, as if I could walk from room to room, making no impression on solid earth, as if not even walls could stop me. I did not wait to say any more to Margaret, or to hear what Margaret would say. She let me walk away, as if she could not see me. There was nothing left between us. Margaret could not touch me now; I was as safe as if I were invisible.

I packed my things. I had to stay in my room; I felt my own weakness, as if something hidden and growing had been taken from my body. I was light now; my body was high again, and dexterous, and clever. But I was weak; I felt the delicious shakiness of an invalid in the first stages of his cure.

I slept. I could see, in my dreams, my own body hovering over the bed, or traveling, or visiting strangers. The light was beginning to come up. I heard a car stop in front of the house. I looked at my watch. It was quarter to three. I looked out the window. Eleanor got out of the car. And Liz. Liz stood beside her, menacing to strangers as a charioteer. I took my two suitcases in my hands and walked silently down the stairs.

My two friends stood waiting for me on opposite sides of the car. The queer light made them bodiless and I felt weightless, as if I had no body.

"Ready?" said Eleanor, a beautiful, reluctant thief, sure to be caught but magically safe from punishment.

Liz looked at me, her eyes flicking up and down in quick judgment.

"Who did your hair? Annette Funicello?"

The three of us laughed. It was a miracle to me, the solidity of that joke. Even the cutting edge of it was a miracle. And our laughter was solid. It stirred the air and hung above us like rings of bone that shivered in the cold, gradual morning.

"I'll have to stay at Eleanor's for a while until I lose this weight. I can't let anyone see me as I am right now."

"Of course," said Eleanor, making another ring above us. It was so simple and so definite. I knew what I would do. How I loved them for their solidity, for their real and possible existences, nonetheless a miracle. For they had come the moment I called them, and they were here beside me in the fragile and exhilarating chill of the first dawn.

"Let's go," I said.

We got into the car without touching. I looked behind me. The small house grew smaller and more thwarted as we drove. I folded my arms and leaned them on the top of the seat where my two friends sat in front of me. I rested my head there for a moment. Then I sat up straight. It was a great pleasure simply to be near them. There was a great deal I wanted to say.

ABOUT THE AUTHOR

MARY GORDON was born in Far Rockaway, New York. She attended Barnard College and the Writing Program at Syracuse University. Her short stories have been published in *Ms., Redbook, The Ladies' Home Journal, Mademoiselle, Virginia Quarterly Review,* and *Southern Review.*

Women of all ages can look

and feel their best with these bestselling guides to wardrobe, weight loss, exercise and skin care.

Bestsellers from BALLANTINE

G-2

HELP FOR THE WORKING WOMAN

         AL-31